DREAMS OF YOU

Dreams Trilogy #1

CARINA ADAMS

May all your dreams come true!

♡ CarinaAdams

Books by CARINA ADAMS

The Bama Boys

Forever Red

Out of The Blue

The Bastards MC Series

Lay It Down Duet

Unfinished Business

The Dreams Trilogy (Coming 2022)

Dreams of You

Glimmers of Me

Echoes of Us

Standalone Novels

Almost Innocent

Ruffles & Beaus

Lucky

Sidelined

Sweary Mom

For Trouble, *who is anything but.*
You're my mirror and my shadow.
The big sister I never had.
You remind me every day that...
Mirrors never lie, shadows never leave,
and blessings come when you least expect.

Chapter One

Lennon

I leaned a hip against the counter in the break room and sighed as the coffee trickled into the pot. I was exhausted and ready to be home in my pajamas. Unfortunately, the segment I'd spent the last week researching had taken a hard left a few hours before. I couldn't leave until it was adjusted and ready to air in the morning, even if that meant pulling an all-nighter. Caffeine and fuzzy slippers would have to be my saving grace for the next few hours.

Finding the biggest mug on the shelf, I tapped a short, chipped and chewed fingernail against it, silently glaring at the ancient Bunn, willing it to hurry. I wasn't sure why the powers that be had never replaced the machine that was older than I was, especially in an office where everyone seemed to exist solely on coffee, but I didn't have time to be picky. There was too much to do.

I should have gone back to my office and worked while I waited, but I knew from experience that I'd get absorbed in the story and lose track of time. I couldn't count how many times the damn pot had grown cold by the time I'd remembered it. This was definitely a hot and fresh kind of night.

With an impatient sigh, I let my eyes linger on the clock. Most of my friends were home getting their families ready for bed. The rest were meeting for cocktails and dinner at their favorite pub before going dancing at one of the many clubs they frequented. Even if I weren't stuck at work, I'd be the boring one, bailing for the privacy of my apartment.

I'd spend another night cuddled in pajamas on the couch, eating takeout straight from the container, while the first few seasons of *One Tree Hill*—back when Lucas and Peyton made me believe young love could survive the tests of time—streamed on a loop.

Better than the alternative, I reminded myself harshly. My Friday nights *could* be spent tucked into the ancient, stained, over-stuffed chair in the corner of my bedroom, wearing a ratty, too-big tee that smelled like desperation and broken dreams, watching the latest comic book superhero franchise-made-movie, praying my phone would ring, and then crying myself to sleep when it didn't.

Oddly specific, I know.

It hadn't been my finest hour. Okay, so it'd been more like a month. A dark time Dylan and I never spoke of.

As if on cue, the obnoxious ringtone I'd programmed for my best friend broke the silence, startling me. I normally let personal calls go to voicemail. If it had been anyone else, I might have. Dylan never called me on my work phone.

I could practically see the Bat Signal flashing across the sky.

Forgetting the coffee, I ran for my office on the other side of the building, dodging desks and a pile of files someone had left on the floor. I grabbed it just in time, slightly out of breath, and frowned as I lifted it to my ear.

"What's wrong?"

She scoffed. "Why does there have to be something wrong?"

"Because I can count on one hand the number of times you've called me since we got cell phones," I retorted with a laugh. "All of them emergencies. And you never use this number."

I was the one who usually initiated verbal contact between us. Yes, we'd been typical teens. Some nights the two of us had spent hours on the phone, giggling and gushing over whatever had been exciting in our lives. However, if it were up to Dylan, we'd only talk via text now. Some of those conversations would be conducted entirely in emojis or gifs. She was *that* girl.

The line was silent for a moment. "Good point," she snorted. "What are you doing tonight, beautiful?"

Relief that she seemed fine—that there was no life-altering crisis—flooded through me as I dropped into my worn-out chair and spun toward the window, gazing out over my beloved city. "Sitting in an ivory tower, watching a chaotic kingdom," I sassed.

"So, you *are* still at work?"

Bracing for the disapproval I had no doubt was coming, I wrinkled my nose. Dylan loved her job as a physical therapist assistant, but at the end of her shift, she went home and put the day behind her. She'd struggled for years to understand why I spent more time in the office than I did at home, and why a forty-hour workweek wasn't in my vocabulary.

"I am. And yes, I know it's a Friday night."

She didn't criticize. "You're not alone, are you?"

The lack of a lecture threw me, yet it was the way she asked that made the hair on my arms rise. Maybe she'd finally taken her concern about my work ethic to another level. However, if I'd learned anything after over two-and-a-half decades of friendship, it was never to underestimate her. Dylan always had a reason.

Suddenly uncomfortable, I frowned and turned back toward the newsroom.

My uneasiness immediately melted away as I looked through the glass walls of my office, over the sea of desks. There were no dividers or cubicles because the powers that be believed an open-space design fostered collaboration between all team members, no matter what their official title. Most days I thought the lack of privacy was a pain in the ass, but at night it was nice because I was able to see who had gone home and which dedicated souls were burning the midnight oil. The migraine-inducing, overhead fluorescents had thankfully been turned off hours before, but five or six desk lamps dotted the room like stars in the night sky.

"There are a few people still here. Even if I was alone, I wouldn't really be by myself. We have twenty-four-hour security downstairs, and you need a badge to access this floor." I didn't know if I was assuring her or myself.

"What about Penny? Have you seen her? I tried to call her earlier, but it went straight to voicemail."

I resisted the urge to roll my eyes. I'd never understood Dylan's friendship with the lifestyle producer. Yes, Penelope Young was as incredibly sweet and kind as she was smart and articulate.

It was her love of celebrity gossip, which she passed as cold-hard fact, that irritated me. Someone as talented as Penny shouldn't waste energy worrying about the lifestyles of the rich and famous. Yet, she was in her element when she put together a story on something as senseless as the latest Hollywood buzz.

I quickly scanned the glass-lined offices that, like mine, created a perimeter around the newsroom. "No. The rest of the producers are gone. Even Penny," I confirmed as my eyes narrowed. "Are you going to tell me what's going on? I can put on my investigative reporter hat if I need to. Just know that I can be brutally intrusive."

Dylan's laugh sounded forced. "I'm coming to rescue you, that's what. Dinner and drinks on me. I miss your face. I need time with my bestie."

"You know I'd love that. But it's a really bad time right now. I can't..."

"You can." She ignored my attempted excuse, talking over me instead. "I'll even make a pitstop at Starbucks on Beacon. They're open late. That way, you'll be energized when you go back to work. I mean, if you even want to go back that late."

Something was off. Dylan barely tolerated my coffee addiction. She only indulged my love of caffeine when something was so wrong that she either wanted to distract me or needed a distraction for herself.

"Okay," I caved cautiously. Not because cold-brew was my obsession —it was—but because I wanted answers. I stood, pulled my wallet and keys from their hiding space on the crammed bookshelf, and glanced around to see if I'd forgotten anything. "Want me to meet you somewhere?"

"No. I'm already on the block. Be outside in five."

I glanced up as the elevator doors opened across the room, and Penelope hurried onto the floor.

"Hey," I muttered into the phone, amazed at my co-worker's perfect timing. "Penny is here. Want me to ask her to join us?"

"Penny is there? Now? Like right now?" The panic in Dylan's voice made me grip the phone tighter.

The petite brunette spotted me, waved frantically, and headed my way.

"Yep, right now. She's coming over. Am I inviting her or not?" My voice dropped to a whisper. "Either way, you're going to tell me what in the hell is wrong."

Screeching her hurried steps to a halt outside my office, Penelope slapped her hands on the glass on either side of my door and leaned into the room. Her eyes were wide and sparkling, delight mixed with irritation all over her beautiful face, and she was practically vibrating with excitement. I knew before she uttered a word that something important had happened in Hollywood. I couldn't tell if it was good or bad, but it had to be big news. Nothing else would elicit that kind of reaction from her.

Trepidation washed over me. If she'd come back to the office on a Friday night, it was to produce a segment for the morning. That meant my story—the one that would actually impact and possibly change lives—wouldn't air the next day. Probably not until much later. Lord knew I'd been bumped enough times that I should just expect it. Even though I'd have some extra time to clean it up now and wouldn't have to pull an all-nighter, I felt like a balloon that had just been poked with a pin.

"I was at dinner when the story broke. WHDH," she sneered our competitor's call sign, "beat us to it. Again."

She kept talking as Dylan started to yell. "Lennon! Are you listening to me? Len!"

I shook my head as if they could both see me. I was too tired to deal with whatever in the hell was going on in Penny's world, disappointment burning a bitter path through my veins. "What's wrong?" I didn't know who I was addressing, maybe both of them.

"Cullen James got engaged an hour ago," Penelope announced excitedly, sinking her teeth into her bottom lip as if she were the lucky girl who'd landed Hollywood's Golden Boy. Clapping, she hopped into the air twice like a deranged bunny. I didn't know if I was trying to process the words she'd uttered, or horrified by the announcement, but I stood frozen, my mouth open.

Without warning, Penny seemed to remember she wasn't supposed to be happy, and her face turned dark. Throwing her arms into the air in dramatic disgust, she growled. An actual growl. One that would come from a scared, feral animal, not a perky little pixie.

"Once again, we're late breaking the news. I rushed over as soon as I heard and called in the rest of my team on the way, but we're still late. Damn it!" Her eyes flicked to the watch on her wrist. "They should be here any minute. Is there coffee? I should have Garrett grab some, just in case. We need to post an announcement online and prep a segment for the morning. I have a call out to New York to see if we have a quote from their reps, but..."

Penny continued to ramble as she headed for her own office, almost like I'd never been there at all. It didn't matter because I hadn't really paid attention to another word she'd uttered after she'd made her announcement. On the other end of the line, Dylan was still talking, her voice full of reassurance.

"You *know* how the tabloids are. They'll say anything to make a buck. This isn't a big deal. Yes, there are pictures online, but pictures don't always tell the real story. Len, this is *Cullen* we're talking about. Our Cullen. He's made some pretty fucked up choices, but he wouldn't do this."

Her words tugged me out of the fog. She was right. It *was* Cullen. I didn't have her confidence. I didn't know what to expect from him anymore. That's what scared me the most.

He was no longer the boy I'd once known.

I meant to mutter a goodbye before I ended the call, but I wasn't sure it came out. I dropped my phone and grabbed my laptop. Without sitting, I typed his name into my favorite search engine. The results popped up immediately. Photos of Cullen and his current rumored love interest lined the top of the page, but it was the headlines that jumped out at me.

Cullen James and Briar Bennett: ENGAGED at Last?

Where There's Smoke, There's an Engagement Ring, and Cullen and Briar are On Fire!

He Put a Ring on It! Cullen James, Briar Bennett Finally Tying the Knot?

I rolled my eyes at the article titles. Clearly, no one had taken the time to think of something half-way decent, too concerned with being the first to break the news. Journalism at its finest, folks.

I clicked on one, then the next, ignoring how pathetic they were, desperate to see the proof. The pictures weren't new. In fact, most of them I'd seen so many times I could describe each in great detail.

I opened the videos tab. The headlines were more of the same, all stating that the man of the hour, the untamable playboy, was finally ready to settle down. With America's Pop Princess, no less. I scrolled through them, past the entertainment magazines and basement blogs to the actual news channels. ABC, NBC, and CBS all had posts, which meant their local Boston affiliates had, in fact, beaten us to the punch.

At that moment, I didn't care about the ratings, rivalries, or who bested who. The only thought in my mind was that they were credible stations with producers too afraid of lawsuits and their reputation to print something without fact-checking. I clicked on the first one, mentally bracing myself for a truth I might not want to face.

The anchor, a young woman with straight, pearly whites and the perfect amount of bronzer, smiled at the camera. "Up next, congratulations are in order. This time for Cullen James and Briar Bennett." She faded from view but continued the story in a voice-over as a slideshow began.

"The couple we all fell for in *Dangerous Night* had been rumored to be dating on and off for almost a year, but it was only last month that Bennett took to Instagram to confirm."

A picture of the two of them grinning—Cullen's arm around Briar, holding her tightly as they sat in the audience at an awards show—dominated the screen as Briar's post was highlighted beneath. "I love this guy so much I just can't stand it. He's the only one who can make me smile this big," the reporter read for those who might not be able to see the giant words that still, three weeks later, made me sick to my stomach.

"Now it appears the couple has taken their love to the next level. Earlier today, as they were spotted leaving Crustacean, the trendy Hollywood restaurant, Bennett was photographed wearing a large diamond and sapphire ring on her left hand, leading many to speculate that the Academy Award Winner popped the question during a romantic lunch."

Pictures flashed across the screen, showing Cullen gazing down at Briar with adoration on his face. When they zoomed in, a diamond that looked suspiciously like an engagement ring sparkled on her left hand. I swallowed hard. Then again, desperate to clear the lump lodged in my throat.

"When asked for comment, reps for both responded with a joint statement saying, 'Cullen and Briar have found happiness. When they're ready to share that with their fans, they will.' So, there you have it, folks. Sometimes fairy tales do come true. Our congratulations go out to them."

The clip ended. For a moment, I stared at my screen. One small piece of me began to plant seeds of hope in the back of my mind. *Maybe it's a publicity stunt. Maybe the ring was a present that wouldn't fit any other finger. Maybe it's anything but what it appeared to be. Maybe there's a perfectly acceptable explanation.*

There wasn't.

I wasn't stupid. Although, I'd never felt more foolish.

The truth swept over me like a bitter January wind. I slammed the laptop shut with one hand as the other attempted to rub away the throbbing in my temple.

The worst part was that I'd known something was wrong. My intuition had become so overwhelming a few weeks before that I'd woken up in the middle of the night in a panic. With tears in my eyes, before I could stop myself, I'd dialed his number because I'd needed to hear his voice.

Dean Cullen had been such a huge part of my life for so long that we'd become connected in a way I couldn't describe without sounding certifiable.

I couldn't have explained what, but I'd felt that something big was looming around the corner, that whatever it was, it was definitely not good. Half of me had expected bad news to be delivered every day since, while the other half wondered if I'd open my door one night to find him sitting in his chair, waiting for me to come home.

What I hadn't anticipated was *this* news.

Or finding out this way. Anger pulsed through my veins. I was pissed at myself for being such an idiot for so long. Yet I was infuriated with Dean, because he hadn't had the balls to pick up the phone and tell me himself.

Screw him. He wasn't going to get off the hook that easily. If he was ready to move on, if he wanted out, he had to say the goddamn words.

He owed me an explanation. I wasn't going to sit around and wait for him to break me. I'd waited on him long enough.

I snatched my cell phone and dialed the number I knew as well as my own.

I took a deep breath as his phone started to ring.

It was all an act. The strong, adamant, yet bitter woman I'd become. This woman he'd come to know.

Inside, I was trembling. There, deep within the safety of my walls, was the girl who loved him with every ounce of her being. She needed him to lie. She wasn't ready for the truth. She would believe anything he said, no matter how crazy his story was, and cling to it like it was her only lifeline. Because *she* wasn't ready to let go.

I didn't know which version of me would appear when he answered.

After the second ring, I half expected him not to pick up, to send me to voicemail. He was no doubt celebrating his joyous news with his fiancée. My fingers gripped the phone tightly.

When Joan's voice greeted me, acid pooled in my stomach, and I clenched my teeth. Of course, he'd have her do his dirty work. Nothing surprised me anymore. The only words I could manage were harsh and forced.

Bitter and angry it was then.

"Put my husband on the phone."

Dean

The damn phone had buzzed non-stop since we'd gotten into the Town Car. I didn't keep track of who'd called, letting my manager deal with the nosey pricks instead. Normally, she loved when my name was on everyone's lips; the way shutterbug stalkers fought each other for the best candids, like seagulls fighting for scraps. Today was a different beast altogether. She'd earned every penny of the outrageous salary I paid.

For anyone who didn't know her, the sickly-sweet tone Joan had used all afternoon sounded over-exaggerated, like she'd spent too much time in Los Angeles. Those of us in her inner circle recognized it for what it was; she was so infuriated that steam was about to billow out her ears, losing her shit was a real possibility and it would take only the smallest spark before she blew. I pitied the poor, unfortunate soul on the other end of the call when that happened.

If people would just mind their own fucking business, it wouldn't be an issue. Not that anyone in this damn industry could manage that.

When the cell vibrated again, her deep sigh echoed around the car, as if bracing herself for whomever was on the other end of the line. As Joan cleared her throat and adjusted in her seat, she reminded me of a general readying for war. I didn't know who was calling, but it was obvious that she dreaded answering as much as I feared talking to my social media manager.

My lips quirked in amused relief as I watched the traffic out my window. At least she was as miserable as I was. This was her fault, after all.

"Lennon, darling," Joan drawled in greeting.

My head snapped toward her as my breath caught and everything else faded away. Joan's eyes narrowed on me in a glare that would stop the most ruthless and dangerous in their tracks. Words failed me, but I gave a subtle shake of my head, to let her know I wouldn't take the call. *Not now.*

Joan's nostrils flared in fury.

I ignored her. There was nothing she could say or do that would make me talk to Lennon in that moment. I glanced at my watch and did the calculation without a second thought. It was a little past nine on the East Coast. There were only two reasons Len would call me on a Friday night. Since it was too early for a drunk dial, I knew she'd heard the news.

I swallowed and rubbed my suddenly sweaty palms on designer denim as I tried to force myself to relax. That was not a conversation I was going to have in front of anyone, especially not the women in the car with me. No, I needed to be home, a bottle of scotch in hand, mentally prepared to brave the force that was Lennon James.

Beside me, Briar went rigid. For a few heartbeats, I wasn't sure she even breathed. Slowly, her hand covered mine. "News travels fast."

With a small nod, I pulled my eyes from Joan to focus on the breathtaking blonde next to me.

When her gaze met mine, Briar offered a small, apologetic smile, but there was no joy on her face. "I'm sorry."

"Don't be."

Without thinking, I lifted a hand to brush a loose curl behind her ear, an attempt to ease her worry and distract myself, but she batted me away. *Idiot.* I knew Briar hated when I played with her hair. She thought it was juvenile and pathetic, but old habits died hard. Some actions were second nature, and my body reacted before my mind remembered.

Instead of calling me out, or slapping the sense back into my pathetic ass, Briar leaned toward me, her mouth next to my ear.

"You should talk to her." Her voice was little more than a murmur as if afraid Len could hear.

Surprised, my lips twisted in disgust. "Why?" The scoff came out much harsher than I'd intended, but I refused to backtrack.

"Because rejection hurts, even when you lose to someone like me. That's what's going through her mind. She could probably use a friend right now. Maybe even an explanation."

Briar Bennett was one of the most important people in my life. I didn't know where I'd be without her and not because our chemistry set the silver screen on fire and sent everyone's imaginations into over-drive. But Lennon was off limits. I didn't want to hear anyone's opinions of her. Ever.

There were many things I wanted to say. I bit back the snarl, but just barely. Instead, I nodded. "I'll call her later."

Briar's eyes closed, and she let loose a long sigh laced with disap-pointment that reminded me of my mother. I didn't know if she was upset with me, the situation, or both. However, I did know that Briar wasn't talented enough to hide her exasperation. When she opened them again, they were cold, her jaw tight.

"When your wife calls, you take the damn call."

I smirked cruelly before I could stop myself. "Is that concern for Lennon I hear or are you worried I'll start to dodge yours next?"

Briar's eyes widened in agitation at my words. She crossed her arms over her chest, tipped her head slightly, and arched a single brow. All signs that meant Briar had reached her limit.

Good. So had I. I'd set clear boundaries around Len. I wasn't backing down for anyone.

"I know the people and laws in New England tend to run a little slower than the rest of the country, but bigamy is still illegal in all fifty states."

I took a deep breath and counted to ten. This, *whatever this was*, was going to get ugly if I didn't stop it. After everything that had already happened, a war with each other was the last thing we needed.

Outwardly, I mimicked her expression, but the corners of my lips curled up, feigning amusement at her behavior. She may have hurled the insult and expected a direct hit, but I refused to show that she'd affected me at all. She could rage with the best of them, but I didn't have to play into it, no matter how infuriated I was.

I *was* that good at my job. There might not be cameras aimed at us, but this was just another role. I'd been playing it for so long, it was second nature.

When the reaction she'd hoped for never came, she rolled her eyes. "She deserves the truth, Cullen."

Truth. I almost laughed. The truth was all about angles, how a person looked at something. We could be standing side by side, watching the same event unfold, yet our versions would be different. Didn't mean that either of us was lying. We simply hadn't seen it the same way.

"Stop being so cruel. Take the damn phone and put her out of her misery."

Briar's voice was much louder than moments before, the car almost silent. Too late, I realized that Joan had stopped talking, even though the phone was still pressed to her ear. I didn't know what Lennon had heard, but from the look on my manager's face, it wasn't good.

Regret had become my constant companion. It weighed heavier on my shoulders in that moment than it had the rest of my life. I couldn't simply take the phone and talk to Lennon, even if I'd give every dime to hear her voice.

There was too much history between us. No one understood. They couldn't because they hadn't been part of it.

Hell, I'd had a starring role, and I still didn't grasp the enormity of it all. I turned my attention to the world outside the car and let myself remember.

Chapter Two

Lennon

The Past

I couldn't breathe.

Dylan, the sadistic brat I'd once foolishly labeled best friend, typically found pleasure in making me giggle until I peed my pants. Today was worse. She was trying to kill me as she recalled her night out shopping with her mom.

Fat tears rolled down cheeks that burned red in embarrassment, I'd started to wheeze, and my sides hurt from laughing at her crazy stories. That didn't stop my best friend, though. Oh, no. She had no mercy.

"Oh my God! Did I tell you about the guy on the bike?" Dylan didn't give me a moment to respond. She leaned forward on the chaise lounge, face pinched in concentration. "When he pulled up next to us at the red light, I looked over because—hello! Hot guy in tight shorts, ya know? Some of those guys have muscles for days, and those shorts show *everything*."

She paused, smirking as I shook my head. Nothing she said shocked me anymore, no matter how much she tried.

"So, he stops next to us, balances for a few seconds, looks over, and sees my mom watching him. He smiled at her, lifted his chin all flirty and shit, pulled off his sunglasses, and went to put his foot down. Totally hitting on her. Apparently, he'd forgotten he was wearing those hideous shoes that clip to the pedals or whatever, so he couldn't actually get his foot loose. For a second or two, he struggled. Then, the dude just toppled over. Like his entire bike fell onto the grass. At the same second, the light turned green."

Tears burned my eyes as my shoulders shook. I could picture it. "What happened then? Did you stop to help?"

She shrugged. "You know my mom. She gave him a little finger wave and drove off."

I couldn't stop the obnoxious giggle. It was totally something Aunt Tasha would do. Not only was my mom's best friend a hoot, but she and Dylan always had the funniest, most random, things happen to them.

"What's so funny?"

I choked on my laughter as Dylan's brother stepped onto the patio and closed the slider behind him. Back muscles bunched under his henley as he moved and his lips curled up in a knowing smile that made him even more attractive, if possible. As he turned toward us, I tried to ignore the fact that everything about him dissolved my insides into mush.

I felt Dylan's eyes on me in that silent, watchful way of hers, but I refused to meet her stare. Instead, I turned around, pretending I hadn't checked out Dean, and focused on the neighbor's back yard as Dylan answered him.

It was a harmless little crush. That was it. *Nothing to see here, folks. Move along.*

Only it wasn't little anymore. If I continued to let it fester, or gave it too much attention, it could be detrimental.

When I was five or six, I'd woken up screaming, sheets and PJs soaking wet from sweat, shaking in fear. The nightmare seemed so life-like that I refused to believe it wasn't real. I'd stayed awake for days straight to avoid sleep.

Worried, my parents had taken me to the doctor. He prescribed medication to help me relax and trick my mind into rest. The diagnosis wasn't anything exciting, a sleep disorder I'd eventually outgrow.

Only I hadn't.

As I got older, I'd started paying attention to the dreams, determined to figure out what my subconscious was trying to tell me, convinced each held an important buried message. At some point around fourth grade, I'd convinced myself I could see the future.

I wasn't clairvoyant. Unfortunately, I hadn't been born a seer or a witch doctor or an oracle. I wasn't trapped in a fantasy realm where I was sent to fulfill a prophecy and save the world. As disappointing as that truth was to accept for a geek like me.

In reality, I fixated on the details of each dream, obsessing over them on a Freudian level, and inevitably, some came true.

Like the time I crashed my bike because I was watching for a hungry-eyed wolf to attack from the woods. Dream Lennon had survived the random attack but had ended up with her right arm in a sling, bandaged after she'd been mauled. Real me got a cast after breaking my arm in three places because I hadn't paid attention to what was in front of me.

Not all the dreams were bad. Sometimes, fantastic things happened to me. In seventh grade, I'd dreamt the new kid kissed me at a dance. I'd gotten up the next morning infatuated with him. We did kiss at the dance, but only because I'd made it my life's mission to find out everything I could about Seth from South Carolina and made sure he'd noticed me.

Seth. I hadn't talked to him in months. I made a mental note to message him as soon as I got home.

The dreams weren't a superpower, but they did mess with my head. When I'd woken up a few months before, drenched in a cold sweat, I sat on my bed, shaking my head at the craziest dream I'd ever had. There was no way Dean would fall in love with me, and there wasn't a chance the two of us would ever spend the night together in the back of his truck. He didn't even own a truck, for goodness sake. The entire thing was pure insanity. Laughable, really.

However, I could still see us—clear as day—every time I let myself remember. If I didn't stop myself, I could almost feel his fingertips on my skin...

No. Nope. Not letting my mind go *there*.

My sudden attraction to him shouldn't have been a surprise. Not after that dream. Although, I did wonder if he'd become hotter overnight or if it was all because of the stupid dream.

Whatever the reason, I planned to ignore his beauty, and my attraction to it.

I'd lose interest eventually. Someone cuter, funnier, and even more perfect would catch my eye and haunt my dreams. Although, I was pretty sure the mold had broken with Dean. There wasn't anyone more attractive, as hilarious, or as perfect for me.

It didn't matter. Best friends didn't perv on their best friend's big brother. It was against girl code. Especially when said friends had been besties since they could talk, and that big brother had seen me naked.

It wasn't as scandalous as it sounded; we'd gotten carried away playing in the back yard, covered from head-to-toe in thick mud. Disgusted, our moms had stripped the three of us and plopped us into a bathtub overflowing with bubbles. Even though he'd been naked too, I didn't remember anything.

Actually, it wasn't just the three of us, now that I thought about it. Tate had been there too. Three-year-old me saw a hell of a lot more action than fifteen-year-old me.

I was relatively sure my mom had photographic evidence of said bath. I needed to find it and destroy it. If Dean or Tate saw it, I'd die from embarrassment.

That wasn't the only suggestive picture from when we were young. My favorite photo from childhood was glued to the cover of my notebook and went everywhere with me. In it, a very young Dean sat on the couch with an even younger me. He'd just given me his lollipop. In exchange, I'd kissed him.

No one had stopped me. They all knew I adored him. Instead,

someone had snapped a picture, forever capturing the sweet moment between two innocents. Our families were so great like that.

The biggest barrier of all was probably the saddest. I wasn't sure Dean realized we weren't actually related. Most people thought we were.

"Earth to Lennon," Dean teased as he pushed my feet aside and sat on the end of the chaise.

I gave him a small smile as my heart started to beat the rhythm of doom against my ribcage. "Sorry. Lost in thought."

His grin lit up his handsome face as he teased, "Why am I not surprised?"

I shrugged. It was a side effect of being an only child. Sometimes the only person you had to talk to was yourself, so you got comfortable with your thoughts. "How was rehearsal?"

It was Dean's turn to lift his shoulders as his brow furrowed. "I think it went okay."

"Just okay?" I prodded. The show's director was new to the organization and according to Dean, a total hardass. The cast had been struggling for weeks now.

He sighed. "We're not amateurs. It's not like we don't know our lines or how to do our jobs, but he keeps changing the blocking and cues, which screws everything up and makes half the cast nervous, so they mess up their lines." His grin was so cocky it was adorable. "You don't have a clue what I'm talking about, do you?"

"Not really, but I don't need to know to listen."

Community theater was not my idea of a good time, but he loved it. Six years before, Dean had become the youngest actor ever cast. He'd gotten a role in every performance since.

The annual show ran for two weeks to a sold-out house every night.

I'd listen to whatever he had to say, and not because of the recent dream. It was our thing. I didn't know anything about soccer or relationships either, but I was an ear when he needed to vent about anything in his life.

Just like he was mine. I'd tell him about whatever social cause had piqued my interest, the latest issue I was having on the student paper, and the normal woes of being a teen with overbearing parents. Neither of us knew everything, but we could always count on the other to offer advice or support. We were friends; it was what we did.

He reached out and tugged on a piece of my hair before he tucked it behind my ear. "Thanks for that." His eyes grew wide, and he cleared his throat as he leaned away from me and looked around the backyard. "What are you guys doing out here? Aren't you freezing?"

His words reminded me how cold I was and I rubbed my hands together before absentmindedly glancing at the neighbor's house again. The reason Dylan had dragged me outside on a cool New England spring day had nothing to do with the sunshine that had finally graced us with its presence and everything to do with the shirt-less boy working out next door. Out of my peripheral, I saw Dean twist and follow my gaze.

"Seriously?" His annoyed tone almost made me laugh as he spun back toward his sister. "Tell me you're not."

"What?" Dylan answered innocently as she intently inspected her nails. "It's gorgeous out."

"You talking about the weather, or my best friend?"

Dylan groaned, annoyed. "Whatever. You know Tate's hot."

For a moment, Dean watched his little sister with a blank face. His eyes shifted to me, lips quirking.

"Tate's hot?"

I wasn't sure if it was a real question, or if he was merely trying to make his sister uncomfortable. I swallowed a laugh. "A legend in his own mind."

Dean's focus on me was so intense, I almost squirmed. Then, he winked. Before either of us could stop him, he cupped his hands around his mouth, "Yo, Griffin! You've got peepers over here, man. Might wanna cover up."

"Dean Fitzgerald Cullen," Dylan admonished with a harsh whisper, her mouth falling open in shock. "You are an asshole."

Dean only laughed, eyes sparkling in pure glee.

Next door, Tate Griffin, arguably the hottest boy in school—as long as you asked Dylan or one of his other many admirers—turned toward us and raised a hand in greeting. Abandoning the weights, he grabbed a towel, wiped the sweat from his chiseled body in a way that would make even my grandmother's mouth water, and started our way.

"Hey, hey," he called as his long legs ate the distance between the two houses.

Once, years before, a flower garden separated the properties. We'd tried to be careful when we ran between the homes, but we'd ruined Aunt Tasha's beloved gladiolus so many times that Uncle Chad had finally stepped in and built her a raised bed at the back of the yard. Now, the only border was crushed rock, decorated with kitschy gnomes.

Tate leapt onto the deck, bumped fists with Dean, lifted an empty wooden chair as if it weighed nothing, and dropped it in the space between Dylan and me. "Ladies," he greeted with a lift of his chin as he fell onto the seat. "Enjoying the weather while it lasts?"

Dean and I stared at Dylan, waiting for her to answer. She was the one who'd dragged me out there specifically to spy, and she was the one who always had a good cover story on the tip of her tongue. When she didn't respond, her face a disturbing shade of green, I felt bad.

I cleared my throat, torn between sending her a dirty look and asking if she was okay. Instead, I smiled up at the too-attractive-for-high-school boy, forcing myself to remember that I didn't need to be nervous around him. I'd known him forever. The four of us had once been inseparable and had countless sleepovers.

Of course, that was before Tate turned into an athletic god most women couldn't think straight around. Even my mom, who never got flustered over anything. It was mortifying.

This was Tate. *Our* Tate. I'd spent the last few years avoiding him because he seemed larger than life now. Well, until recently, when Dylan convinced me to help her stalk him from a distance.

Before the town had adored him, we'd been his only friends. Almost instantly, I conjured up an image of an overweight, acne-prone tween laughing so hard at something silly that he'd snorted milk out his nose. Just like that, he was no longer Mr. Popular Jock and simply an old friend who I didn't get to see enough.

When I realized Dylan was going to remain silent, I answered. "I'm so sick of winter. I need fresh air and beach days."

Tate nodded his agreement. "We haven't had a beach day in forever." His eyes shifted to Dylan. "We should do one this summer. Skip school and have a flashback day."

"A flashback day?" I asked, desperate to cover for my friend, who looked like she might throw up.

"Yeah," he shot a grin my way before looking at Dylan once again. "You know, the five of us. Hanging out like before. Sans the old people, of course. Maybe even make a weekend out of it."

"Oh," Dylan breathed loudly. "Mm-hmm."

Clearly, it wasn't the answer he'd expected. With a confused frown etched on his handsome face, Tate turned his attention back to Dean. "We still on for tonight?"

"What's tonight?" Dylan demanded, nosiness overriding embarrassment.

Dean's lips twisted in amusement at her sudden change. It was fun to see Dylan so flustered, but I didn't know if her brother realized why. Sometimes it felt like you couldn't simply hint; you had to put the message on a flashing billboard with a picture of a giant cheeseburger just to get teenage boys to take notice.

"That's why I was looking for you," Dean explained as he leaned back.

Had he been looking for us? I tried to recall what he'd said when he'd joined us, but I couldn't remember. I had no right to give Dylan shit about the way she acted around Tate. I barely knew my own name when Dean was nearby.

"You two still going to the movies?"

Dylan nodded. "Yeah."

"You coming back here after?"

"No," Dylan's voice was full of caution as if she suspected her brother was leading her straight into a trap. "Ana's for a bit before we crash in the treehouse. Why?"

"Will you cover for me with the 'rents?"

Dylan didn't miss a beat. "Absolutely."

One of the things I loved the most about the Cullen family was how close Dean and Dylan were. I didn't know what their parents had done differently than so many others, but the two of them didn't hate each other. They never had. Instead, they liked spending time together. Even though they argued about the silliest things, they never fought in an angry way and always had the other's back.

As an only child who had once wanted a house full of brothers and sisters, it made me extremely envious.

"Thanks."

"Wait a minute," Dylan lifted a finger as Dean attempted to stand. "Why am I covering? Don't you have a date with Vicky tonight?"

"We broke up."

Her eyes practically bulged out of her head, her shock unmistakable. "When?"

"A few days ago."

"Seriously? How did I not know? Why in the hell didn't you tell me? No one at school said anything. Does anyone know? Where are you going tonight?"

Dean took his sister's rapid-fire interrogation in stride. Like it was the most natural thing in the world. "Eastman's party."

Dylan sat forward, eyes intense. "In hopes of running into her, so you can get back together?"

"Fuck, no." Dean looked at me sheepishly. "Sorry." Before I could laugh it off—it wasn't like I hadn't heard him swear—he pushed himself off our chair. "We're done. I'm over it, over her. She won't be there tonight. I'm going to have fun with my friends."

"Why are we covering then? Why not just tell your parents?" The question was lame, but I was curious. The Cullen siblings rarely kept secrets from each other or their parents.

"You know how my mom is. If Vicky calls here looking for me, Mom will feel bad, and she'll try to help. I don't want her to tell Vicky where I am."

"Yeah, but if she wanted to see you that much, she could just go to the party."

"She doesn't know about it," Tate explained as he stood too. "Eastman's parents left this morning on a last-minute weekend getaway. It's gonna be hella crazy." He ran a hand through his chestnut hair, yet all the movement did was draw attention to his bare torso.

My eyes swept over him. I didn't want to admit I'd noticed, but it was hard not to see how stacked he was.

"No one will tell her about it. We don't invite kids." He snapped his fingers as if he'd had the best idea ever. "Hey, you should bring the sisters, man."

"Sister," Dean and I corrected at the same time.

It didn't matter that I'd gone to school with almost the same group of people since I was five and that everyone knew I wasn't biologically a Cullen. Our families had been inseparable for years; almost everywhere they went, we went and vice versa. Somewhere along the way, I'd become an extension of Dylan, and in essence, Dean's second little tagalong.

I hated it.

"Whatever. Bring *Dylan* and *Lennon* tonight." Tate smirked at me as he popped an eyebrow. "Better?"

"They're sophomores," Dean argued. "Dude, you just said we don't invite kids to party with us."

Tate snorted. He knew Dean's reasoning was ridiculous. Other tenth-grade girls went to their parties. Vicky had been a constant when she was Dean's girlfriend. She'd be invited again as soon as they got back together. Given their history, that'd be in about five minutes.

"Kids?" Dylan rolled her eyes and threw a flip flop at her brother. "Irish twins, you ass. We're almost the same age."

Dean still thought of Dylan and me like we were ten, instead of only a few months younger than him. It hadn't always bothered me, but the thoughts I'd had about him lately changed that. I wanted him to see I'd grown up too.

A long moment of silence passed while Dylan and I each held our breath. Dean was the gatekeeper. For us, the only way in was through him. As long as he said no, we'd never get invited. I didn't even know if I wanted to go to a real party, but I definitely wanted to know I could.

He finally nodded. "Yeah, okay." Pointing at Dylan, who was so excited she'd started to wiggle in her seat like a puppy, he narrowed his eyes. "It'll actually be easier this way. They'll think we're going to the movies together."

Tate held out a fist to Dean. "Later." He was halfway back to his house when he turned and started walking backward. "For the record, ladies, I knew you were watching. Hope you liked what you saw."

Dylan's face flamed.

"Busted." Dean laughed all the way back into the house.

Chapter Three

Dean

My sister thought she was a master at hiding her crush on Tate, but everyone knew. In fact, the more she tried to downplay it, the more obvious it became. It'd be kind of cute if it were anyone else following him around, hanging on his every word, making sure she ran into him in the most random places like a thirsty stalker.

But it was Dylan.

I was stuck in the middle, trapped in the back seat of someone else's car as they careened toward the edge of a cliff, and I had no way to stop it.

Dylan was the most tenacious person I knew. Once she got an idea in her head, it took an act of God to change her mind. Tate was never going to look at her as anything more than the little sister he'd never had. He'd grown up next door, spent more time at our house than his own, and in his mind, Dylan was family.

He was just as protective of her as I was. Of both Dylan and Len, actually. So was Shaun Eastman, my other best friend.

The girls might not realize it, but the three of us didn't watch out for them because we wanted to be assholes. It wasn't some pathetic attempt to keep them from having fun either. I didn't care what they did, as long as they weren't putting themselves in danger.

I wasn't a hypocrite.

I'd never taken them to a party because they weren't ready. My friends were hardcore. We'd hit the high school scene running and hadn't slowed down. There was a reason freshmen weren't invited to hang with us, not even when we'd been the ones in ninth grade.

Shaun, Tate, and I had never talked about it, but somewhere along the line, we'd stopped including the girls. If our childhood had proven anything, it was that the two of them thought they were as tough as we were. When one of us had done something, Dylan and Len had done it too, just to prove they could.

Which was fine when you were attempting a new bike trick at the skate park or trying stupid stunts at the lake. Worst that would happen was that one of them would get hurt and we'd get our asses beat when we got home.

It was a totally different ballgame when you got so wired you were on top of the goddamn world and thought you could do anything, smoked until you were too tweaked to function, or drank until you were so hammered you didn't know where in the hell you were, what in the fuck you'd done, or who you'd been with.

I wouldn't have done half the shit I had if Dylan had been with me, I would've been too worried about her to let loose and have fun.

If Len had been around, *well fuck*, I would've been a boy scout. I didn't want her opinion of me to be stained by actions fueled with alcohol or drugs.

The adults hadn't objected to the change. In fact, there had been pure relief on my dad's face the first time I left the house without the girls tagging along. He wasn't so old that he'd forgotten what it was like to be a teenager. He knew the shit we did even if he'd never admit it.

I was only nine months old, not walking or talking yet, when Dylan was born. My parents hadn't planned to have two kids, let alone both in the same year. The day they brought her home, or so the story goes,

Dad put her into the crib next to me and introduced us by saying, "Meet the best friend you'll ever have. You're a team now; take care of each other."

As we grew older, we heard it over and over again. We were the only people who would understand everything we'd go through in life. Our bond unbreakable.

I didn't remember the day I'd become a big brother, but I'd never forget the day I'd gotten Len. She'd been three when my parents' best friends bought the house across the street and altered all our lives. After Uncle Trev and Aunt Gayle went back to their new home, leaving Lennon to play with us while they unpacked, my dad pulled me onto his lap and told me that Lennon James was mine to protect. I needed to take care of her and watch out for her the same way I did Dylan. Even at four, I knew my job was important.

She might not be blood, but she was family just the same. I'd protect her and have her back—always. The way my parents looked out for Len's and vice versa. It's what you did for family.

I'd started that day, thirteen years ago, and had never stopped.

I left the girls on the patio and hurried to my room, desperate for a few minutes of silence.

Rehearsal had been a shitshow. Vicky had blown up my phone most of the day. I didn't have to listen to know she'd filled my voicemail, first with pleading, then hate-filled messages. It was her M.O. When guilt and manipulation didn't work, she got nasty.

I needed a smoke, a bottle of Jack, and to sleep for days.

Now, I didn't even get the night to kick back with friends and relax. Instead, I was on babysitting duty.

I'd never admit it to anyone, even if I could, but I was nervous about taking the girls to Shaun's.

Yeah, sophomores partied with us all the time. But they seemed older. Different.

While every other teenager was out trying new things and living their best life, Len was content to stay in her bubble of innocence. Jesus, if she had her way, she'd spend her weekends at home with her parents, face buried in one of the ten books she still borrowed from the library every Wednesday after school. There was no doubt in my mind that the only reason she ever went anywhere was because my sister dragged her along.

Dylan had a vision of what high school should be—she'd been obsessed with teen dramas as a kid—and she wanted to experience it all, but she didn't want to venture off without Lennon. I didn't know if it was because she didn't want to leave her best friend behind, or if it was because Len was her security blanket. Whatever the reason, she'd made it clear that wherever she went, Len went too.

It wasn't that I wanted to keep them young. As a big brother, I felt the need to shelter them. I'd spent enough time around other people our age to know that Dylan and Len weren't the typical all-American teenagers.

As we'd moved on without them, the girls had eventually made their own group of friends and let the three of us off the hook. We still kept our eyes on them. We knew what they did, whenever they did it.

I just wasn't sure I was ready to introduce them to *my* world.

When my cell rang, I almost ignored it.

I couldn't avoid Vicky forever. Unfortunately. With a sigh, I pushed myself out of the chair and reached for it, relieved when I saw Shaun's name.

"My cousin is a douche," he snarled when I answered. "So much for only a small group from King. Someone from the Academy just invited me to my own party. The one at *my* fucking house."

I scoffed. "Did you really expect it to stay small?"

Shaun's parties were always huge. He was an only child, but his cousins lived two towns over and took full advantage of his parents' frequent absences.

He didn't answer. "You're still coming, right? And bringing the sisters."

The last part wasn't a question. News traveled fast.

"That's the plan."

He chuckled at my flat tone. "Fucker, if your car gets a mysterious flat on the way, I'm coming to get your ass and dragging it back here, girls in tow. This whole night is for you, so you better be here."

"I told you I didn't need a party." I groaned, annoyed. I broke up with Vicky, not the other way around. I didn't need my friends to attempt to cheer me up when I wasn't sad to begin with.

"The best way to get over one chick is to get on top of another."

Closing my eyes, I rubbed my forehead in exasperation. He was an idiot. Casual sex was his thing, not mine, no matter how many times he'd tried to convince me otherwise.

"I'll be there," I assured him.

"With the girls."

"Maybe it's not a good night."

"They're not naïve little kids anymore. They don't give two fucks what you do."

"I know," I insisted. "I only said I'd bring them because I thought it was going to be small."

"You are so full of shit," he laughed. "Ya know, in a few weeks, there'll be summer parties everywhere. If you don't start letting them come to ours, they'll go to their own. Where we can't see what they're doing. Or who they're doing it with. At least here, you can establish ground rules and shit. Stop being a controlling dick and bring 'em."

I didn't point out that setting rules was the definition of being a controlling dick. I liked the idea too much. Maybe Dylan would be so pissed about having rules she'd back out, and I wouldn't have to be the bad guy.

"That's actually a good idea. First rule: The girls are off limits."

His laugh was unrestrained. I rolled my eyes while he struggled to get control of himself. "Shit. That's hilarious."

"I'm serious, you dick."

"That's what makes it so funny. They're the little sisters, man. They've *always* been off limits. Every upperclassman knows that. Our college friends know that. No one touches—hell, no one even looks at —the little sisters. Unless they want to drink their meals through a straw for the next six months."

"You know I only have one sister, right?"

"I do." He paused for a moment. "Wait. Does that mean that Lennon's fair game now? 'Cause she wore a skirt the other day that made my mind go all kinds of places it shouldn't. I felt dirty for a hot minute."

My fist tightened around the phone. *Fuck him.* I knew exactly which day he was talking about because every time I'd seen her, I'd fought the urge to rip off my shirt and tie it around her waist. It had distracted me all damn day. I would've insisted she go home and change but didn't want to deal with her accusations of misogyny or hear a lecture about how our culture objectified women. She would have just told me that if her clothes made me uncomfortable, I didn't have to look.

Like I could actually see anything else, no matter what she was wearing.

"No," I ground out, failing my attempt to sound neutral. "Simply pointing out that calling them the little sisters is weird."

"Only for you, 'cause you want to tap that."

"Fuck off." I most certainly did not want to "tap that." But I also didn't want my friends to want "tap that" either.

"Don't even try to pretend you don't wonder what her milky-white thighs would feel like as earmuffs or that your pants don't get tighter every time her cheeks hollow out as she sucks on one of those damn Tootsie Pops. I swear Mr. Padilla gives them to her just to watch her lips wrap around it, the sick fuck."

"Jesus. Really?" I wasn't going to think about Lennon's legs wrapped around my shoulders, squeezing my head. I wasn't. Yet, as soon as I closed my eyes, that's all I could see.

I forced the image out of my mind and tried to focus on the other half of what he'd said.

Mr. Padilla was the one who supplied Lennon with the damn suckers she had every afternoon? I needed to ask her about that. And keep an eye on the communications teacher.

One thing at a time.

"Asshole. What did I just say?"

"You only have one sister, and Lennon is fair game." Before I could reply, he snorted. "I'm messing with you. You know virgins aren't my thing. Too complicated. Too clingy."

Oh, for fuck's sake. We were not talking about her sexual experiences. Or lack of.

"She's too young for you. She's just a kid."

"Yeah," he scoffed. "Like Vicky was too young for *you*? They're in the same class, dipshit."

A fact I ignored whenever someone pointed it out. Len and Vicky were so different, worlds apart really. It was easy to think my ex was older than she was.

"I gotta go hide all my parents' expensive crap before strangers invade my house. Any other laws you need to lay down?"

"No." I sighed. "They're not for you, anyway."

"At some point, Dylan's got to realize she doesn't have a chance with Tate, right? There's nothing she could do that would make him change his mind about her. That's not on you. You didn't draw a line in the sand. He did."

That's what worried me. One day my sister was going to figure out that it wasn't me keeping Tate away from her; he truly wasn't interested. That reality would break her heart.

Yeah, he flirted shamelessly. He did with every woman he talked to; moms included. Half the time, I didn't think he knew what he was doing.

Tate always tried to include Dylan because she was his friend, not because he was secretly in love with her. He wanted Lennon to join us too. We were his family, something he wanted to hold onto as long as he could.

"One day, she will. Until then, let me be the bad guy."

He thought about it for a minute. "Give 'em more than one rule. Don't make it so obvious."

"Like what? Don't talk to strangers?"

"Yeah," he scoffed. "No, asshole. Shit like don't drink anything they don't open themselves. Don't leave the party with anyone until they've told someone where they're going and with whom. Don't have sex with someone until they know his real name, marital status, and really want to sleep with him. Basic rules all women should follow because we're a bunch of pigs." He paused. "See you in a few hours."

"I'll be there. With the girls."

Something told me I was going to regret taking them.

Chapter Four

Lennon

"You're so not wearing that."

Dylan's words greeted me before I'd even shut the front door behind me and stepped into the foyer. I glanced up, finding her leaning against the hall railing, glaring down at me.

I almost snorted. Poor thing was obviously freaked out. When Dylan got nervous, her neurosis started to show.

As soon as she'd told her parents that Dean was going to drive us to the movies, they'd made him promise to get us home safely and bailed. They were on the way to the city with my parents to do whatever old people did. Which meant Uncle Chad wasn't around to police her outfit, Aunt Tasha wasn't there to critique, and Dylan was going all out.

I motioned to my clothes. "It was either this or track pants. I thought you'd prefer jeans."

"Uh, you have shorts. Or that dress your mom got you a few weeks ago."

I couldn't stop the horrified laugh. "The sparkly Easter monstrosity I wore to church? Yeah, totally not wearing that to a party. It's thirty degrees out there. They said it might snow." I eyed the black halter and plaid mini she wore accusingly. "I'm not going to freeze just so I can look good."

"Lennon." The whine threw me, but the way she stomped her foot in exasperation made me shake my head in bewilderment. "You have UGGs."

"You've lost your mind if you think I'm wearing shorts with boots. What's wrong with my outfit?" I glanced down at the mini vest over the black tee I'd paired with my favorite low-rise denim and Converse. I'd even slapped on lip gloss and mascara and triple checked it all before I'd left the house. I didn't look bad. Plain, maybe even boring. But not bad.

"You look like you're going to a job interview."

My snicker was completely unladylike, but she was obnoxious.

"We're not hanging out with friends. We're going to a *party*." She sighed dramatically as her gaze shifted behind me. "Tell her she can't wear that."

Surprised, I glanced over my shoulder. Dean was propped against the entrance to the living room, one foot crossed over the other. I hadn't seen him there when I'd walked in. I hadn't heard him come in either.

His eyes roamed over me slowly, from the sneakers I'd drawn on to the colorful streaks in the hair I'd left down instead of hiding away. I braced myself; Dean always found an issue with the clothes I wore. They were either too tight, too short, or too low cut, even though nothing I owned fit into any of those categories.

He was worse than my dad.

Instead, Dean dismissed me with a small shrug. "Actually, you are hanging out with friends. She looks fine." He pushed himself off the wall and swaggered into the middle of the foyer. "Can we go now?"

With an annoyed groan, Dylan turned and slowly descended the stairs, flipping long dark hair over her shoulder. Glowing, probably from all the self-tanner she insisted she needed to get ready for spring break, she looked more like a fashion model than a teenager playing grown-up with smudged kohl liner and full-blown smoky eyes. For a moment, the briefest heartbeat, I was envious of my best friend's beauty and style.

Dean rolled his hand, hurrying us along as he yanked open the door and held it for us. Before we could step outside, he slammed it shut again.

He held up a finger as if he'd remembered something important. "We need to set some ground rules."

Dylan rolled her eyes at me. "Of course, we do."

He ignored her. "Don't drink anything in a cup. Not even if someone you think you trust gives it to you. Not even if you get it yourself. Bottles only. Don't leave your drink alone for a second. If you set it down or take your eyes off it, get a new one."

Unease crept up my spine. I wondered if I should back out. Parties at Ana's were lowkey, with our closest friends passing a few stolen bottles around.

"You seriously think someone would be dumb enough to drug one of us?" Dylan asked like it was the most absurd idea she'd ever heard.

"Not if they want to live." Dean's face was hard.

I had no doubt he meant it. I'd seen his hands bloodied and bruised more than once when he'd defended our honor.

"I don't know who'll be there," he continued, "which means they might not know who you are. If they don't know who you are, they won't know you're related to me, which means they don't know the shit they'll be in if they fuck with you."

"Fine." Dylan crossed her arms over her chest, following his rambling. "What else?"

"Don't go into a room alone with someone you don't know."

"Please," Dylan sneered, "that's a given. Len and I use the buddy system."

His eyes narrowed on me in accusation before moving back to her. "When I say it's time to leave, you come with me. No questions, no arguments."

"Makes sense," I answered before Dylan could argue.

Dean was our ride. We were leaving when he was ready, even if she wasn't.

"One more. My friends are off limits."

Dylan's arms fell as she glared at her brother. "That's not fair. You're friends with *everyone.*"

She had a point. While we all knew everyone in our high school—small-town problems, kind of like first world problems, but, you know, smaller—Dean didn't belong to one specific group. He had such a busy personality he seemed to fit into all of them. However, he also had friends in every group, which meant that even if someone wasn't his friend, they were a friend of a friend. Around there, that meant something.

It wasn't only in school either. It seemed like Dean knew everybody, everywhere. He couldn't walk into a store in town without someone stopping him to chat.

Maybe it was because of his connection with the theater, maybe it was because he'd helped make soccer a sport people wanted to watch, maybe it was because he talked to everyone like they were his long-lost friend. Whatever the reason, people didn't just know him. They loved him.

Screw Kevin Bacon. It was like the six-degrees of Dean Cullen. It was annoying as hell.

"Nah," he shook his head dismissively. "There are a few freshmen I don't recognize on sight."

"You want us to sleep with children?" Her horrified jeer drew a smile from me.

"I don't want you to sleep with *anyone,*" he clarified. "But I really don't want you to flirt with my friends. Or talk to them. Hell, don't even look at them unless you have to."

After a moment, Dylan's hands moved to her hips. "What if your friends flirt with *us?*"

Dean bit his cheek as he fought a smile. "They won't."

He sounded so confident in his answer that I didn't doubt him. He'd either had the same conversation with his friends, or he knew that they weren't interested in either of us.

"Little sisters are off limits," he explained, answering my thoughts.

Dylan narrowed her eyes on him. "Then my friends are off limits to you too."

He didn't spare a glance in my direction. Instead, he let out a low, bemused chuckle. Clearly the idea he'd like one of her friends was absurd. "Deal."

"That means *all* my friends." The way she stressed the word made me think she had someone specific in mind. I wondered which of our pals she thought had caught his eye.

"All your friends. Got it."

"I mean it, Dean. If we're going to follow these stupid rules, you are too."

"I mean it too, Dylan," he mocked. "All my friends, including next-door neighbors who don't mind if you look, but you really can't touch."

"I hate you."

He laughed as he ruffled her hair, ignoring her attempts to bat him away. "You love me."

The meteorologist had been right. It started to storm before we left our cul-de-sac. So much for the warmer temps from a few hours before sticking around. There went my Sunday plans of sitting on the deck, reading in the sun.

Dean parked in the closest spot possible, but the walk to the Eastman's McMansion was still miserable. Sleet and freezing rain pelted us, each step more unpleasant than the last. By the time we made our way inside; my feet were soaked, Dylan's arms and legs were bright red, and we were shivering.

Dean, on the other hand, looked warm and comfortable in ripped jeans, boots, and a heavy zip-front hoodie. I should have worn a coat, screw fashion.

When I stalled by the door, shocked by the number of people crammed inside, Dean put one hand on the small of my back, one on his sister's shoulder, and pushed us farther into the house. People called to him in greeting, but I didn't recognize a soul.

Tate's description was spot-on. It was crazy. Nothing like the parties I'd been to. Not that I had a lot to compare it to.

Dean led us to an enclosed porch at the back of the house. Thankfully, it was both heated and filled with familiar faces.

"Jesus. Somebody get the little sisters a drink," Shaun hollered as he offered his fist to Dean, his eyes glued on a shivering Dylan. "They're going to freeze to death without it."

"You good here for a minute?" Dean asked us as Shaun turned toward a table filled with bottles.

I wasn't. I wanted to find a quiet corner and hide. If I admitted that, though, he might not leave my side. Instead, I nodded. One of us should have fun.

"Remember the ground rules. I'll find you when it's time to go."

Before either of us could answer, he moved away, joining Tate and a group of girls on the other side of the room. They were all dressed similar to Dylan, hair and makeup done to perfection. As Dean leaned down to hug one, leaving his arm around her shoulders, jealousy burned in my gut.

It was only a dream; I tried to remind myself. I was not crushing on Dean Cullen. No way.

Yet, I couldn't tear my eyes away. Thankfully, big, bulky shoulders stepped in front of me, blocking him from view. Shaun smirked down as he lifted two miniature bottles of vodka, offering them to us.

I shook my head as Dylan nodded. He opened both, pushed one into her open hand, and downed the other. Beside me, Dylan smiled and lifted it to her lips.

"There's whiskey and Goldschläger too, if you want those instead."

"I'm good. Thanks."

Shaun—the guy always good for a laugh—reached out a hand and grabbed my fingers. "You're freezing, Len. Drink something before you get hypothermia."

Shaun was both calming and familiar. For a moment, I longed to step into the safety of his arms and let him block off the chaos around me. I took a small step in his direction, but when I glanced to his right, my feet faltered.

A small group of juniors and seniors stood close, watching us. While most of them seemed curious, a few didn't bother trying to hide their agitated expressions and angry scowls. They might not have uttered any words, but I got the message loud and clear. I was tolerated because of Dean, but I wasn't welcome.

Someone handed me a beer. I accepted, only to have something in my hands so I wouldn't reach for my friend. I craved Shaun's warmth, but the nasty looks I'd gotten from the girls around us made me feel uneasy. Unwanted attention always did.

Flailing for something to say, I recalled the words he'd said a few minutes before. "Alcohol actually doesn't help you get warm."

Shaun raised an eyebrow in challenge. "It warms you up. Like hot coffee but better."

"No, it doesn't. It makes your blood vessels dilate. You'll feel warmer a few drinks in, because there'll be extra blood warming your skin. But once you stop drinking, you'll get cold really quickly."

He watched me warily for a moment, trying to figure out if I was being serious before he barked out a loud laugh. "Easy fix, sis. Don't stop drinking."

Sis. Gah. My fingers tightened around the bottle at the annoying nickname. I was not related to Dean, damn it. "Not his sister."

Shaun's eyebrows rose at my snappy tone, genuinely surprised. He took a step closer and dropped his voice so only I could hear it. "A fact that never bothered you before."

Stupid dream. I met his intense stare with one of my own. I didn't know if I was daring him to ask why I'd had an abrupt change of heart or begging him not to. I wasn't sure how to answer if he did.

"Or," my best friend started, oblivious to our whispered conversation, "you drink so much you forget you were cold."

"I like the way you think." Shaun laughed and tossed an arm around her shoulders, tugging her close, his eyes still on me. "Or I could warm you up."

If Dylan's smile got any bigger, her face would break. Completely in her element, she beamed up at the giant oaf as he rubbed her arm. Maybe Dean had given his friends the same "off limits" chat he'd given us, but it didn't seem like Shaun listened any better than Dylan had.

Not that Dean had to worry about the two of them. Shaun was sickeningly in love with drawing and sports. They came first. He'd briefly dated over the years, but he was infamous for his hook-ups with random strangers–during the regular season only. Girls were a distraction he wouldn't tolerate during playoffs.

As for Dylan, Shaun definitely wasn't even on her radar. No, she was hopelessly head over heels for Tate. He was all she focused on, all she could see. She wanted to impress Dean's friends, yes, but only to get Tate's attention. Maybe even prove she was worthy of him.

I hated that thought process. No one should ever have to prove their worth. You either liked someone, or you didn't. You were either attracted to someone, or you weren't. You couldn't force another person to feel something they didn't.

"So that's a myth, huh?"

I glanced over, surprised to find Ross McKinney, a senior who played soccer with Dean, standing close. "It is. Alcohol actually lowers your core temp. But you knew that already, Mr. Honor Society."

"Tell me more," he demanded with a lift of his chin, ignoring my jab. "I love it when you talk nerdy to me."

"I do what I can." I chuckled, raising a shoulder. "We all have to be good at something, right?"

"Lennon James," he drawled, voice deep. "I almost didn't recognize you without your notebook and pen." He inched even closer, pressed his shoulder into mine and lowered his voice to a sharp whisper. "Are you undercover?"

"You caught me," I held a finger to my lips. "Don't tell."

"Not a word." He moved his fingers over his mouth in a zipping motion. "What's the story?"

I pursed my lips as my eyes moved quickly over the crowd. "Quiet, dorky girl crashes party to see how the in-crowd lives?" It sounded awful, even to me.

"I like it. Now that you've had unfettered access to the other half, what do you think?"

"That I should have stayed home with a good book and fuzzy slippers and enjoyed my night off."

Ross laughed. "I thought reporters never took time off because there was always a story somewhere?"

"Pretty sure those are real reporters. Ya know, the ones who don't work at the *King High Chronicle,* in exchange for an elective credit."

His grin grew wide as he pointed the neck of his beer toward me. "Don't knock it. I've read your articles. Today, it's a student paper. Tomorrow, the *Associated Press.*"

I didn't argue. That was the goal, my dream. Not to be a newspaper journalist. Hell, no. Broadcast news. Television segments. One day, I'd produce stories that mattered. Until then, I'd take any experience—and every compliment—I could get.

"I was shocked as shit when you walked through that door. You were pretty much the last person I expected to see here tonight."

"Right?" I agreed as I surveyed the room one more time. "I may be a little out of my element."

"Not at all." His eyes burned into mine. "But I thought hell would freeze before Cullen got his head out of his ass."

I didn't know what he meant.

Seeing my confused frown, Ross clarified. "You came with him, didn't you?"

"Oh. Yeah. He brought Dylan and me."

I glanced in her direction. She was still talking to Shaun, his arm around her waist. A senior named Jenna had joined them and was telling Dylan a story that had my friend cracking up. The sight made me smile.

As I watched the two of them, Ross's words from a moment before sunk in. Realizing what he meant, I spun back toward him. "Oh! Dean and me? No. He was my ride. That's it."

"So, you aren't together?"

I forced a laugh, but it came out more like a strangled gurgle. "God, no."

"Sorry," Ross shifted as he cleared his throat. "When I heard he and Vicky broke up, then saw you here with him, I just assumed."

I hated how uncomfortable he looked. I shrugged, hoping to ease the tension swirling around us. "They're fighting, but they'll be back together as soon as the guilty party apologizes or the other one gets lonely."

"No," he shook his head. "This time it's final." He motioned to the room around us. "Or we wouldn't be here." He paused for a moment, watching me closely. "This is his breakup celebration," he finally explained.

"His what?" I didn't know if I should be horrified or intrigued.

Ross's lips twisted in amusement. "It's a thing. When you're done with your ex, really over them, you let the world know you're available again with a party. Tonight is all about Cullen letting go, to commiserate his loss with his closest friends, remember that he still has goodness in his life, and let himself heal. Vicky's probably having her own."

"Wow. That is the most absurd thing I'd ever heard."

Ross chuckled. "It's high school. It's all insane."

I looked around again, finally understanding why most of the girls were dressed the way they were and why so many of them were watching Dean like he was the waiter about to serve tiramisu. The constant attention was a typical occurrence, yes, but they seemed overly interested tonight. He was, after all, quite the catch.

Rebound groupies. Apparently, it was a real thing. I was ashamed to be a woman.

"By 'goodness in his life,'" I used air quotes, "I'm going to assume you mean hook-ups. It's a party to show the girls in town he's single and ready to mingle." The mirth in my voice was unmistakable.

"My, my. Aren't we cynical?" Ross snorted. "No, it's not code for other options. It's so he doesn't get depressed and drink himself half to death thinking he lost the best thing that happened to him."

Vicky was hardly the best thing that had happened to Dean. I wouldn't even put her in the top ten. I couldn't say that in my out loud voice though. Instead, I shook my head and argued another way.

"I call bullshit. Everyone wanted an excuse to get wasted. Not that they've ever needed one."

Ross chuckled. "You didn't feel the hate emanating from every chick and half the dudes here when you walked in the door? They all thought you were with him."

"I'm always with him," I explained. "People see him. They just don't notice me."

"Believe me. People notice you. And not because of Cullen."

It was the sweetest thing he could have said.

"Thank you."

It was his turn to look confused. When he started to say something, I cut him off.

"Not for saying that, even though it totally made my day. You're the only person here who hasn't called me his little sister," I explained. "It's nice to know that someone remembers I'm actually not. I could kiss you I'm so happy."

"Yeah?" Ross popped an eyebrow playfully.

I laughed.

The back door opened, giving me a view of the massive yard, as a gush of cold air washed over the room. I started to shiver, my teeth began to chatter, and I slid closer to Ross almost involuntarily, desperate for body heat.

"Here," Dean appeared out of nowhere and thrust his sweatshirt at me. "Put this on before you get sick."

"You can't catch a cold from being cold," I argued as I snatched the hoodie and slid it on without objection. "Thank you."

It was still warm; the strong scent of cedar and citrus clung to the fabric. I felt like he'd wrapped me in a comforting hug and was holding tight.

"Another myth?" Ross moaned playfully. "I love it when she goes all nerdy, man."

Dean glowered. "What?"

I shook my head with an embarrassed snort. "Nothing."

"It's not 'nothing.'" Ross grinned. "Lennon is like our own personal MythBuster. It's hot as hell when she starts blurting out random facts."

"Is that so?" Dean crossed his arms over his chest, his narrowed eyes aimed at me.

He thought I was breaking one of his stupid ground rules. I wasn't. Neither was Ross. Not really.

Unless he'd been serious about not talking to his friends. Which was impossible. They were the only people he let us interact with.

An awkward silence settled between the three of us as I waited for Dean to leave. For the first time, I heard music blaring from the other room and hummed along absentmindedly. I lifted the beer to my lips, dreading the bitter taste I hated, but desperate to do *something*.

Before I could tip the bottle back, Dean ripped it out of my hands.

"Did you open this?" He demanded as his face twisted in an angry scowl.

"I... um...," my eyes widened as I tried to remember. Realizing I hadn't, that I didn't know who had given it to me, my mouth fell open as I shook my head. "Shit."

His features softened slightly. "Len."

He didn't need to say more. I felt awful.

"I gave it to her," Ross interjected, his tone sardonic. "Let me guess, lil' sis isn't allowed to have a beer?"

"Coors Light isn't beer. It's watered-down horse piss." To make a point, Dean handed the bottle to the first person who walked by. They took it without explanation. "And no. She's not."

"Hey, party people!" Dylan, oblivious to the tension, looped one arm through mine, the other through her brother's, saving me. "We're going to play beer pong. Want in?"

I didn't. I'd seen it played in movies but had zero interest in learning the rules or embarrassing myself in front of everyone. However, I needed the escape.

"No. But I'll come watch."

"You can be my cheerleader," Dylan grinned, let go of her brother, and pulled me behind Shaun as his large body cleared a path through the crowd for us.

The dining room had been converted into a game room, and the table had been turned into a giant ping-pong arena. The two teams playing quickly cleared out when they saw our group roll in.

Shaun claimed Dylan as his partner, making a large group of girls sigh in disappointment while my best friend beamed. As Jenna and Tate teamed up to take them on, I grabbed an unopened water from a tub of ice and leaned against the wall, content to fade into the background. Dean joined me, settling in to watch.

We didn't talk during the first game other than to cheer on Dylan as Shaun carried them to a crushing victory. When another team stepped in to challenge them, Dean slid closer to me so I could hear him.

"Any warmer?"

"Yes, finally. Thank you, again." I reached for the zipper as my eyes met his. "Do you want your shirt back?"

His hand covered mine, stopping me. "No. I was just making sure."

Everyone around us cheered, but I couldn't look away from him. Wearing his shirt was one thing but having him so near was pure torture. Images from the dream flashed through my mind, screwing with my memories, confusing me until I didn't know what was real and what wasn't.

Dream Lennon would grab Dean, pull him close, and kiss him until we both forgot we were in a room full of people. Of course, dream Dean wouldn't object like the real version would. For a moment, I let my mind get lost in the alternate reality and could almost feel his weight against me, pushing me back into the shelves.

"You okay?"

The question, full of concern, snapped me out of my fantasy. Too late, I realized I was staring at his mouth, my heartbeat wild, lungs working overtime. I tucked my water into one of the giant pockets on the sweatshirt and wiped sweaty palms on my thighs.

"Yeah, I'm fine," I lied as I pretended to watch the game. "You don't have to babysit me, you know?"

He huffed out a laugh. "I'm not babysitting you. Although I should be. I left you alone for five minutes and look what happened." His fingers found one of my rainbow curls and gave it a tug. "Who knew you'd be such a little rule breaker?"

I snorted. It was one rule. Maybe two, but only if—and that was a big *if*—he counted my talking to Ross. I pushed myself away from the wall. "I need a beer."

"You don't drink beer."

I turned narrowed eyes on him. Big mistake. He was so damn attractive it wasn't funny, especially when his hair was slightly messy like he'd just run his hands through it.

"What makes you think that?"

His cocky smile was instant. "I know what you like to drink, what alcohol makes you sick, and which kind you hate." He shrugged as he tapped the side of his head. "I pay attention. Good memory, remember?" He took a step forward. "Stay here. I'll get you something."

My hand was on his arm before I realized what I was doing. He stalled instantly but didn't pull away. "I can get it. I don't need you to take care of me. Go. Have fun with your friends. Celebrate being single." I tipped my head toward the group of seniors from earlier.

"I'm not celebrating be..." he broke off midsentence. "Who told you that? Never mind." He rolled his eyes, annoyed. "McKinney. Really?" He shook his head as if he couldn't believe it. "Out of every one here, you and Ross Mic-fucking-kinney?"

I glanced around to make sure no one was listening. Thankfully, everyone close enough seemed engrossed in the game. "Why do you keep saying his name like that?" I snapped, at the end of my rope. "Is this the part where you tell me he's a closeted scum bag? Reveal some big secret? Because unless you know something I don't, I can't figure out what your problem is. So, let's have it. What's wrong with him? Is he the reason you were afraid someone would drug our drinks? Does he have some weird sexual fetish you don't want me to find out about?" I crossed my arms. "He's into furries, isn't he?" I shook my head in mock sadness. "It's always the quiet ones."

His forehead wrinkled. "What? No. Ross is a great guy." He frowned. "I don't know what in the hell a furry is, or how that's a fetish, but now I'm more concerned that you do."

An uncomfortable laugh escaped, and I bit my lip in an attempt to stay serious. "If he's so great, what's your problem? I didn't break your precious rules, big man. Ross and I have a study hall together, so technically, he's not just your friend. He's mine too. You said your friends were off limits. You never said mutual friends were."

My eyes grew wide as I forced myself not to slap a hand across my mouth. I wasn't sure why I'd said that. I wasn't interested in Ross.

46

Although, if people thought I was, maybe they wouldn't figure out that Dean was the object of my every fantasy lately.

"Nothing is wrong with Ross," Dean snarled. "It threw me, you flirting with him."

"You shouldn't be surprised. He makes me laugh. When he's around, I feel both smart and pretty, which most guys our age seem to think is an oxymoron. He isn't afraid to nerd out with me. He's totally my type."

"Type?" Dean dismissed the idea with a cruel laugh. "You're fifteen. You don't have a *type* yet."

Again with the age. Irritation coursed through me. He'd turned seventeen last month, and my birthday was around the corner. It was irritating that the dates fell just right, and for almost three months every year, Dean was technically two years older than me. During those few weeks, he never let me forget it.

"You know, you're right," I challenged. "I don't know what attracts me the most. Like, I never thought I'd be into muscles, but watching Tate lift weights makes me lose my mind and does things to me I can't explain. I want to touch every inch of him to see if they're as hard as they look. I love that Ross gets my humor, but you know who cracks me up? Shaun. I never stop smiling when he's around. He's such a goofball. He's so big that he makes me feel safe. Plus, he's nice to look at." I shrugged as if I didn't have a care in the world. "I might not have a type yet, but it'll be fun figuring it out."

Lies. Big, fat, ugly lies. My pants were going to engulf in flames at any moment.

His jaw started to tic. Seeing him annoyed was almost satisfying. Yet, all he said was, "You done?"

His lack of response irked me in a way I couldn't understand.

"I know what I don't like though. Domineering asshats who are so full of themselves they expect everyone to do what they say without reason or explanation. Good thing or I'd be helplessly attracted to you."

Dean stared down at me, oblivious to the beer pong game going on behind him or the people crowded around us. Finally, he nodded slowly as his lips turned up in a small smile. "Yeah, good thing."

I couldn't think of a single comeback. Not having a response to wipe the smirk off his face made me even angrier.

"Stay here. I'll grab you a drink you'll actually like. Then you can get drunk enough to tell me what in the hell a furry is."

"Nope. I'll never get that drunk. That's what they made Google for. Just clear your search history. Your mom will freak if she sees it."

"We'll see."

I didn't want to smile. I definitely didn't want to laugh. Yet as I watched him walk away, I chuckled. Dean drove me absolutely insane. One minute I wanted to smack him, the next I wanted him to grab me and kiss me breathless.

Stupid, stupid dream.

Dylan was at my side before I had a chance to look away. "What was that about?"

I tried to feign ignorance. "What?"

Her knowing smirk was so much like her brother's it annoyed me. "What'd you do to piss off Mr. Broody?"

"Ross gave me an open beer. Then he, get this, talked to me."

She cackled. "Oh my God. The horror." Her fingers wrapped around mine as she started to back up, pulling me with her. "Come on. Everyone's moving to the garage. Let's join them."

I dragged my feet, hesitating. "But—"

"No." She shook her head. "You've had time to acclimate to your surroundings. Now it's time to have fun. Tell me all about your conversation with Ross."

I glanced over my shoulder as she pulled me from the room but couldn't see Dean. Maybe he wasn't going to bring me a drink anyway. Maybe it had been his way to escape. With a sigh, I turned back to my best friend and vowed to relax and attempt to have fun.

Chapter Five

Dean

"You crashing here?"

"I've had two drinks all night." I didn't bother to look up from the fire. "I'm sober as a priest."

"How do we know priests don't drink? All that wine. Regretted vows of celibacy. I bet you they're lit half the damn time," Tate sat in the lawn chair next to me. "I wasn't worried about *you*. Little sisters are tipsy as fuck."

Across from me, Shaun chortled. "Tipsy? You mean drunk off her ass."

I didn't miss the way he'd changed the topic of conversation from "sisters" to Dylan. Or the look he shot me as he did.

I'd escaped to the covered patio an hour before and started a fire in the pit to keep myself from following the girls around. If I was honest with myself, I could admit it was only Len I was trailing. But as Dylan dragged her from room to room, refusing to let Lennon out of her sight, it felt like I was spying on my sister. I hated it. So, I'd put down my whiskey, declined the pipe passed in my direction, and headed outside to let the stormy air clear my head.

Shaun joined me, an unlit joint hanging from his lips, not long after. I'd sat with my back to the house in an attempt to avoid seeing anything, while he'd moved his chair to have the best view possible. We hadn't said much, but I knew from his agitated sighs and irritated groans that he'd kept an eye out.

"Why in the fuck are we all straight?"

The question didn't need an answer. It was obvious. The three of us had never intentionally stayed sober at a party.

"Next time—" Shaun started.

"Next time?" I shook my head. "This was a one and done."

"Next time," he flipped me off as he continued, "we'll take turns being party guardian. No reason for all three of us to miss out on the fun."

"Fuck that," Tate took the words out of my mouth. He leaned forward, scrubbing his hands over his face. "I'll do it." He gave each of us a hard look before we could argue. "We can't keep excluding them. All three of us don't need to spend the next year and a half like this. I can't get twisted around her; I'm afraid of what will happen. I'll do it. I'll be the Designated Dry."

"Dude, it's Dylan. She's all of five-feet-nothing and weighs maybe a buck-ten soaking wet. It's not like she's going to wait for you to pass out and take advantage. She's too fucking sweet. Plus, let's be real. I doubt she'd know what to do."

"No." I shook my head at part of Shaun's argument and ignored the rest—it was my baby sister we were talking about after all—as I watched Tate. He looked completely defeated. "He's afraid he'll hurt *her.*"

"I'm gonna tell her," He snapped defensively as he dropped his head back to stare at the ceiling. "Jesus. I can't stand the thought of disappointing her, so it's not like I can hook up with someone else to get the point across. But fuck," he dragged the word out, "the way she looks at me..." his swallow was so loud I could hear it over the crackling of the fire. "She sees everything I do."

"At some point, she's got to realize it's one-sided and move on," Shaun offered.

This was uncharted territory for us. Usually, when we talked about chicks, it was because we wanted their attention, never because we were trying to avoid it.

"Will she?" He sighed. "You guys keep saying that, but then it gets worse. I know she's not really my sister, but it's weird as fuck." He lifted his head. "Like the thought of you and Len. Can you imagine Lennon following you around, trying to flirt and shit?"

I ignored the way my muscles tightened at her name.

Shaun coughed, trying to cover his laugh, but it was painfully obvious. Then the asshole opened his mouth. "Len's not the little sister though. If she came onto me the way Dylan's been after you, I'm not sure I'd say no."

Fuck him. Dickhead. He was trying to get me to react. I flipped him off with both hands.

"I would," Tate assured us. "We grew up together, man. She'll always be a little sister."

"Not mine. Think about it this way," Shaun didn't finish. Instead, he cleared his throat. "Shit. Incoming."

"What are you guys way out here?" My sister asked, mixing two phrases together, as she attempted, and failed, to step onto the brick patio, her words as fucked up as she was. "You're missin'."

Before I could stand, Lennon took her hand, leading her slowly, trying to offer help.

Dylan had only taken a few steps when she stumbled again, tripping over her own feet. Lennon steadied her before the three of us could offer help. However, when Dylan started to tilt to the side, Shaun reached out and pulled her into his lap.

"What are we missing?" he asked as he helped Dylan move wet hair out of her face.

She looked at him, then around the fire, surprised to see us. "I don't know. What?"

"Someone had fun tonight."

"Yeah. One of us." Lennon smiled. "Unfortunately, I don't think she'll remember it."

Tate held out a hand. "Come 'ere. We only keep three chairs out here. That way, unwanted company can't stay. You can sit with me."

I didn't miss the way Len glanced at my sister before she tucked a bright rainbow-colored chunk of hair behind an ear and shook her head. "I'm good. Thanks."

Dylan wasn't paying any attention. Sprawled across Shaun as if she were boneless, she giggled at something he'd whispered in her ear. She was going to feel miserable in the morning. Thankfully, our parents wouldn't be home until the afternoon.

"Any chance you're ready?" Lennon asked me quietly. Her eyes were full of hope, almost as if she were begging me to say yes.

"You never answered me. You crashing here?" Tate repeated the question from earlier.

I tore my eyes away from Len and shook my head. "I've gotta get the girls home. Need a ride?"

My best friend hesitated for a moment, trying to decide. "I'm gonna stay."

"I don't blame you." I pushed myself up. It was still early. The music was blaring, drowned out only by laughter. The storm was still raging. People wouldn't start clearing out for hours. I touched Len's elbow lightly. "What about you? Wanna head out?"

Relief washed over her face. "You have no idea."

"You're so lucky," Dylan told us. For the umpteenth time in ten minutes. "Jenna says it's gonna be the bomb. *The* party of the year."

"So you've said," I mumbled under my breath. "Everyone is going to be there. Except you."

"Dean!" Lennon hissed quietly, her tone more amused than scolding, as she backhanded my stomach lightly. "Stop."

"Everyone who is everyone is going to be there," my sister whined. "But me."

"She can't go because she's going to be stuck on a sunny tropical paradise with your grandparents," Len whispered, predicting Dylan's next words. "Can you imagine how awful that will be?"

"A tragedy, really." I nodded, my eyes glued to the road. I'd driven in the snow and on icy roads so many times I was perfectly comfortable. However, I was afraid if I looked at my passenger's seat, I'd stare at Len —she never rode upfront. I liked having her there entirely too much. "I'm the lucky asshole who gets to stay home for a week alone, instead of being forced to go to the Caribbean."

"It's not fair," Dylan cried again from where she laid across the backseat.

I couldn't see her, but I had no doubt she had one arm flung over her forehead dramatically with tears streaming down her cheeks.

"I'll be stuck on some stupid island in the middle of nowhere, instead of at the one party that actually matters. Not you! *You* get to go. You'll all be having fun. It's just not fair," she wailed. "I'm joining drama next year."

"Wow. With that performance, maybe you should. Dean belongs to the community theater, not the drama club, babe. Even with a brilliant performance like this one, you wouldn't make the cut."

I couldn't stop my laugh. Lennon rarely got snarky with my sister, but apparently, even she'd reached her limit.

"I'm not sure if I should be worried or impressed. A few hours ago, you were biting off my head. Now you're trying to defend me?"

"Don't flatter yourself. Maybe if she hadn't screamed so loudly that the entire block heard her when she found out your grandparents were taking your family on a cruise, I'd be more sympathetic. But it's all she's talked about for months. It isn't like you didn't want to go. Seriously, you're missing the trip of a lifetime. She's missing a party. It's not a big deal."

"Yeah, but 'it's the party of the year.'" I pointed out, repeating my sister's words as I pulled into my driveway.

I was thankful to find our houses still dark. Yes, the parents planned to be gone all weekend, but in the back of my mind, there was always a nagging fear that one day I'd come home, higher than a kite, and they'd catch me. I definitely didn't want them to see Dylan tanked.

"Yeah," Lennon scoffed. "Aren't you glad you get to avoid white sandy beaches and swimming with dolphins, so you can go to Jenna's party?"

Dylan pulled herself up and attempted to push open her door. "It's so not fair."

With a sigh, I got out and scooped my sister into my arms. There was no reason for her to kill herself in her obnoxious sky-high heels. Who wears stripper heels in a snowstorm? My sister, that's who.

"I can walk."

I'd almost believe her, except each word was emphasized with a hiccup.

Leaning her head on my shoulder, she closed her eyes. "I'm wicked dizzy."

"Hey," I jostled her, trying to keep her awake. "Keep your eyes open, or you'll get sick."

I was all the way to the door before I realized I'd slipped my keys into my pocket so I could carry Dylan. "Len?" I glanced over my shoulder.

One step ahead, as usual, Lennon was already on her way to the hide-a-key rock where my mom kept the spare. When she turned empty handed, I groaned. I'd taken it out the week before when I'd been too drunk to drive, and Vicky had brought me home after curfew. I'd forgotten to put it back.

"What are the chances you've got your spare?"

"It's in my purse." I followed her gaze as she looked across the street at her dark, empty house.

No way in hell was she going over there without me. We lived in an upper-middle-class development full of cookie-cutter homes in the middle of nowhere, but that didn't mean it was safe for a teenage girl to be home alone. Crime didn't discriminate. If someone wanted to rob a house, they'd probably target our neighborhood. Especially if it looked like the owners were away.

"I think I'm going to barf," Dylan moaned, her eyes closed again.

"Shit." Adjusting my sister's weight slightly, I turned my side toward Lennon. "My keys are in my pocket. Can you get them?"

Her eyes widened, and she bit her lip, but she nodded. "Sure." Her voice broke over the word, clearly uncomfortable.

"It's just my pocket, Len." I chuckled as she slunk toward me. "I won't bite."

"It's not you that I'm worried about. I remember the crap you once stuffed in there." Her breath hitched as she got close enough to touch me. With one hand on my back to brace herself, she slid her other over my hip and down into my jeans. "Got 'em. I didn't find a worm this time."

"Nah, nothing wiggly or slimy anymore. The worst you'll find now is something to suck on," I joked back.

As soon as the words were out of my mouth, we both froze, her hand still in my pocket, a groaning, drunk sister in my arms. She'd been kidding, teasing about the time she'd found worms in my jeans when she'd been looking for gum or lollipops. I closed my eyes and swallowed, realizing exactly what I'd said.

Fuck me.

Len pulled out her hand so fast you'd think she'd gotten burned, keys locked in her grip. Before I could apologize, she'd started to giggle. Her shoulders shook as her laugh turned into a howl as she struggled with the lock. Once inside, she tossed my keyring onto the table and flipped on lights, cackling the entire time.

"Slimy. Wiggly." She gasped between snorts. "Suck on."

"Shut up, brat. You knew what I meant."

She only laughed harder.

I followed her up the stairs to Dylan's room. While Len tugged off my sister's shoes and tucked her into bed, I got water, painkillers, and moved her trash can closer. We had to force her to sit up and take meds, but she passed out as soon as her head hit the pillow.

Once she was all settled, I turned to Len. "You're staying tonight." It wasn't a question, but I still waited for her to reply.

"Yeah." She looked down at a snoring Dylan, sprawled across the queen bed. "We were supposed to sleep in the treehouse, but I'm not going out there alone. I can't share a bed with her like this; she'll kick me all night. Guess the floor it is."

There was no room on Dylan's floor. My sister took messy teen to an extreme. "She'll be fine alone, Len. I'll even check on her later."

"You think so? I guess I can crash on the couch in the den."

"Take the master," I insisted as I ushered her into the hall. "They're not coming back."

She closed Dylan's door before she answered. "God, no. I don't even want to sleep in my parents' room, and in my mind, they haven't had sex since I was conceived. I'm so not sleeping in that bed, knowing what I do about your mom and dad."

I groaned. "Please don't tell me." Mom liked to overshare with Dylan, who in turn, told Lennon. Unless they'd progressed to the point where my mom filled her in too. Thankfully, they kept me in the dark. Dad and I didn't talk about that shit for a reason. "I'll take their room. To me, it's only a room with a kick-ass bed. You can crash in mine."

For a moment, she looked like a deer caught in headlights. "No, I'm good."

"It's not like you haven't slept in there before."

Her eyes narrowed as she frowned, but instead of saying whatever was on her mind, she bit her lip. I tried to ignore the rush that hit me along with a sudden urge to kiss her. It was late; I was exhausted and grateful for her help with my sister. That was it.

"Spit it out, Len. While we're still young."

"You and Vicky never..." she cleared her throat. "You know? In there?"

I crossed my arms over my chest and cocked an eyebrow. "No. I don't know. Did Vicky and I ever what?"

"Don't be an ass. You know exactly what I'm asking."

My lips twitched. "I don't. Did we talk about the future? Study? Fight? What do you want to know?" Her glare was amusing as hell, as was the way her fists braced themselves on her hips. "Ohhh, you mean have sex?"

She nodded, but her eyes fell to the floor and studied the carpet like it held the most interesting pattern she'd seen.

"What an odd question to ask," I teased. "Do you ask all your friends if they slept with their ex? I wonder what McKinney's answer was."

"God, you're so annoying."

"Feeling is mutual. Yes, Lennon. We had sex. Lots and lots of noisy, sweaty sex. That's what you do when you're seventeen. However, there was a strict 'no cameras allowed' policy, so unfortunately, I can't offer video evidence."

"Sixteen."

"What?" For a moment, her response threw me. I'd expected her to blush, or blanch, or maybe even hit me. Not correct me.

"You were sixteen when you started dating her. She was fifteen." Without pausing a beat, she switched topics. "I'll sleep in the den."

"What? Why?"

"It grosses me out. I don't want to sleep in someone else's..."

"You are so weird. Sheets wash."

"Night." With a shrug, she turned and started to walk away.

I reached out, my fingers closing around her arm to stop her. I didn't know why, but I needed her to know the truth. "No. Okay? I'm just messing with you." I raked my empty hand through my hair. "Vicky never stayed here. The only girls who've slept in my bed—metaphorically or literally—are you and Dylan."

"Honestly?"

"Yeah. Can we go to sleep now? I've got nothing left."

She nodded, giving in, and reached for my door as I headed for the other end of the hall.

"Hey, Len?" I asked, hand on the doorknob, and she turned, face blank. "If sleeping somewhere I've had sex grosses you out so much, you may want to avoid the showers and couches. And my car." Her face turned red, but I didn't know if she was blushing or pissed. "Definitely the treehouse."

"You didn't!"

"Night," I called with a wave over my head as I laughed my way into my parents' room.

Chapter Six

Lennon

"Wakey, wakey, eggs and bakey."

I stifled an exhausted groan and sat up, pushing the rat's nest that was my morning hair out of my face. Dylan sat in Dean's comfy chair—the one that was my absolute favorite in the entire world—with one knee propped up in front of her, holding a ginormous cup of coffee. She didn't look hungover. Hell, she didn't even look tired. Meanwhile, I hadn't had more than a drop of alcohol and felt like a garbage truck had backed over me before dumping its contents on my maimed body, then crushed me again as it sped off.

As I caught her gaze, her eyes darted to the nightstand. I turned, finding another giant mug. God bless her. I slid back, braced myself against the headboard, and cupped my salvation.

"You are a goddess. I'm a little in love with you right now," I murmured as I took a long, glorious sip.

She waved a finger in the air next to her head. "Oh, I know. But I can't take the credit for the coffee." She lifted a shoulder, and the wide neck of her top slipped down her arm, exposing her shoulder. "It's all Dean. He made some wonder breakfast too. It's supposed to be the cure-all. I told him I'd come get you. In his room," she gave me a look I hadn't had nearly enough caffeine to decipher. "I definitely want to know why you're in here. You're not getting off the hook. First, though, I need details."

I didn't have to ask what she meant. "What do you remember?"

She groaned. "Not much. Do I have to run away and join an animal-free circus?"

"Leave all this glory behind? Please, that's like leaving a job at McDonald's to work at Burger King. Plus, you can only join the circus if they'll let you."

"True," she nodded, a wistful expression on her face. "I'm thinking when they say, 'Circus Freaks Wanted' they're not looking for someone with my many non-talents, weird attachment disorder, and stalker tendencies."

I chortled. "Probably not."

"So, on a scale of 'It's fine; everyone was drunk and acted the same way' to 'I can never show my face again and need to transfer schools,' how was last night?"

"Somewhere in the middle. Almost everyone was drinking, but I think the moment that cemented your infamy was when you took Mr. Eastman's guitar out of the display case and gave us an acoustic performance of "Wonderwall." It was...well, I have no words."

Her mouth fell open. "Not Stevie Ray Vaughn's autographed Fender?" Her voice was little more than a squeak.

I nodded. According to Shaun, it was irreplaceable.

Dylan's hand covered her mouth. "But I don't know how to play the guitar."

I shook my head. "Nope. You really don't."

Her eyes got huge. "Len," she whispered. "I don't even like to sing in the shower."

"I know, honey." I bit the inside of my cheek to keep from laughing, but the muscles in my stomach started to shake. "Now everyone at the party knows why."

She closed her eyes as she lifted her empty hand to rub her forehead. "Out of every song in the world, "Wonderwall?" I hate it. Why would I try to sing it?"

"Well," I started slowly, staring at the wall, avoiding her gaze. "Whoever was in charge of music added it to the playlist. You heard it and said it made you think of Tate."

"No." She gasped. "Tell me I didn't."

I slid my attention back to her. I couldn't give her the confirmation she needed. She'd made a complete and utter ass out of herself.

Thinking about her horrid, howling performance, and the way she'd tried to figure out how to play the expensive instrument, I couldn't keep the giggles at bay anymore. I was an awful friend. She needed to fire me.

"Why didn't you stop me?"

"I tried." I tsked and lifted my shoulders. "You pushed me away. It felt like I was making it worse, drawing unwanted attention, so Dean tried. You made him take your picture so you could send it to NASA."

"NASA?" she parroted, clearly confused. "I didn't realize that was an acronym for anything else."

"Oh, it's not. NASA, as in the space program."

"What?" Her face scrunched in confusion. "Why?"

I shook my head. She didn't want to know.

"Lennon? Why would I want Dean to send my picture to NASA?" Her tone was worried, scared almost.

"Because," I cleared my throat, desperate to keep a straight face, "you're a star." I coughed once when her puzzled frown was too much. Then again. Finally, I forced out, "You said they needed to know about you, so they could put you on their map. Document the one they missed."

"Fuck my life." She moved her hand to her eyes as if trying to hide away from the truth. "That settles it. We need to move. I can never show my face again."

"It's really not that bad," I assured her. "There's a bright side. Shaun gave you a standing ovation. He was sober and said you did a great job. Even though you kept asking him if he was listening and dedicated the performance to him, Tate wasn't embarrassed. In fact, he never left the room. Instead, he threatened everyone with a cell phone. I actually thought he was going to break a few. Or maybe maul the guys who wanted to film you. So, I don't think any evidence will pop up online." I tipped my head. "Which is actually too bad. I'd watch it again."

She threw a pillow at my head. Thankfully, I knocked it away without spilling any coffee. Dean made it the way I liked, and I didn't want to waste a drop.

"You are such an asshole." She'd started to chuckle, and her words didn't hold much heat. "Oh my God. I'm never drinking again. Thank God I'll be gone for Jenna's party. Can you imagine?" She puffed her cheeks and blew out a long breath.

I didn't point out that the highlight of my night was definitely the moment she'd started to cry and told me I was a horrible friend because I wouldn't go on the cruise in her place and was making her miss said party. She had enough on her plate and didn't need to be even more embarrassed. I could only hope that no one else said anything.

After a long sigh, Dylan rubbed her eyes with the heel of her empty hand. "Distract me. Tell me a story. Better yet, explain why in the hell you slept in this pigsty."

"Because trying to find a place that isn't tainted by your brother and Vicky is almost impossible. Apparently, they've had sex everywhere."

She nodded as if it weren't a big deal. "Yeah. Between them and my parents, there aren't many surfaces in the house that haven't been christened. I think my room and this one are the only spaces safe enough to use a black light."

I shook my head, unable to keep the disgusted look from my face. I didn't need to have the mental images of Dean and Vicky getting it on in every room. I'd struggled to fall asleep as it was. His sheets smelled like him and had sent my imagination into overdrive.

"That's so nasty. How are you okay with it?"

It was her turn to snort at me. "It's just sex, Len. It's not that big of a deal. It's like pooping. Everyone does it. Eventually. Except for me because I do idiotic things like get wasted and sing the ultimate creeper song for the one guy I actually want to sleep with. I'm going to die a virgin."

"I legit have no words for you right now."

"Luckily for you, I have plenty. Also lucky for you, this is me and not someone who would read much more into your reaction." She chuckled. "If I didn't know about your weird fetish, I'd think you were jealous of Vicky."

I *was* jealous of Vicky, even though I was ashamed of that fact. Stupid dream me had planted seeds in my head, and now real me was apparently envious of Dean and his ex. Awesome. Best day ever.

That wasn't something I could admit to her though. It was a secret I hoped to take to my grave.

"It's a phobia, not a fetish," I clarified. "It's perfectly normal."

It wasn't. If I could be honest, tell her the real reasons, I'd seem a hell of a lot less neurotic. Yeah, the idea of my parents grossed me out because, hello, it was my mom and dad. Eww. No.

However, I didn't want to sleep anywhere Dean had been with Vicky because I didn't want to think about the two of them together. I'd fixate on it and be curious about all sorts of things I had no business wondering about.

"Did he say anything to you about her?" she asked, sitting forward slightly, stretching her back, her lips twisted in thought. "I want to know why they broke up, but he won't tell me a damn thing."

"Rumor is," a deep voice drawled from the door, "there's someone else."

Tate Griffin, dressed in baggy gray sweats and a henley with the sleeves pushed up to his elbows, showing off muscular and veiny forearms that would make The Rock proud and every female in existence have unholy thoughts, was not someone I'd expected to see. With a smirk full of mischief, he gave us a heartbeat to let his presence sink in.

"Mornin'. I'm supposed to tell you that breakfast is getting cold, and you need to get your lazy asses' downstairs."

Well, that explained why he was standing in the doorway.

Before we could greet him, his attention settled on Dylan. "I want to know how you're feeling, Superstar, I do. But first," his entire body swung toward me, ignoring Dylan's flaming red cheeks "what are you doing in Dean's bed, looking all fine and shit, Lenny?"

Ignoring the suggestive way his eyebrows moved up and down, I tried to get him to backtrack. "Someone else? Like one of them met someone else? Or slept with someone else?"

"I'm starting to wonder if I'm looking at the answer."

"Ohhhh," Dylan started to interrupt, too slow on the uptake after the night she'd had. Unfortunately, her voice cracked.

Tate held up a finger in her direction. "Don't try to talk. Your vocal cords need to rest after your concert last night, there, Killa." He jerked the finger to point at me. "You, on the other hand, spill."

"Why are you even here?"

"I wanted to check on you two, see how you were holding up after your inauguration. Maybe torture Dylan a little bit. Plus, boozy brunch," he said it like it was an obvious reason to show up. "Finding this though?" He lifted his chin toward the bed. "Is pure fucking gold."

"Please," I scoffed. "If Dean had spent the night with me, he'd still be in here. He sure as hell wouldn't have the energy to make your hungover ass breakfast."

Dylan choked on her coffee. I didn't know if she was impressed that I'd had the balls to say it, or shocked as shit that I had. Either way, I could see her gaping at me in my peripheral vision.

Tate rubbed his chin in a way that shouldn't look normal or sexy on a teenager, yet it did. "That is a valid argument. He doesn't usually cook after he gets laid. His grumpy ass certainly wouldn't be as moody. So that leaves you."

Dylan squirmed as his gaze swung back to her.

"Didn't you say breakfast was ready?" I attempted to shift the attention from her once again.

When he nodded, I threw the covers back and slid from the bed, not caring that they'd see me in a pair of Dean's boxers and one of his favorite shirts. Maybe it would distract them.

I lifted a hand, still clutching my mug with the other. "Lead the way, buddy."

When my phone chirped with a text message notification, I knew it was from Dylan before I looked. It wasn't a surprise to find the *'I'm sick. Can't go to school tomorrow'* excuse. There was no doubt in my mind she'd spent the few hours since I'd left her house worrying herself into a tizzy.

With a sigh, I tossed my latest read aside and dialed her number.

"Oh, honey. What's wrong?"

"Definitely the flu. Nasty headache. Nausea. Chills. My body hurts all over. I may have to miss school all week."

I smirked. *Sure.* "That's awful. As soon as our parents get home, have your mom take you to the emergency room. It could be malaria."

"Malaria?" Her shriek was vicious, and I had to pull the phone away from my ear.

"Well, I haven't heard of a flu outbreak; have you?" There weren't any mosquitos out yet either, so malaria wasn't a real possibility, but I left that little fact out.

"Food poisoning?"

"Maybe, but I ate the same things you did. I'd be sick too. Hmmm," I hummed in fake thought, "I can Google your symptoms." Before she could say no, I grabbed my laptop and typed in 'faking sickness to get out of work.' I quickly scrolled through the results. "Hmmm... I think it might be malingering."

"Malingering?" Dylan's voice cracked, full of worry. "Is that like Malaria? I don't know what either is. Will I lose my hair?"

"I actually don't know. Let me check." I clicked on another page, reading all about it. "Ohhh. I think this is definitely it."

"Yeah?" She was entirely too engaged and worried for someone who was actually sick.

"Yep. This is definitely it." I sighed sadly.

"Maybe it's not," she started to backpedal. "I might just be hungover and need electrolytes."

"Most common symptom?" I asked, closing my computer and lying back on my bed. "Feigned or grossly exaggerated physical symptoms in order to avoid school or other uncomfortable social situations."

There was a long pause. "You're an asshole."

I snorted. "You're a chicken shit. We're the perfect pair."

She groaned and let out a long, aggravated sigh. "I don't know how to face them."

"Who is this 'them' we're speaking of?"

"Everyone."

"Dylan, I love you, so please listen to me when I say this. Not everyone is going to care what you did last night. Even if there is a small group of people talking about it, the big brothers will take care of it. You have nothing to worry about."

"The big brothers?" Amusement tinged her words. "When did you start calling them that?"

"It hit me at breakfast. They're so damned determined to refer to us as the 'little sisters,' it only makes sense for us to return the favor. I'm not sure why we never thought about it before."

"It's perfect." She sighed. "I really can't get out of school?"

I shook my head, smiling. "Nope."

"Shit." She yawned. "I guess I'll see you in the morning. Night."

"Night, beautiful."

The next morning Dylan barely said two words to either Dean or me. Instead, she snapped open the passenger's mirror and attempted to smooth out makeup that wasn't messy to begin with. After it looked the way she wanted, she fussed with her hair the rest of the way to school. I knew she was nervous, but I didn't know how to make it better.

By the time lunch arrived, it was clear her worries had been unnecessary.

There wasn't a single story floating around. Not one rumor. No one laughed at her when we walked down the halls. No one taped paper stars to her locker, even though I was tempted to, just to make her laugh.

The only thing that was slightly different was how the upper-classman treated us. They didn't nod a simple hello in our direction anymore. Instead, they stopped to talk to us or joined us at our lockers.

It was weird.

When we headed to classes after lunch break, Dylan giggled and gossiped, back to her old self. I was relieved to see my friend act normal. I was also uncomfortable as hell because suddenly it felt like everyone had eyes on us, and every move we made was watched carefully.

I blamed the big brothers.

The week both flew by and dragged on. On one hand, I wanted it to end because I was desperate for spring break. I needed time off, away from everyone.

On the other, I dreaded it. For the first time ever, my family wasn't joining the Cullens on vacation. Aunt Tasha's parents had retired earlier in the year and cashed out a pension, so they'd decided to take all their children and grandchildren on a nine-night Southern Caribbean Disney Cruise.

We hadn't been invited. Not that we'd expected one. We weren't really family.

Dylan's parents had been upset, though. Instead of dropping subtle hints, Uncle Chad had flat out told my dad to ignore his in-laws and book a room on the same trip. He got all the information for them and urged my parents to try to get an adjoining cabin to his.

They hadn't. Without talking about it with me, Mom and Dad had decided this would be our first spring break on our own. I didn't know all the details, but it felt like the excuse my parents had given wasn't the whole truth. Yes, my mom suffered from severe motion sickness, but there were drugs to battle that.

Plus, the Simmonses adored my dad. He'd grown up down the street from Tasha, and the two had been in the same class and friends as children. Not only had they known him his entire life, but they'd also once been close with my own grandparents.

When I was six or seven, we'd rented a cabin in the mountains for Christmas with the Cullens. At the last minute, Aunt Tasha's parents surprised her with the gift of their presence for the holidays. We'd all had a blast, and I remembered my dad telling Dylan's grandpa that we would do it again one day.

Yet, Mom and Dad had avoided the cruise like it was the Black

Plague. Whenever I asked, they'd offer bullshit excuses. Something didn't add up.

At first, I thought it was because they'd planned to go somewhere else, just the three of us. Maybe Florida, so we could absorb some much-needed Vitamin D. Or maybe the Grand Canyon, because they'd always talked about it.

I didn't know if I was relieved or upset when they'd told me they couldn't take the time off from work. Dad had some big project, while Mom wanted to save her vacation time for a family trip. So, not only were we not going anywhere fun, we weren't going anywhere, period. In fact, I was going to be home alone for the majority of the week.

When the new theater director had told Dean he couldn't miss a week of rehearsal so close to opening day and that he had to stay while his entire family went away, the Cullens, while upset their son couldn't go, were suddenly grateful we were going to be home, and my parents had a reason to justify their decision. *Everything happens for a reason, you know.* It wasn't that the adults didn't trust Dean to stay alone that long; it was like everyone felt better knowing that he wouldn't truly be by himself because he'd have us across the street.

Until Dylan launched a full-on campaign to have me go in his place. She argued that the trip was non-refundable, and someone might as well enjoy his ticket. She was relentless and didn't give up until she'd convinced her grandparents to let me tag along.

My parents said no. Part of me felt like it was a pride issue. They didn't want me to go because they hadn't paid for it. The other part of me worried that it was something more, something I wasn't seeing or didn't understand. Maybe it was to punish me for asserting my independence.

Trying to make the best of it, I was looking forward to sleeping in, taking a break from school, and being lazy. But I also hated the idea that Dylan and I were going to be separated for so long.

When I slid into my chair in study hall Thursday afternoon, I glanced at Mr. Guy's desk to make sure he wasn't watching before I snuck my cell out to reply to Dylan's latest freak-out. She was leaving in the morning, and we still had so much left to pack it wasn't funny. To say she was a nervous wreck was an understatement. I pulled out a notebook and started to make a list of things she needed in her carry-on, something she'd put off all week. Engrossed, I zoned out as the room filled and the bell rang.

"Lennon James," a voice drawled from my left, startling me.

My hand paused, but I didn't look up. I'd know that raspy sound anywhere. "Ross McKinney," I replied in a whisper.

The legs of his chair scraped against the floor as he moved his desk closer to mine. I lifted my eyes to scan the classroom, but no one was paying attention. His breath hit the back of my neck as he leaned over to see my paper. "Whatcha working on?"

I didn't try to hide it from his prying eyes. "A last-minute packing list for Dylan."

"Isn't she leaving tomorrow morning?"

I gave in and looked at him. "That's why it's a last-minute list," I sassed quietly.

For a moment, he surveyed me, his eyes moving across my face then down the rest of my body, which made me feel oddly self-conscious. "Yeah," he shook his head absentmindedly as if he couldn't make up his mind. "I don't know which version of you I like better. Nerdy or witty."

"Wit lacks an edge. It's self-deprecating. Sarcasm, on the other hand, has a bite. It's mean. It's like saying, 'yo, dumbass, you're really asking me a question when the answer is obvious?' in a much more condensed form." I grinned. "Only you would mistake my blatant sarcasm for wit."

"I love sarcasm. It's like punching someone in the face with words." He bit his lip as his eyes lit up. "Tell me I'm the only one who finds your nerd talk sexy."

A snicker escaped, even though I tried to suppress it. "I can promise you, you're the only one who thinks that."

"Sexy as Sin Lennon, what are your plans for spring break?"

"I don't have any, Bullshitting Ross. What about you?"

"Go out with me tomorrow night."

Completely off guard, I jerked away from him, choking on my saliva. "What?"

He didn't flinch. "Let me take you to dinner and a movie."

Neither had been a question, just a simple demand. Somehow, it wasn't as appalling as it should have been. In fact, it was kind of hot.

I didn't know if it was that surprising revelation or the fact that he'd asked me to begin with, but my face fell into a confused frown. No one had ever asked me out, especially not an upperclassman. Maybe the big brothers warned people away, maybe it was because of my age—I was the youngest sophomore at the school—or maybe it was or because I wasn't pretty enough to be as geeky as I was. Whatever the reason, it never happened.

"Isn't there some big, must-attend party you can't miss?"

His lopsided grin bordered on arrogant yet was attractive as hell. "There's always some big, attendance-mandatory party. It's part of high school. This week, it's not until Saturday. Tomorrow, I'm all yours." He didn't give me a moment to think. "I'll pick you up at six."

I liked Ross. He was cute, funny, and wasn't an asshat, but I wasn't drawn to him. Dreams of Dean still haunted my nights, leaving me with warped expectations and a skewed sense of reality. If I could get him out of my head, maybe I'd feel differently about the boy in front of me.

However, the truth was clear. The only way to stop thinking about Dean Cullen was to start thinking about someone else. I took a deep breath and jumped in.

Raising a finger, I nodded. "As long as you don't tell anyone." I continued when he popped an eyebrow. "It's not a big deal. I just don't want three chaperones."

Understanding was clear on his face. "I won't tell anyone because I don't want three shadows tagging along, sitting behind us in the theater, trying to steal our popcorn, or harassing me when I finally make my move." He leaned down close once more. "But this *is* a big deal. We only get one first date." With a wink, he slid his chair back into his normal spot.

I turned my attention back to the list, but I couldn't concentrate. I had no idea what in the world had just happened, or how I'd actually agreed to go on a date with Ross. My first instinct was to text Dylan because she'd know what to do.

I couldn't do that, though. Discretion was not one of my best friend's many talents. If I wanted to keep the date off the radar, I definitely couldn't tell Dylan.

I hated keeping secrets from her. First, the dream about her brother, and now this. Although, maybe if things went well with Ross, he'd become the new object of my affection, and things could go back to normal with Dean.

After that, I'd simply explain why I hadn't told her about the date. She'd understand without a doubt. I mean, we all had that one crush even our best friend didn't know about.

Things might actually be looking up.

Chapter Seven

Dean

"Well, well, well, look what the pussycat dragged in."

I laughed at Shaun as I lifted a fist to his, my other arm thrown around Chelsea. "Yeah, yeah. Rehearsal ran late."

That was the understatement of the fucking year, but no one needed to hear how bad my day had been. If I hadn't promised Chelsea we'd go to Jenna's party, I would've blown it off altogether and crashed. I was exhausted, both from the day and an almost sleepless night.

My family had left for Boston at five-thirty the morning before, where they caught a flight to Orlando to meet up with my aunts, uncles, grandparents, and cousins. Once the entire *fam damily* was there, they'd boarded a chartered bus and made the trip to the cruise ship in Cape Canaveral. That's when their fun started.

I hadn't missed a single step of their journey because not only did my little sister insist that she keep me up to date and recap every conversation that was happening, but my mother also felt the urge to check in on me every hour. All night long. Until they'd reached international waters and had to turn off their phones.

I was looking forward to the peace and quiet of the next ten days. I had a few plans, but other than that, my days would be filled with rehearsals and my nights with absolute solitude. By the time my family came back, I'd probably miss them.

In that moment though, I was almost glad they were away.

Chelsea and I downed a handful of shots as soon as we'd stepped through the door. I grabbed each of us a drink, and we'd gone in search of my friends. Dylan had sworn it was going to be the party of the year, but she'd been lost in her drunk fog. It had been nothing out of the ordinary.

Jenna's parties were always a bit crazy. People came from every school in a fifty-mile radius. It didn't matter who was there, or where the party was. King High students always ended up together in the back of the house to start off the night.

We found everyone gathered on a deck, overlooking the still-covered pool. It wasn't warm enough to be outside, but the snow and slush from the week before had at least melted away. I glanced around, looking for an empty spot, not surprised when the seat next to Tate miraculously opened up. People always moved out of my way like they were afraid.

I dropped into it, starting to feel pretty good, and took the blunt he offered as I balanced my drink in the other hand. I didn't have to drive home, I wasn't keeping an eye on the little sisters, and I was free to enjoy the night any way I wanted. I wanted to get fucked up.

Shaun was the first to speak. "You're late, man. You missed all the fun."

"Yeah?" I settled back into the chair while Chelsea perched her boney ass on my lap like she belonged there.

I didn't miss the pointed look Tate gave Shaun when I wrapped an arm around Chelsea's waist and pulled her back into me to make it more comfortable for both of us. Or the way Jenna's eyebrows rose when my hand lingered on Chelsea's leg, careful not to spill my drink on her. I knew it was weird for them to see me with someone other than Vicky, but it was hella different for me too. They could all fuck off.

Chelsea and I had been friends since kindergarten. We'd dated a handful of times over the years, but never had anything serious. She was fun to be around, and I liked hanging with her.

I took a long hit and offered it to Chelsea before I tipped back my head and stared at the sky, blowing smoke out slowly. It was almost comical the way my body relaxed immediately, like someone had turned a key and forced all my muscles to go lax.

"Where're the little sisters?" Someone asked, their voice far away.

"Dylan's on a cruise," Tate answered for me.

I closed my eyes, enjoying the weightless feeling.

Chelsea shifted slightly. "What about Lemon?"

Lemon? I laughed. It was funny. I wasn't sure why I'd never thought of it before.

Forcing myself to open my eyes and lift my head, I found too many people watching me. "I don't know where Lemon is," I admitted with a chuckle.

Warning bells went off in my head. Why didn't I know where Lemon—fuck, Lennon—was? That was a first. I knew her schedule better than I knew my own. Probably because Dylan never stopped talking.

"Relax," Tate's voice was quiet. He took a hit and passed it back. "She's at a sophomore party."

That's right, a sleepover at her friend Ana's. There hadn't been any lights on at her house, so her parents must have been gone for the night.

"So, what did I miss?"

When no one supplied the information they'd seemed so eager to give moments before, I glanced around the circle of familiar faces. Worry settled into my gut, threatening to ruin my high. Thankfully Dylan was in the middle of the Atlantic Ocean, on her way to Aruba, or I'd assume it had something to do with her.

"Somebody gonna tell me, or do you want me to try to guess?"

"A brawl between two Academy kids. And some random gossip."

I frowned at Jenna. Why would I care about either? My friends were clearly higher than Mount Washington already, not that I could say much because I was well on my way. Either that or they'd hit Jenna's mom's homemade moonshine hard. That shit fucked us all up last time. I'd even—not kidding—seen little purple fairies flying around.

Tate shook his head while Shaun laughed uncomfortably. Totally fucked up. All of us.

"Tell him." I didn't know who he was talking to, but Shaun's face held entirely too much trepidation for it to be something good.

"I don't think we need to," Tate muttered, his eyes glued on something over my shoulder.

"Fuck," Shaun whispered loudly, biting his damn fist as if he couldn't believe what was happening. "Shit's about to get real all up in here."

The fuck?

I tensed. Vicky. Someone must have brought Vicky. It was the only thing that made sense.

Joke was on them. It didn't bother me in the least. We were done. *Adios-ed.*

I didn't have the energy to give her my attention. I didn't care who she was with. Maybe she'd be happier with this new mystery guy than she'd been with me.

"Hey," Jenna said with a smile, lifting her hand in a mini wave that told me she hadn't hit the hard stuff yet, "you made it."

"We got sidetracked," Ross answered as he pulled Vicky out into the circle, smiling at her in a way that should have made my stomach burn with jealousy.

None came. Instead, I felt relief. I wasn't sure why.

I'd never have put the two of them together. They didn't have a single thing in common. Good for them. Maybe now he'd be too distracted to look Lennon's way.

Vicky moved into the light, and I realized how wrong I'd been. I sat up suddenly, every muscle taut again as rage flooded my body. The fuck was she doing here? The abrupt movement almost pushed Chelsea off my lap, but I didn't try to steady her. "Len?"

To her credit, Lennon seemed as surprised to see me as I was her. As my eyes scanned over the two of them, I realized she hadn't just come to the party with Ross. Oh, hell no. Her fingers were locked around his, and she seemed to be clinging to him for support.

Go ahead and hold him now, sweetheart. It'll be the last time he ever gets a chance to touch you.

I would remain calm. I would not slap a bitch, no matter how much my fist wanted to connect with his smug face. For a smart guy, McKinney was a fucking moron. It hadn't even been a week since I'd made it clear Len was off limits.

He clearly had a death wish.

Wide-eyed, I glanced at Tate. He was watching the newest couple, unmasked suspicion on his face. Clearly, I wasn't the only one who felt like they'd fallen down a damn rabbit hole.

If Ross felt the sudden tension that descended over our group, he didn't acknowledge it. Instead, he lifted his chin in greeting to me, wrapped his arm around my girl, and smiled down at her.

Wait. No. That wasn't right. Not my girl. *Sister.*

Ugh...not my sister either.

Fuck.

My Lennon. Yeah. That's what she was. *Mine.*

McKinney was a dead man. He stood there, looking like he didn't have a care in the damn world, arm wrapped around my Len, as if it belonged there. And she moved into him like he was her safe space.

I'd missed a step. *Fuck me,* I'd missed an entire act.

"A little birdy told us," Shaun started, his hands fisting and un-fisting in his lap, "that you two were at the movies last night."

Ross looked down at Lennon, deferring to her. Others might not realize it, but that action spoke volumes. It meant that he didn't know how much she wanted shared, so she could control the flow of information. It was the only response I needed. Fuck the audience, I wanted to grab him and beat the smirk off his face.

Lennon's arm wrapped around his back, her hand fisted his shirt. My eyes narrowed on her. How had I not seen it, not known about the two of them?

"Guess now we know it wasn't just a rumor," Jenna interjected as she forced a welcoming smile on her face. "We're all here now. Can we go into the game room? I'm freezing."

She didn't give us a chance to say no. Instead, she stood, pulled Shaun to his feet, and headed for the house. Everyone else followed, including Len and Ross.

Jenna's game room was exactly what it sounded like. Long and rectangular, it ran the length of the pool. A wall of floor-to-ceiling windows made sure you never missed a thing happening in the back yard. The opposite wall held a flat-screen you could see from the water. A bar was tucked in one corner, a poker table with twelve chairs was in the other. In the center of the room were two tables, one for billiards, the other air hockey.

Dylan would be impressed. I had been the first time I'd seen it. But now the only thing I cared about was getting to the bar and consuming my weight in alcohol.

Surprisingly, no one bothered me as I grabbed a jar of moonshine and poured a large glass. Other than a few worried glances from Shaun and Tate, everyone left me alone to drink in peace.

Everyone except Lennon.

I had to give her credit, she had balls the size of Atlas stones. Dylan would have avoided me, but then again, Len faced her problems head-on.

Which meant she thought I was a problem. I tipped back another drink without so much as a flinch. The bite of the moonshine was nothing compared to the bitterness swirling in my gut. She went on a fucking date with Ross McKinney?

I didn't even know why I was so fucking angry.

Not true. I knew exactly why it made me want to kick his scrawny ass. I just didn't want to admit I knew why I was pissed.

I thought about walking away. Dodging the situation wouldn't make it go away. So I poured myself another drink and waited for her lecture.

Finally, after she stared at me with disapproving eyes for what felt like an eternity, she sighed sadly. "I didn't know you'd be here tonight or I wouldn't have come."

"No?" I snickered, not believing a word. There was no way in hell

McKinney would miss a party. Especially not with her on his arm. He was trying to make a point. *Fuck him.*

Len dragged her teeth over her bottom lip. It distracted me, made me forget what I'd been about to say as my body reacted. The urge to kiss her, to nibble on her mouth overwhelmed me. I frowned at the thought.

"No." She didn't offer an explanation as she crossed her arms over her chest, which pulled my attention away from her mouth to other parts I shouldn't be staring at. The fuck was wrong with me?

"Did you go on a date with him last night?"

Lennon glowered at me and let out a long, annoyed huff. "That's none of your business."

Before I could respond, Tate joined us. Eyes glazed over, a slight smirk stuck on his face, he definitely wasn't feeling any pain, but he wasn't as wasted as I was. I didn't know if he was there to referee or defend, friend or foe.

I pointed at her. "You broke the rules."

She shook her head. "No, I didn't." She lifted a finger, "Don't drink anything in a cup or a bottle I didn't open myself." A petulant shrug. "I'm not drinking, dumbass. Two," she put up a second finger, "don't go into a room alone with someone you don't know. Ross isn't a stranger. Three," another digit joined the first two, "your friends are off limits. We've already established that particular rule doesn't apply in this situation because Ross is my friend too. Mutual friends are excluded."

I narrowed my eyes on the cheeky little shit. "No dating."

She tossed her hair over one shoulder. "Not a ground rule. You can't amend them now. It's not like you can keep either Dylan or me from dating."

"Why didn't you tell me about it?" I demanded.

Len's eyes lit up. Oh boy, she was pissed. "Because," she snarled haughtily, "the big brothers don't need to know everything."

"Big brothers?" Tate interjected.

Her angry gaze settled on him. "If we're stuck with the stupid little sister label, the three of you are now the big brothers."

My best friend leaned back, nodding like an asshole. "I like that."

Traitor.

Len's scowl shifted my way.

I stared her down, but she refused to budge. "Len," I finally growled between clenched teeth.

"Jackass," she snapped back.

"I told you—" I didn't get to finish my thought.

Len slammed her hands on top of the bar, seething. "It's time you realized that we aren't little anymore. We're not going to do whatever you tell us to."

"When have you ever done what you were told?" I poured another glass, downing it in one movement. "That's right. Never."

"Guess you should have made that one of your stupid rules then."

Something she'd said triggered a thought. I snapped my fingers. "Four. When I say it's time to leave, you come with me. No questions, no arguments."

She gave me a look that clearly said she thought I was an asshole who had lost my mind.

I had her. *Brat.* I barely kept my smug smile at bay. "It's time to go."

Lennon's nostrils flared. "What?"

Oh, yeah. I had her good. "It's time for us—" my words were slow so she wouldn't have any trouble understanding me as I motioned between the two of us, because there was no way my speech had turned sluggish from the alcohol, "—to go home."

"I didn't come here with you," she challenged, anger seeping from every pore.

"No. But, my friend's party, my rules. No arguments."

She pursed her lips, and I was sure she'd argue. Instead, she raised her hands in defeat and took a big step backward. "Fine."

"Okay, that's my cue," Tate stepped closer to me, his hand on my shoulder. "As much as I hate to interrupt this..." his attention bounced between Len and me, "I don't even know what the fuck this is. Cullen, you're staying here. You're drunk. You're not driving."

I agreed with that. There was no way I could get Len home safely. I'd had too much to drink.

However, I did have a standing claim on one of the guest rooms upstairs, had for years. Wheels started to turn. We could tell people we were leaving and go up there instead. No one would know.

Unless Len was willing to crash there with me, the entire plan was pointless.

"I've got him, Lenny." Tate lifted his chin toward the other side of the room. "McKinney is waiting for you. Go."

Len barely acknowledged him, her eyes glued to mine. "No. Rules are rules. I promised I'd follow them."

If I'd been even a hair less wasted than I was, the tone of her voice would have warned me that she had something up her sleeve.

"Lennon," Tate warned.

She cut her gaze to him. "Dean says he's ready to go home. I'll take him."

Tate let out an uncomfortable wheezing laugh. His voice was low when he finally spoke. "You can't drive him home. It's on the other side of town. You can't even drive yourself yet. I won't let you take that chance."

The hurt flashed on her face. The fact that she didn't have her license yet, even though almost everyone in her class was older and had already crossed that goal off their bucket list, cut her like a knife. I liked that she was my little Len, but she hated it. For three entire months, I got to point out that she was much younger than me.

"Trust me?" The way she asked had me nodding like a fool. I did trust her, damn it. "Let me tell Ross. I'll be right back."

As soon as she'd turned away, I reached for another drink.

Tate grabbed the jar before I could. "Shouldn't you be slowing down?"

"Why?" I knew the answer. My words sounded slurred even to my own ears.

"Because you need to get Lennon home," he ground out.

He was right. I dropped my hand. I'd already had too much. If I'd known I was going to see her, I wouldn't have touched a drop.

Len was beside me before I had a chance to process she was gone. "Let's go." She slipped her arm around my waist to help me walk. I laughed at the absurdity of it. She was half my size. I took care of her, not the other way around.

Until I stumbled and fell sideways, leaving her to hold me up.

"Let me do it," Tate practically lifted me off the ground as he took my arm and wrapped it around his shoulder, "before he hurts you."

"Dean would never hurt me."

"I don't know what's wrong with me," my voice slurred as they walked me outside, my toes dragging with every step. "I didn't drink that much."

They ignored me. It was like they couldn't understand my words.

"Do you want me to come with you? I can help get him into the house."

The sound of Lennon's laughter made me smile. It always did. Not her evil, Medusa chortle. No, that one made me want to put my hands over my balls to protect the family jewels. This happy lilt reminded me of Tinker Bell and trips to Disney.

Weird. I'd never thought about it like that before. It was so fitting. Lennon was tiny and annoying like Tink. Everyone knew that Peter Pan and the little fairy were secretly in love and meant to be, even if he had gotten sidetracked by that witch Wendy.

That was us. I was Pan with his band of lost boys and Lennon was Tinker Bell, the annoying but beautiful fairy guiding my way with her insatiable light.

"You're barely standing upright," Len told him. "There's no reason for you to leave early too. Not when I've got this."

We stopped by a car I didn't recognize.

"Okay, buddy, in you go." Lennon opened the backdoor before attempting to guide me inside.

"Lennon James, you're my hero." Tate started to laugh. I joined in, too drunk to ask what was so funny.

Without warning, he gave me a shove. I landed on my stomach with a groan, unable move.

"Tate," I yelled as loudly as I could, my voice sounding muffled and slurred. "Chelsea." I couldn't remember the last time I'd actually seen my date.

"I'll make sure she's okay," he promised as someone tucked my legs inside and slammed the door.

I tried to push myself into a sitting position, but my arms gave out. Shit, I was fucked up. This was definitely a first.

Two more car doors shut, and we started to move. Lennon thanked someone and started to apologize, but I couldn't stay awake long enough to hear the rest of the conversation.

Seconds later, Len called my name loudly as she yanked me from the car. I blinked at her. I could see my house over her shoulder. Then I noticed the fuckwad behind her.

"Let me help you," Ross insisted as Lennon pulled me to my feet.

She shook her head. "I'll get him from here." We stumbled past him and up the front steps. I outweighed her, yet somehow she managed to hold me up and keep both of us on our feet. Once inside, Lennon left me to hold up the wall and turned back to shut the door. "I'm so sorry," her voice was low, little more than a whisper.

McKinney chuckled. "Don't be. He's family. Family comes first."

I tried to roll my eyes, but it made my entire head move and I smacked my forehead into the wall. "Fuck!" I rubbed at the tender spot, almost losing my balance.

The door closed, the lock clicked into place, and Len was at my side in an instant. She laughed—the one I loved—as if I weren't the most annoying thing on the planet and pulled my arm over her shoulder. "You are such a sloppy drunk. Never would have pictured that."

I couldn't argue. I was a mess. Jenna's Moonshine, man. That shit messed you up.

"You're staying tonight." I didn't want her walking home alone. I didn't know what time it was, but it was well after dark. I should have insisted McKinney take her home. I could have crashed on the couch.

"Yeah. I'm supposed to be at Ana's anyway. My parents are gone."

Again? God, they were MIA as often as mine.

I wasn't sure how she did it, as tiny as she was, but somehow, she managed to maneuver my dead-weight upstairs and into my bedroom. Maybe pixie dust was involved. I started laughing at the idea.

"This is like bad déjà vu," she muttered as she pulled back my covers. "Feels like I've done this recently. Like maybe last week."

"Smartass."

"Ew, Dean," she chastised as she helped me lie back. "You haven't changed your sheets."

"How'd you know?" I could have washed them. I hadn't. But I could have.

She tugged on my pillow, moving it slightly. "That's my mascara."

I snorted as I looked at her horrified expression. "They smell like you. I like it."

Too shocked for words, she stared at me. I loved it when she couldn't find a comeback quickly. Then again, I loved it when she mouthed off too.

With a shake of her head, she finally managed to spit out one word as she started to pull off my boots. "What?"

"The sheets won't smell like you anymore if I wash them. I smell you and go to sleep happy. I wake up harder than steel, imagining all the things I want to do to you."

I snorted as I looked at her horrified expression. "You're cute when you're grossed out. And sad. And happy. But when you're pissed off, mad at me, that's my favorite."

"You're drunk."

"Yeah." I laughed. "Drunk me is just like sober me," I assured her as she pulled the covers over me. "Just twice as honest and ten times as horny."

Her breath hitched as I reached up to tug on a piece of the purple hair that I dreamed of pulling while I pounded her from behind. *Holy fuck.* I'd never admitted that, not even to myself. Instead, I always pushed every inappropriate thought of her away because she was Lennon. Little Lennon. Who wasn't so little anymore.

And yet tonight, not a single fuck was given as I let myself think of the fantasy that taunted me.

I watched as she swallowed nervously, the urge to lick her throat almost too much to deny. "They say the only honest people left in the world are either drunk or under five."

"And leggings." I pushed her hair behind her ear. "Leggings always tell the truth. Yours say you have a fine ass that I want to bite." I started to laugh so hard my breath wheezed.

"Oh my God. You're so wasted. And a little insane."

"Fuck," I groaned as I closed my eyes, wishing the pounding would stop. "This isn't one of those fake conversations we have in my head, is it?" I couldn't keep track of the shit my mouth was spewing. God only knew what I'd admitted. "I said all this shit."

"Did you mean it?"

"Every goddamn word. But tomorrow, Imma pretend I didn't say a thing. 'Cause I don't want you to know."

The bed shifted slightly, as if she were bracing her weight on it, and I tensed, expecting her to slap me. She should hit me. The things I wanted to do to her...man, she should beat my ass.

Her dad would kill me if he knew. Fuck. My own dad would bury me in the back yard if he could hear the thoughts I'd had about his precious Lennon. This certainly wasn't what he'd had in mind when he told me to protect her.

"I'm not going to hit you," she whispered softly.

Instead, hair brushed across my cheek right before warm lips pushed against mine. My eyes flew open as I realized—much slower than normal, thank you, alcohol—that Lennon had kissed me.

Was kissing me.

My hands fisted in her hair, loving the silky strands, as I took control. In that moment, she didn't belong to anyone but me. It was Lennon and me against the world.

My hands trailed down the sides of her body until I found her hips. Regaining strength I'd lost hours before, I pulled her down until she straddled me. My arms circled around her as my fingers slipped under her shirt to caress smooth, perfect skin.

I couldn't get close enough; she still felt a million miles away. I wanted to consume her. Devour her.

Fingertips danced along my forehead as she deepened our kiss. A deep moan escaped from one of us, but I couldn't tell who. I never wanted to stop.

Clutching the nape of her neck, I pulled her away, bracing my forehead against hers. "Stay with me."

Her eyebrows pinched together. "Dean, I..."

My fingers tightened in her hair, afraid she'd run, desperate to hold onto her. "Len, we're alone. Stay. I'm too fucking drunk to do anything more. Let me hold you tonight."

Her eyes never left mine as she gave a slight nod and toed off her shoes. I tried to roll to my side, but the entire world went into a tailspin. "Jesus, fuck." I was falling without a parachute.

Suddenly she was there, thin arms wrapping around my body, grounding me. Saving me. Instantly, I locked my arms around her waist and buried my face in her neck. She smelled like home.

Chapter Eight

Lennon

For the second Sunday in a row, I woke up in Dean's room.

Unlike the week before though, the man of the hour was nestled behind me, one arm holding me tightly, the other tucked under my pillow, as he snored softly into the crook of my neck. I stretched, trying to work out the kinks that came from sharing a bed with an aggressive cuddler, without waking him.

I'd known where I was and who I was with instantly. It was like my brain hadn't shut off, trying to remind me all night that I wasn't having another dream; I really was with Dean. Which explained why I felt physically refreshed but emotionally exhausted.

I didn't know what had pulled me from slumber. I could have sworn I'd heard a door slam, but since the rest of the Cullen family was gone, I knew that wasn't possible. For the few moments I laid there, walking the line between sleep and consciousness, my ears strained to hear anything out of the ordinary.

"You know," a lazy voice began quietly, startling me so much I jerked in surprise.

The entire bed shook as I let out a high-pitched yelp that could have woken the dead. By some miracle, Dean kept snoozing next to me. Heart pounding so loudly I could hear it pulsate, I pushed myself up onto my elbows and glared at the man in the overstuffed chair.

Tate paused, chuckling at my reaction, before he started again. "I'm not sure what I expected to find this morning. There were a few different scenarios that seemed more likely than others. Finding you, in here again, second week in a row, was definitely not something that ever crossed my mind."

I groaned, fell back onto the bed and flung an arm over my eyes. "Why are you here? Don't you ever go home?"

"Not if I can help it." He chuckled. "Neither of you answered your phones. I wanted to check on my best friend and make sure you'd taken care of him. Never in a million years did I think you'd *taken care* of him."

I wanted to laugh. If he only knew. Instead, I attempted to explain. "It's not what it looks like."

"Hmmm," he mused. "It looks like Dean didn't have the energy to get his ass out of bed this morning."

"He drank a lot last night," I defended.

"Never stopped him before. Dean's typically up before the damn sun, no matter how hungover he is. However, last week *someone* pointed out that he'd never be able to drag his ass out of bed early after a night with her. It's almost ten. He's still passed out. With a certain *someone* sleeping next to him. I'm simply connecting the dots."

I tittered as I remembered the words I'd slung at Tate the week before. My snark had a nasty habit of coming back to bite me in the ass.

I tried logic instead. "He could barely walk. The dude was slurring every single word and saying the craziest things."

"Yeah, he does that every six months or so."

I attempted a different angle. "I've spent more nights in here than I can count. You should know. You were here for most of them."

His chuckle was low and dangerous. "This doesn't look like any sleepover we've ever had. Maybe next time, you'll invite me along again, so I can see for myself. I could use a good night's sleep."

So many thoughts hit me at once. All of them rated R. No way I could handle one of these boys, never mind two. I fought the blush I felt moving down my face.

"Hate to disappoint, buddy." Carefully, I slid out from Dean's tight grip and eased off the bed, motioning to my clothes to prove I was still fully dressed. "Not your kind of party. Totally PG-13."

I stumbled over the words as memories of Dean's mouth on mine overwhelmed me. I cleared my throat in a pathetic attempt to hide my embarrassment and turned to cover Dean with the blanket. He rolled into my spot, burrowed into my pillow, and started snoring once again.

"*Titanic* is PG-13," Tate argued. "I wouldn't use that as an argument to prove nothing happened between the two of you. Considering that's the movie that taught me how to—,"

"No!" I whisper shouted as I slapped a hand over his mouth. "There are some things I never need to know. Whatever you're about to say is one of them."

Tate gripped my wrist and pulled my hand away as his eyes twinkled mischievously, probably thinking about all the ways he could torment me. "Just saying, there's some heavy petting in PG-13."

I ignored him. "Now that you've seen he's fine, let's go make boozy brunch."

"When'd you learn how to cook?"

"Better question is, why haven't you?"

With a snort, he pushed himself out of the chair and followed me down the stairs. "Don't think I didn't realize you changed the subject."

I found my purse in the foyer and tugged out my phone. Without looking to see if I had missed calls or messages, I moved into the kitchen and plugged it into the docking station. Familiar tunes started to play.

Tate sat on a stool on the other side of the counter, typing away on his phone. I wasn't *Top Chef* material, but we wouldn't die from food poisoning. We actually might even enjoy the meal too.

Once the coffee had started to brew, I pulled ingredients from cupboards and started mixing our favorite breakfast foods. I made the mistake of glancing up and found Tate watching my every move intently.

My heartbeat increased, and my palms got clammy as reality sunk in. I tried to recall the image of my geeky pre-pubescent friend I'd conjured up the week before, but it wouldn't come. It was stupid but having him this close to me made me feel clumsy.

"You're making me nervous."

"Why? 'Cause I'm watching you?"

"Because you're Tate Griffin and you're watching me."

Hearty laughter filled the room. When I didn't smile it cut off abruptly. "Wait. You're serious?"

"Yeah," I snapped, refusing to look up.

"You're not kidding right now?" He sounded horrified.

"I'm not." I whipped the eggs harder.

"Lenny," his tone was soft, almost full of pity. "I don't understand."

Taking a deep breath, I forced myself to meet his stare. His face was pinched in hurt confusion. "Do you not realize how much of a big deal you are?"

He gave me a disgusted look and clicked his tongue, waving a hand to silence me.

"Everyone loves you. Every guy wants to be you, every girl wants to sleep with you, most fantasize about marrying you, and half of them would die if you actually talked to them. When you're on the field, people think you're a god. When you walk down the hall, people move out of your way. Lord help us when you give someone that stupid dimpled grin of yours. I've seen people actually swoon. You're a big deal, whether you realize it or not."

His eyebrows rose, and his eyes bulged like he hadn't believed a word. "That's a gross exaggeration and you know it."

I crossed my arms over my chest and lifted my chin. "Fine, Mr. Bigshot. Why else do you think so many people get tongue-tied around you? How many people, on a weekly basis, act embarrassed when you're near?"

A thick *V* formed between his eyes as he considered my words. His face fell. "Is that why you ignore me at school?"

"Please." It was my turn to be dismissive. "I couldn't ignore you if I tried. You're everywhere."

"Bullshit. In fact, until a few weeks ago, you avoided me completely. This is the first time we've talked, just the two of us, since I started high school."

"No, it's not," I argued.

I tried to remember a time, even once, that we'd sat and chatted. Or that I'd approached him. I couldn't.

"All this time, I thought you were mad at me. I never would have guessed that you, of all people, would feel insecure."

"You're popular. I'm not." I argued as if it made all the sense in the world. "That's not me being insecure. That's a fact."

"What does my social status have to do with you not talking to me? You ghosted me, not the other way around."

"I didn't ghost you. I stopped being clingy. Let you have freedom."

He scowled. "I may be popular, but I'm no Dean Cullen or Shaun Eastman. Your argument doesn't even make sense."

"What's that supposed to mean?"

"I play ball, yeah, but I worked my ass off to get here. If I get hurt, or I fuck one thing up, my career will end in high school. Then all I've got is a pretty face and rock-hard abs to carry me through." He winked, an attempt to be playful, but the hurt and worry in his words were clear.

"Dean, on the other hand, has more natural talent in his pinky than I have in my entire body. He's going places. The entire fucking state loves him. And Shaun? There's no way in hell he doesn't get drafted. Scouts have followed his career since we were twelve. If by some random twist of fate that doesn't happen, his parents will make sure he has a great life. He's got his humor and his art to fall back on. You're not shy around them. Hell, I see you talking to Shaun all the time. You and Dean are..." he paused with a sigh, "whatever it is you are. So, knock that shit off around me."

I heard every word, let each sink in. He was right. I felt like shit. "I'm sorry."

"Don't be sorry, Len. Just remember that I'm your friend. That didn't stop because I got hot and you decided you want me." He smirked. "You know me better than most ever will. We have history."

"We do," I agreed. Recalling his words from the beginning of the conversation, I sighed. "Why in the world would you think I'm mad at you?"

With a long sigh, he shook his head. "Because we left you guys behind and grew up without you. Because we try to protect you and do stupid shit like make dumbass ground rules or attempt to scare away potential boyfriends. Because I'm going to break your best friend's heart. Take your pick."

"I'm not mad, Tate. I've never been upset about those things. You're the big brothers. It's what you do." I shrugged. "Since we're being so blunt and honest, I've spent a lot of time feeling like I wasn't good enough to be around you."

"It's all in your head." The way he stared at me, deep gray eyes almost penetrating mine, felt invasive. "The five of us may be best friends, but Dean and Dylan are a pair, and so are you and me. When I call you the little sisters, it's because you're mine."

Well, shit. "I'm an asshole."

His lips twisted. "Yeah. But you're my asshole. I love you, kid." He tipped his head toward the bowls of breakfast food I still hadn't cooked. "Now make me breakfast, brat. I'm hungry."

I turned on the burners, heating up the skillet and the cast iron frying pan and grabbed the bacon from the refrigerator. As I hummed along to the song, I thought about what he'd said. One thing stood out more than the rest. *Because I'm going to break your best friend's heart.*

He knew about Dylan. I wasn't that surprised. I mean, he hadn't seemed shocked by her off-key serenade at the party. In reality, she hadn't hidden her crush very well.

It also meant that he didn't feel the same way about her. I wasn't shocked by that news either. Tate had a type, and those tall, blonde beauties were quiet and almost shy. Polar opposites of Dylan.

It made me sad. Dylan had loved him for as long as I could remember. She'd convinced herself that one day Tate would wake up and realize he felt the same way about her, and they'd live happily ever after.

Well, as much of a happily ever after as two teenagers could have.

It could have happened. I hadn't known I was attracted to Dean until that stupid dream. Before that, he'd been the boy who hadn't seen me as anything more than his sister's best friend at best, his little sister at worst.

At least, that's what I'd believed.

Now, I was utterly confused. I had more questions than answers. I didn't want to think about most of them. I had to prepare myself for what was sure to be one hell of an awkward conversation between the two of us, but I dreaded the possibility that he'd made a drunken mistake.

I slipped the pan of bacon into the oven, set the timer, and ladled batter onto the skillet.

"What kind of pancakes are those?" Tate put down his phone to watch me once again, but I heard the hope in his voice.

"Purple." I couldn't stop my grin.

It was silly, really; a piece of our childhood I'd never let go. Every Saturday morning, Aunt Tasha had let us decide what went into the pancakes. We'd created some of the worst and most disgusting recipes, throwing in random candies, berries, and even meat.

When I was nine, we'd discovered the Holy Grail of flapjacks. Grossed out by the Sour Patch Kids concoction we'd had the week before, the five of us made a deal. The boys would pick one ingredient, Dylan and I'd pick another, but we wouldn't tell the other side what it was. They chose white chocolate chips, while we picked wild Maine blueberries. We'd been shocked when the batter had turned a hideous shade of purple. Yet, they were the best damn things I'd ever tasted.

"I love purple pancakes."

The voice, deeper and raspier than normal, was like a shot of lust straight into my veins. Goosebumps broke out all over my arms, and a fierce shiver ran down my spine as I looked up into eyes so brown, I couldn't see the pupils from a distance. I wanted nothing more than to grab his hand, tug him back to his bedroom, and spend the day kissing him.

Dean's nostrils flared slightly as if he knew exactly where my thoughts had gone and he felt the same.

"Mornin', sunshine," Tate grinned. "How you feeling?"

Dean yawned in answer, lifting his hands over his head to stretch. His shirt rose up, just a smidge, revealing a small patch of bare skin above the pajama pants that hung dangerously low on his hips. He hadn't been wearing them earlier, but holy hell, they did something to me. Realizing I was staring, hyper-focused on parts of him I shouldn't be, I bit my lip and turned my attention back to the food.

Dean grabbed a cup and poured himself coffee. "A little confused."

That made two of us.

"My memory is a little hazy."

Tate snorted. "I'm surprised you remember anything. Chelsea said you guys lined up shots as soon as you got to the party. Did you drink the entire bottle? She didn't drink the rest of the night, and she was pretty trashed."

"It's that damn moonshine." Turning to lean his back against the cupboard, Dean sipped his coffee as he watched me. "Oh, I remember everything important," he assured us. "It's the little details I'm still trying to work out. You hungover?"

I wasn't sure if he was talking to Tate or me, but the former answered. "A little headache, but it could've been worse. Thank God for hair of the dog."

"That actually doesn't work," I interjected without thinking. "Drinking more when you're hungover only delays the inevitable. Once you stop drinking, you'll feel it. Hangovers aren't caused by withdrawal. Unless you're drinking copious amounts every day, you're not getting sick because your body needs more booze."

"So," Tate mused, leaning back in his stool and bracing an arm over the one next to him, "You and McKinney, huh? He may have a valid point with his 'nerdy is sexy' argument."

A flush of embarrassment washed over me and my cheeks turned bright red. I could almost feel Dean's eyes burning into my back. "We went on one date," I answered with a nervous chuckle. "I think it's safe to say there is no Ross and me."

"You went out Friday. Does that mean last night wasn't a date?"

I didn't know how to answer that. Thankfully, the timer went off so I didn't have to. Dean took out the bacon while I scrambled the eggs, and Tate started carrying everything into the dining room.

I plated the eggs and moved to make my own coffee when Dean stepped up behind me, caging me in. My breath caught as he leaned down and kissed the sensitive spot where my shoulder and neck met. He'd discovered how much I liked it only a few hours before and had taken delight in torturing me.

"You left me," he growled against my skin before nipping my ear. "I woke up all alone."

I gripped the counter as my eyes rolled back in my head and I fought the urge to melt into his warm body. "Tate," my voice cracked over the word. I didn't know if I was giving him an explanation for why I'd left or warning that we could be discovered.

A strong hand cupped my jaw, turning my face towards his before he captured my lips in a kiss that turned my blood to lava and instantly drove away my worries. He leaned back but didn't release me. "Later."

Before I could ask what he meant, Dean slid sideways, putting distance between us. In seconds, Tate strolled back into the kitchen. "Is it ready? I'm about to waste away."

As we sat around the table and dug in, I was lost in a sea of emotions.

Dean had kissed me. While he was sober. With his best friend only a room away.

A hot-as-hell, toe-curling, heart-racing kiss that set my entire body on fire and sent my mind whirling. I could have imagined our first interaction this morning to go in a million different directions, and that would haven't even made the top fifty. It was unexpected, yet absolutely the best way to put my mind at ease and give me a teasing glimpse of what was to come.

The things he'd said the night before had been an ego boost, but part of me hadn't believed he'd truly meant them. I'd expected him to wake up and apologize, to take them all back. The relief I felt knowing he didn't regret them was indescribable.

When he'd claimed me with his lips, he gave me hope. The way he kept staring at me like he wanted nothing more than for Tate to leave us alone, made my body tingle and caused butterflies to invade my stomach. I didn't know if his feelings and attraction were as new as mine, or if they had been there for a while. As curious as I was, all that mattered was that we were hopefully on the same page now.

Not that I knew what that meant. As hundreds of questions flew through my mind at warp speed, it was clear that I was more confused and excited than I had been in my entire life.

Chapter Nine

Dean

Lennon hadn't been gone more than a half hour when Shaun walked into my house and fell into my dad's favorite recliner. "It's the start of spring break," he grumbled as his way of greeting. "Are we just going to sit here and do nothing? For reals?"

"I don't have the energy to do anything," Tate answered lazily from where he was sprawled over the loveseat across from me. "Len made us breakfast. She put me in a carb coma."

"Nothing a six-pack and a pick-up game won't fix. What about you?"

I didn't look up from my laptop, even though I knew he was talking to me. "I have to be at the theater at one."

My director had sent the entire company an email outlining the newest round of updates and changes. We were expected to have them memorized by the time we arrived. I didn't know whether to laugh or dig through my drawers to see if I had a joint stashed away. I was stressed the fuck out.

The Actors' Equity Association had labeled Nilo Kessering one of the best directors of our time. He'd worked with more Broadway stars and Hollywood A-Listers, before they made it big, than any other. It was said that one production with him would hone your craft. There had been nothing but excitement when we'd heard the Board of Trustees had snagged Nilo for this performance.

Eccentric on his best day, belligerent on his worst, we'd all had a bit of a learning curve to overcome. Now though, the man was tripping balls.

"Wait. Seriously?"

"Yeah," I chuckled at the utter surprise in Shaun's voice. "I told you I had rehearsals all week."

"I figured you said that to get out of going on vacation with your family."

Tate snorted at the absurdity.

I tore my eyes away from the screen to stare at him. "They went to the Caribbean, dumbass. Why would I want to get out of that?"

"Empty house. Freedom from the little sisters. No one riding your ass. Empty fucking house."

"How in the hell were you the sperm that won?"

He lifted a middle finger in my direction. "So, we're not doing anything this week?"

"I don't know about you two, but I'm out."

I didn't explain that technically, I only had to be at the theater in the afternoons. Half our cast and crew were hobbyists who had nine-to-five professions while the rest were your typical moody artists with night owl tendencies. Even if Nilo had demanded our presence first thing, no one would show.

I *could* spend my mornings on the courts or on road trips with my friends. I didn't want to. It was selfish, but I wanted to ask Lennon to hang when I had free time.

"You can party this weekend though." This time it was Tate who spoke. "We're still hitting up the bonfire, yeah?"

Fuck. I'd forgotten. I groaned inwardly. My mind had been filled with thoughts of a nerdy girl. Everything else seemed to be taking a back burner.

"I, uh," I cleared my throat, "I'm supposed to take Chelsea."

Shaun sat forward and braced his elbows on his knees as he exchanged a look with Tate. "Come on, man. You can't bring her."

I closed the laptop and slid it onto the coffee table, hoping there was a valid reason I couldn't. Like, maybe she'd hooked up with someone at the party. "Why not?"

Tate sighed. "I know you have this weird fixation with her—"

"I say it's cannabis lube or ecstasy in her vag," Shaun interrupted.

"But she's a shark," Tate finished, talking over our friend.

I glanced back and forth between them, a frown on my face, trying to decide if I should laugh or not. "I haven't fucked her, so I wouldn't know what kind of magic pussy she has. There's no fixation. She's *our* friend."

"Eh, she's your friend. We just tolerate her."

"Which was easier to do when Vicky was around because at least then she knew her place."

I stared at Shaun, then Tate. They were serious. I'd had no idea they felt that way. "I already invited her. I can't simply decide not to take her."

They were quiet, digesting my words. I knew they disagreed with me, but I wasn't going to budge. I was a lot of things, but being a complete douche was where I drew a line. Chelsea was my friend.

Finally, as I was about to reach for my computer, Tate snapped his fingers. "Then don't. We'll go as a group. I'll bring Len."

Shaun nodded in agreement. "That works. But weren't you going to ask that blonde from the Academy?"

"You're assuming he knows which blonde you're talking about," I deadpanned, unable to resist the dig.

"Fuck off, assface." Tate laughed, not even trying to disagree before turning his attention to Shaun. "I was going to ask her, but—"

"Then I'll take Len," Shaun interrupted with a shrug. "You can take Blondie."

"The point is for us to take people we don't want to sleep with." Tate's eyes narrowed on our friend. "That way, we don't get distracted, and Blue and our boy aren't alone."

Shaun pursed his lips and nodded his head again, somehow

following along with everything Tate had said. "Makes sense. I'll ask Jenna. You take Lennon. They'll help us."

Wait. What? I looked around the room. "Why are you talking in code? Who in the hell is Blue?" I swallowed, dreading the answer to the next question. "If the object is to go with someone you don't plan to fuck, either one of you could take Len, right?" My tone held a twinge of accusation, but I couldn't help it.

"Blue," Tate started almost apprehensively, "is Chelsea. Blue sharks are one of the fastest and most deadly. They have no problem attacking people, which is why so many people are afraid of them. I think that comparison is pretty self-explanatory."

"You almost sound like Len and her bottomless pit of useless facts," I goaded playfully.

He grinned. "She's actually the one who told me."

Of course she was, my little know-it-all. "Why did we start comparing our frien–,"

"Your friend," Tate corrected, talking over me.

I gave him a dirty look and continued, "to a blue shark?"

"She's not afraid to be aggressive to get what she wants," Shaun answered. "She'll devour anything that stands in her way."

It was starting to make sense. "And you think she wants me?"

"No one thinks. We *know*. Plus, she looks like a shark."

Shaun nodded. "That big ol' nose, the giant eyes…"

"The constant vacant expression, her inability to smile," Tate added without missing a beat. "The feeling of doom one gets when she's around."

"You're both giant dicks." I rolled my eyes.

"When the shoe fits," Tate trailed off with a shrug. "This time it's the fins and jagged teeth that fucking fit. So Blue it is."

"Both of you can fuck off." I refused to acknowledge the rest of their shit-talking and focused on Shaun. "We know why he can't take the blonde, but that doesn't explain why you can't take Len."

Shaun adjusted uncomfortably under the heavy weight of my gaze but had the balls to meet my eyes. "Thought now that she'd gone out with McKinney, she was fair game. Figured I'd stake my claim before any other prick tries to take what's mine."

"Yours?" The word barely made it past my lips.

"Mine." He used both hands to point at himself with his thumbs. "It's not like I've ever hidden my appreciation of all that is Lennon James. Her sass makes me hard. She's easy on the eyes; the girl has seriously grown over the last few years. It's sure as shit not difficult to see the way she looks at me. I'm sick of pretending we don't notice each other."

I clenched my teeth as my jaw tightened and my hands formed fists. This fucker. I was going to beat his dumb ass bloody before the day was over.

The two of them shared a long look. I leaned forward and braced my arms on my knees as I tried to find words, a death glare on my face. Before I could voice my rage, the idiots started to cackle like two old maids.

"You should see your face," Shaun wheezed out as he fell over the arm of his chair.

"Chill. We're just messing with you," Tate explained with a sad shake of his head. "I can't believe you fell for that."

"I told you," Shaun pointed at Tate. "I fucking told you."

I glared at them. "Told him what?"

He shrugged. "You're jonesing for lil' miss. *Hard.* Have been for months."

My jaw clenched as my muscles started to tic. I refused to admit anything to these assholes. Instead, I tried to distract. "Lil' miss?"

The bastard smirked. "Yeah. As you pointed out last week, you only have *one* little sister. I've been calling Len that since she was a kid. It's a hard habit to break. Knowing she spent the night in your bed makes it really fucking wrong. Since Lennon is now tainted and can no longer be little sis, from this moment on, she's lil' miss."

"You know there's no cure for stupidity, right?"

They started roaring again.

"Shit. You're not even going to try to deny it, are ya? She spent the night with you."

"It's not like that," I started, trying to protect her, but the look of disbelief each wore was too much to handle.

"Damn. He's in over his head."

"Yeah. He's screwed."

I ignored them and glanced at my phone. "I've gotta go. Lock up when you leave."

Their laughter followed me out.

Fuckers.

Thankfully, the house was completely dark when I drove in hours later. I hadn't expected them to be hanging around, yet the worry had lingered in the back of my mind. I turned off the engine and sat, relishing the quiet for a moment.

Exhausted, I leaned my head against the seat and sighed. Rehearsal had been hell. No one had memorized the changes, some hadn't even seen the email.

Insults, props, and tantrums had been thrown. Tears had been shed. A script had been torn in two and tossed into the air.

Nilo hadn't responded well to the cast and crew either.

Actors, man. Some of us had a flair for the dramatic. Occupational hazard or plausible justification, I wasn't sure which.

I was worn out. Physically and mentally. I should have gone inside and headed straight to bed.

Instead, I slid from the car, flipped up my hood, tucked my hands in the kangaroo pocket, and walked toward the white, two-story colonial that sat on the lot diagonal from ours. My steps slowed when I realized there was only one car in the garage. Aunt Gayle, my mother's best friend, had backed her Camry in, yet left both doors open.

Typically, that meant Uncle Trev was expected home. However, the outside lights had been turned out. In fact, as I came to a stop at the end of the stone walkway that led to their front door, I realized the entire first floor was dark. Even the nightlight that was a constant in their kitchen was missing.

I tipped back my head, scowling. The second floor was just as black as the first, not even blue light from the television splattered across the walls or reflected in the windows. I checked my phone. It wasn't *that* late.

I hurried around the corner, eyes still skyward. My lips spread in a wide smile when I saw the soft yellow illuminating Lennon's bedroom. She never closed her curtains or shades, insisting that no one could see in because she was on the second story and the trees blocked anyone from trying to peep. Since she didn't need to use them for privacy, she claimed the room felt bigger when the windows were left bare.

Scaling the ancient oak, I crept along the thickest branches to the roof and catwalked to my destination. I'd made the trip so many times I could do it in my sleep. For a moment I perched, watching. Lounging on her bed, knees bent, and book propped on her thighs, she was absorbed in the story. I wondered what mythical land she'd transported herself to. Knowing her as well as I did, it was probably some epic fantasy where good was battling an ancient evil, and it was up to a feisty, young heroine to save them all.

I lifted my hand to knock, then hesitated. She looked so sweet and innocent, so young, that regret started to ooze through me. I was supposed to protect her, keep her that way forever, my little Len.

Yet, memories from the night before had replayed in my mind almost all day. I couldn't forget the way she'd kissed me, the feeling of her hands as they'd roamed my body. There was nothing little about her anymore. I could try to deny it, pretend it hadn't happened, but the harsh reality was that Lennon James had grown up sometime after I'd stopped watching.

It was only a matter of time before everyone else realized it too. The idea of some other dude, some ass like Ross, standing outside her window, watching her, made me long to climb into her room, dirty her up, make her mine.

Dirty her up? I groaned as I shook my head at the absurd thought. I wasn't sure where it had come from, and I certainly didn't trust that dark part of myself. At least, not around Len. I was clearly horny as hell and fucked up from the breakup.

Deciding to follow my first instinct, I started to turn when Lennon sat up, adjusted the book, and gave me a perfect view of the cover. My eyes widened. Fantasy novel, my ass.

The Len I knew didn't read romance. She'd made fun of the stash of old Harlequins we'd found in the attic one day and sworn she'd never waste her time on drivel, as she called it. The one in her hands, with the half-naked dude on the cover, looked more risqué than any of the books her mom had kept hidden away.

Eyes wide, fully engrossed in the words in front of her, she bit her lip, and adjusted again, one hand moving to her stomach and drifted downward. I moved without thinking. The window was up, and I ducked into her room before I'd even realized I'd decided to stay.

Startled, Len squeaked and dropped her book as she scrambled to sit up and scoot back against her headboard. "Dean!" She hissed, breathless. "You scared the crap out of me."

I closed the window and pulled the curtains together with a quick snap, not caring that she liked them open. I wanted to be alone with her, in our own world.

When I turned back to her, Len was watching me with a mixture of wearied amusement. "Whatcha doing?"

She was a smart girl. She knew exactly what I was doing as I toed off my sneakers and pulled the hoodie over my head. A few strides later, I was on the bed next to her.

I'd climbed in that window more times than either of us could remember, had millions of conversations and spilled my heart out within those walls, and spent countless nights on the floor. Yet, as I laid my head on her lap, my heart began to race. This version of Lennon made me nervous.

To cover this new, unwanted, feeling, I reached out and tried to tip the book up so I could see the title. "What're you reading?"

Before I could see it, she leaned forward, snatched the book from my fingers and tossed the paperback onto the floor almost carelessly. "Nothing important. Research for a project I'm working on."

I stretched out, propping my head up with a hand and gazed up at her. "It's spring break. You should be doing something fun, not working."

Len rolled her eyes as she repositioned, lying down next to me, tucked her bottom arm under her pillow, and grinned at me. "Reading *is* fun."

I smiled back. It was such a Lennon thing to say. I didn't know another person our age who would rather spend the night reading than going out with friends.

Unless, of course, they were reading the smut she'd been. I was tempted to steamroll her and snatch the book off the floor. The only thing that stopped me was that I didn't want to read about kissing when I could do the real thing with her.

"If I kiss you, will you hit me?"

Her shrug was nonchalant. "Guess that depends on when you kiss me. And where."

My lips twitched as I lifted a hand and tugged on a piece of her green hair. "Right now, brat."

She moved a few inches closer and tipped her chin up, giving silent permission, probably without realizing it. "Isn't that why you snuck in my window?"

I tucked the hair behind her ear before letting my thumb caress her cheek. Her skin was silky-soft, almost calming to touch. I adjusted my gaze to meet hers. "No. I didn't want your parents to know I was coming over so late."

Her eyes grew wide before she rolled over, away from me, and shot to her feet as she checked her phone. "Shit!"

I sat up, realizing exactly how little she was wearing. I'd gotten so caught up in seeing her that somehow I'd missed the lack of clothing. I forced my eyes upward and away from the barely there tank that made my blood begin to boil. "What's wrong?"

Thankfully, she didn't notice the way my voice cracked over the words as she shook her head.

Shoving her feet in slippers, she threw open her door and rushed into the hall. "They're gone," she told me over her shoulder. "I was supposed to lock up hours ago."

I frowned as I followed her from the room and down the stairs. It seemed like Len had been left at home alone a lot lately. I didn't like it.

"Gone? Where are they?" It was Sunday. Even corporations took a day off to rest.

"Dad has that big project at work," Len explained as she moved through the dark house without stopping to turn on any lights. "There was some black-tie dinner last night he couldn't miss. They were supposed to come home today but decided to stay because Mom has the day off tomorrow."

My eyes started to adjust as she made it to the other side of the kitchen and opened the small door that led to the attached garage. She leaned around the corner and I heard the motor for the automatic door engage as she stepped back into the kitchen. Shutting and locking the side door, she turned back to me with a grin. "In all honesty, I think they needed a weekend to themselves."

She was off again, headed toward the front of the house this time, before I could respond. If they'd called hours before, that meant she'd been home alone all this time with every door in the house unlocked. I wanted to wring her little neck.

I was irritated with her parents. Len couldn't drive yet. My family was gone. God only knew if Tate was home. If she'd needed something or had an emergency, she would've been all alone.

"Why didn't you call me?"

Len hesitated as she lifted a hand to slide the deadbolt. After the door was secure, she turned back to me and cleared her throat. "I wasn't sure what to say." She walked toward me slowly. "Every text I wrote sounded like an invitation." She lowered her voice to a sultry tone, "Hey, my parents aren't home. Come over." She snorted. "See? So, I deleted 'em. You'll probably have a message from my parents when you get home. Gotta watch out for clueless little Len, ya know? She can't possibly spend the night alone."

I hated the contempt I heard in her voice, even though I agreed with the theory. "That'd be a first."

She was close enough that I could see the confusion on her face, even though the house was still bathed in darkness. "What is?"

I stepped forward, my hands finding her hips. Her curves were driving me out of my mind. They had been for months, even though I hadn't realized, or admitted what that meant. "My girl's parents asking me to spend the night alone with their daughter."

Her eyebrows pinched, but she didn't try to jerk away like I'd expected. "Your girl?" She grunted. "I kissed you once. If you're staking a claim on all the girls who've kissed you, there's a long, long line in fro—"

My fingernails dug into her flesh as I yanked her into my body. "It wasn't just once."

She smirked. "It was one time. It may have lasted for a few hours, but it was only once."

"Yeah?" I challenged back. "Let's make it twice."

Before she could pull away or say another word, I cupped her jaw and captured her lips with my own. Full of surprises, she didn't fight me. Instead, her arms slid around my back and she met me kiss for kiss.

It was hot as hell.

Once we'd sucked the air from the room, our lips swollen, and nothing but need for her flowed through my veins, I stepped back. Every instinct told me to toss her over my shoulder, carry her back to her room, and spend the rest of the night getting to know her body, but my conscience wouldn't let me.

Instead, we stood there, staring at each other as we both struggled to catch our breath. I was trying to figure out what to say when her stomach growled. As if hearing a sympathetic beast, my own answered the call and sent up a battle cry.

"Sorry," I said with an embarrassed laugh, "I didn't have a chance to eat."

She shook her head slightly before switching on a lamp next to the couch. "I actually forgot."

"Forgot? How does one forget to eat?"

"Good book?" She shrugged.

"Must be quite an interesting read. Is it a school project or something for the paper?"

The flush that stained her cheeks made me want to grab her and kiss her stupid all over again. "Um..." She stared at me, completely flustered. "Personal development?"

Unable to resist, I prodded. "You seem very confused by this. What is it, like a self-help book? Don't be embarrassed, Len. We all need support sometimes. If you tell me what you're looking into, maybe I can help."

She shook her head, unable to meet my eyes. "Nope. All good."

"You sure?" I teased, "If it's something like, *Fifteen Ways to Tell Your Best Friend You Want Her Brother,* I've got some ideas."

Her nose wrinkled as her beautiful mind formed what I was sure would be a spectacular comeback. Then her eyes lit up, and she grinned, teeth digging into her bottom lip in a way that made me bite my own and suppress a groan. She didn't pay any attention, too focused on her plan.

"Well, you're half right," she twisted her lips as she nodded sadly. "I can't handle the guilt anymore. I need to confess, tell Dylan everything. I think I might be in love with Tate."

Little brat. I looped an arm around her waist as I fell back onto the couch and dragged her with me. As she twisted against my unbreakable grip, I leaned down and nipped the bottom of her ear.

"Don't lie. It's me you think of when you're reading that bodice ripper upstairs, isn't it?"

She froze, muscles taut. I expected a denial, her to pull away, to question how I knew. Instead, she leaned back so she could see my face. "Sometimes," she arched one eyebrow in challenge. "It depends on the scene and what kind of hero he is. Most of the time, like if he's a good kisser or has muscles for days, I imagine Shaun."

It was my turn to stop dead. My fingers tightened on her thighs, almost involuntarily. My stomach growled again, but I barely heard it or felt the hunger pain, too focused on her.

She'd found my weak spot. I'd kill both my best friends without hesitation.

Laughing, Len tapped a single finger to my nose. "You're adorable most days, but when you get jealous, you look perfectly murderous." With a wink, she pushed herself off my lap and held out a hand. "Come on, let's see what we've got in the kitchen, so we can at least tame one beast tonight."

I wasn't sure about much, but one thing I felt deep in my soul; Lennon James was going to drive me out of my mind. If I weren't careful, she'd destroy me.

Chapter Ten

Lennon

After a thorough search of the refrigerator and cupboards, Dean turned to me. "What in the hell were you supposed to eat? There's nothing here."

Annoyed, I lifted my head and pointed my chin toward the box of cereal I'd pulled out ten minutes before. "There's milk. Soup or cereal is quick and easy."

He crossed his arms over his chest as his eyes narrowed and his jaw clenched in agitation. "They seriously took off without leaving you food?"

He didn't have to spell out who he was talking about. I rolled my eyes. "I'm fifteen, you ass. Not five. My parents don't need to make me dinner if they're leaving for the night. I can cook. In fact, I made you a huge meal a few hours ago."

"Yeah, if there's something to make."

With an agitated sigh, I slid off the stool and yanked open the freezer, pointing to the overflowing shelves. "Nope. You're right. Nothing." I shut the door with a slam and shoved my way past him to reach for the cereal. "The door's over there if you'd rather eat at your house."

Dean moved fast, and before I could stop him, he'd backed me into the cupboards, arms on either side, blocking me in. "I don't know what's going on with me lately."

Surprised, I tipped my head back as far as I could in order to meet his eyes. "What do you mean?"

"I'm being a dick for no reason. Maybe it's the stress of the show; I don't know."

I lifted a hand to the middle of his chest and pressed lightly against his heart. "Or maybe it's because you just broke up with your girlfriend and refuse to admit you're sad about it." The words burned, and I hated how my own ticker seemed to ache at the thought of him going back to her. "Give yourself some time."

His eyes narrowed as if he didn't want to hear it.

"Plus, it's not like you're being any more douchey than normal."

Orbs so warm and dark they reminded me of my grandmother's beloved mahogany desk grew wide. Amusement pulled at the corners of his mouth. "I am not a douche."

"Please," I scoffed.

His expression didn't change, yet he watched me with intense interest. It was almost as if he had no idea. I didn't buy it. No one could act the way he did and remain clueless.

"I'm not," he insisted. "In fact, once, not that long ago, you told me I was the coolest person you'd ever met."

I shook my head in pure amusement. I'd been ten. It wasn't like I'd met that many people yet.

"Correction. You *were* cool. Then you graduated from eighth grade and become Deputy Dickhead. You took a little break when you were with Vicky and were only a halfhearted hag. But now the Alpha is back, baby, and it's like you expect us all to fall into line and obey when you bark a command."

An eyebrow quirked in challenge. He thought I was nuts. There was no way he didn't realize what a controlling ass he turned into whenever he thought he could get away with it. Which was the majority of the time.

"Okay. Let's refresh, shall we? You try to frighten away any guy that shows the slightest interest in Dylan or me. You complain about my clothes constantly, boss us around, manipulate situations to fit your needs, and even created ground rules for us to follow before you let us go to one of your stupid parties. Now you're treating me like I'm a child. That's all in the last two weeks." I sucked my teeth. "Hate to tell ya, buddy, but if it talks like a duck, and it walks like a duck, you're a douche." My stomach rumbled in protest once more. "I'm hungry. Quack, quack and waddle along so I can eat."

His eyes narrowed as he leaned close enough for our noses to touch. For a split second, I thought he might kiss me again. "I'll order pizza. Apparently, someone gets cranky when she's hungry."

He stepped away, leaving me speechless. He'd already pulled out the phone and started punching in numbers when he glanced over his shoulder. "TV while we wait?"

I nodded in exasperation. Dean Cullen was driving me crazy.

"Do you know how bad that is for you?"

Dean shook his head, but he didn't stop sprinkling garlic salt all over his pizza. "Nope. But I bet you're going to tell me, Ms. Know-It-All."

"Too much sodium can lead to high blood pressure, heart disease, and stroke. It might not be that big of a deal at our age, but give it ten years and you're doomed. I bet your levels are already abnormally elevated."

"Doubt it. Doc says I'm as healthy as a horse."

"Yeah, a charley horse. Annoying like one too." I grinned at his glare.

"Don't knock it 'til you rock it." He held the piece out to me. "Come on, just one little bite."

"Ew. No." I shoved his hand away and watched in horror as he devoured the entire slice in three bites. I wiped the grease and cheese from my lips, shaking my head. "Boys are so gross."

"I'm anything but gross. You don't know what you're missing."

I wasn't sure if he meant him or his pizza, so I shrugged, popped my last piece of crust into my mouth, and chewed thoughtfully. "I'll take my chances."

His answering grin was full of mischief. Before I could retreat, long fingers closed around my ankle, and he gave it a swift tug. Unprepared, my butt slid across the carpet, and my top half fell backward, cushioned not only by the thick, plush rug but also Dean's arm that suddenly appeared under my head to soften the landing. The rest of him stretched out next to me, too close for it to be casual.

I looked everywhere else but at him until his pull was simply too strong. As soon as my eyes met his, he pinched my chin and leaned in. The kiss was soft, yet not. Demanding, but gentle.

His tongue traced the outline of my lips, asking for entrance. With a sigh, I surrendered, letting him take control. In moments, I was lost in him, my fingertips scratching his skull as I held on for dear life. I didn't care that he tasted like sea salt or garlic. In fact, I was relatively sure it was now my favorite combination.

We'd tried to watch a movie, but since we'd been unable to agree on one before the pizza arrived, we'd given up once it was delivered. Instead, we'd sat at the coffee table and inhaled the food while we talked. As much as I loved listening to him, and I'd be happy to anytime, lying in his arms, kissing him until my lips were sore was my new favorite pastime.

All too soon, he groaned and pulled away. "It's late."

His voice was full of regret. I knew he didn't want to stop any more than I did, but I let him pull me to my feet anyway. He knew what he was doing, and I trusted him enough to follow along.

He grabbed the nearly empty box and carried it to the kitchen, while I trailed behind him with the rest. Once our glasses were deposited into the dishwasher, and the trash thrown away, his eyes drifted toward the door. It was time to say goodbye, even though I didn't want to.

"Stay?" I hated the pleading in my voice. I was sure he'd say no. It was the smart thing to do.

Dark eyes searched my face before his nod instantly washed away my anxiety. His fingers laced through mine as he snapped off the kitchen light and pulled me up the stairs behind him. Safe in my room, he locked the door and started to pull the comforter off the end of my bed, preparing to make a bed on the floor, the way he always did when he spent the night.

"You can sleep with me."

My words jerked him to a stop but he didn't look up. "I've slept on this floor hundreds of times. Pretty sure I can handle once more."

"We shared a bed last night. Pretty sure we can handle it again."

Still not looking at me, he dropped the blanket back into its place and pulled my sheets back. "Get in."

I didn't argue. He turned the light off before I settled into my spot, covering us not only in the black of the night but also in silence. I don't think either one of us even breathed as he hovered next to the bed.

"I can't sleep in pants sober."

I grinned at the ceiling, biting my lip so I didn't laugh. Not only had it sounded ridiculous, but I knew for a fact he couldn't sleep in them drunk either. That's how his jeans had ended up on the floor the night before.

"Then don't."

My face fell, and my eyes grew wide, shocked not only by my words, but also the tone I'd used. If he hadn't been in the room with me, I would have smacked my forehead in embarrassed disgust. Who was I?

The hiss of his belt sliding through loops as he tore it off pulled my attention back to him. Next was his zipper, the sound magnified in the silent room, followed by jeans falling to the floor. My heart pounded as the bed creaked and shifted when he slid in next to me, close but not touching.

Neither of us moved as if we were both too scared. Seconds ticked by, yet slumber stayed just out of reach.

"How was rehearsal?"

The question was whispered, in case he'd fallen asleep. I'd meant to ask him earlier, but every time I tried to bring it up, he'd dominated the conversation.

"Hell," he answered with a whisper of his own.

I rolled toward him, bunching my pillow. I couldn't see his features, but I wanted him to know he had my full attention. "Tell me?"

"Nilo, the director, is a genius. He doesn't do things like others."

As he walked me through the nightmare that his practice had been, his hand found mine. His voice was like warm milk and honey, soothing comfort. I fought to keep my eyes open, to stay in that moment with him for as long as possible.

The last thing I remembered was him kissing my forehead before he wrapped his body around mine.

I didn't know how late it was when I felt the pull of morning. Usually, the sun liked to coax me from sleep. Yet, *someone*—a very arrogant and bossy someone—had closed the curtains the night before, and my room was unusually dark.

That same someone was still behind me, almost as close as he could get, playing with my hair. Closing my eyes once more, I relaxed into him happily. The dreams had stayed away, almost as if they knew I had the real thing and he was much better. I'd finally had a decent night's sleep.

"Morning," I mumbled with a yawn.

"Mornin'," his greeting rumbled through his chest.

I'd started to drift back into oblivion when he spoke again.

"You never did tell me. Why'd you dye your hair?"

I knew he wasn't being nosy, the question full of genuine curiosity, which is why I answered honestly. "I asked for a tattoo. Told the parentals I'd settle for piercings. The furthest they'd budge was streaks because hair isn't permanent. I'm sure they pictured subtle lowlights or highlights, something Dylan would get. When your mom offered to take me to her salon, they gave in. I came home with this. Dad said I looked like Rainbow Brite and demanded I change it. Which shows you what he knows because Rainbow Brite didn't have colored hair."

Dean chuckled. "How sad is it that I knew that?"

It wasn't sad at all. It was sweet that he knew. I smiled and leaned back against him more. He'd always been my safe place, but lying in his arms escalated that feeling. In that moment it seemed like nothing in the world could hurt me.

"Pretty sure you put up with way more than any big brother should have."

He tucked his chin into the nape of my neck. "Tate and I definitely spent more time playing dolls and dress-up than anything else. All to make you two happy."

I grinned at the memory. "Clearly, it paid off. I mean, obviously, Tate learned everything he needed to know about women or he wouldn't be... well, Tate. He's going to be a great dad one day. And if you think about it, what is acting if not an adult version of dress-up? So, you're welcome."

"Touché." His arm tightened around me in a welcome squeeze. "You kept the hair even though your dad hated it."

"Yep. He says it's a bullshit power struggle. I'm banned from all his work functions until I stop rebelling. Jokes on him because the last thing I want to do is play the dutiful daughter in front of a bunch of old rich dudes who measure my worth by how small my waist is and look at me like they're waiting for me to be eighteen so they can cop a feel."

Dean's body went taut as if he was suddenly on alert. I wasn't sure if it was the bitterness in my tone or the words that caught him off guard the most. I'd been a daddy's girl for so long that recent developments had thrown everyone for a loop.

"It hasn't gotten any better?"

I rarely talked about how upset I'd grown with my father. I wasn't sure if Dylan even realized the depth of my disappointment, but her brother had been the ear I'd needed more than once. "Only worse."

My father had been avoiding me. He could pretend he wasn't, but I knew the truth. I was almost positive that Aunt Tash and Uncle Chad saw it too. It felt like Dad was struggling with the fact that he had a teenage daughter and that his once little buddy no longer followed him around, telling everyone she wanted to be just like her daddy when she grew up.

"It's like they've forgotten they spent years teaching us to be the people we are, and now they're terrified they're about to lose all input in our lives, so they tighten the grip instead of trusting us."

"That's exactly what this is."

I nodded and rolled over. If possible, Dean was even hotter first thing in the morning with messy hair and half-lidded eyes.

My heart ached when I saw my hurt reflected on his face. Without thinking, I cupped his cheek. I wasn't the only one with dad issues. "He still won't listen?"

With a small shake of his head, he reached up and tugged my hand down between us before he laced his fingers through mine. "He insists acting isn't a real job. I can't change his mind, so I stopped trying."

Uncle Chad, while proud of his son, had started to push Dean to figure out what he wanted to do with the rest of his life. He insisted that Dean needed to grow up sometime. In Chad's mind, that didn't mean age, it meant having Dean leave his acting dreams behind.

A few weeks before, the tension between the two had reached an all-time high when Dean found out he couldn't go on the cruise and his dad had insisted he didn't have any choice but to go. He'd crawled in my window that night too. I hadn't been able to offer much other than to let him know he wasn't alone.

"Enough of the depressing bullshit. We're on vacation. They're old. What do they know anyway? I like the hair. I hope you keep it."

I grinned up at him. "Oh, I am. Until they'll let me get a tattoo. Or take me to get pierced."

"A tattoo? You're totally fucking with me."

"Nope."

"You, really?"

I nodded.

"Yeah? What big, badass symbol did you plan to permanently etch onto your virgin skin?"

I ignored the way his words made my body tingle. "Promise not to laugh?"

He shook his head as a smile teased his mouth. "Not even a little bit. Let me guess, Tinker Bell?"

I snorted—he would assume I'd want a cartoon. "Why would I get Tinker Bell?"

He shrugged. "It fits."

My forehead wrinkled as I watched his eyes glimmer with mischief. I twisted my lips, waiting for him to explain. He didn't.

"No. An owl." I pushed myself up, leaning over him, as I reached for the nightstand drawer on his side.

I hadn't thought about how little I was wearing, or the fact that he was naked except for his boxers. From the sudden way he inhaled and went still, he hadn't forgotten. His hands immediately found my hips and gripped them tightly, almost as if he were afraid for either of us to move.

For a split second I considered throwing a leg over him and leaning down to kiss him until we were too far gone to stop. Instead, I tugged out the small piece of paper I kept hidden away before I dropped back into my spot and held it out for him. He waited a moment, his pulse pounding vigorously in his neck, and let out a long breath before he reached out, letting his fingertips brush mine.

He took my beloved treasure cautiously, eyes widening when he saw the sketch of a wise old owl, glasses perched on his beak, sitting on a stack of unopened books while reading another.

"Did you design this?"

"Kind of. I told him what I wanted, but Shaun took my idea and created a masterpiece."

"Shaun drew this?" Dean studied it closely, impressed. "This isn't his usual style." Not many people knew how talented our friend was. It seemed like he wanted to hide that piece of himself from the world. "Wow."

"Knowledge is power. At least, that's what it symbolizes."

Dean handed it back to me, eyes focused on my face. "It's perfect."

I tucked the sketch back into its hiding place and settled into my spot again. "Right?" I shrugged. "I thought maybe telling them I wanted to pierce my tongue or lip would scare my parents into agreeing to the tattoo. I was wrong. So, rainbow hair it is."

He reached out and tugged lightly on another piece before twirling it around his fingers. I didn't know if it was meant to irritate or to comfort, but over the past few years, it had definitely fallen into the latter category. I loved when he singled me out and touched me in such a simple yet intimate way, even when there were other people around. It made me feel special.

Which was dumb. Little girls weren't supposed to like it when boys pulled their pigtails and told them what to do. In fact, we'd been taught how wrong it was. Yet here I was, mooning over how special he made me feel when he acted like a bully. Ugh. I was hopeless.

"This is perfect too. The hair, I mean," he assured me. "It's unusual. Bold and bright. So, *you*. If that makes any sense at all."

"Are you saying I'm unusual?"

He laughed. "Did you not know? I'm sorry to be the one who finally told you. I would've thought the way you dress might have tipped you off a few years ago. Or the fact that you spout random facts about the weirdest shit at the drop of a hat. You, Lennon James, are a giant enigma wrapped in a teeny package."

I grinned. "You think I'm mysterious? Me?"

"You definitely confuse the fuck out of me," he admitted. "I can't figure out if you want the whole world to notice you or if you simply want to hide away but can't seem to do it because you were born to stand out."

"I don't want to hide," I assured him. "I hate being the center of attention. I struggle sometimes when I'm out of my comfort zone. Hiding would mean I have something to be ashamed of. I don't. In fact, I like me."

"Good," his eyes narrowed slightly. "I like you too."

"You like to kiss me," I teased. "The rest of the time, I annoy you."

As if the words reminded him, his attention dropped to my lips. "I really, really like kissing you."

I smiled, scraping my teeth over my bottom lip as I did. I had no idea how I was going to explain this recent development to Dylan. Not that it would matter much because I had no doubt Dean would get sick of me before spring break ended. I forced the thoughts from my mind as he leaned closer.

With a quick peck to my temple, Dean rolled over and out of bed. He was glorious to look at, even more so than the Dean in my dreams.

"You're leaving?" I pouted as he pulled on his jeans, one leg at a time.

He waited until his shirt was securely in place before he turned back to me. Carefully sliding his belt through the loops, he twisted his lips. "It's late. What are your plans today?"

I yawned and stretched. I had absolutely nothing on my agenda. My parents would be home later, but until then, I could be lazy.

"Reading smut and dreaming of Shaun?" I teased.

He snorted as he reached for his shoes. "Spend the day with me."

"You don't have rehearsal? Or something better to do than babysit?"

"Yeah. 'Cause that's what spending time with you is, babysitting." He rolled his eyes as he pulled the second sneaker on. With swift movements, he put one knee on the edge of my bed and leaned over me, holding himself up on straightened arms. "Get dressed and come over. I'll make breakfast." He pressed a quick kiss to my lips and backed away.

He didn't give me a chance to say no before he pulled open my curtains, practically blinding me, and left the way he'd arrived.

Chapter Eleven

Dean

I forced myself to jump from the tree and jog across the street as I ignored the pull to go back. I unlocked my front door, took the stairs two at a time and hurried into the bathroom without bothering to grab clean clothes. I was home alone. No one would see me; no one would complain.

The water was too cold, but I was desperate for something to help. Lennon drove me all kinds of crazy. I had hundreds of thoughts running through my mind at any given moment. One minute I was overly protective, the next, I was pissed at her for nothing, and then before I could stop it, I was hard, my dick begging for her attention.

It was too much, too fast. I was caught in a goddamn typhoon. A brilliant storm with a rebel heart, rainbow hair, and doodled Chucks. Eyes so blue they were almost purple and a snarky streak a mile wide. *Fuck me.*

I leaned my head against the shower wall, letting the frigid spray cascade over me. I needed to hurry so I could have breakfast ready when she got there. Yet, my body wouldn't cooperate. Instead of cooling me down, I was even more turned on, every nerve ending on alert, begging for release.

I hadn't rubbed one out in the shower since I was in junior high. I hadn't needed to. Now, the idea sounded really fucking appealing. It would be so easy, picturing Len in the skimpy, almost see-through pajamas she'd worn.

With a groan, I turned the tap to hot and let thoughts of her take over.

When I stepped out of my room twenty minutes later, boner-free and fully dressed, the smell of brewing coffee met me. With a smile, I ran down the stairs, thinking Len had beat me to it. As I rounded the corner into the kitchen, my face fell.

"Mornin', sunshine," Tate crooned from his regular spot at the counter, sweaty from one of his workouts. "You got up late and still look awfully chipper. That never happens. Sleep well?" His tone held a note I couldn't identify but put me on edge.

I hesitated. He hadn't been around when I'd gotten home, the house had been too quiet, so there was no way he could've known I'd stayed out all night.

I walked lazily to the coffee pot, determined to act like I didn't have anything to hide. "I did," I admitted as I poured a cup, adding cream and sugar slowly. I turned and leaned my back against the counter, ready to ask about his night, to talk about anything other than the girl on my mind, yet his smirk stopped me.

"I'm guessing you didn't sleep on the floor then."

I couldn't hide my guilt fast enough. His eyebrows rose, daring me to deny it. I wouldn't. I'd never lied to him. I wasn't about to start.

"No." I didn't know what else to say. Clearly, he'd figured out where I'd been. I wasn't sure how, but he knew.

"I saw you climbing out her window on the way back from my run, dumb ass," he answered my unasked question with a chuckle. "You're lucky it was only me. It was broad daylight. Anyone could have seen you."

"I stay at Lennon's all the time," I pointed out.

"Yeah, I've slept over too," he countered. "Just not in her bed. And definitely not when her parents weren't home."

I couldn't argue with that. We'd both climbed through her window. It had always been innocent. Most of the time, I'd left after a few minutes, but there were a few times where Len and I had talked almost all night.

We hadn't been alone in the house then. I certainly hadn't had my hands or lips on her. It felt like a lifetime had passed between then and now.

He sat back and crossed his arms over his bare chest. "The fuck you doin'?"

I pinched the bridge of my nose as I set my coffee down. "I don't know." I hated admitting it, but it was the damn truth. "She's in my head. I can't get her out."

"It's Len. She's been in your head since we were five."

"Not like this, man." I swallowed as I shrugged and clutched the counter by my sides.

"Exactly like this. The stakes are just higher now."

I frowned, unsure of what he meant.

He rolled his eyes as his lips quirked up on one side. "For as long as I can remember, there's been a push and pull between the two of you. You're tight one minute, at each other's throats the next. You could boss her around, push her almost to the point where she'd break before you backed away, but if any other guy disrespected her, you'd beat him bloody. Do you remember when you kicked Charlie's ass in sixth grade?"

I nodded as he spoke, agreeing with him. As soon as he finished, it was my turn to cross my arms, mimicking his pose. "He shoved her down and called her names."

Tate narrowed his eyes. "Because he was trying to be cool and copy you. You'd tormented her all morning."

I wanted to argue, but I couldn't remember if he was wrong. All I could recall was seeing her crying and letting the rage take over. I'd been mad at myself as well as at Charlie. It was my job to keep shit like that from happening, and I hadn't protected her well enough. To punish us both, I'd lunged at him in front of the teachers.

I'd gotten suspended for three days, and my parents had grounded me for what felt like forever. Len had come over after dinner, and hugged me, thanking me for sticking up for her. That moment had made the punishment and sore knuckles completely worthwhile.

"I could give you a hundred more examples."

"I would've done the same thing for Dylan." I pointed out. "That's my job. I'm the big brother."

"Nah, that's the story you try to sell. You're the only one buying it."

"I've spent the last decade watching out for both of them."

"You have. But differently. There's nothing you wouldn't do to keep Dylan safe, no matter what the consequence. You'd lock her in a tower and throw away the key if you had to, no matter how much she fought back, no matter how much she might hate you in the end. On the flip side, you've always known where Lennon's line in the sand is, and you'll do anything except cross it. You'll toe the fucking thing, walk along the edge, but you'll never step over it. Ever ask yourself why?" He didn't give me a chance to answer, good thing because I didn't have one anyway. "Because she isn't stuck with you. She could leave. That scares the fuck out of you."

I opened my mouth to argue, yet nothing came out as my mind whirled in an entirely new direction. He was right, damn it. The entire situation was a fucking disaster. I scrubbed my hands over my face, frustrated beyond belief. When I looked up, my best friend was grinning like a madman.

"I'm glad you think this is so fucking funny."

"Well," he started slowly, "it was only a matter of time."

"What's that supposed to mean?"

He snorted. "You broke up with Vicky for no reason. You watch Lennon like a hawk, eyes always glued to her. When she's around, you act like you don't know whether you want to shove her away or keep her close, kill her or kiss her."

I had a valid reason to end things with Vicky. I was seventeen. There was no reason to stay with a girl who bitched and moaned about everything I did and acted like she hated me most days. Especially when I didn't know if I liked her or not.

I had to keep an eye on Len because she was always doing something crazy like wearing clothes that showed too much or going on dates with fuckwads who didn't deserve an ounce of her attention.

"That's because I don't know," I grumbled under my breath. Half the time I wanted to throttle her, then hold her tight.

"No shit." The asshat's arrogant smile irritated the piss out of me. "Trust me when I say that she's always been in your head. Whatever it is the two of you have going on was always going to happen."

"You're okay with that? Didn't I hear your dumb ass tell her yesterday that she was like the little sister you never had?"

"She is. If you hurt her, make her cry, or break her heart, I will wreck you. Never doubt that." His face hardened as he gave me a death glare.

"I'd never hurt her intentionally."

"I know that. But we're not kids anymore. We don't bounce back like we did. Your actions don't only affect the two of you."

"Yeah, yeah. You and Shaun will kick my ass. I'll even let you."

"You've got bigger things to worry about than the two of us," he chuckled gleefully. "You keep sneaking in her window, Len's parents are going to figure it out. If by some miracle they don't kill you, they'll sure as shit tell your parents. Something tells me Papa-Pain-in-The-Ass is going to have a thing or two to say. I can only imagine what a shitshow that'll be."

"Fuck him," I grumbled. "He doesn't get a say about this."

"Keep telling yourself that. More terrifying than any of that, though, is the fact that your hooking up with her best friend was never part of Dylan's five-year plan. When she finds out, she's going to flip her shit."

He was right. I didn't know what to do about my sister. Before I could dwell too much, the front door shut. Len strolled into the kitchen moments later.

"Well, well, well. Look what the cat finally dragged out of bed," Tate drawled before he took a sip of coffee, his eyes never leaving her.

"Decided to give up on the quiet and loneliness at your house and join us for an orphan's meal, eh?"

"How'd you know I was alone?"

"Your mom called my house last night and asked me to check on you."

"Yet you're here and not across the street?"

"I knew you'd make it over here eventually."

"That's funny, 'cause I didn't." Lennon grinned as she slid onto a stool next to him. "I figured I'd come over to see what you bums made me for breakfast."

Tate flipped over his cell dramatically and checked the time before he shook his head. "Tsk, tsk, lil' miss. Did you forget our conversation yesterday? Dean's an early riser. He never sleeps this late. He's probably already eaten and is ready to start his day."

Her smile didn't waver as her eyes drifted to me. "Well, some of us don't need beauty sleep."

"Cause they can afford Botox?" Tate asked playfully.

Len shook her head, eyes still on me. "True. But it's not like it would help. Poor Dean would look like a troll either way."

My best friend snorted and choked on his coffee. "Touché."

I couldn't bring myself to break eye contact, let alone think up an appropriate comeback. She was absolutely gorgeous. I couldn't believe I'd never realized the magnitude of her beauty before. It wasn't only her looks, though she was hot as hell. It was the way her nose wrinkled the smallest bit before she smiled. The happiness that shone in her eyes. The kindness that oozed from her pores. Her genuine nature too magnificent to be hidden away.

"So, whaddya say, chef? You open for business, or is the kitchen closed?"

"We actually closed due to illness. I'm sick of cooking. I've been sending everyone to the diner downtown." I winked at her before I could stop myself. I fucking winked. I wanted to punch myself in the damn traitorous eye. "What do you say...my treat?"

"You had me at 'diner.'" She slid out of the chair and glanced over her shoulder at Tate. "You coming?"

He shook his head and finished off his coffee. "Hell no. I'm training. I already binged on carbs once this week."

"They do have eggs and bacon," Len pointed out.

"Can't do it. I'm a carb addict. I see them and need to make them mine. I get all stabby and shit. Can't be trusted." He stood and carried his cup to the sink. "You crazy kids have fun." He pointed at Len, a wicked grin on his face. "Remember, pancakes go straight from the lips onto your hips. Make sure you get a double stack. That ass is looking a little flat." He hustled out the back before I could smack him for talking about Lennon's glorious backside.

Bastard better not look at it again.

"Your ass isn't flat," I assured her as we walked through the house.

"Thanks?" She snorted. "I don't care if it is. The boy gave me an excuse to eat pancakes. I'm going to inhale my weight in the fluffy deliciousness. It's true, by the way. There was a study done where scientists found that even short periods of bingeing on junk food can leave the body more prone to weight gain for years. Unfortunately for many women, fat cells seem to congregate on their hips."

"I don't even want to know how you know that."

She shrugged. "I told you. I'm a wealth of useless knowledge. Come on, I'm hungry. Someone promised me food. Don't push me. You won't like me when I'm hangry."

"Learned that the hard way last night, remember?" I teased as I ushered her out the door. "Double stack of pancakes to keep the monster at bay?"

Once we were in my car, backing out of the driveway, she nodded. "Yep. Plus, I'd love a fat ass."

Only Lennon.

Rehearsal had gotten out on time for once, but I'd stayed a little later to talk to Randy, our costume designer extraordinaire. The man was a genius who had vision and approached each character's look as if they were a real person. He knew how to dress every actor so when we stepped out on the stage opening night—and every show afterward—we were full of confidence and knew we looked good. We'd had a great discussion, and I left with a smile on my face, eager to call Lennon.

I pulled out my phone and turned it on as I strolled down the path, not paying attention to anything else. The town might roll up the sidewalks at sundown, but the police patrolled the historic district regularly. The streetlights outside the theater were bright, and I wouldn't have been surprised to find there were at least three cameras following my every move.

Reading the text messages Lennon had sent was my only priority.

As I sent my reply, asking if I could see her, I trotted down the wooden steps that led to the parking lot. I glanced up and did a double take. It wasn't the fact that someone was leaning against the back of my car that had thrown me off. It was the *who*.

"Inconceivable," I muttered sardonically as I started to walk again.

Chelsea pushed herself off my trunk and gave me a perplexed smile as I got closer. "What?"

I knew she'd heard me. She just didn't have a clue what I was talking about. Len, on the other hand, wouldn't have missed the *Princess Bride* reference.

I pulled my keys out of the pocket of my messenger bag. "Nothing. I'm just surprised to see you."

That was an understatement. Waiting for me, like this, felt like she thought there was more between us than there was. I could practically hear Tate with his, "*I told you so.*"

"Good," she stepped into me, up onto her toes, and threw her arms around my shoulders; I gave her a half-assed hug in return and attempted to pull away, but she wouldn't let me. Instead, her arms tightened. "That was the point."

"What are you doing out here all by yourself?"

If the question sounded harsh, Chelsea brushed it off. "I missed you." The words were a whine right before she buried her head in my neck.

I was stunned for a moment. Before I thought too much about it, I reached up, pulled her arms down and took two steps back. I didn't want the scent of her perfume all over me.

My eyes scanned the lot. "Where's your car?"

"The girls and I were headed to a movie when I saw you were still here. I had them drop me off. Figured we could hang."

My phone beeped with an incoming text. I glanced down, happy and relieved to see the name lighting up my screen. Chelsea kept talking, but I drowned her out as I gobbled up Lennon's words.

Tink: I was tempted to ignore your ridiculous question. Because, duh. Then I realized you were asking instead of telling. I think we should celebrate this momentous milestone when you come over.

I'd started to tap out a quick reply when Chelsea reached out, laying her hand over mine, blocking my phone. "Hey. Did I lose you?"

I shook her off, told Len I'd call her in a few, and hit send. When I lifted my eyes, Chelsea was glaring.

"Nope." Acting on instinct, I tucked my phone into my back pocket, almost like my subconscious was telling me to keep it far away from her and attempted a small smile.

"Hot date?" If her tone hadn't given away her displeasure at the idea, the way her nostrils flared before her mouth puckered like she'd smelled something rotten certainly did.

My phone beeped again. "No." I wasn't giving her more than that. "I wish I could tonight, but I'm out. I'm exhausted and have to come back to do it all over again tomorrow."

The phone sounded again, another text message. Then one more. I was dying to see what Len had written, but I did my best to focus on the girl in front of me and ignore the one I wanted to give my attention to.

Chelsea crossed her arms over her chest, attitude oozing from her as she lifted her chin. "Needy friend."

The unasked question hung in the air for a moment. I didn't owe her an explanation. She wasn't my girlfriend, and it was none of her business who was blowing up my phone.

Another beep. I didn't know if they were all from Lennon, but I had a pretty good idea they were. She was probably giving me entirely too much information as she spouted off some random fact. Or she'd had another fight with her dad and was venting. Either way, I needed to ditch my present company so I could find out.

"Do you need to answer those?"

If I didn't give her something, Chelsea's questions would get bolder, more forceful. She demanded your full attention and hated to be ignored. If something started to steal her spotlight, she'd point it out. Or do something to make you focus on her.

It typically didn't bother me. Yeah, it'd been annoying as hell when I'd been dating Vicky. When I was single, though, I usually had no problem answering her questions and playing along.

I wasn't technically taken, but I wasn't single either. A lot had happened over the past two weeks, and I didn't know how to describe any of it. The need to protect Lennon, to keep her off Chelsea's radar, was overwhelming. I didn't want to share Len with anyone.

"Well?" Chelsea demanded when I didn't answer. "It's obviously important."

"Just Eastman. I'll hit him back later."

She ran her tongue over her teeth as she gave me a knowing look, almost as if to silently say, *yeah, fuck you, you lying ass.* "From the movie?"

My eyes widened. Movie? "What?" I hated how clueless I sounded.

Narrowed eyes surveyed me. "Shaun's texting you from the movie?"

That got my attention. "The movie you bailed on to come here?" It was taking me a little while, but I'd started to catch on.

Chelsea nodded.

Fuck me. This was exactly why I didn't lie usually. I always got caught. I stuck with the truth this time. "I have no idea where he is."

She was quiet for a moment. "He told you, didn't he? I swear, he gossips more than my girlfriends."

The hair on the back of my neck rose, but I forced myself to play it cool. "Maybe." I shot her a cocky look. "Why don't you tell me what you're talking about, so I know if he told me."

Her smile was villainous. "There's a nasty rumor going around about you and Lennon James."

My mouth went dry. "What?"

"Right? That's how I reacted. As if." She smirked, completely amused. "Supposedly, the two of you were on a date this morning." She rolled her eyes. "Jenna's cousin said she saw you at the diner. She claims you were flirting and holding hands and that you even paid. Don't worry, no one believes her. Unless hell froze over, you'd never be on a date with Lemon." She chortled.

I was torn. I hated the way she said Len's name, fucked it up, like me being with her was completely out of the realm of possibility or something to be ashamed of.

On the other hand, I hadn't realized our quick breakfast date would cause such a scuttlebutt so damn quickly. I hadn't seen Jenna's cousin. Not that I'd paid attention to anything other than the girl with me. She'd stolen all of my attention.

It didn't matter to me, but Lennon would hate that we were the subject of small-town discussion. If we weren't careful, if I didn't put a stop to the rumors, Dylan would hear about it before we had a chance to tell her.

Len and I were having fun. We didn't need to get serious yet, and we definitely hadn't talked about what to tell my sister.

I longed to ask Len how she wanted me to handle it. Unfortunately, I couldn't call her while Chelsea was staring me down, waiting for me to respond. As if a sign from a much higher power, my phone beeped again, a text from Lennon, no doubt.

I settled for somewhere in the middle. The truth to an extent, but one that wouldn't draw anymore unwanted attention Len's way and hopefully would never reach Dylan's ears.

"We went out for breakfast." I lifted my shoulder in a careless shrug. Rehearsal may have ended, but here I was, playing another part. "I bought her pancakes."

"God, why?"

The venom in her voice made me grit my teeth so I wouldn't say something I regretted. "She's my sister's best friend. Do I need a reason?"

There wasn't a single person in our school who didn't know how close Len and Dylan were. That's why everyone called them my little sisters.

She barked out a laugh. "Yeah. She's a loser."

"Len's not a loser," I snapped.

"Please," Chelsea snorted, either not smart enough to pick up on the vibe I was sending out or too dumb to care. "She's a clueless nerd who dresses like she just walked off the set of a bad eighties music video."

I chuckled, not because I agreed with her statement, but because I could totally see Len rocking out in an Aerosmith video. She was hot enough to get the part and a total badass, in an understated way.

"I knew you'd agree," Chelsea muttered, dropping her arms. "We've been friends a long time, Cullen. You've never spent any time with Lemon unless you were forced. Why now?"

In that moment, she sounded more like a jealous girlfriend than anything else. I didn't correct her because it wasn't worth it. I was wasting time that could be spent with Lennon.

"Dylan's gone and Lennon didn't have anything better to do. Plus, I owed her for getting me home Saturday."

Chelsea's forehead wrinkled. "Ross took you home."

"Because he was at the party with Lennon. He only took me home for her."

"Wait." She held up a finger. "Lennon James was at the party this weekend?"

"Yeah." I was so done with her and this useless conversation.

"With Ross McKinney?"

"Yeah." The answer left a nasty taste in my mouth.

Chelsea frowned. "They were there together? Like on a date?"

I cracked my jaw in irritation at the reminder. "You were there too."

"I don't remember her at all."

It was my turn to give her a dirty look. "What do you remember?"

"Not much." She giggled like it was the funniest thing in the world. "Shots with you. Us sitting out back. The rest is a blur. I woke up without you the next morning. Eastman told me Ross had taken you home."

"I never meant to drink that much." It wasn't a lie. The moment I'd seen Len at the party with McKinney, I'd gone overboard.

Chelsea laughed merrily and stepped into my personal space again. "I don't blame you. It's hard to focus on anything else when I'm around." Her fingers closed around my shirt. "There'll be no escaping this weekend."

"Actually," I stepped around her to get to my car, forcing her to let go of my shirt as I did, "I told Tate and Shaun we'd go as a group."

She groaned, following a step behind. "Whatever. They'll both do their own things, so we'll still have our tent."

I opened the back door, lifted my bag over my head, and tossed it in. "Actually, no." I turned to face her, "We're also bringing Len."

She crossed her arms over her chest as she propped a hip against the fender and popped an eyebrow. "Why in the hell would we bring her?"

With an annoyed sigh, I realized I'd squandered too much time already. The urge to drive away and leave her there was strong, yet I couldn't do it. Instead, I tipped my head to the side and moved to the passenger's door. "Come on, let me take you home."

It was a pleasant surprise when she didn't give me more lip. "Always the gentleman." She smiled sweetly as she slid into the seat. Before I could close the door, she reached for me. "Since your parents are out of town, maybe we could go back to your house..." she trailed off as her fingertips tiptoed up my arm.

"They're gone, but I'm still under surveillance. The neighbors keep pretty tight tabs on me. If I bring a girl home, they'll know."

Chelsea gave me a pout. "Fine. Take me home. But this weekend, you're mine."

I'd never be hers. I didn't bother to argue. It wouldn't have done any good.

Chapter Twelve

Lennon

"Len?"

Marking my spot with a finger, I tipped my book down and looked over at the boy sitting on the deck across from me, a silent question on my face.

"Go camping with me tomorrow night."

I snorted, an absurd unladylike sound. There were so many things hilariously wrong with his non-question demand that I didn't even know where to start. I waited a few seconds for him to tell me he was kidding. When he only stared back, his handsome face blank, I realized he was serious.

My idea of camping was a cozy cabin in the woods with a real bed, running water, and electricity. Dean liked to hike miles into the middle of nowhere, carrying everything he needed in a backpack, with only a thin piece of foam to sleep on. It was April, for crying out loud. There was still snow in the woods.

I didn't say any of that. Instead, I asked the question that had been on my mind for the last three days. "Aren't you sick of me yet?"

His dark brows met. "Why would I be sick of you?"

"That's not an answer."

"No. It's a valid question in response to your asinine one. Why would I be sick of you? I like spending time with you."

I choked on my chuckle. "No, you don't."

He dropped the script he'd been furiously studying—even though he knew his lines—and glowered. "Okay, smartass. If you're going to argue with everything I say, then you tell me. Why don't I like spending time with you?"

"That's actually a good question. I'm fun and quite snarky. I make great observations. I always keep you on your toes. I'm a bottomless pit of random information. I can cook. Why wouldn't you want to spend time with me? "

Dean growled. His frustration should have made him unattractive. Yet the way his eyes lit up and his jaw clenched pulled on all the right strings deep inside. It made me want to kiss him again.

"Lennon," he ground out, "what makes you think I don't like having you around?"

"Oh gee, I don't know. Maybe the fact that you do whatever you can to avoid me."

"You are the strangest, most difficult person I've ever known." His face twisted in exasperated astonishment. He sat forward, elbows on his knees, hands clasped in the space between his thighs—something I'd noticed he did when he was irritated. "I've either been with you or thinking about you every waking moment all week. You're the first thing on my mind when I get up, the last before I sleep, and half the time, I dream about you. In fact, last night, I laid in bed next to you and thought about all the things I wanted to say to you as soon as you woke up. If you think that's me avoiding you, you're stalker-level needy."

I laughed at his absurdity. "I'm not talking about this week, you goof. We're on vacation, in our own little bubble. It's like a break from reality. This doesn't count. I meant normally."

He took a deep breath and I braced myself for whatever he might say. Instead, he released a long sigh as he sat back. "What if I want this to be our new normal?"

My heart started to race and I could feel the pulse in my neck pound. In an attempt to avoid his intense gaze, I let my eyes wander around the back yard as a hundred ideas bounced around my mind like tennis balls. I liked him more than I wanted to admit. I refused to get my hopes up.

"Our new normal?" I parroted back, daring to look at him again. "Explain that to me."

His answering smile turned my insides to mush. I was such a sucker. Because every time he looked at me that way—with his beautiful eyes and gorgeous grin that said I was the only girl in the world who had his attention—it pathetically made my day.

"You. Me. Doing exactly what we've done for the last week. But on a much larger scale."

"So, you'll sneak in my window every night, spend the night without our parents knowing, then we'll spend the days together before you go to rehearsal only to do the same thing all over again in a few hours? Wash. Rinse. Repeat."

He nodded. "Exactly. Sounds pretty great, doesn't it?"

It did.

"Just a few problems with that. You know, like school. Family. The fact that Vicky is coming home on Sunday."

"My ex-girlfriend," he didn't miss a beat, "and where she is or what she does has no impact on you and me."

"Mmm."

I couldn't shake the nagging feeling that once she was back, they'd work through whatever problems they'd had. The two of them had been a couple forever, but it wasn't like this was the first time they'd called it quits.

It was the one thing he wouldn't talk about, no matter how many times I brought it up. I still didn't know why they'd broken up. If it was something stupid, I wouldn't stand a chance against their history, no matter what he thought right then.

I pushed my fears away and focused on the other elephant in the room. "What about Dylan? Or your friends for that matter?"

He stood and pulled me out of my chair in one fluid move before his arms closed around me. "We'll figure it out. As long as you're in this with me, everything else will fall into place." His fingers twirled a piece of my hair. "Come with me tomorrow night."

I didn't care that once again, he'd told instead of asked. Or that we were going camping. I didn't remind myself that whatever he and I had was temporary. I didn't worry about how I'd explain the new plans to my parents.

All that mattered in that moment was the way he made me feel when he looked at me like I was the most important thing in his world.

I nodded. "Okay."

———

"Where have you been?"

I gasped as the voice startled me, making me jump. Breath gone, heart pounding, I took two steps back and leaned against the doorjamb of my father's office. "You scared the Beetlejuice out of me."

For a quick moment, his features softened and he was the dad I missed so much.

"You were lost in your own world again." A small smile tugged on his lips. Once it had been reserved for me, then I'd developed opinions of my own, and for a long time, it felt like I had a better chance at seeing Halley's comet than seeing his happy smile again.

I nodded, even though he didn't need an explanation. I'd been lost in thoughts of Dean. Apparently so distracted I hadn't noticed my dad's car. "What are you doing home so early?"

He motioned to the blueprints that covered not only his drafting table but also his desk and parts of the floor. "The office was too loud, too many distractions."

That was my cue. With a nod, I stood. "I'll let you get back to it."

"Lennon," he called, voice stern, as I started to turn away. "Where were you?"

"At Dylan's."

"She's home already?"

"No. I was with Dean."

Any hint of a smile disappeared as he tensed, his angry frown back in its usual place. "You're too old to play with boys."

I almost laughed. It was the first time I'd been told I was too old to do anything. My father usually liked to remind me how young I was.

"I wasn't *playing* with him, Daddy. I was helping him run lines and reading when he didn't need me." I held up the paperback as if it offered proof.

"Why didn't you answer your phone?"

"It's upstairs. I forgot to charge it last night."

Not entirely true, but not entirely a lie. After Dean had snuck back out my window in the early hours of morning, we'd talked until I'd fallen asleep with it in my hand.

Dad's eyes narrowed.

"It's not a big deal." I argued weakly. "Dean needed help and Aunt Tash and Dylan are gone, so I'm the next best thing."

He watched me closely as if he could see right through me and for a moment it felt like he knew my secrets. "If he needs help again, have him come here."

I opened my mouth to argue, but he silenced me with a finger.

"This is non-negotiable. You're fifteen. You're not allowed to be over there again without adult supervision."

And there it was. Again with the age. The man was infuriating.

"I'll be sixteen in a few days," I snapped.

I didn't understand why everyone got so caught up on a damn number. It might seem like I was young to someone who hadn't met me, someone who saw my age on a page, but I had as much knowledge and experience as any other sophomore. More than a few. "I'm at their house unsupervised all the time."

"This isn't up for debate."

"Of course it isn't. Why would I get a say in my own life?"

"Your life?" He shook his head. "Lenny, your life hasn't even started yet."

"How will it, if you're going to micromanage every decision I make?" I threw my hands into the air. "I'm not a bad kid. I get good grades. I don't party every weekend. I don't lie or steal or put you and Mom through hell on the regular. Why is it so damn hard for you to trust me?"

"It's not about trust. It's about you not being able to see the big picture. You're brilliant, yet you make stupid and impulsive decisions that could impact the rest of your life. You want to put holes in your face and ink on your skin, but what happens in five years when you can't get a job because that's all the interviewer sees? Or in ten when you decide you actually want to be in front of the camera, but no one will promote you to newscaster because you don't have the right look? Or better yet, you get invited to the White House Correspondents' Dinner and can't find a single dress to hide the way you've scarred your body? All your life you've wanted to be a reporter, yet right now, you're so focused on pissing me off that you can't get out of your own way. You can't see how your decisions could negatively impact your future."

"I actually like piercings and tattoos and crazy hair. How I look is not about you. It's not a reflection of you. As unbelievable as it may seem, I don't make decisions to piss you off," I repeated his words angrily. "Did you stop to think that it's a different world now than the one you grew up in? My work will be judged on quality, not my appearance."

"If you believe that then you're not as smart as I thought you were." He shook his head.

There was no happy medium here. We'd go round and round, the same way we had hundreds of times over the last two years. "What does any of that have to do with me being at the Cullens'?"

"It's my job to protect you from yourself."

"Fine. Whatever. But I'm not doing anything harmful."

He sighed angrily. "You know, I'm not as old as you seem to think I am. I'm also not as stupid. When a girl like you and a boy like Dean get mixed up, it becomes a mess, and there are only two possible outcomes. Both end with you being devastated and me never forgiving the boy I think of like a son."

"A girl like me?" I repeated, my voice breaking along with my heart.

"I won't let my only daughter throw her future away because he was bored and lonely and she was the only thing around. Is that honestly what you want? This is Dean we're talking about." I hated the way Dad said Dean's name, like he was something dirty and unredeemable. "Do you think he'd give up his dreams to help you take care of a baby?"

I jerked back as if he'd hit me. That escalated quickly. Not only did my dad think I needed to focus on my looks because I was too stupid to succeed on my own merit, he apparently expected me to end up a teen mom. "Wow."

"He wouldn't. That kid has been hyper focused on one thing and one thing only since he could talk. He's got stars in his eyes, Lenny. He's leaving all of this—everyone and everything—behind, as soon as he can. He'll barely remember your name in five years."

Ouch. His words would have hurt, even if I hadn't started crushing on the boy across the street. Our lives were so deeply intertwined that Dean Cullen was part of me. I'd never forget him. He'd never be able to forget me, either.

My relationship with my dad had been strained over the last few years, but I'd always assumed we'd come out of it stronger because we had an underlying mutual respect and never-ending love. All teens fought with their dads at some point; it was hard to grow up and, according to my mom, even harder to watch someone you love struggle to find themselves. Dad had taught me to think on my own, to be unafraid to try new things, to be my own person. Yet here he was, telling me he didn't trust me to do the very things he'd ingrained.

Arguing was pointless. Done with him and the conversation, I turned away and took the stairs two at a time. He didn't call after me. I would've ignored him if he had.

Once in my room, I grabbed my cell, shocked to see my hand shaking. I needed to get out, away from home, from him. I refused to bother Dean while he was at rehearsal. Dylan and the rest of my friends were gone. Desperate, I scrolled through my contacts until I found a number I hadn't dialed in years.

"'Sup, lil' miss?"

The name threw me for a moment, and I blurted out the first thing on my mind. "Are you busy?"

The music in the background cut off suddenly, leaving it so eerily quiet I was worried we'd gotten disconnected. "What's wrong?" Shaun's voice was full of concern.

It was strange to hear him so serious for a change. Swallowing, I closed my eyes, desperate to keep the tears away. It was stupid to be so upset over a fight with my dad.

"Nothing. I'm fine. I just..." I trailed off, not knowing what to say. I cleared my throat. "Are you busy?".

"Never too busy for you. You at home?"

"Yeah."

"Tate and I are on the way to the mall. You want in?"

Relief poured through me. "Do you mind?"

"Nah. More the merrier. I already turned around. Be there in fifteen."

I didn't tell my dad I was leaving. Instead, I sent my mom a text, told her dad and I'd had another fight, and that I was headed out with friends. Her response was immediate.

Mi Madre: Take a coat, it's supposed to rain. Your father is stressed over his deadline. He didn't mean whatever he said. I love you. Have fun. Text if you won't make curfew.

At least I had Mom. So many girls my age couldn't stand their mothers. Not me. I didn't know what I'd do without her.

Chapter Thirteen

Dean

One of the unwritten rules in theater was that you turned off your cell phone before you walked through the door.

Especially if you had a costume fitting.

The experience itself was daunting. After standing around in nothing but your skivvies while people poked and prodded, you were left feeling bare, vulnerable. The last thing you wanted was someone to have a cellphone out, camera at the ready.

I'd been so wrapped up in my thoughts of Len that I'd forgotten to power mine down. I'd just changed into the white mock-up of my first costume for the first fitting and was waiting for the team to arrive when it started to ring. I glanced at Randy while pointing at my bag, a silent question on my face. Everyone knew the costume designer held all the power; you didn't piss him off unless you wanted to look like an idiot.

If he told me no, I'd ignore it.

Instead, Randy nodded and turned back to the draper.

I slid into the corner. "Perfect timing, asshole. Another minute and I'd be on the stool. What's up?"

"You're not at practice?"

"Rehearsal," I corrected as my lips curled in amusement. "I am. In wardrobe, actually. I just put on a pair of muslin trousers that need major alterations. They're too short and make my ass feel fat."

"You know, if someone else said shit like that to me, I'd call them a pansy."

"Go ahead. I dare you. Might be the last word you say for a while, but do it."

"I may look stupid, and I may act clueless so people won't expect much from me, but I'm not dumb. I like my face the way it is, thanks. So, what are you doing?"

He was right. I'd beat his ass. It didn't matter that he outweighed me. When someone threw insults about theater, how it made me feminine or less of a man, I had a reason to fight.

"It's a fitting with the costume designer," I explained. "I have to stand still for the next hour so they can draw on my clothes while they figure out what style line they want to use and envision the final version. Then I strip and do it all over again for each costume change I'll need."

"Waterboarding sounds more appealing. You're busy, so I'll hurry," he continued, finally getting to the point. "Lil' miss called me crying. Any idea why?"

I gripped the phone tighter and took a step toward the wall. "Len doesn't cry. Ever."

"I know."

"What in the hell is going on?"

"Your guess is as good as mine, brother. We wanted to make sure we weren't getting in the middle of something before we intervened."

Middle of something. It was his way of asking if I'd done something to hurt her. Except it felt less like a question and more like an accusation.

"You think I did something horrible enough to make Lennon cry and then came to rehearsal like a careless asshole?"

"Slow your roll, dipshit. Chill the fuck out. I don't know what's going on with you two. I don't need to. I just wanted to check with you before I got myself into the middle of something I had no business being in."

"When I left her, she was smiling. We have plans to pack for the bonfire after I'm done here."

"That's all I needed to know."

"She didn't give you any clue why she's upset?" My worry had slowly begun to transition into full-blown panic. Not only was she crying, but she'd called Eastman of all people, not me. "Let me change, and I'll—."

"No," he interrupted. "We've got her. Tate and I are almost at her house. She's coming with us to the mall."

The mall? Lennon never went to the mall, not even when my sister begged. "I don't—"

"We've got her. Do your thing."

"Thank you." I didn't know what else to say. I wanted to go to her, to find out what was going on, but realistically, there was no way I could leave. "Take care of my girl."

"Always."

Apprehensively, I ended the call and faced the room. Randy had his notebook in hand while the draper had a swatch of fabric samples. I turned my phone on silent, slid it onto the dressing table, hoping my friends or Len wouldn't need me right away and stepped onto the stool.

A few hours later, I backed into the shadows of stage right and pulled my phone out of my pocket. I'd been trying to check it since I'd felt it vibrate twenty minutes before, but I'd been too busy. Plus, both the stage manager and the director had kept eyes on me as if they knew I was distracted and were waiting for me to screw up.

Before I could open the text messages, Nilo called my name. Stifling a sigh, I shoved it back into my jeans and stepped out into the light. Opening night was officially days away. Both the cast and crew were mentally and physically exhausted after the intense week we'd had.

"Dean," Nilo motioned me toward him. "Come sit with me."

I glanced at the castmates closest to me. It was highly unusual for Nilo to single any of us out for something good. I'd never seen him call anyone down to sit. He usually pulled us aside to talk about our craft or offer ideas to improve a scene.

I jogged down the makeshift stairs on stage left and hurried toward his perch in the third row.

He pointed to the chair next to him. "Sit."

I didn't argue.

"That's it for tonight," he spoke loudly, his voice carrying in the empty auditorium. "I'll see you tomorrow."

We waited in silence as the theater cleared. Some eyed us with confusion as they filed out. Others glanced at me with worry.

Once it was the two of us left in the large auditorium, he tucked his clipboard into the chair on the opposite side of him and gave me a long look. I prepared myself for the worst.

I'd been off. Preoccupied. I hadn't missed any cues or screwed up any lines, but my mind was miles away.

"Acting requires tremendous openness and vulnerability. Those of us who direct are asking you to reveal your most private self, to convey your character with truth. If we're harsh or unreasonably critical, our cast will not perform well. However, if we don't set expectations, they won't connect with the audience and their acting will be perceived as stiff and cliché."

I nodded and hoped he couldn't see my heart thundering with worry in my chest. I understood exactly what he was saying. I tried to focus on his words instead of the unease washing over me.

"Directing young actors, or those just starting out, is particularly challenging because we must also protect them. Directors cannot ask them to do this stressful job unless we create a safe environment. I've worked with many young actors during my years. Some have found a home on Broadway. Others prefer television or film on the West Coast. Unfortunately, a few discovered that the pressure of chasing their dreams was too much and they live normal lives now.

"A handful of times, I've had the pleasure of working with actors who showed tremendous promise. These young men and women didn't just possess a natural talent that would make others jealous, they also had a deep drive. They were eager to learn, anxious to improve, and full of determination to make sure they were the best."

I nodded again, still unsure of what we were talking about.

"Where do you see yourself in five years?"

I didn't hesitate. "Acting. That's all I want."

It was his turn to nod. "I won't lie. It will be hard. There are more actors than there are roles. There will always be those with more experience, more knowledge, or those who are typecast. However, it's your raw talent that fills these seats. Most lack that, even with years of training because it's something that can't be taught. Dean, when you step onto the stage, patrons take notice because they know they are going to see something magical."

I was speechless. It was high praise coming from someone as talented and knowledgeable as Nilo. I dipped my head. "Thank you."

"Don't thank me. That's all you. But you still have a lot to learn." He reached for a folder tucked into a bag at our feet. "There are many summer workshops around the country. However, there is only one that is the best." He held out a thick packet. "For eight weeks, Emerson University's esteemed acting faculty takes a group of handpicked high school juniors and seniors under their wing to teach a distillation of the University's revered program.

"Not only will you have courses that will teach and strengthen your abilities, you'll live on campus and submerse yourself into theater with your fellow actors. Students conclude their experience with a live performance for industry professionals. The best management organizations and the most reputable talent agencies will have representatives in that audience. There is also a special showing for family and friends before that."

It sounded intense. Overwhelming. Perfect for me.

"Is this the application?"

"No, no." He chuckled. "Applications were due *last* July. That is your welcome letter and all the information you need, including the script for the show you will be performing in August."

"I don't understand." I glanced up, completely thrown. "I didn't apply last year."

"It is incredibly rare to find an actor your age with your abilities. Now that I have, I will help any way I can. An old friend heads the department. I spoke with him on your behalf. He'll be coming opening night and is excited to welcome you as a late addition to the program."

I locked my jaw to keep from gaping at him. "You got me into the summer acting workshop at Emerson University?"

"Your abilities and talent got you in. I only told a friend about those talents."

I shuffled through the paperwork quickly, trying to hide how much my hands were shaking. The price tag jumped out at me, and my heart sank. There was no way my parents would send me to a summer workshop that cost as much as a new car. I could ask my grandparents for the money, but I wasn't eighteen. I couldn't go unless my parents gave their okay.

As if reading my mind, Nilo reached out and tapped a paragraph halfway down the page. "They're also extending a full scholarship, room and board included."

I lifted my eyes to meet his. I didn't know how to thank him. Or if I ever could. "This could be life-changing."

"Not *could*. It *will*. It will be grueling. There will be days you wished you'd stayed home. Students who complete this workshop become the next wave of Hollywood and Broadway stars. They will be household names within ten years."

"I don't know if my parents will let me go," I admitted sadly. If it were up to my dad, the answer would be no.

"Let me handle your parents. Keep your focus on this show, and then worry about finishing the school year so you can dedicate yourself to the workshop. Don't let yourself get distracted by anything else. Eye on the prize and you'll grab it in no time."

"Thank you." I shook my head. "It doesn't seem like enough to say for something like this."

"I don't say this lightly, Mr. Cullen, so remember it when you hit your lows. Because you will hit rock bottom; we all do. I expect big things from you." There was no hint of amusement or humor on his face. "It won't come easy, but when it comes, it will be worth everything you'll have to sacrifice." He stood. "I'll see you tomorrow."

Dismissed, I hurried backstage to grab my bag. This was huge. No. This was gigantic.

I wanted to scream my excitement from the rooftops. The acting workshop at Emerson was an opportunity I'd never thought I'd have. I didn't know how my dad would react, but my mom and Dylan would be overjoyed. Shaun and Tate would want to celebrate.

It was Lennon that I wanted to talk to first, however. She'd be happy for me, even though the school was taking me away from her for the summer. Len always saw the big picture. She'd understand that this was a make-or-break deal. A chance to have all my dreams come true.

Yet, all I could focus on was the fact that I'd have to leave her. It felt like a lifetime could fit into eight weeks. That scared me.

Chapter Fourteen

Lennon

I'd once told Dylan that our friendship wouldn't survive if she expected me to go shopping with her again. It wasn't the act of going to a store and buying new things that bothered me. It was wasting an entire afternoon at the mall only to visit the same three stores, all in different wings, ten times each.

For some reason, I'd expected it to be different with the guys. It wasn't. Only this time, I was dragged into stores I had absolutely no interest in.

When Tate called a timeout a few hours after we'd arrived because he was hungry, I almost hugged him. It was safe to say that I still hated the mall, no matter whom I was with.

"So, you comin' to the bonfire or what?" Shaun asked as we snagged an empty table in the food court.

"Nope." I pulled the straw out of my coffee shake and sucked the bottom.

"Yeah, she is," Tate answered, ignoring me.

"I'm not. I, uh..." I hesitated, unsure if I was supposed to tell them

I'd made plans with Dean. This was all new territory. I didn't know the rules.

"You, uh...uh...what?" Shaun teased with a smile.

"Have plans?"

"You asking or telling?" He shoved a handful of fries into his mouth.

I watched him, totally amazed, and a little grossed out, by how much he could fit in his giant cakehole at one time. Boys were gross. "I definitely have plans."

"Yeah. To come with us."

"I don't even know what bonfire you're talking about," I admitted as I reached over to steal a mozzarella stick from Tate.

"I forget you don't pay attention to shit like that." Shaun lifted his fountain drink and took a long sip from the straw before he pointed the cup at me. "It's tradition. Every year, the outgoing seniors host a bonfire on the beach. It's the incoming seniors who decide who gets invited. State parks haven't opened yet, so they aren't monitored. No one bothers us. We hike in, pitch tents on the sand, have a night to remember. It's the party of year."

"I thought the party of the year was last weekend."

They both laughed.

"Fuck, no. That was one of Jenna's. Who said that?"

"Dylan was wasted." Tate rolled his eyes as he answered for me. "She heard us talking about the bonfire, but then Jenna's party was mentioned. She got the two confused."

The mention of Dylan made me miss her. I hoped she was having a blast on vacation, but I was ready for her to come home.

"Just make sure you pitch your tent near the dunes, not down on the water," Tate said with a chuckle, eyeing Shaun. "Or you'll get a surprise the next morning."

"It was one time, motherfucker. *Once.*" Shaun threw a fry at our friend with a laugh then looked at me. "I was wasted. It was a mistake I'll never repeat."

"The tide came in?"

His answer was a small affirmative tilt of his head, making me snort.

"You don't need to worry about it. You'll be with Cullen. He always goes in early to claim the best spot," Tate assured me.

"So, when he invited me camping, he actually meant…"

"Beach camping at the bonfire."

"I don't know if that's better or worse than what I'd imagined."

"Better. This way yo—" Tate's word cut off suddenly. With no warning, he pulled my chair across the tiles with a loud squeak, so close to him that there was almost no room between us.

Shocked, I glanced from him to Shaun. Neither looked at me, both focused on something else. I turned my head, groaning when I saw the group of familiar faces walking our way. I sighed. After the fight with my dad, I was in no mood to play Social Suzie.

Tate's fingers closed around my wrist, and he gave it a gentle, but warning, squeeze.

"Hey! You didn't tell me you were coming down." Des, a junior who'd made the varsity cheer squad her freshman year, pushed against Shaun's shoulder playfully before straddling his lap and pressing her lips to his.

He didn't pull away. Instead, he grabbed her and yanked her farther onto him before he started to eat her face. My nose wrinkled, and I grew queasy when she began to make disturbing grunts. I hadn't known they were a couple, but now that I'd seen it, bleach wouldn't be enough to wipe it from my mind.

Unable to watch the public display of affliction—there was nothing affectionate in their actions—I turned to Tate, hoping he'd be as disgusted and want to leave. He didn't look at me; instead, he watched the newcomers with a bored expression. His fingers tightened on my hand once more. I wasn't sure if he was trying to offer moral support or telling me to keep my mouth shut.

"Hey, hey," Chelsea Turner greeted as she dropped into the last chair, uninvited. "Last minute supply run?"

"Yeah." Tate didn't offer any further explanation. Instead, he lifted his head in greeting as more people crowded around, some stealing chairs from other tables.

I knew who they all were, but I hadn't spoken to most of them since elementary school. It wasn't only that we ran in different circles because we most definitely did; it was that I'd never had anything in common with them, other than the big brothers.

It's believed that the great Eleanor Roosevelt once said, "No one can make you feel inferior without your consent." While there's no proof she actually said the words, and believe me, I'd tried to find a credible source—the saying was linked to her because it seemed like something she would have said. While I'd been one of the millions who had taken comfort in those words, I also knew that if dear ol' Ellie had been in high school in the twenty-first century, she'd have a different take on things.

The popular crowd didn't need your consent. They sent the message that you were worthless with a dismissive flick of their eyes. The girls weren't just mean, they were vicious. They might have hated themselves and each other, yet they *despised* anyone who didn't worship them.

I definitely fell into that last category.

"Lemon," Chelsea greeted with a fake smile, using the nickname she'd bestowed upon me years before. It wasn't one created from kindness, but instead cruelty. We'd never been friends, even though she liked to pretend in front of certain people. "I heard you're joining us this weekend."

Not coming to the party. Not going camping. *Joining them.*

She was so good at being a mean girl that she could put me in my place with a smile on her face while having everyone else think she was being nice. I got her message loud and clear. I was an unwanted guest.

"She is," Tate ground out before I could answer.

"Word gets around fast," I tried and probably failed, to sound unimpressed and bored. I knew by the way Tate clutched my hand that it wasn't smart to engage.

Chelsea's eyes lit with delight as she lifted a bare shoulder. As she started to talk, her lack of appropriate clothing distracted me. I was in jeans, boots, and a sweater with a raincoat draped over the back of my chair. A cold front had moved in over the last few hours, and the early warmer temperatures had turned bitter.

Sure, her shirt was stylish, and she looked like a million dollars. Everyone wanted to show off what the good Lord gave them, and Chelsea had been given plenty. But did no one my age think about how they'd look if they lost appendages to frostbite?

I shook my head. "I'm sorry. What were you saying?"

Beside me, Tate coughed in an attempt to cover what suspiciously sounded like a snort. Chelsea, on the other hand, tucked her tongue into her cheek as her nostrils flared. She sat up a bit straighter and braced her elbows on the table.

"Cullen told me you were coming with us."

"Oh," I nodded. "That makes sense."

"We met after his rehearsal the other night to try to finalize plans," she went on. "We were gonna go to the party, just the two of us, but decided it would be more fun if we went in a big group. You know, since we can go on a date any time. So many of our friends are seniors, for one night we should focus on them instead of each other. But it works out because this way, you can tag along, too."

I hadn't known Dean had seen her after rehearsal. He'd never said anything. Then again, we weren't a couple. He didn't owe me any explanation.

It would've been cool to have gotten a heads-up, especially since it felt like she was using that information to get me worked up. But I couldn't be mad. Annoyed, yes, but not angry.

I tried to think of an appropriate response. None came. Instead, I settled on, "Cool."

It wasn't the reaction she was looking for. She drummed her fingernails on the tabletop for a moment before trying again. "It's so exciting, your first beach bonfire. Cullen and I went to our first together. That was the year Eastman's tent got flooded." Everyone laughed, some throwing insults at my friend.

Chelsea never took her eyes off me. "He took Vicky last year. It's like a tradition now, him bringing a freshman."

I didn't bother to correct her. She knew I was a sophomore. It was a pathetic attempt to make me feel insecure.

There were many things I could say about Chelsea—most of them negative—but I had to hand it to her. She was observant and knew how to get under my skin. She'd been friends with Dean almost as long as I had and never missed the chance to take a dig at my looks, actions, or age.

I wished Dean was there because he always knew what to say to shift Chelsea's attention elsewhere.

Tate dropped my hand and stretched his arm over the back of my chair. Chelsea jumped on the action like a bloodhound on a criminal's scent.

Her lips twisted in glee. "Looks like Dylan's going to come home to quite the surprise."

The words hit their target. Tate and I both tensed as I realized what he'd done. In his attempt to defend and offer moral support, he'd sent a message that could be interpreted in many different ways. None of them good.

Dylan would understand. It would take some explaining and lots and lots of groveling. I'd have to admit the truth about what I'd been doing with her brother. But she'd forgive me for being linked to Tate.

At least, I hoped she would.

"Chelsea, we all know you're a bitch. You don't need to remind us," Shaun snapped, taking a break from his make-out session.

Her eyes lingered on him a breath too long and she popped an eyebrow. "What? Dylan's going to flip when she finds out that Lemon and Tate were hooking up while she was gone."

I shook my head. "Noooo." My hand danced between Tate and me as I pointed at each of us. "That's not what this is."

Her face twisted into a challenging expression that said she didn't believe a word. "Look at you, making the rounds. First McKinney, then Cullen, now Tate. Three of the most popular boys in school. Makes me wonder what—or who—is next." She pursed her lips in thought. "I've heard you're Mr. Padilla's favorite." Her eyes lit up in excitement as they drifted to Shaun. "Or maybe it'll be someone closer to home."

My eyes narrowed as my temper rose. I normally ignored the stereotypical, mean girl bullshit, but after my dad had been a major ass about Dean, I wasn't going listen to someone else spout off when they didn't have a clue. Before I could tell her where she could shove her outlandish theories, Tate came to the rescue.

"Usually, I'm impressed by your ability to create drama out of absolutely nothing. This time, it's even more pathetic than normal. Your jealousy is showing," he sniffed the air, "and it reeks. Unless that's just you."

A quiet settled over the table. Everyone averted their eyes except Chelsea. Her glare was fixed on me. I wanted the floor to open and swallow me whole.

As if the moment couldn't get any worse, Ross walked up to us, an oblivious smile on his lips as he greeted his friends. When he spotted me, confusion replaced happiness. "Len?" His eyes followed the arm over my shoulders to Tate.

I hadn't talked to him since he'd driven Dean and me home Saturday night. I'd expected him to call, maybe even text, but nothing came. Under different circumstances, I would've bitten the bullet and taken charge. Instead, I'd become so enamored and gotten so distracted by another boy that poor Ross had barely crossed my mind.

"Hey!" I stood and grabbed my still-full shake, desperate to move our awkward reunion far from an audience. "I've got to get something. Walk with me?"

I didn't give him a chance to say no. I grabbed his hand and pulled him behind me as I tried to escape without looking like I was running away. Tate yelled my name, loud enough to make me wince, but I didn't stop until we'd gotten halfway across the mall and hidden in the back of a shoe store.

"Don't take this the wrong way, but I can't see you in stilettos," Ross mused as he lifted a mile-high heel off the shelf. "Especially not at the bonfire. They'll sink in the sand."

I snatched the shoe from his fingers, smacked him on the arm, and shoved it back into its box in one swift movement. He glanced around, eyeing the handful of middle-aged women around us, and shot me a sheepish grin as he leaned in close. "If you'd wanted me this badly, you could've asked. Don't get me wrong, this aggressive side of you is hot as hell. But you never struck me as someone who'd want an audience."

Jokes. I was stressed the hell out and he had jokes. "You're so not funny right now."

"No? 'Cause that's a smile you're fighting."

I chuckled, even though I felt more like crying than laughing. "Today has been so messed up," I admitted with a sigh as I collapsed onto one of the benches in the middle of the aisle. "The whole week, actually."

"Yeah," Ross sat next to me and bumped my leg with his playfully. "I've heard."

I rolled my eyes. "Of course you have."

Chelsea seemed to think she knew something, which meant everyone else did too.

"Doesn't mean we can't change it. Come on, Len. Give me one of your random facts. Tell me how shoes like those," he pointed to the mile-high heels he'd had out a moment before, "ruin your feet."

"It's actually not just your feet," I muttered. "Because the angle disrupts the natural form of the body, people who spend lots of time in heels pull their muscles and joints out of alignment. It's not unusual for them to have back, neck, and shoulder pain. There are exercises you can do to combat long term effects."

He was grinning like a fool when I turned back to him. "There she is. I love it when you talk nerdy to me."

I shook my head playfully. "You're insane."

"Nah." He grew serious. "I just know what I like."

I swallowed and met his eyes. "I'm sorry I never called you after the party."

"That's my line."

"Yeah?"

He nodded.

"Then you're forgiven."

"You're not going to ask why I didn't call?"

"Nope. Thought I'd let you let me down easy."

"Oh?" His tone was full of humor. "No hard feelings then? You're not going to cause a scene?" He poked at my shake. "Throw that at me? Dump it over my head?"

I snorted. "You're right. I totally seem like a person who'd have a public meltdown."

"It's always the quiet ones that do the things you least expect."

It was my turn to smile. Before I could answer though, Shaun and Tate stomped around the corner like they were on a mission. I had no idea how they'd found us so quickly, but when Shaun's eyes narrowed on us, either pissed that we were together or mad that we were sitting so close, there was no doubt in my mind they'd been looking for me. He blocked the path, legs spread, arms crossed over his muscular chest, intimidating as hell.

Tate, on the other hand, stopped in front of us, my forgotten jacket in one hand, and reached for me with the other. "Let's go, lil' miss. Time to get you back to the boss man."

My eyes darted from his outstretched hand to his face and back again. "What?"

I felt like I was in the middle of one of my crazy dreams. Everything had gone sideways and absolutely nothing made sense. I had no idea what was happening.

"Dean," he said the word like I was an idiot. "You know, your boyfriend. My best friend. He's waiting for us."

"Dean's not my boyfriend."

Tate shot me a challenging look that said he didn't believe a word I'd said. "Yeah, okay." Tate tipped his head toward Ross. "Say goodbye. It's time to go."

I didn't have a chance to say anything. Before I could even manage an apologetic shrug, Tate reached down, closed his fingers around my wrist, and hauled me to my feet. An instant later, he was pushing me through the store, Shaun on our heels like an overly cautious bodyguard.

I barely had a chance to wave at Ross over my shoulder.

"I almost didn't recognize you without a cheerleader glued to your lap."

Shaun didn't even crack a smile as he ignored my jab and moved in next to me, matching his steps to mine. "Less talking, more walking."

"Dean's not even out of rehearsal yet. What's the rush?"

"He got out early and went home to pack." Tate answered, his grip on my wrist still lock-tight. "Told him we'd drop you there."

"How'd he know I was with you?"

"Do I look like I have a death wish?" He scoffed. "We told him, of course."

I couldn't stop the eye roll. "My non-boyfriend is not the boss of me. I can do whatever I want with whomever I want."

"He's not. You can." Shaun agreed from my other side. "Chelsea likes to run her mouth. If she thinks she knows a secret, she'll use it in any way she can, to get what she wants."

"Knowledge is power." I could appreciate that.

"Exactly. It's better for everyone if everything is out in the open. She can't twist anything if we all know what actually happened."

"You sound like you're speaking from experience."

When Shaun shrugged noncommittedly, I turned my attention to Tate.

He watched me out of the corner of his eye. "We've been down this road a time or two."

"That's all you're going to give me? What happened to laying it all on the table, no secrets?"

Shaun snorted while Tate shook his head as he held open the door and ushered me into the parking lot. "Between the three of us. Cullen, Eastman, and me," he clarified. "That way, we can protect each other. And you."

"Me?" I sneered. The idea was archaic. "That's always been your problem, Tate. You've never seen Dylan and me as anything more than something you have to take care of, keep safe. We're not your property. You can't stop us from growing up. You can't protect us forever."

His face hardened. Clearly, he disagreed. I didn't want to argue with him, though.

"I'm not afraid of Chelsea and her lies." I assured them as we reached Shaun's Jeep.

"I'm not trying to protect you from Chelsea." Tate pulled open the passenger door and leaned the seat forward for me.

"No?" I didn't believe him for a minute. He'd gone all caveman as soon as she'd appeared. "Then who is the big bad wolf I need you to save me from?" I inquired as I settled into the backseat.

"Did you ever stop and think that maybe I'm trying to protect Dean?"

"From me?" I gaped at him, horrified at the absurd statement.

"From the one thing that could destroy him." With that, he pushed his seat back and hoped in front. Conversation over.

He never answered me.

Chapter Fifteen

Dean

As soon as I'd gotten home, I'd bypassed the house, opened both garage doors, and headed straight for the storage area on one side. Some dads had a workshop with tools lining the walls, others had a mancave. Not mine. He'd insisted it was the driest and best place to keep things that could get musty and ruined in the basement.

Over the years it had become a camper's paradise.

I halfheartedly pulled gear from shelves and stacked it in the spot reserved for my mom's car. I'd gone camping with my friends enough to know what I'd need without making a list. In reality, it was a mindless task to keep me busy while I waited.

I was on edge the entire time.

Part of it was because of the excitement and worry over the upcoming workshop at Emerson. I'd Googled it. It was a huge honor to be accepted and would challenge me like nothing had yet.

The rest of my anxiety was because I had no idea why Len was upset.

I hated talking about feelings, almost as much as I detested when girls cried over senseless shit. When we were a couple, Vicky had wanted to talk everything to death only to dig up the damn grave and talk about it some more. She'd also tear up when I asked her hard questions like what movie she wanted to see or where she wanted to eat. Apparently if I really loved her, I would've been able to read her mind.

My sister was the same way. Dylan cried and stomped her feet like a petulant child whenever she didn't get her way and sobbed all the way home from a party when she'd discovered she couldn't go to the next one. Then, she'd wonder why people thought she was spoiled. It made me shake my head.

I didn't want to compare Len to anyone else, but it was hard not to sometimes. She was nothing like the other girls in my life. She voiced her thoughts once and wasn't upset if I didn't take her advice. Sometimes, she didn't even feel the need to offer her two cents. Instead, she listened and let you figure things out on your own.

Lennon was the type of person you could sit with, not say a word, and walk away feeling like it was the best conversation you'd had all day. I admired that about her.

It wasn't like she never cried. God knew, I'd pulled some shady shit more times than I wanted to remember, and almost every one of those times had ended with her in, or on the verge of, tears. Looking back, I wondered if Tate was right and I'd pushed her to her breaking point on purpose.

I'd teased and tormented until Len had gotten so mad, or sad, she'd cried. That's how I knew it was time to stop. Any further and she might not forgive my stupidity.

It was a different story when someone else was the cause of her pain. I'd always done whatever I could to protect her. I'd gotten in more than one fight, worn black eyes like trophies, whenever some asshole tossed a cruel insult her way or did something that I'd deemed unacceptable.

Hell, I'd even bailed on state championships freshman year, letting my team and friends down, so I could hold her while she sobbed after her grandmother lost her battle with cancer. It was the only thing I could do to offer a little bit of comfort, but it meant the world to her. I didn't regret any of it.

I needed to talk to her. Until I knew why she'd gotten upset enough to call Shaun, I'd continue to drive myself crazy imagining the worst. I couldn't fix it if I didn't know what was wrong.

When headlights cut across the side of my house and lit the garage, I abandoned the last few supplies and hurried out to meet them. Lennon beamed at me as she hopped out of the Jeep, obviously as happy to see me as I was her.

Her face scrunched with worry almost immediately. "What are you doing home early? Is everything okay with the play?"

I nodded as I stepped into her space, ready to pull her into my arms and promise to explain later. I needed answers about her tears, the rest we'd talk about afterward. I reached for her, desperate to hold her, when she took a step back, her gaze focused on something over my shoulder, and her face fell.

"Lennon."

I spun, surprised to see her dad at the end of my driveway. I'd been home for hours, watched every car as it pulled into our cul-de-sac, yet I hadn't seen him come home. Aunt Gayle had beeped and waved as she'd driven by, as had all the other neighbors, but I hadn't realized Trev was home yet.

"Uncle Trev," I greeted lamely.

He didn't acknowledge me. He didn't even spare a glance in my direction. His arms were crossed, jaw clenched, and fury radiated from him with every breath as he glared at his daughter.

"Get your things. Go home."

I couldn't remember seeing him as angry as he was in that moment. While Trev could be a first-class pain-in-the-ass to his kid, he usually had a level head. He was the one who always saw the other side of any argument, put himself in the other person's shoes, the one friend who could talk my dad down.

His behavior would raise red flags by itself, but add in the fact that it seemed directed at the pint-sized pixie behind me, and I was completely on alert.

When Len tensed at his tone and heated stare, everything clicked. He was why she'd been upset earlier. She'd tell me what happened when she was ready. Until then, there was no way in hell I was letting her go home. Not when he was acting like a volcano ready to erupt after being dormant for fifteen years.

Without thinking, I sidestepped, forcing her behind me, blocking her from her father's view. Uncle Trevor's arched an eyebrow.

"You don't want to do that, son. This doesn't concern you."

Everything about Lennon concerned me. I wasn't dumb enough to tell him that, no matter how much it killed me to keep quiet. Sensing the situation could turn ugly any minute, both Shaun and Tate moved, flanking me.

Trev watched us with a flicker of amusement on his rigid face. He might be old, but it was a timeless gesture. Mess with one of us, you get two more for free.

"Oh, for heaven's sake," Len mumbled as she shoved me out of her way.

I hadn't expected her to cower or hide behind me. Every interaction we'd ever had proved that Len simply didn't have it in her DNA to let someone else fight her battles for her. I had hoped she'd at least let me try to shelter her from whatever storm was coming her way.

Instead, she marched straight for her dad, shoulders back, head high. He might infuriate the hell out of her, but she was a little hurricane herself. She wasn't about to back down.

For a brief moment, I wondered what would happen when a hurricane crashed headfirst into an erupting volcano. No doubt it would be an epic battle leaving nothing but chaos and destruction in its wake. A disaster like nothing we'd ever witnessed before.

My money was on her.

Right before Len got to him, she veered to her left and cut across my lawn. She glanced over her shoulder once and gave us a little wave. "Night, guys."

As we echoed her goodbye, Lennon quickly crossed the road and headed straight for the stone-lined walk in front of her house. Movement on the porch caught my eye, and some of my tension dissipated when Aunt Gayle wrapped a comforting arm around her daughter. I watched until the two were safely inside, the door closed behind them, and the outside light snapped off as if a giant "screw you" to Uncle Trev.

I slid my attention back to him, surprised to find him not only in the same place but his expression still fixed in an angry sneer. This time, it was focused solely on me.

I lifted my chin and met his glare. I loved him, thought of him like a second dad, but I wouldn't cower to my own father, and I sure as hell wasn't about to bow down to Trevor James. *Not today, old man.*

His attempt at the quintessential, overprotective dad role was bull-shit. He didn't know a damn thing about his daughter, or he wouldn't be causing a scene. Lennon didn't need anyone fighting her battles for her, and she hadn't done anything wrong.

Shaun shuffled his feet while Tate cracked his neck. Neither Trev nor I would back down, look away. It was a battle of wills, and Lennon was clearly more mature than either of us. The minutes ticked by as we continued our attempt to stare the other down.

A throat clearing surprised us both. I don't know who looked away first, but my gaze darted from Trev to the slightly older version of Lennon, who had appeared at his side. Somehow, I'd missed their outside light coming back on *and* Aunt Gayle crossing the street to join us.

Ignoring the tension, she tucked her arm through her husband's as if nothing was wrong and smiled sweetly at us. "Boys," her voice held nothing but kindness, "it's getting late. You should clean all this up. You can finish packing tomorrow."

"Absolutely."

"Yes, ma'am."

"Trevor?" She glanced up at him.

Trev took a deep breath as he gazed down at his wife. Whatever he saw on her face made him nod. He let her turn him toward their house. Before they reached the road, he turned back to me.

"Dean, just so you know, I've decided to sleep in Lennon's room until your parents come back."

Gayle shook her head as if she didn't know what to do with him and tugged on him once more. He finally gave in, but not before he motioned to his eyes with two fingers and then pointed at me in the, "I'll be watching you," gesture. I didn't move until they'd gone into their own garage and shut the door.

"That was the weirdest fucking thing," Shaun muttered as he picked up some of the camping gear I'd left laying out. "Was he just admitting that Gayle tossed him out of their bedroom?"

"No. *That* was a warning shot," Tate answered for me as he carried a load into the garage.

"For what?"

"For anyone who might be stupid enough to sneak into Lennon's room in the middle of the night."

I glared at Tate. He watched me with a smug look on his face. Shaun's attention bounced back and forth between the two of us for a moment before realization dawned.

"Are you fucking for real right now?"

I held up my hands in surrender. "It's not what you think."

"It never is." Before he let me explain, Shaun turned to Tate. "So much for everything being out in the open." He headed for the door, a chuckle of disbelief echoing behind him. "I'll catch you guys tomorrow."

Confused, I took a step after him, wanting to clear the air. Tate stopped me. "He needs a minute to process." He backed out of the garage. "You should take one too."

He was gone before I could argue.

The incessant knocking dragged me from a restless slumber the next morning. I'd tossed and turned most of the night, sleep staying just out of reach until the sun started to come up. The blanket was too scratchy, my favorite pillow too lumpy, my arms painfully empty. I'd longed for Lennon, and somewhere around three or four had decided that sleeping alone was not something I ever wanted to do again.

With an agitated sigh, I dropped my arm over my eyes and tried to ignore the noise. When it came again, pounding this time, I gave in and sat up. I grabbed my phone, swearing when I saw how early it was.

I yanked a shirt from my floor, pulled it over my head, and pushed my arms through the sleeves as I trotted down the stairs. No one I knew knocked, they all just strolled in as if the house belonged to them. Whoever it was better have a damn good reason to be on my doorstep at the ass crack of dawn on a Saturday morning.

I didn't check the peephole, too tired and cranky. Instead, I yanked open the door. And immediately wished I'd ignored it.

"Uncle Trev."

I didn't know if I was more surprised or annoyed. Uncle Trevor had never knocked. In fact, we trusted them so much that each member of the James family had their own key. They were the only ones, other than Tate and Shaun, who knew where the spare was hidden. If he wanted in the house, there was no reason whatsoever for him to wake my ass up.

He didn't wait for me to invite him in. Instead, he pushed past me into the foyer. I didn't have the energy to do more than watch as he turned and held up a brown paper bag in one hand and a drink tray in the other.

"I brought breakfast. We need to talk."

He spun around and walked toward the kitchen, leaving me standing in the open doorway in nothing but my boxers and yesterday's tee, gaping at him like he'd just lost his mind.

That was it. The last straw. I needed a fucking vacation from my life.

Suddenly a vision of me and Len, secluded in a cozy cabin in the middle of nowhere, hit me. Nothing sounded better than lazy days on a mountain top followed by steamy nights in a hot tub under the stars. One day that would be our life.

For now, I was stuck there, alone with her dad.

Fucking fantastic.

I kicked the door closed and followed him, feeling like a death row inmate headed for execution. There was no hope for me now; the end was near. Nothing good could come from his arrival.

As soon as I stepped over the threshold, Trev handed me a cup of coffee and pointed to the island. "Sit."

I didn't hesitate. I was too tired, too worried about what he wanted, too desperate to get him out of my house. I took the java and did what he said.

"You look like hell."

No shit, Sherlock. I felt worse. "Thanks?"

"Your bed probably isn't as comfortable as Lenny's, eh? I always sleep better when I'm next to Gayle."

I kept my face blank. For all I knew, he was fishing for information. As long as I refused to give him any, he'd only have wild accusations and crazy theories. It didn't matter that they were probably all true.

He smirked, finding humor in something. My head spun. I was getting whiplash from the rapid change.

This was not the man who'd been outside my house the night before. No, this was my dad's best friend, the one with quick wit and a faster smile. I was dealing with a modern-day Jekyll and Hyde.

He took a long sip of his coffee. "Did you know that your dad and I bought home video surveillance systems last year?"

The question threw me. He'd not only surprised me, he'd also caught me off guard. And from the look on his face, the smug bastard knew it.

I cleared my throat and forced myself not to glance around the kitchen looking for hidden cameras. "I didn't."

He nodded as he pulled a donut from the bag. "Yeah. Back when there were some burglaries around town. Don't worry, they're not in the house." He chewed the bite and continued, "They're strategically placed where they'd do the most good. Pointed on driveways, doors, the back yards. One of yours has a great view of the treehouse. One of ours produces a quality shot of the roof outside Lennon's windows."

As much as I tried, I couldn't stop the blood from draining from my face. I didn't know if the knowledge that I'd been under surveillance was the most horrifying thing about this, or if it was the fact that Vicky and I had probably been recorded having some pretty wild times in the treehouse. The worst thing though, was that I'd been caught red-handed sneaking into Lennon's room. There was no way we could get out of it now.

"Neither of us take time to watch it usually. There's no point unless something happens. So whatever you're thinking about right now, whatever act you think you were recorded doing, it was never seen. Or you'd have been grounded long before now. And it won't be seen now, because anything older than a month is automatically wiped."

I almost sighed in relief.

He tipped the bag toward me, offering me a donut. I grabbed one and took a bite. I was still chewing when he started to talk again.

"Yesterday afternoon, I decided to clear out footage to make space on my hard drive and found there is one major problem with the program. Before any recent footage can be manually deleted, it requires you to scan the last few days of surveillance. You can either wait for it to auto erase, or you can take a few minutes and watch."

He glanced in the bag nonchalantly, checking out his options the same time my heart seemed to stop. Warning bells sounded in my head. *Danger, Will Robinson. Danger.*

"Lennon is grounded."

I dropped my Boston Cream onto the counter. "What?"

"My daughter doesn't typically lie to me. At least that's what I would have said if you'd asked me yesterday. Yet, as I watched more and more footage, I was blown away by the half-truths and blatant non-truths Lenny has told her mother and me. When confronted, she did the right thing and confessed."

"Lennon doesn't lie," I defended. "She may have omitted a few details here and there, but she always tells the truth."

"Having a young man spend the night in her room every night is omitting a few details? Telling us that she's going to a sleepover with a friend and then staying here, alone with said young man instead isn't lying?"

He had me there. I swallowed, uneasy.

"You feeling okay? You look a little green."

The humor in his voice did nothing to ease my sudden panic. I felt like I was going to hurl.

"Relax. I'm not going to tell your parents." Trevor picked up his coffee and gave me a knowing yet almost predatory smile, as he lifted the cup to his lips. "You are."

He'd misread my concern. I knew how my parents would react. Dad would flip his shit, yell a bit, tell me I was stupid for screwing up a perfect friendship. Mom would worry. Not just about me, but about Len too. She'd sit us down, attempt to have an embarrassing talk about our bodies and how lust is natural. Then she'd hug us both and pretend it had never happened.

She'd done it before.

I didn't care about me or how much trouble I might be in. I was worried about Len.

"It's my fault, not Lennon's. She only stayed here because I'd had too much to drink, and she was worried. I'm the one who climbed into her window, not the other way around. You can't punish her for my actions."

He watched me for minutes that stretched on. "Lennon is in trouble for her part in this, not yours. She can't make decisions for you, any more than you can make them for her. If you do something wrong, you own up to it, ask for forgiveness if necessary, and move on."

I nodded. I'd heard him say those words so many times they were embedded in my brain. "Is that why you're here? You want me to apologize?"

He set the Styrofoam cup down and gripped the edge of the island casually. "No. I'm here because my wife thought it was time for you and me to have a little chat." A wistful smile lit up his face. "I learned a long time ago that when I don't do the things my wife suggests, it can get very ugly, very fast. I make a point to always listen when she makes a suggestion."

I smiled, forgetting for a moment how serious the situation was. I admired many things about Uncle Trevor. His love for Aunt Gayle was one of them.

"I know I don't have to explain how hard living with a teenage girl is. One moment she's happy and loves everything, the next the world is against her and you're trying to ruin her life. You have to learn to ignore the eye roll because it's her response to everything and all you can do is hope they don't get stuck like that. Sass is the new norm, and you'll swear she's going to be a lawyer one day because she can find an argument for anything. You go to sleep one night as her favorite being in the world; when she wakes up the next morning, you've become the devil incarnate."

I thought of Dylan. I couldn't wait for my little sister to get home, but he'd hit the description head-on. "Exactly."

"Lenny and I have struggled, no more than most fathers and daughters, I imagine. We're both trying to adapt to this new reality. I'm not handling it as well as I should. I've said things I didn't mean, things I regret. I'll own that. I miss my little girl. One day, God willing, many, many years from now, you'll be in my position, and you'll understand. My family means everything to me."

"I know they do." I swallowed. "Len means—,"

"No," he held up a hand, interrupting me. "I don't need to hear it."

I frowned in confusion as my heart started to pound with worry.

"Whatever you're going to say is between you and my daughter. You need to tell her." He stood back and crossed his arms, leveling me with angry eyes. "She's going to be sixteen soon. Lord knows I'm not sure how that happened already. But, as my loving wife pointed out, I can't keep Lenny little by sheer will alone. Who she wants to spend her time with is none of my business. If that person is you, however, there are some things you need to remember."

Here we go. This was when he'd tell me about his shotgun, not that I believed he actually had one, or explain that if I hurt her in any way that everything I'd done to her, he'd do to me. She'd have to be back at their house by ten, my hands were to remain on the outside of her clothing at all times, that he didn't mind going to jail. The same song and dance I'd gotten from every father before I'd dated their daughter.

"The rules for dating my daughter are," he arched a brow, "you ready?" At my nod, he held up a finger. "I don't make the rules. You don't make the rules. Lennon makes the rules. It's her body, what she says goes."

I stared at him, waiting. When the death threat never came, I was confused. There had to be a catch.

"She can make her own decisions. Plain and simple."

"You really wouldn't have an issue if I asked her out?"

"Son," he shook his head, "if that's a serious question, you haven't heard a word I've said."

"I heard you. I can't tell if you're serious or not."

"I would never joke about this."

It was hands down the coolest thing I'd ever heard from a dad, mine included. I was impressed. He knew he didn't have to act like an overprotective ass or guard his daughter's virtue because he trusted her.

"How long is she grounded?"

"I'm sure she'll fill you in at school on Monday." He fought a smile. "Your parents will be home then. You'll be able to compare punishments."

Ugh. I didn't want to think about how they'd react. Or the fact that I now had two entire days without Len.

Uncle Trev lifted his cup and turned around. He was almost out of the kitchen when he paused. "Next time my daughter invites you over, don't creep in her window. We have a front door. Use it."

Chapter Sixteen

Lennon

There'd been a time when peaceful, quiet weekends at home were my norm. I'd go to the library ahead of time and borrow the maximum number of books allowed, lock myself in my bedroom, and get swept away into a fictional world or two. Sometimes I'd go a little crazy and take on a babysitting job.

When Monday morning rolled around and all my friends shared stories of parties and mayhem, I'd sit happily and listen, not envious in the least because I'd had just as much fun doing my own thing.

It was an entirely different story when that solitude was forced on me.

Not only had I missed the party on Saturday, I hadn't been able to take Dylan's calls Sunday morning when she'd made it back to port. Or seen her when she'd arrived home late that afternoon. I'd lost access to both my phone and laptop. Without them, there was no way to communicate with the outside world, so I was completely out of touch. I'd even been forced to decline any sitting jobs I was offered.

Being grounded sucked.

The worst part came Monday morning when my dad announced

that I wasn't allowed to ride to school with Dean. My options were the bus, which I hadn't stepped foot on in years, or Dad. I almost chose the cramped seats and stale air of school transportation but decided at the last minute that being stubborn would only punish myself further.

Thankfully, Dad insisted we had to leave at his normal time. He thought it would be a punishment, but it was really a blessing. We got to school so early the student parking lot was bare. I forced a goodbye as I jumped from the car and hurried into the building. Even though the halls were practically empty, it felt like those who were there were staring at me. It was unsettling.

I hid in the computer lab and worked on an assignment for the paper until it was almost time for the first bell.

I was at my locker getting everything I needed for first period when a familiar voice squealed my name. I turned just in time to see Dylan sprint down the hall, arms open wide, backpack bouncing behind her. She didn't slow as she got closer, and I wondered if Tate ever watched helplessly as other football players mowed him down on the field. Her speed forced us back into the metal as she all but tackled me, and I barely kept us from falling.

"Len, Len, Len!" Her arms wrapped around me and squeezed tight. "I've got so much to tell you."

I snorted with glee as I hugged her back, no doubt in my mind. Dylan always had a lot to tell me, and we were never usually apart for more than a few hours. I couldn't imagine how many stories she had now that we'd been separated for so long. "I missed you too. And I can't wait to hear all about it."

"Hey."

My breath caught when I heard his voice, and I immediately opened my eyes to search for him. Dressed in jeans that were just a bit baggy, a fitted, plain black shirt, and his baseball cap on backward, he was hotter than I remembered. *If that were even possible.* He lingered a few feet behind his sister, backpack slung over one shoulder, fingertips halfheartedly tucked into his pockets. I wanted to lunge into his arms, to hold him as tight as his sister clung to me, and kiss him until he understood just how much I'd missed him every moment over the last two days.

I couldn't do that, though. One, I'd look crazy, almost obsessed. Two, I didn't know what he'd told Dylan, if anything. Three, something about the way he looked at me, an expression I couldn't identify, made my hands clammy and butterflies invade my stomach. Maybe my worst fears had come true and whatever we'd had was simply a spring break fling.

The anticipation would kill me if I didn't know.

"You okay?"

"He's been worried about you." Dylan rolled her eyes in disgust and stepped back as she shot him an annoyed look.

Not a month before, I would have felt the same annoyance she did, frustrated by the overbearing, big brother attitude. Now his attention didn't feel anything like that.

"See? She's fine." Dylan shooed him away with her fingers. "Now go away."

Dean narrowed his eyes on her, but she was too busy watching me to notice. "When Mom told me you'd been grounded, I laughed. I totally thought she was kidding. What in the hell did you do, Ms. Goody Two Shoes?"

I hesitated. I hadn't planned out or rehearsed what I'd tell her or others who asked. I didn't know how to answer.

I glanced back at Dean. His head was tipped slightly to the side as he watched me intently, waiting for my answer. His lips quirked in amusement and I knew that no matter what I said, he'd follow my lead.

That didn't help. My eyes slid back to my best friend, who was waiting patiently for an answer. I sighed.

"It's a long story."

Dylan chortled. "The great ones always are."

Before she could demand details, a giant arm dropped onto her shoulders. "Look who's back, all tan and shit. Lookin' good, lil' sis."

Without greeting him or Tate, Dylan's arm whipped backward, connecting with Shaun's stomach so hard we all heard it. "Hands off. I'm taken."

Shaun winced playfully and rubbed the spot she'd hit as the rest of us gaped at her in varying degrees of confusion. She lifted a shoulder and glanced around our group. When her eyes fell on me, she winked. "See? Lots to tell."

That was apparently an understatement. No one said a word while we all waited for her to explain. Instead, she lifted a hand and inspected her nails.

"So, this is where everyone is." Chelsea strolled up to our little group and ducked under Dean's arm like she belonged there. "I thought we were going to meet in the café for breakfast?"

What? My entire body tensed as I watched her smile up at my boyfriend, looking like she belonged on his arm. The universe apparently believed I hadn't reached my mental limits and decided to test me a bit more.

Wait. No. He wasn't my boyfriend.

I just wanted him to be.

I spun around to my locker before anyone could see me react. There might be some answers I could avoid giving Dylan right away, but there was no way in hell I'd be able to hide how much seeing Dean and Chelsea together hurt. I tuned out the conversation going on around me and told myself I didn't care. I had more important things to worry about.

I'd known this would happen anyway.

Sensing something was wrong, Dylan stepped closer to me and hovered. Once I had everything I needed and slammed my locker shut, she grabbed my hand. Together we walked away, ignoring the boys and the friends who had joined them.

"She's such a hag," Dylan muttered as we moved through the crowded hall toward her locker. "She was at my house when we got home yesterday afternoon, and no matter how many hints Dean dropped, she wouldn't leave. Mom finally had to kick her out at like ten."

My jaw flexed as my hand tightened around my books involuntarily. "Why was she there? Didn't he have rehearsal?"

"I think he had a costume fitting or something earlier in the day. He was home when we got back." She shrugged as she entered her combination and yanked open the metal door. "She's like a parasite that just won't go away. You should have seen her, hanging all over him. I don't even want to think about what they did at the house without my parents there." She shuddered dramatically. "So gross." Then she laughed. "Maybe we should buy a blacklight to make sure my room is still safe."

I tried to keep my face emotionless, to act like the news didn't bother me as much as it did. Part of me had hoped Dean would blow off the stupid beach party and sneak in my window. I'd kept my door locked and my radio on low, to cover us, just in case. He hadn't tried to join me.

Dylan grabbed her books, still talking, no clue she'd delivered the momentous blow that might rip my heart out. "It's not like it'll even matter. Once he goes to that camp, he'll completely forget her."

Wait. What? I'd missed a step.

I touched her arm to slow her down. "What camp?"

Her face lit up. "I totally spaced that you didn't know. He told us as soon as we got home, before we'd even unpacked. He got into some exclusive summer theater camp at Emerson University. It's a huge steppingstone for him. Even Dad was excited about the news, so you know it's ginormous."

"Wow. That's amazing." Pride swelled in my chest. I'd known he was talented and brilliant for as long as I could remember, but the moment he'd stepped onto the stage for the first time, the entire room had known too.

"Yeah," she tucked a lock of hair behind her ear as she nodded. "He's gonna be a star someday, Len. He's got the talent, he's got the looks," she pretended to stick a finger down her throat and gagged playfully. "All he needs is his big break, and this might just be it. I guess the actors who go to this camp are all on their way to greatness. We're talking Academy Awards and Tonys. The big time."

I shook my head in awe as we started walking again. "That's huge. He must be so excited."

"Yeah. We're all wicked proud of him. My point is that he's on his way. The girls that go to that camp are going to have beauty, brains, and talent. You really think he's going to stay with some girl he dated for a hot minute in high school? Please. Chelsea can't compete with that. She'll be nothing but a memory before June ends."

I swallowed against the lump in my throat, but it wouldn't budge. I couldn't compete with all that either. I wasn't sure if I was trying to convince her or myself when I mumbled, "That doesn't sound like your brother."

"You're right," she sighed. "He's loyal to a fault. I hope he doesn't change too much, but I don't want to see him get screwed either." She chewed on her lip as we stopped next to her classroom. "He needs to stop dating. Like last week. We can't let anyone hold him back."

"We? What exactly are *we* going to do about it?" My tone was snippy, irritated by her assumptions that every girl was the same and none had his best interests in mind. Maybe some of them wanted nothing but the best for him. Maybe some would treasure the time they'd had and watch quietly from the sidelines while he shot for the moon.

"You need to talk to him," she insisted, like it was the most obvious answer ever.

"Me? How'd we go from we to me?"

She laughed. "You're better with him than I am. He listens to you. He humors me and my ideas, but he actually hears what you say. Plus, he's always there to protect us. It's our turn to watch his back."

"You want me to tell your brother that he can't date anyone on the off chance she might try to keep him from chasing his dreams? You realize how idiotic that sounds, right?"

"It's not dumb. It happens all the time. There are two types of girls who date boys with bright futures. Those who would try to keep him from going to Hollywood or Broadway or wherever he wants to go because they're afraid to lose him and know they will if he goes. Then there are those like Chelsea, who will dig their claws in and keep him close, so he'll take them with him. It happens all the time. Look at the cleat chasers. They latch on if they think their guy will go pro."

"He's a high school junior. I think we're a little way from red carpet walks and Oscars. You don't have to worry about wedding bells."

"Not if there's a baby."

"Cheese and rice. Now you're bringing in an imaginary baby?"

She chortled. "I can tell you've been grounded. You sound just like Uncle Trev. The only dad in existence who uses mom swears more than his wife." She adjusted the books in her arms. "So, when are you going to tell me why you're in trouble?"

"I lied."

Her face pinched. "So, you're not grounded?"

I almost laughed. "No, I am. I'm grounded *because* I lied."

Her surprise was almost comical. "No."

I lifted a shoulder noncommittally. "Yeah, I lied. I got caught. Now I'm grounded."

"Oh, honey. That's why you can never lie. You're horrible at it. You're supposed to let me do it for you."

The warning bell echoed off the lockers around us. We had five minutes to get to class.

"You'll talk to him, right?"

I shook my head at the ping-pong game that was our conversation. "What am I supposed to say? You want me to scare Dean away from his hypothetical entrapment and fictional child. That's crazy, even for you."

She grinned, not taking offense to my insult. "You're right. I just don't want to see him fall in love with some awful girl and get stuck here."

She loved her brother and only wanted what was best for him. I knew that. Yet I had to argue anyway. "As opposed to falling in love with an amazing girl?"

"If he feels bound to this hell hole, or she uses him, I don't care how wonderful she is, I'll hate her."

"He could fall in love with some wretched witch out there too. You know that, right?"

"Yeah, but at least he'd be out there, following his dreams. No one here is good enough for him, Len. No one." She took two steps toward her classroom as I started to back toward mine. "We'll talk about this later?"

I nodded. "See you at lunch."

I t wasn't Dylan who sat across from me a few hours later. Instead, it was the boy who'd taken up the majority of space in my head all day. There were hundreds of things I wanted to say, but only one came out.

"Congratulations."

He didn't return my warm smile. Instead, he watched me apprehensively. "For?"

"Getting accepted into a summer acting camp, silly. I'm so proud of you."

"I didn't apply."

"That means they found you. Even more impressive."

"I wanted to tell you, but there wasn't a chance." He reached across the table and tugged on a piece of stray hair. "We need to talk."

I resisted the urge to lean into his hand. "You don't owe me an explanation."

"Oh, you totally owe me one," Dylan snapped as she dropped her tray onto the table. "You both do."

Dean snatched his hand away from me, but his face remained a calm mask. Unlike me, who'd started to panic. Lord only knew what she'd heard. Rumors around here spread faster than gonorrhea on a school-sponsored trip, and after the seniors spent a week in Florida over February vacation, we all knew just how quick that was.

"What could I possibly owe you for an explanation?" Dean frowned, appearing utterly perplexed by the idea.

If I hadn't known the truth, I would've bought his act.

"I just came from gym, dumbass. Girls talk, you know?"

His eyes darted to mine, and one brow lifted ever so slightly. It was the cutest thing. I could stare at him all day.

"And you!" Dylan slapped the table in front of me. "Seriously? Ross McKinney?"

I stared at her, feeling like a deer in the headlights. Eyes wide, mouth open slightly, I tried to find words. I couldn't.

"You didn't feel the need to mention that this morning? Way to bury the lead."

The sad truth was that it hadn't even crossed my mind. "I was going to tell you," I assured her. "You still haven't told me any of your stories."

"I was gone for a week, and I feel like I don't know you anymore. Dating a senior. Public displays of affection. Sneaking out to go to parties. Graphic make-out sessions at the mall." She counted each one off on her fingers. "Really? Who are you, and what have you done with my best friend?"

I shook my head—I hadn't done half of those things—but before I could answer, Dean forced a laugh. "Who are *you*? My sister would never buy into locker room gossip. Have you been tested for heatstroke? You should be. That doesn't sound like Len at all."

"Oh, don't even get me started on you." Dylan turned wild eyes on her brother before I could answer. "Haven't you messed with that poor girl's emotions enough?"

"Which poor girl?"

"Vicky." Dylan was fuming, but the word was hissed. "Weren't you supposed to take her to the bonfire Saturday night?"

"No," he scoffed. "I haven't talked to Vicky since we broke up."

Dylan crossed her arms, smugly. "Oh, really? So, who is the mystery sophomore everyone is talking about in hushed tones? Word on the street is that you've been stringing some poor girl along to make Chelsea jealous."

"Word on the street?" He shook his head in indignation as he avoided looking my way. "You're ridiculous."

"You're ridiculous!" she snapped back. "Chelsea? Out of every girl in this school, you chose her?"

"Not that it's any of your damn business, but I'm not *with* Chelsea."

"Really? I heard a very different story. Everyone at the bonfire saw you two together. It's all anyone is talking about. Are you trying to say she didn't spend the night in your tent? Don't bother lying. Every single person there saw it."

"Almost every single person there was wasted," he snarled. His eyes moved from his sister to me, his agitation disappearing, eyes almost pleading. "Chelsea slept in my tent. People saw her leave the next morning. It's no big deal."

"To you, maybe. But Chelsea seems to think it is. I had to hear all the gory details," she shook her head in disgust. "I thought I knew way too much about mom and dad. Ugh," she groaned. "At least Vicky never bagged and bragged. I'm sending you the therapy bill."

I hadn't had much experience with the whole heartbreak thing. I'd been lucky. In that moment, I realized acting wasn't in the cards for me. I didn't know how to sit there and pretend to be indifferent to Dean's words.

Dylan groaned disgusted. "Boys are predictable and gross. Newsflash, jerkface. It doesn't matter how you label it. Sex means something, even to heartless hags like Chelsea. Now, because you're dumb and let your dick make decisions for you, she thinks she's getting happily ever after, and I'm stuck dealing with her. If you marry her, I'll stab you in your sleep."

I didn't know which of us was more shocked by her outburst, but both Dean and I stared at her. Something had set her off, and it felt like it was much more than just her brother and Chelsea hooking up. It wasn't as if he acted like a saint before he'd started dating Vicky.

"Of course, here she comes. Can't let you out of her sight for two minutes, not even to have lunch with your sister." Dylan pointed over his shoulder as she hissed. "You should go sit with your new girlfriend with the rest of your asshat friends. I really don't have the capacity to be nice right now."

Dean pushed himself up, eyes boring a hole into mine. "We're talking about this later."

Thinking he was talking to her, Dylan twirled a piece of hair on her finger as if she didn't have a care in the world. "Can't wait."

He glanced at me over his shoulder twice as he walked toward his friends at their usual table. I watched him with feigned indifference. I might not have anything to say to him, but I wasn't going to let him know how much my heart ached.

"So, Ross? I knew you liked him the night of the party." Dylan pulled on my arm and grinned like she hadn't just bitten her brother's head off and threatened murder.

Our friends appeared out of nowhere, almost as if they'd been waiting for Dean to leave. "I'll fill you in after school," I promised, feeling like a broken record as they sat and started asking her a gazillion questions about her trip.

I didn't know if I was thankful for the interruption because it seemed to calm her and gave me more time to think about what I was going to say or stressed because it meant we had to put off the conversation once again. In reality, probably a bit of both.

Even though I didn't want to look, my eyes betrayed me and drifted to Dean's table more times than I wanted to count. Each time I'd find his attention on me, yet Chelsea's hands on him. I couldn't handle it. Before the period was half over, I told my friends I'd see them later, tossed my uneaten food in the trash, and went in search of Mr. Padilla, my favorite teacher.

"Lennon James," he called cheerfully as I peeked my head around his classroom door. "Shouldn't you be at lunch?"

"Why be there when I can be here, avoiding awkward encounters and internally rehashing my every reaction?"

"I'm supposed to tell you to go back to the cafeteria." He lifted half his sandwich and held it in my direction. "But as the adult currently avoiding the teacher's lounge for those very reasons, I say, 'welcome.' How was your vacation?"

"Awful."

"I don't like the sound of that. Tell you what, you tell me all about it, and I'll fill you in on all the things your favorite three-year-old has discovered."

I grinned, imagining the tiny terror I babysat sometimes. He liked to drive his parents and big sister crazy. I missed him. "Deal."

With help from Mr. Padilla and a fictitious mysterious project he told other teachers he absolutely needed my help on, I managed to avoid almost everyone for the rest of the day. I lingered in his classroom, working on homework, long after the final bell. Then I made my way to my locker and outside to wait for my dad.

I was sitting on the bench by the pick-up lane, kicking my feet back and forth in the dirt, counting how many licks it took to get the middle of a Tootsie Pop, forcing myself to think about anything other than Dean, when a shadow fell over me.

"You know you can't actually dig your way to China, right? A smart girl like you should already know that."

I squinted up at the giant that was Shaun. "My dad is late. I'm bored."

"I know," he admitted. "About the late dad part, I mean. But I figured you were bored by the way you're ruining your Chucks."

I smiled around my lollipop. Shaun was probably the only person on the planet who wouldn't think they were already ruined by my doodles. "What brings you out here? The cool kids have their own lot. This is where us losers come to hitch a ride with people even more dorky than themselves."

He lifted my bag from the bench. "Come on, I'm taking you home."

"No, you're not. I'm in enough trouble already."

"Your mom called me. Your dad is stuck at work, and she can't get here for another hour."

"My mom has your number?"

"Okay. Your mom called Tate, but he's got practice, so he messaged me."

"My mom has Tate's number?"

"Lil' miss, there are some things even I don't question."

"Good point." I took the hand he offered and let him pull me to my feet, even though I didn't need help. "I'm surprised Dean wasn't option number one."

"No, you're not," he laughed, repeating my words from a few minutes before. "You know damn well your parents wouldn't call him.

My guess is that you're more than a little relieved he wasn't the first choice."

"Am I that obvious?"

"Not to most. To me, yeah." He scanned the lot as we walked toward his Jeep. "So, how long do they have you on house arrest?"

I happily let him change the subject. "Until my birthday."

He gave me a horrified look. "Which one?"

I chortled. "Sixteen. If it'd been up to my dad, I'd be locked away until I'm twenty-one. Thankfully, Mom talked him down. I'm not sure I could handle much longer."

"Does that mean there's a big birthday bash in our future? A giant sweet sixteen?"

"Yeah, no. Not a chance in hell. I'm pretty sure my partying days are behind me. Plus, you and I definitely don't hang with the same crowd."

"Didn't feel that way last week."

I shrugged, ignoring the memories that wanted to bombard me. "Things change."

He unlocked the car with his fob but held open the passenger door for me. "You can't avoid him forever."

"Maybe not. But I can try."

He shut my door and moved around the front quickly. "Seems like a lot of effort to put in for a non-boyfriend."

"You're not going to let me off the hook and make small talk so we can ignore the elephant in the room, are you?"

"Not a chance."

I groaned. "You're supposed to be my funny, easy-going friend who hates to be serious."

"I'm your only funny, laidback friend. Dylan's good for some laughs, but good Lord, that girl is high maintenance."

I didn't say anything as he maneuvered around the school, past the fields where the baseball team had just started practice.

He waited until he'd pulled out on the main road before he tried again. "I might not look like I'm paying attention, but trust me, I notice everything. You can talk to me, Lennon."

Shaun never used my name. I think I'd heard him use "Len" a time or two, but most of the time it was whatever nickname he'd bestowed upon me at the time.

I tucked my Tootsie Pop into my cheek. "And what, screw the bro code?"

"Bros before hoes doesn't really apply here. Sister from another mister, maybe?" He laughed.

I turned to watch him as the realization hit. "He asked you to talk to me, didn't he?"

"Who is this *he* you speak of?"

I crossed my arms and narrowed my eyes as he tried to hide his playful smirk. "Shaun."

"Nah. Cullen didn't ask me to talk to you." He shook his head. "He won't say a word about it, either."

"That's because it's a disaster."

"Whenever feelings are involved, things get messy. Which is why I don't do it."

"Have feelings?"

Sean smirked. "Date, smart ass."

"We weren't dating."

"Hate to break it to you, Lil'-Miss-Know-It-All, but you're wrong. You definitely were. Think about it for a second. What's the definition of dating?"

"I don't know. To go out with someone you're romantically interested in?"

"Go out with. Spend time with. Be around all the time. Spend the nights with. Want me to keep going?"

I shook my head, horrified I'd missed it. Dean had never said anything, so maybe he didn't realize it either. We'd never defined us.

"From where I sit, I didn't see either of you break up with the other. So technically, you're still dating. You should talk to him."

"I may not have a ton of experience, but I'm pretty sure that when you're dating someone, you don't let someone else hang all over you. And you definitely don't sleep with them."

"Yeah, I won't even pretend to understand what's going on with that whole crazy sitch. For the record, I heard what Dylan said earlier. She's wrong. But that's a truth you need to get from your boy."

"That's hard to do when I'm grounded, and he's got an audience the rest of the time."

"When did you, of all people, turn chicken shit? Tell him you want to talk to him and watch as he drops everything and follows wherever you go."

"Then what?"

"Is that fear I hear in your voice? Is it possible that you've finally found something that scares you? Something you can't research your way out of?" He grinned at me as he turned onto my road. "This is life. We're all just figuring it out as we go. Things either go our way or they don't. Either way, just talk to him so you're both on the same page." He pulled up to the curb in front of my house. "No matter what, you've got friends to get you through."

I watched him for a minute as I thought about his words. Shaun always had the best advice. He was wrong about one thing. The people who would get me through weren't just my friends. They were my family.

Chapter Seventeen

Dean

"Late night?"

I grunted a response, not willing to waste precious energy on words.

Dylan was quiet for only a moment. "You're more broody than usual. Trouble in paradise?"

I refused to justify her ridiculousness with an answer.

"Look, I already said I was sorry for the Vicky confusion. I can't understand what you see in that other troll, and I won't pretend I do. But I am sorry. Can you please stop being a dick now?"

She'd been nothing less than a hag since she'd gotten home from the cruise, but it was me who was a dick and needed to get control of my attitude. Seemed legit. I'd get right on it.

Ignoring my sister and the stupid faces she made as she inspected her makeup in the visor mirror, I cranked the radio. It'd been a long-ass week, and I didn't want to talk to her. I didn't even want to hear her voice.

Flo Rida's "Right Round" blasted from the speakers, the mainstream beat irritating me even further. I flipped the station, only to find the new angry, man-hating tune from Briar Bennett that had oversaturated the market. If I never heard her songs again, I'd be okay.

I stabbed another button, bringing up a sappy love duet between Nate Kelly and Molly Ray that I knew by heart because Dylan played it on repeat whenever Tate ignored her. With an angry growl, I chose another preset. This time, Kelly Clarkson sang about how much her life would suck without the dysfunctional dude she loved.

Fuck that.

I turned off the radio, stabbing the button too hard. We didn't need music anyway. Silence could be refreshing and comfortable. A guy could get his head straight in the quiet.

Of course, it was thoughts of Len that invaded as soon as I let my guard down and tried to relax.

Thankfully, Dylan didn't attempt to talk again. A few times she'd looked at me for far too long as if she were trying to find a way to start a conversation. Once she'd even opened her mouth but then thought better of it. When we parked in the student lot, she didn't even bother to say goodbye before she lunged out the door and practically ran up the steps.

I didn't want to be at school. It was tech week—Hell Week, if you asked the cast and crew—and I'd been at the theater extremely late every night. This morning, I'd strolled into the house a little before three and would've loved to catch up on sleep instead of going to American History, but I was Dylan's unofficial chauffeur.

Hell Week was the craziest part of any show and took more work than the rest combined. The point was simple: rehearse the show with all the technical elements in place so the actors could get used to the sets and costumes, the production crew could catch unforeseen problems, and Nilo could ensure everything came together. It was never that simple, though.

In theory, everything that went wrong during one rehearsal would be fixed by the next day. We all spent a massive amount of energy to make sure timings and cues were correct, costumes didn't restrict movement, props looked natural and weren't awkward to handle, and that everything sounded fine once microphones were live. Yet, no matter what we did to fix the issues, they persisted in one form or another.

We were out of time. Ready or not, our final stages were happening over the weekend. Saturday morning was the final Q2Q Tech Rehearsal where the show was run from cue to cue, to help get the actors and crew in sync. Saturday afternoon was the costume parade where the cast would act out the entire play silently, transitioning from one scene to the next with no stopping, to make sure there were no surprises once the lights came up. Sunday was the dress rehearsal, where everything would come together.

Previews—public performances open to very specific groups—started Monday night with members of the theater and their families, along with critics and reviewers. Tuesday night was for drama clubs from surrounding junior and senior high schools. Thursday was opening night.

I dragged my feet as I followed my sister into the school, both dreading and excited about the days ahead. The performance was what I lived for. The energy from the audience, the thrill of being on stage, the joy of seeing all the hard work come together was indescribable. However, once the play was over, Len would no longer be grounded, and I'd have only days left with her before I headed to Emerson.

I hadn't gotten to see my parents much since they'd gotten home, but whenever I had more than five minutes with them, they talked non-stop about the workshop and how proud they were. They'd done research and found out just how prestigious it was. I'd looked into it more too, and was horrified by the rules I'd have to follow. No cell phones. No home visits on days off. No distractions whatsoever.

Two and a half months without Len seemed worse than Chinese water torture. It'd only been a week since I'd held her, and I was hanging on by a thread. I had no idea how I'd make it all summer with little to no contact.

Tate was waiting for me at my locker. I dropped my backpack by his feet and fell back against the cool metal, too tired to do more than mutter a greeting.

"You look like shit."

I rubbed my eyes with my fingertips and pinched the bridge of my nose. "I feel worse, trust me."

"Late night?"

I groaned as I forced my eyes open and ignored the way they burned. There wasn't enough Red Bull in the world to help get me through the day. "Yeah. I almost called my dad to come get me because I wasn't sure I could make it home safely."

"Speaking of dads..."

I'd started to enter my combination but stopped, hand still in the air as I watched my best friend, waiting for him to finish. When he didn't, I asked, "Did he finally call?"

"Not mine," he scoffed as if the idea that his deadbeat had finally reached out was absurd. It was, but I'd never tell him that. "Do we know if Uncle Trev is still driving Len?"

I frowned as I started turning my lock. "Not a clue. I haven't talked to her since Monday. Why?"

He cleared his throat. When I didn't look at him, he cleared it again. Catching on, I glanced his way, only to follow the tip of his head. "We may have a situation."

Situation was a fucking understatement. Lennon strolled down the hall, eyes on the notebook in her hand, chewing on the cap of a pen, lost in her head. Getting so caught up in a potential article or book that she was oblivious to the world around her wasn't that out of the ordinary for Len. It wasn't her actions that had caught the attention of more than just Tate.

"What the fuck is she wearing?"

Tate shook his head and shrugged. "From this angle, it looks like her dad's sweater and nothing else."

He was right. The cardigan she wore was at least three sizes too big. The bottom fell slightly above her knees, the sleeves bunched up on her arms, the lapels overlapped each other. If she had anything on under it—and I was going to assume she hadn't worn an old man sweater as a dress—no one could see it.

It should have been weird. It made me want to pull her into the closet and peel it off her, just to see what was hiding underneath. From the way she held the attention of almost every asshole in that hallway, I knew I wasn't the only one thinking it.

Her rainbow hair was mostly on the top of her head in a messy bun, but a few bright curls cascaded over her shoulders and framed her face. It was a style that would have taken most girls hours to get right, but there was no doubt in my mind she'd pulled it back to get it out of her face, and the rest had simply fallen into place.

Leave it to Len to look hot as hell wearing what could only be described as homeless chic. She was a walking wet dream.

When McKinney called her name, I forgot about Tate, my bag, my locker and whatever I'd been about to grab from the inside. I stalked toward her, not giving a damn how obvious I was. I'd given her space, waiting for her to come to me all week. She hadn't. I was done waiting.

I made it to her before Ross could, and I propped my shoulder against the locker next to hers, blocking him from her view. "You're here bright and early."

Startled by my words, her eyes grew wide as she glanced at me. "You scared me." She started to frown before I could respond. "What's wrong?" She lifted a hand to my forehead. "Are you sick?"

I didn't answer or tell her how tired I was. I wanted her to touch me, any part of me, and I knew if I explained why I looked like death warmed over that she'd stop. Instead, I stood still, watching as she surveyed me with concerned eyes.

Her hand slid down my face as she lifted the other to cup my cheek. "You don't have a fever. You look miserable, though, like you're fighting something off. You should go home and get some rest." She patted my cheek gently. "Seriously, you look exhausted."

"And you look bright-eyed and bushy-tailed. Been here a while?"

As if remembering what she was doing, she turned back to her locker. "There was a *Chronicle* meeting this morning. I got here hours ago."

Unable to stop myself, I tugged on the tan and brown monstrosity she was using as a robe. "New style?"

She frowned and glanced down. Seeing the sweater, she let out a small, embarrassed laugh. "No. I thought I had a hoodie in here. I didn't. Remind me later to check with Dylan to see if she borrowed it."

I nodded. I probably wouldn't remember, but I would do anything to keep her talking to me. I missed her not being mad at me. "So, where'd this come from?"

"Mr. Padilla."

I tensed. "I'm sure I have something in my locker that would fit you better. Hell, here." I started to unbutton my flannel.

Her hand covered mine. "You don't have to do that."

I paused, lost in her eyes. "I miss you."

"Good." Blush tinged her cheeks as she looked at the floor. "Because I miss you."

I barely heard her whisper above the typical morning noise in the hall, but she dropped her hand and glanced around as if making sure we hadn't been overheard.

I slipped the last button through the hole and shrugged out of my shirt, holding it out. Her eyes moved around the hall again, then she quickly removed the sweater, tossed it in her locker, and grabbed my shirt, slipping it over her arms before I had a chance to blink.

She was adorable all the time, but in my clothes she was irresistible. I didn't know what it was, but something about seeing her dwarfed in the shirt I'd just had on made me want to go all caveman and claim her. It took every ounce of self-control not to grab her and kiss her breathless in front of the entire school. Especially when she smirked up at me as if she could read my very dirty thoughts.

"How're rehearsals?"

"Slow. Stressful."

"Hell Week always is. It looks like it's taking more of a toll than normal."

"That's not the only reason I'm not sleeping."

She'd started to roll my too-long sleeves up her arms but paused to meet my eyes.

"This is where you've been hiding." Chelsea attempted to tuck herself into me, but I sidestepped and crossed my arms over my chest.

"I looked everywhere." She glanced down at Len in feigned surprise. "Oh. Morning, Lemon."

Len sent her a half-hearted wave, annoyance clear.

"What an interesting little outfit." Chelsea narrowed her eyes in concentration. "*Gossip Girl* called. They want their wardrobe back."

Lennon glanced down at clothes that were now only half-hidden under my shirt—an itty-bitty plaid skirt and plain, tight gray tee, complete with a thin, matching plaid tie—before starting back at Chelsea. "Oh, you mean the show? Cute. I'm a *One Tree Hill* girl myself, and they don't wear uniforms, so I'm not really sure what you're talking about. I'll check it out though. I'm always looking for new inspiration."

"The clashing plaid really secures your spot as a fashion icon."

"Right?" Len ran her palms down the outside of the shirt I'd practically forced her to wear. "I was going for more of a punk, private-school-dropout vibe, but Dean insisted I wear his shirt. He didn't want me to get cold." She shrugged and if I didn't know her as well as I did, I might assume she was innocently explaining how she'd ended up in my clothes. "He wouldn't take no for an answer. I mean, he practically stripped right here."

Chelsea propped thin arms on her hips. Before she could spout off whatever venom she'd planned to spit at Lennon, Dylan joined us, her hand on Chelsea's arm. "Hey, I've been looking for you."

"Why?"

It was no secret that my sister hated her, but the way Chelsea spoke to Dylan made my teeth grind.

It was one thing for Chelsea to hate Len. She had a really good reason—I watched Lennon in a way I'd never look at anyone else. Len needed to realize that out on her own and stand up for herself, stake her claim. If she didn't, girls like Chelsea would walk all over her for the rest of our lives, no matter what I did to discourage them.

Dylan was another story. She was family. No one spoke to my baby sister that way.

Before I could intervene, Dylan stepped a little closer to the intruder. "I wanted to pick your brain about party ideas." She gently started leading Chelsea away as she spoke. "It's almost opening weekend, and you know my parents always throw a party the Sunday after. This year…" I couldn't hear the rest as the two were swallowed by the crowd.

It almost felt like Dylan had intervened on purpose to give Len and I time to talk. I forced the absurd idea away. There was no way she could know about us. "You're going to miss opening night."

Len nodded sadly. "I am. But I'll be there closing night. I already bought my ticket."

"I would have gotten you a ticket," I argued, but she gave me a look that told me to stop talking. I took another approach. "Come with me to the cast party after the show that night."

"Isn't it just for the cast and crew?"

"No. Plus ones are welcome. Be my date."

"Okay." She didn't even think about it. "I'll see if I can get a later curfew."

"It's your birthday weekend. I can't see your parents saying no."

"If you'd asked me a few weeks ago, I couldn't have imagined my parents grounding me."

"Touché." My chuckle was drowned out by the warning bell. I didn't even have my books yet. "Eat lunch with me."

"I'm not an exhibit. I actually prefer to eat without an audience. If you sit with me, everyone will watch us."

"Fine. What about if you eat with me in the tutoring room?"

She shook her head as if the idea was absurd. "No one would ever believe you're tutoring me."

I chuckled. The teachers all adored little miss straight-As. "They might believe you're helping me pass this bullshit chemistry class that I'm on the verge of failing."

"You're almost failing chemistry?" Her appalled look spoke volumes. "I'll be there. But we're eating too. It's my only break today."

"Yes, ma'am." I hurried toward my locker and was halfway down the hall when I turned back toward her. "I like how you look in my clothes. I'm going to cover you up more often."

Her middle finger was my only answer. I smiled through all my morning classes, exhaustion forgotten.

"Do you think there are cameras in here?" I'd inspected the room twice, but unless they were really well hidden, I couldn't find them.

"Every inch of the school is on camera, so I'm gonna say yes. Why?" Len took a giant bite of her sandwich, her face still glued to my chemistry book.

"Just wondering who was going to be watching when I kiss you."

That got her attention. She finished chewing and gaped at me. "A bit presumptuous, aren't you?"

I leaned my forearms onto the table, closing the gap between us. "We spent almost every night of spring break in the same bed. I haven't kissed you in over a week. If you thought I was going to get you alone for more than a minute and not have my lips on you, you don't know me at all."

"Don't act deprived. Or like you miss me that much. You had a backup."

I'd hoped she wasn't going to bring it up, that we could avoid talking about Chelsea. Wishful thinking. "That's fair. Ask me anything you want to know."

She hesitated.

"I'm not keeping secrets from you, Len. But I'm not a mind reader either. If you want to know something, ask."

"Did you sleep with Chelsea?"

I'd assumed she'd ask about Chelsea eventually but never imagined she'd believe those rumors. "Not a chance. Even if I'd drank as much as everyone else, which I didn't, I wouldn't have done that to you. People think we shared a tent because she slept in mine. You're asking the wrong questions, Len. Sometime you should ask McKinney who he bunked with."

Her look said she was skeptical at best. "Why is she hanging all over you all the time?"

"Because it's better than her targeting you." I adjusted in my seat, dreading admitting this truth out loud. I shouldn't be this pathetic.

"Chelsea and I have always been each other's backup. If we need a date and we're single, it's an unspoken rule that we'll call the other. She's always been clingy. I've always let her. If I tell her to back off, she's going to know there's someone else. She'll dig until she figures out who I'm seeing, or she'll make up shit and start drama. You and I haven't had a chance to talk about us, and she kept hinting about you and me, so I made a split-second choice. I'm sorry if it was the wrong one."

Len frowned and the most adorable little wrinkles appeared between her eyebrows. "That actually makes sense."

"The truth sometimes does." I smiled. "You're the only one I want. When you're ready to go public, she's the first person I'm telling."

"Speaking of Chelsea," she blew out a breath, ignoring my words as if I wasn't waiting on her to make us official. "I'm supposed to talk you out of dating her."

"Good thing I'm not. Mission accomplished. Now kiss me."

She grinned and shook her head at my impatience. "I'm serious. Dylan worked hard to help set this lunch up."

Out of everything she could have said, I didn't expect that. "Huh?"

"She thinks you'll listen to me." Nervous, her hands twisted the pen. "I'm supposed to convince you that high school girls aren't worth your time, and you should focus on the bigger picture."

"What's the bigger picture?"

Len's swallow reverberated off the walls of the small room. "You, off living your dreams. Without anyone from here holding you back."

"Is that how you see it? You think you'd hold me back."

Her eyes widened slightly, the irritation in my voice unmasked. "We're not talking about me."

"Why not?" The wall behind me suddenly became very interesting and drew all her focus. "I feel like we've had this conversation before. Apparently, it didn't get settled then, so explain it to me one more time."

"Which part?" Her voice broke into a nervous squeak that would've been cute if I wasn't annoyed.

"You said Dylan didn't want anyone to hold me back, which is completely absurd and pathetic, by the way. The only one who could possibly hold me back is me. But what I want to know is if you feel the same way. Do you think you'd keep me from chasing my dreams? Because there is no one else. Only you."

"There isn't anyone else today. Next month, you'll be in a totally different world. The girls there aren't awkward and geeky. They're going to be beautiful and talented and perfect for you."

"If you're that worried about Emerson, I won't go."

"Damn it, Dean." She slammed a small fist onto the table before pointing at me, anger sparking from her eyes. "That, right there, is exactly what I'm talking about." She dropped her hand as she shook her head sadly. "Dylan called it. Your biggest strength is also your biggest weakness."

My own anger started to rise. "Oh, yeah? What's that."

"Your loyalty. You'd give up the best thing that has ever happened to you if some girl asked you to stay because she was insecure."

"Emerson isn't the best thing that has ever happened to me." *You are.* It was on the tip of my tongue, but she was already spooked and looked ready to bolt. "It's a great opportunity, but it fell in my lap. More will come."

"What if more chances never come? You'd have given up everything because some random girl asked you to put her happiness ahead of her own."

"You aren't 'some random girl.' I'm not some guy you just met and have a thing for. I'll play along, just for shits and giggles. Would you do that? Ask me to stay here?"

"Oh my God. Never. I'd rather spend every night imagining the worst, twist myself up in knots, than watch you give up on your dreams."

"Exactly." I crossed my arms over my chest and leaned back in my chair. "In this crazy scenario you and my sister cooked up, you didn't factor in all the variables. You left *me* out. I'm not an idiot. I may let my dick make some decisions, but I can and do, use my brain. I'd never connect myself to someone who is not only self-centered but apparently extremely needy. I'm Dean. Not Shaun. Not Tate. Give me some fucking credit."

She chewed on her lip at a loss for words, as she let mine digest. "Sometimes, I feel like we're really good friends. Others, it's like we're more than that–we're connected in a way I can't explain. But there are times, I feel like I don't know you at all and we're total strangers."

There were some days I had to remind myself that Len wasn't just younger than me; she was completely inexperienced. She was clueless when it came to dealing with the opposite sex. In comparison, I was light years ahead of her.

"That sounds about right. A good relationship has a little bit of everything. You have to be friends first because if you don't like each other, what's the point? There has to be more—a spark, an attraction, a draw—something that makes both of you want to cross that line. Or you really are just friends. And if you knew everything about each other, the magic would be gone. That mystery will keep us on our toes, keep us trying. As the years go by, we'll mature and change. The goal is to grow together."

"He really is more than just a pretty face."

I couldn't stop the smile at her taunt. "I really am. This week without you made me realize that *you* are so much more than I ever expected. I have friends, but you're the only one I tell every single secret. When I walk into a room, I always look for you. I want to be around you all the time, even if you're being an annoying pain in the ass like right now, because it feels like something important is missing when you're not there."

"Wow."

"Yeah." It wasn't the reaction I'd hoped for, but then again, I'd laid everything out, and it was a lot to take. At least she wasn't running away. "Thankfully, I have the show. If I didn't, I'd lose my mind while you're grounded. Not being able to talk to you whenever I want is seriously fucking with my head. I spend most of my time hoping this isn't one-sided."

"You don't have the slightest idea how much I like you, do you?"

I had a decent idea by the way she looked at me. Yet, Len didn't talk about her feelings as openly as every other girl our age, so I worried that I might have imagined the hunger in her eyes. I watched her, waiting for her to explain.

"Everything you just said, that's how I feel. But it scares the hell out of me."

"Why?"

"Because we're kids. It's moving too fast. This isn't normal. It's not just you and me in this. There's Dylan. Our parents. Our friends. What if they don't understand?"

Dylan was my biggest concern. I didn't know what to do about it. In theory, she'd be happy that Len and I were together. Best friend, big brother—what could be better? Yet, Dylan had been pretty clear more than once. Her friends were off limits.

Add in the fact that we'd spent all vacation together and never told her, and it could get ugly fast if she thought we were keeping secrets or lying. I didn't know who would bear the brunt of her anger, the brother who broke his promise or the best friend who betrayed her trust. I wasn't looking forward to finding out.

"This all happened really fast, after one of my dreams. It was like I went to sleep one night and you were just Dean. When I woke up the next morning, I was obsessed with you. You didn't like me before then. What happens if I put some weird spell on you and all these feelings go away once it wears off?'

"A weird spell on me?" I rarely lost control when I laughed, but her question, combined with my overall sleep deprivation was too much. I pushed my chair back, bending over and dropped my forehead to the table while I howled.

When I finally looked up, Lennon had crossed her arms over her chest once again and narrowed her eyes on me. "I'm not kidding."

"That's what makes it so funny," I wheezed between chortles. "It's perfect, Len. One day, some interviewer will ask me about falling in love so young. I'm going to tell them it wasn't my fault. You cast a spell on me, you little witch. I didn't stand a chance."

She watched me wearily until I got control of myself. "It wasn't that funny."

I shook my head and wiped my eyes. "Oh, Len. I don't know what I'd do without you."

"Clearly, you'd fail Chemistry." She lifted the textbook in front of her, ready to get back to business.

I let her steer us back to schoolwork. We both had a shit-ton to think about. I felt better and hoped she did, too.

It didn't click that I'd used the *L* word until I was in bed hours later, the conversation on replay in my mind. She'd never said a word, never called me out, so maybe she hadn't heard it. Now that I'd realized it, I couldn't let it go.

I was in love with Lennon James, and I didn't know what in the hell I was going to do about it.

Chapter Eighteen

Lennon

"You still haven't told us what you want for your birthday."

"The only thing I want is to not be grounded." It was true. It felt like I'd been under lock and key for months and I was ready to have my freedom back.

"Lennon." This time it was my dad. "That's not a present. What else would you like?"

I pushed the baked chicken around my plate as I debated the timing of my request. I'd planned to wait until Saturday morning once I was free and clear of the invisible chains they'd bound me with. That was only two days away. I should wait.

I met my father's eyes. "A later curfew. And for you to understand that Dean and I want to be a couple."

There was no yelling. Dad's eyes didn't bug out of his head. Mom didn't have to intervene.

Instead, the two of them shared a long look I couldn't decipher. When Mom took a deep breath, put down her fork, and pushed her plate forward, I knew I was in trouble. She braced her arms on the edge of the table and leveled me with a brutally intense stare.

"Your father and I have been debating this for a while now."

My gaze darted to the man on my left, but he only dipped his chin. I turned back to Mom.

"You get an extra hour. You need to be back in this house no later than eleven. I have agreed to renegotiate once summer comes, depending on circumstances and your behavior. If Dean is going to spend the night, it has to be on a weekend. He needs to clear it with both his parents and us, and your door will stay open at all times." She glanced at my dad, almost as if she needed encouragement. "You and Dean also need to talk to his parents about your relationship. There will not be any sneaking around."

I was in the damn *Twilight Zone*. If not, this was a dream, and I was going to wake up and be seriously disappointed. There was no way my parents would acquiesce that easily.

"However, there are some additional rules," my dad interjected. *Of course, there were.* "If Dean has a drop of alcohol, a single sip, you are not to get in a car with him. Call us to come get you. If we aren't here, and you're not safe to stay where you are, call a cab and put it on the emergency card."

"What emergency card?"

My mom nodded. "That goes for any driver, not just Dean."

"A quarter of all car-related teen fatalities are caused by alcohol. Last year alone, there were almost six-thousand teens killed. Sixty-three percent of those were being driven by another teen. The statistics are overwhelmingly scary. Trust me, I'm not getting in any car with anyone who's been drinking. Ever."

My dad dropped his fork onto his plate with a clang while mom's eyebrows disappeared. "Change of plans. You're not going anywhere ever again."

Shit. There was a reason I'd stopped relaying random facts to my parents years before. I smiled despite the seriousness of the topic. "I promise you that Dean would never put me in danger."

"There's no doubt in my mind. That boy would walk through fire for you." They exchanged another look. Dad slid an envelope across the table. "It's for emergencies only."

I lifted the flap and reached inside to find a Master Card with my name printed on the front. I was shocked. They'd never said anything about getting me my own card. "Is this a birthday present?"

Dad shook his head. "No. It's a way to make sure you always have options. There will come a day when Dean isn't there, for whatever reason. In those moments, take care of yourself. If the opportunity arises, make sure you take care of him, too."

"Always."

"Again, those are not presents. So, what do you want for your birthday?"

I shook my head, clueless. They'd already given me everything I wanted and more.

"Happy Birthday!" Dylan squealed, wrapping her arms around me from behind. "You're finally free!"

"Finally," I groaned playfully as I spun to find her and two of the three stooges standing behind me, a large bundle of balloons above them. They'd been so quiet I'd never heard them sneak up.

"You said you wouldn't go to a party." Shaun grinned as he stepped around Dylan and slipped the balloons' string through the vent in my locker before tying a knot inside the door. "You didn't say we couldn't bring the party to you. Whatcha think?"

I stepped back to get a better look. I normally hated attention, but it was my birthday. I was no longer grounded, and even the most embarrassing displays couldn't get me down. The mismatched menagerie of messages—from a giant rainbow "16" to "Welcome Home" and "You Did It" to "Happy Birthday"—made me snort with glee. Even the beautiful cartoon owl was perfect, considering the tattoo Shaun had designed for me. However, one didn't seem to fit.

"A vulture?"

Tate cracked up. "He told them he wanted a jailbird. That's what they sent."

"I love them!" I practically assaulted poor Shaun as I jumped up to hug him. "Thank you!"

His strong arms tightened around me. "Happy sweet sixteen, lil' miss." Once my feet were safely back on the ground, he reached out to ruffle my hair. "If you want to change that whole, 'never been kissed situation'," he teased, "you know where to find me."

Dylan shoved him out of the way. "I think McKinney might have something to say about that." Her eyes lit up. "Do you guys have plans tonight?"

No matter how many times I'd told her that Ross and I weren't a couple, she wouldn't let it go. "It was just those two dates. I told you. We're not a thing."

"Oh, right. Sure." She winked conspiratorially like we knew something the big brothers didn't.

I turned to the boys so they could back me up, but it was Dean I found. He hadn't been there a few moments before. With a lopsided and carefree grin that I had no doubt would soak panties one day, he held out a single daisy. "Just living is not enough. One must have freedom, sunshine..."

"And a little flower," I finished for him, my voice barely a whisper as I reached for it and our fingers touched.

"Happy birthday, Len."

"You two are so weird," Dylan ground out. "You know that, right?"

"Eh. We're all weird." Shaun tossed an arm around Dylan's shoulders. "Let's skip and go to the beach."

"You guys, I legit just got done being grounded. I'm not doing anything to go back."

"Good point." He nodded. "I'm disappointed, Cullen. I expected a *Braveheart* monologue, not some shit about a flower."

Dean shook his head, his eyes on me. "It's not a movie quote. Len hates Hans Christian Anderson. She told me once that the only thing he'd written that she could tolerate was that poem."

"That's the dude who wrote *Grimm's Fairy Tales*, right? Those things are scary as hell."

Tate snorted. "Asshole, that was *The Brothers Grimm*. We watched the movie, remember—Kate Beckinsale, all that leather? Oooh, yeah."

Dylan scoffed at Tate in disgust. "I don't know if you're talking about *Van Helsing* or *Underworld*, you moron, but *The Brothers Grimm* was Heath Ledger and Matt Damon. Duh." She rolled her eyes as if everyone should know and turned to Shaun. "They all wrote fairy tales, so you're in the ballpark. Len, what's the difference between the two?"

"Anderson wrote tales from his imagination, even though some were based on folklore. The Brothers Grimm, on the other hand, traveled the German countryside and gathered their stories from other people. Both published dark, moral-driven stories aimed at scaring children into doing the right thing. Both have stories that were adapted by Disney into something much lighter and fluffier. I hate both equally."

"Good to know," Shaun nodded. "I might be able to use that later."

Dean beamed at me as if I'd just won the Pulitzer Prize. "That's my girl."

"I still expected movie quotes. What's that one where Mel Gibson's screaming about freedom?"

"I can't help," Tate muttered with a shrug. "The only *Braveheart* quote I know is, 'Englishmen don't know what a tongue is for.'" He nailed the French accent perfectly. "I only remember that because I was determined to find out what a tongue *was* used for." He looked at Dylan and gave her a wicked grin. "For the record, I did. And I know."

"Dude," Dean practically shouted, appalled. "My sister!"

Shaun groaned. "Little sister, man. Not funny." His quiet laugh, on the other hand, said the opposite.

"Figures," Dylan rolled her eyes. "A three-hour movie and that's the only line you remember?"

Tate shrugged, bored now that he'd successfully riled his friends. "You know I don't like classics. They make me fall asleep."

Shaun shook his head sadly. "And you all thought if you typed the word idiot into Google, it'd be my picture that came up. At least I know the definition of a classic movie."

"Whatever," Tate punched him in the arm playfully. "You knew what I meant."

"No. I don't speak moron, cretin." When we all stared, unsure what he was attempting to say, he shrugged. "Or whatever language idiots speak. Lil' miss knows what I'm talking about."

The warning bell sounded.

"Saved by the bell," I joked.

Dean cupped the back of my head and yanked me into him before he kissed my forehead. "Happy birthday, Len."

I stiffened, worried about our audience. Dylan didn't react. Instead, she acted as if it were perfectly normal for her brother to kiss me. Tate stepped in and pressed his lips against my temple, too. Then, Shaun pulled me into a giant bear hug and lifted my feet off the ground.

"Put me down!" I squealed, laughing as people stopped to watch.

"Nah, I like the way we fit. You're so tiny I could put you in my pocket and carry you around all day. Think my teachers would freak if I brought you with me to all my classes?"

Dylan smacked the back of his head. "Put her down, you oaf. Go torment someone else."

With a laugh, after another round of birthday wishes and congratulations on my freedom, the boys scattered off to their classes. Dylan waited while I got my books and walked with me to class. I waited nervously for her to comment on her brother's behavior.

"I think I had a mini-heart attack when Tate winked at me."

"Wait." I stopped walking, not caring that people had to go around us. "I thought you were over the crush. Moving on. You met some guy on the cruise."

"I was. I am. I did. I don't know what's going on. Just when I think I'm over it, over him, he gives me attention for like point two seconds and my heart is all, 'well, hello there.' And it starts all over again."

"Really?" I wrinkled my nose, trying to hide the worry in my gut. She could crush on him all she wanted, but that wouldn't change a thing. "Hey, if you still like him, more power you."

"It doesn't matter how incredibly stupid he is. Or how big of a player he is. He's so damn cute. You can't dictate what your heart wants. My heart wants him, even though my brain is totally against it."

I nodded as the words hit hard. I wanted to tell her I understood because my heart wanted her brother. I hated keeping things from her. I missed sharing all my secrets with my best friend.

"Well, the heart wants what the heart wants." We started walking again.

"Speaking of boys, how'd things go with Dean?"

I paused, panicked for a moment, my mind blank. "What?"

She gave me an odd look. "At lunch. Did he listen?"

Relief washed over me. I'd totally forgotten I hadn't had a chance to talk to her without him around. "He basically told me that he isn't a moron and can date anyone he wants."

"Of course he did." She sighed. "I'll try this weekend. What are you doing tonight, birthday girl? I can't believe we don't have plans. Ugh," she groaned. "You're the one who got grounded, but it was really me who got punished. Want to come over and finally catch up? My parents are going to Dean's show. I can bail. I've already seen it three times. We'll order pizza and eat our weight in Oreos while we trash boys because there are no such things as carbs on your birthday."

"I wish I could. My dad's parents are here for the weekend, and we're doing something with them. Pizza with you sounds a thousand times better." I smiled. "Hey, has anyone said anything about Sunday? Or do you think they forgot?"

The Sunday after a birthday, it didn't matter if it was an adult or a child, the Cullens, Griffins, my family, and in recent years, the Eastmans—if they were home—gathered for a barbeque and cake. Usually, we all talked about it for weeks before, planning the food and what games we'd play. It was odd that no one had mentioned it. Although, I had been in solitary confinement, so maybe I'd just missed it.

"No." She gave me a small, sad smile. "I assumed your parents said no because you were grounded."

"Right."

When we reached Dylan's class, she gave me a hug. "I'm so glad you're free. I'll see you at lunch, birthday girl."

I hadn't told anyone other than Dean that I was going to Saturday's show. Normally I'd feel guilty about that, in case someone else had wanted to go too. As I walked into the theater and handed over my ticket, I didn't have an ounce of shame. I was doing this for me, and if people didn't like it, they could suck an egg.

Usually, I went on opening night with our families, then a few more times during the show's run. Knowing I only got to see it once this year meant I didn't want to miss a single second. Friends were distractions I couldn't risk.

My seat was five rows back, center stage, right between a retired couple who was hard of hearing and a group of four early-middle-aged women out for girls' night. It was perfect, just far enough so Dean couldn't see me—if and when the houselights illuminated the audience —but close enough for me to be completely immersed in the story. Plus, being alone in the middle of two groups allowed me anonymity and let me hide if I saw people I knew. I'd only had to explain to the ticket agent that I was Dylan's best friend and she hooked me up.

I didn't move a muscle for the entire first half. I wasn't even sure I breathed. I sat, transfixed by the raw talent that oozed from the boy I adored. I was biased of course, yet even if I hadn't been, I would've raved about Dean's performance to anyone who would listen.

He'd owned the audience. It wasn't just good character development or witty dialogue. I smiled when his character was happy, cried with him, and was heartbroken when he died at the end.

I wasn't the only one who was enamored with the young star. There wasn't a dry eye in the house as his character did the unthinkable and ended his own life. The way his mother clung to him, telling him it was okay, that he could let go, and her heartbroken sobs when she realized he was never coming back, cut me in two. The woman next to me grabbed my hand not long after the second act started and didn't let go until the curtain fell. The performances were that powerful.

The actors were always brilliant, the sets and costumes eloquently designed, the lighting flawless. Yet something had happened between the last spring performance and this one. The bar had been raised, and every single member of the theater had not only met this new expectation, they'd exceeded it.

We gave the much deserving cast a standing ovation. When Dean had his solo bow, the entire theater roared so loudly I was surprised the roof didn't collapse. The women on my left swooned as if he weren't half their age and they didn't have spouses or kids at home. He laughed, accepted the roses someone placed in his arms, and waved to the audience before joining his castmates once again.

I sat in my seat for a moment after the houselights came on, waiting as the masses filed from the building and couldn't help but overhear the various conversations going on around me. Some were discussing the intricate plot and the surprise twist at the end. Others talked about the cast and crew. More than one mentioned Dean, his unbelievable talent, and many wondered when he'd leave our little community theater behind for bigger productions in Boston.

The thought had never crossed my mind.

Of course, I knew he'd leave one day. Go off to college, get discovered in some university production, and become a household name. In my mind, though, we had years before that happened.

The harsh reality was that we didn't. He only had one more year of high school left. One year before he went off into the world and left us all behind.

It wasn't just the image of a clock counting down that made my stomach churn. It was my line of thought. He wasn't leaving *me* behind; he was going in search of himself. That was a good thing.

Before I had a chance to stand with everyone else, an older man walked down the row and sat next to me. "Lennon, darling." He greeted with a warm smile and a kiss on each cheek.

"Randy G. Your work was beautiful. You outdid yourself. As always."

He beamed. "Please. I'm not a betting man, but if I was, I'd wager you didn't take your eyes of our Mr. Cullen all night. That boy doesn't need any help to look good." He slid closer as he lowered his voice. "I heard a little rumor that our leading man had been snatched off the market. Then I heard your name being tossed around and everything clicked into place. It's about damn time, don't you think?" Before I could answer, someone else caught his eye, and he wiggled a hello with his fingers in the air. Suddenly, he grabbed my hands in his. "You're coming tonight, right?"

I nodded. "That's the plan."

"Good. I'll see you there." He leaned in close and whispered in my ear. "He's waiting for you in his dressing room. Fourth door on the right." Another set of kisses on my cheeks and he was gone like the whirlwind he reminded me of.

I picked my way through the remaining crowd, keeping my head down in case I saw a familiar face. When I hit the hall that led out back, I hesitated. There wasn't a security guard there to check for credentials or tell me I wasn't allowed backstage like there normally was. It threw me off.

Taking a deep breath, I hurried in, searching for Dean's dressing room. As soon as I knocked, the door flew open. A blur grabbed my wrist and tugged me inside. Before I could even let out a surprised squeal, my back was against the wall, and a shirtless Dean stood close, arms on either side, blocking me in.

"You were—" I started, ready to tell him how impressed I was, but he interrupted.

"Later." His finger covered my lips, silencing me, as he stared at me the way a man in the desert eyes a cold glass of water. "Right now, I'm alone with my girl for the first time in what feels like centuries." Both hands moved to my face and cupped my jaw as he tipped my head back. "I need to kiss her more than I need air."

His breath tickled me as he leaned down in slow motion, teasing me, eyes never leaving mine. I could see right through his cocky, self-assured behavior, right down to a boy who seemed worried, apprehensive almost. He'd been drunk the night I'd first kissed him, so he might not remember all the details, but Lord knew we'd gotten some great practice runs in since then.

His lips touched the corner of mine gently, no more than a whisper. They were gone the next second as the tip of his nose circled mine. My teeth sunk into my bottom lip in anticipation as I fought a smile and forced my eyes to stay open. He smelled so damn good, it made my head foggy and my heart pound.

I wanted more. Tucking my fingers into the front pockets of his jeans, I pulled him toward me. He chuckled as my teeth closed around his bottom lip.

"Greedy little thing," he mumbled as soon as it was free. His hands slid upward, clutching the back of my head, holding me still and moved so close that every breath was shared. He hesitated, right before his lips touched mine, as if waiting for me to make the call.

Easiest decision I'd ever made.

Every time we kissed, I lost myself in him so easily I knew that it was only a matter of time before I was completely swept away in all that was Dean Cullen. I wouldn't even try to fight the current. I'd just let it take me and hope I didn't drown.

He didn't hurry. There was no urgency. Instead, his lips moved almost lazily. Slow and steady, as if he had a lifetime to waste doing nothing but kissing me.

Time in his arms was nothing short of perfection. I saw stars, felt like my heart was going to explode from my chest, and longed for more as I prayed the moment would last forever. If I had to choose how I got to spend my last hours on Earth, it would be right there, wrapped up in Dean's arms.

Chapter Nineteen

Dean

Someone knocked on the door, but I ignored it. It was either a castmate wondering if I'd left for the party already or a member of the crew checking to see if I'd cleaned out the room. Castmates could see me when I got there. The crew didn't need to start breaking down the theater until Monday, so they could chill.

I'd waited what felt like a lifetime to have Len in my arms again, and there was no way in hell I was going to stop until she told me to. When she tightened her grip around my neck and she stepped into me, I knew she felt the same.

"Dean, honey, are you still here?"

My mother's voice, followed by another loud knock was more effective than being submerged in a tub of ice water ever could be. Len's arms fell the same time I backed away. Our moment was gone, lost. I made a silent vow to get it back as soon as I could.

I hadn't known my mom was going to be at the last show. I certainly hadn't expected her to bombard me backstage. She never had before.

I grabbed Lennon's hand to get her attention and held a finger to my mouth, silently begging her to be quiet. Maybe if my mom thought I was gone, she'd leave. Len nodded in understanding.

"Nilo said he's back here. Try again."

I closed my eyes as my dad's words seeped through the door. *Shit.* Both parents.

The night just got better and better.

Desperate to protect her from their unwanted attention, I pointed at Len and then slid my finger through the air in the direction of the small, attached bathroom, before poking my thumb into my chest and pointing to the door. Len narrowed her eyes as if to tell me she hated my plan and shook her head.

"I'm not hiding in your bathroom," she hissed.

Another knock and a jiggle of the handle—thank God I'd locked it —had me switching the plan. "Fine. I'll go in there. You answer the door, tell them I've been in there for a while."

With a frustrated shake of her head and a roll of her eyes, she sighed almost silently. "Seriously? They'll ask why I didn't answer the door."

I put my palms together, begging, eyes wide.

With a roll of her eyes, she nodded and shooed me on my way with her fingertips, agitation clear. Fighting a smile, I leaned in and stole a kiss quickly before running to the bathroom on tiptoes and closing the door as quietly as I could behind me.

I turned on the faucet so they'd hear water and pressed my ear against the door just as Len let my parents into the dressing room.

"Lennon?" Mom's surprise was clear. "I didn't know you were going to be here tonight."

Before Len could answer, my dad weighed in. "Len? Is that really you? It's been so long." His teasing laugh annoyed me. "Finally made parole, huh?"

Her response was muffled. If I knew my dad, he'd probably hugged her. Jealousy hit me with a force I hadn't expected. It was my dad, not some asshole trying to hit on my girl. The thought was obnoxious, yet the idea of her in anyone else's arms, even his, drove me crazy.

I groaned and splashed water on my face before I hurried out to rescue her. I stopped short when I saw my dad's arms still resting on her shoulders.

"What's going on?" The question came out gruff.

Len's eyebrows shot up, then furrowed. She'd definitely picked up on it but clearly couldn't understand why I'd gone from happy to infuriated.

"Dean," my mom rushed across the small space and put her hands on my shoulders. "You were..." She paused and glanced toward my dad before beaming at me. "Well, I don't even have the words to describe how fantastic your performance was. I'm in awe of your talent." She hugged me. "We're so proud of you."

I hugged her back. When I stepped back and saw tears in her eyes, I didn't know what to say. The play had been tear-worthy, yes, but my performance hadn't been *that* good.

Dad clapped me on the shoulder. "We're extremely proud, son. You killed it."

I stared at him for a moment, looking for any hint that he wasn't sincere. There wasn't one. I waited for the other shoe to drop, the "but" that typically followed his praise of my acting ability, yet it didn't come. Maybe it was because Lennon was there. Maybe it was because I'd gotten invited to the acting workshop over the summer. Whatever the reason, it made me uncomfortable.

"Thank God you're here," I nodded in Len's direction, "I didn't record any of that, but you can be my witness. They really did say something nice about my acting."

Mom's smile turned to a frown. "Don't be a jackass. Did you watch the play, Lennon? I didn't see you out there."

Lennon nodded. "I did. Dean's best performance yet."

"I wish I'd known you were coming. You could've had Dylan's ticket. She didn't want to come because she's seen it so many times. Last night we invited everyone we knew and practically filled the theater."

It was a gross exaggeration. Yes, my extended family had come to surprise me, but they hadn't made a dent in the three-hundred-and-fifty-seat theater. Even with all of them sitting together, they'd barely filled three rows on house left.

"We thought you all might join us, but your mom said you had company in town."

Len nodded. "Yeah. My dad's parents came up for my birthday. The four of them went to the city tonight. I just assumed you'd be with them."

Mom's frown deepened as Lennon spoke. "You're here alone?"

Len cleared her throat. "Yep. I didn't want to miss it, and since everyone else had already seen it, I got a ticket. Last-minute thing. Didn't even tell Dylan. Just in case something happened and I couldn't come."

"Got out of the crowbar hotel just in time, huh?"

"Dad," I groaned. He made no sense. "She was grounded. Not in jail. Enough with the jokes. They're not funny."

Lennon, on the other hand, laughed up at him. "By the skin of my teeth. There were some dark, depressing times where I wasn't sure I'd ever see the light of day again. I never let myself imagine a life outside, just in case I didn't make it through. The thought of never seeing your son again was just too much for me. And here I am, free at last."

"Okay, smartass. And you say I'm dramatic." I turned to Mom. "I'm glad you came. Everything really came together tonight. But what are you guys doing back here?"

"I could ask you the same thing," Mom shrugged. "You had fans out front, waiting to meet you." She reached up to play with her earing and I knew we were in trouble. "What took you so long to answer the door?"

And there it was. The question I had no doubt she'd been dying to ask since Len opened the damn thing. Mom had been overly curious ever since Aunt Gayle and Uncle Trev admitted that Len was grounded. She'd also been overly skeptical about my self-professed lack of knowledge as to why perfect little Lennon had gotten in trouble. Now that she'd found us together, without Dylan, I could practically see her wheels turning as she tried to piece it all together.

"I was washing this," I pointed at my face, thankful I'd scrubbed the layers and layers of stage makeup off before Len had joined me. "I didn't really want to leave the theater looking like a pirate in drag."

"I don't know why. Anything would be an improvement to what you've got goin' on there." Len tried to fight her smirk and lost.

"Oh, yeah? You like my face, brat. That's why you stare at it so much."

She snorted. "You are so full of yourself. If I stare at you, it's because I'm waiting for you to say something intelligent."

I stepped closer to her, devouring her smart mouth with my eyes. "Oh, little girl, you can pretend you don't hang on every single word I say, but we both know that's a lie."

She cocked an eyebrow. "It's cute you think that. Really."

I couldn't take my eyes off her. If we'd been alone, I'd have pulled her into my arms and spent the night kissing the snark out of her. Before I could attempt a somewhat intelligent response, my dad cleared his throat.

"Okay. I hate to break up this little..." one eyebrow rose as he gave me a hard look, "whatever the hell this is. Actually, that's a lie. I don't hate to break this up. I have no idea what's going on and it's awkward as hell." He chuckled. "You have a party to get to, and we need to get going. Len, want a ride home?"

"I've got her."

Three sets of eyes landed on me, but it was Mom who spoke first. "Don't you have the cast party? It's on the other side of town. You're already late. We can take her to save you time."

I turned to Lennon. She met my stare. We still hadn't talked about how we were going to tell everyone, or what we were going to tell them. My parents weren't dumb. The tension in the room was so thick we could cut it with a knife. They could probably smell the pheromones. If they hadn't figured it out yet, they weren't far from connecting the dots.

With a subtle nod of her head, Len gave me the permission I needed. I reached for her hand, knotting my fingers through hers. "Len's coming with me."

"Oh." My mom froze, her mouth slightly open, eyebrows high. She spun towards my dad.

Dad nodded, not surprised in the least, as if he'd been in on the little secret from the beginning. "Do your parents know where you are,

Lennon?" He held up a finger when I started to object and spoke directly to her. "They're our best friends. I love you like a daughter, but if they expect you home after the play, I'm taking you home."

"They know."

"Hmm." He tipped his head slightly, watching us. "You were grounded for quite a while. It surprised me actually, considering you've always been our angel. Your parents wouldn't say much, just that you'd gotten into some trouble. Whatever you did must have been big."

Well, shit. I hadn't told them. Instead, I'd plead ignorance even though I was pretty sure neither believed my act. Uncle Trev had left it up to me to tell them about my part in all of it, and I planned to do that, there just hadn't been time.

Len chewed her lip the entire time he spoke, digesting every word. "It was. I learned my lesson. It won't happen again."

He looked at me. "Make sure she's home before curfew."

"Of course." I wasn't an idiot. I wasn't going to risk her getting into trouble again, not when I'd just gotten her back.

He put his hand on Mom's back, as if to usher her out of the room, but she didn't budge. Her face pinched in concern. I'd rarely gotten the look from her because she'd always trusted me. Even when Vicky and I started having sex, Mom hadn't been overly dramatic or worried. She'd made sure I had condoms, told me to be safe, and explained that I could call her anytime, tell her anything.

"This is really happening? You're not being a shit right now?"

My answer was to tug Lennon closer to me and step in front of her slightly, almost as if I were trying to block her from whatever my mother might say. "Yeah, this is really happening."

She turned to my dad again. "Did you see this coming? 'Cause I definitely didn't."

He shook his head. "Never. I thought Lennon was smarter than that. Clearly, we've overestimated her."

Mom nodded. "Do you think it's serious or a fling? He is easy on the eyes. Len may have gotten swept away in the Dean Cullen craze that seems to hit this town about this time every year."

"Dean Cullen craze?" I asked with a mock laugh, both embarrassed and astonished.

They ignored me.

Dad lifted a shoulder as his eyes narrowed on my hand, still holding Lennon's. "Well, honey, I think we need to remember it was serious enough that she got grounded."

"Oh, that's a good point. I wonder what happened. And why Gayle and Trevor didn't tell us."

"My guess is that our son was supposed to fill in the gaps."

I lifted my free hand. "We can hear you."

Dad's eyes shot from me to my mom, his face skeptical, almost worried. "I thought he outgrew the belief that we could communicate telepathically two or three years ago."

Lennon snickered behind me, finding humor in a situation that wasn't funny in the least. The two of them always seemed to know what the other was going to say, so of course, I'd believed it as a little kid, ten years before. Not two. *Jackass.*

"Of course, you can hear us, darling. We wouldn't ever say anything about you that we couldn't say to you." She glanced at my dad. "You know what this means, don't you?"

"If he's with Lennon, he's not really dating Chelsea."

Mom nodded, a smile tickling her mouth. "He's not dating Chelsea."

Oh, good Lord. That's what they'd been worried about? I dropped my free hand helplessly, letting it slap my leg.

"Does your sister know?"

My fingers tightened around Lennon's. "Not yet."

Mom's face puckered like it did when she ate something sour. "Oh, that's a bad call, you two. A really bad call." She shook her head for emphasis.

"She's right. You shouldn't have told us before you told Dylan. That was bad planning. Things could get messy."

"Well, considering I hadn't planned on telling the two of you, I'd say this entire thing is a giant fucking disaster."

Mom crossed her arms. "Language, jackass. You can't swear like that around your girlfriend."

Dad shook his head. "You kiss your girlfriend with that mouth?"

Fuck, me.

"The four of us should sit down and chat. Establish some rules." Mom tipped her head to see Lennon better. "What do you think?"

I shook my head. Lennon and I weren't ready for the sex-ed talk yet. We weren't there, and if it went anything like the talk with Vicky, Len would run for the hills before I could beg her to stay.

"I think that's a good idea," Dad answered for us. "Tomorrow afternoon. Lennon, you can come over for an early lunch. I mean, unless you want to join us for our reservation tonight."

"Nope," my voice broke, giving them a knowing look. "Tomorrow works. But I thought we had plans."

"We can do that after our company leaves," My mom smiled smugly. "Looking forward to it."

Fantastic. I rolled my eyes. Just fucking great.

"Perfect. It's a date." Dad reached for the doorknob, ready to go now that he'd ruined my weekend plans. "Dean, you did a great job. Lennon, I'm glad you're finally free and hope to see more of you."

"Have fun tonight. Drive safe. We'll see you both tomorrow?"

"Yeah." It wasn't like we had a choice.

Mom leaned forward, kissed me on the forehead, hugged Len, and they left as quickly as they'd arrived, with much less stress and fanfare.

I shut the door behind them, relieved. "I'm so sorry."

Lennon started to laugh. "That was random. And terrifying. Yet oddly hilarious."

"They should be comedians." My hands found her hips and I pulled her toward me. "You're a saint."

"I adore your parents. They're cute." She lifted her hand and brushed some hair off my forehead. "It wasn't *that* bad. There was no yelling. No one forbid it."

I chuckled. "We're not the Montagues and Capulets, Len. I'm not Tony, and you're not Maria. Our families don't hate each other. We don't belong to rival gangs. No one is going to forbid us to be together."

"You sure about that? Nothing is ever this easy, Dean. Our parents are being overly calm about this entire thing. And we still have to tell your sister."

I wasn't certain at all. Something felt off. Instead of telling her that and freaking her out even more, I held her chin between my thumb and forefinger and kissed her.

I woke up before my alarm, smiling. I grabbed my phone and sent a good morning text to my little fairy, surprised when there was no immediate response. Len was typically an early riser, but I had kept her out late the night before, then up half the night talking on the phone.

Her parents said I had to have her home by curfew; they never said we had to stop talking after she was tucked safely into bed.

Dylan was in the kitchen. "You're up bright and early for someone out so late last night. And how do you look so good after a night of drinking?"

I grabbed a mug and filled it with coffee. "Easy. I didn't drink."

"Bullshit. It was the cast party. You always drink."

I shook my head. "Not this time."

"Who's the girl?"

I ignored the question as I sat at the table. "Need help?"

"Don't deflect. The only reason you wouldn't drink is if you were trying to impress someone. Who is it?"

"Good morning," Mom called as she joined us. "I thought you'd sleep in a little."

"I wanted to help. You only turn sixteen once."

"Technically, she turned sixteen on Friday. But you're right. You only get one party." Dylan lifted the knife in my direction as she smiled smugly at our mom. "Dean has a new girl."

Mom gave me a pointed look I saw right through. I didn't give two shits what she thought. I wasn't telling Dylan right before Len's surprise party. "Oh? Does that mean that Chelsea isn't coming today?"

"Oh em gee. If you invited Chelsea, I will kill you. This is Lennon's day, and you know they hate each other."

Mom seemed entirely too interested. "I didn't know they didn't get along. They're fine when they're here."

Dylan snorted. "Yeah. Because Dean intervenes. If he didn't, they'd tear each other to shreds. Chelsea thinks she's tough and runs her mouth, but Lover Boy always jumps in before Len can retaliate. My girl has sharp claws too, ya know. You should let her use them."

"More like a sharp tongue," I muttered. "I do it for Len, not Chelsea. Just because Lennon can hold her own doesn't mean she should have to."

"We're not babies anymore. You don't have to protect us."

"You're my sister. I'll always protect you."

"Yeah, but Len isn't. At some point, you need to come to terms with that fact."

"I think your brother knows that he only has one sister," Mom intervened with a sigh. "Speaking of the birthday girl, do you think she suspects anything?"

I shook my head. Len was convinced everyone had forgotten her birthday because she'd been grounded. Her parents had given her a gift card to her favorite store, but that was the only gift she'd gotten.

"No," Dylan agreed, "not a thing."

"Your dad and I didn't even wish her a happy birthday when we saw her last night. It felt awful. He almost slipped more than once."

"You saw Len last night?"

Mom's eyes drifted from Dylan to me briefly. She wouldn't lie, not even to protect me. "We did. At Dean's play."

Dylan pouted. "She didn't tell me she was going or I would have met her there."

"It was all last minute, honey."

"Oh, maybe her parents got her a ticket for her birthday. She really didn't want to miss it." Dylan rolled her eyes playfully. "It's like she actually enjoys watching this idiot act."

Mom gave me a long look. "Yeah, maybe." Moving a bag of carrots in front of me, she handed me a knife. "We have a lot of people invading in just a few hours. Get busy, mister."

Dylan and I chopped veggies and cheese until Tate showed up, then my mom put us to work setting up the back yard. Typically, we always got together to celebrate the Sunday after a birthday, but this year was special. Sixteen was apparently a big deal.

Dylan's sweet sixteen had been insane. It was like a wedding without a groom. She'd had two dresses, one for cocktail hour and a giant, puffy ballgown for the reception. She'd had her makeup and hair done. All sixteen girls in her court dressed to perfection to match their queen, and the entire world had focused on her for a day. She'd been in heaven.

I didn't want to think about how much that party—in a ballroom at the trendiest hotel in the city—had cost my parents, but my sister had danced the night away, a giant smile on her face, so they'd claimed it was worth every penny.

I was relieved we didn't have to do it all over again for Lennon. The tux I'd been forced to wear was a pain in the ass, but it was nothing compared to the way my sister's friends stared at me all day long, whispering whenever I was near. I'd felt objectified and gross.

Of course, Len had laughed when I'd told her that. *"I can't imagine what it must feel like to be treated as a mere object simply because of how you look in an article of clothing."* She curled her lips and tugged on my lapels. *"Better get used to it. If you get your way, you'll be objectified on a daily basis by women all over the world."*

How had I not realized then how I felt about her? While Dylan's friends had been watching me, I'd only had eyes for Lennon. I might have been there with Vicky, but I'd spent most of the party with Len.

I sighed as I helped Tate hang a string of big bulbed lights.

Since Len hated attention and had been clear that she didn't want a big fuss for her birthday, Dylan decided to make one for her. Today's party had been in the works for months.

"Dean, you almost done?"

I nodded at my dad before I glanced over my shoulder at the rest of the yard, trying to figure out what else needed to be done. "For a minute. What's up?"

"Come to my office when you get a chance." He disappeared before I could protest.

Tate gave me a knowing look. Going to my dad's office almost always spelled certain doom. "What'd you do now?"

I chewed on the inside of my cheek. "Len."

"The fuck?" He dropped the chair he'd been carrying and sent me a death glare. "Seriously?"

I almost laughed at my terrible choice of words, but I was too afraid he'd hit me. "No. That's not what I meant." I pinched the bridge of my nose. "They found Len with me backstage last night. We told them we'd been seeing each other. They acted fine, but it was too accepting, even for them."

"So, there is finally something to tell?"

For an asshole who hooked up with random chicks all the time, he seemed overly invested in labels. Especially the ones I put on my girl.

"It means she's still off limits."

He smirked. "You're such a pussy. Why not just fucking own it?"

"Because it's Lennon."

"Because what's Lennon?" Dylan asked, juggling balloons.

"The party." Tate covered for me. "Everything here is just so her."

"Right? It's absolutely perfect. I can't wait to see her face. She's going to be so surprised."

"Doesn't Len hate surprises?"

Dylan shook her head. "That's just what she says. No one really hates surprises."

Tate and I shared a long look. My sister was absolutely clueless sometimes. "I'm gonna go find out what Dad wants."

He was in his office, working. On a Sunday. Typical, really.

He and my mom would go out Saturday night, then, if they managed to make it home before lunch, he'd spend most of the next day working. I'd watched him do it, week after week, year after year, only stopping when my mom made him. I'd vowed that whatever job I had when I grew up, I'd reserve Sundays for my family.

I could almost picture it now. Len would have a crazy schedule as a reporter, so we'd have to figure out which day worked best. It didn't matter the day, really, as long as one day a week we put away our computers and phones and focused on just us and our kids.

I knocked lightly.

"Close the door."

"Uh oh. It's never good when I have to close the door," I joked and did what he asked, dropping into the chair opposite him. "This could be about a few different things. Before I die from a panic attack, can you just yell at me and let me go enjoy Len's party?"

He frowned. "I wasn't going to yell at you. Although now I'm wondering what you've done that I need to be pissed about. Anything you want to get off your chest?"

"Like?"

"The reason Lennon was grounded."

I swallowed. "How much did Uncle Trev share?"

"Jesus, Dean." He ran a hand through his hair. "He hasn't told me anything yet. He's been avoiding me. Now I know why. What did you do?"

"Me?" I narrowed my eyes on him. "There are two of us, Dad. Lennon was there too."

He swore. "How long have you been sleeping with her? She's only fifteen, Dean."

"Sixteen." My fingertips dug into my palms. "That's the first thing you think of? I called this, by the way. I knew as soon as you found out that you'd freak. Mom would want to talk about safe sex, sit us down and have a conversation about being open and honest, all kumbaya. But you'd be pissed about it."

"You done?"

I rolled my eyes and crossed my arms in answer.

"How long, Dean? Was alcohol was involved?"

"Len doesn't drink. And we haven't slept together." I sat back, a smug smile on my lips at his confused double take. Screw him and his assumptions. "Not that it's any of your business."

"Why was she grounded?"

"Uncle Trev caught me sneaking in her window on his security footage." I pointed at his computer. "If you check yours, you'll find her here when she wasn't supposed to be."

"You snuck in her window? She's on the second floor."

"I've been going to Len's room via the window since I was ten."

He seemed shaken by the news. Horrified, really. Clearly they hadn't paid much attention to the stupid security footage before.

"We're not having sex," I told him again. I hated that I felt I had to tell him, to share moments of my time with her. "It's not like that. I love her."

He rubbed his forehead as if it were the worst news he'd ever heard. His face was tight, his expression almost sad. Dude acted like I just killed his puppy.

"How can you be upset? It's Lennon, Dad. If things work out, she'd be your daughter."

He shook his head sadly. "That will never happen."

"You don't know that."

"I do."

I fought the agitation that creeped over my skin and held me captive like a net. "What bugs you the most? The thought that she's slumming with me or the idea that I may have tainted her?"

Anger washed over his face. "Your glowing opinion of me never ceases to amaze. I'm not the one upset, Dean. I think you'd make a perfect couple if things were different."

I wasn't following. "If you mean Uncle Trev and Aunt Gayle, they aren't upset. If what things were different?"

"Did the two of you ever stop to think about what will happen when you break up?"

"No. Because in this century, we don't envision something great ending before it's even begun. It doesn't matter anyway, because it's not going to end."

The doorbell rang, and laughter filled the hall. He leaned back in his chair, eyes on the door. "You know what? Len will be here any minute. We'll talk later, after the party."

"Aren't Len and I supposed to sit and talk to you and Mom soon?"

He shook his head. "That's why I called you in. Your mom and I were caught off guard last night, finding the two of you together. When I suggested us talking, I wasn't thinking. To be honest, I'd forgotten about the party. We need to sit together later this week. And have Gayle and Trevor to join us." The doorbell rang again. "Go. Before Lennon gets here. I've got to finish this before the party starts."

I left because I wanted to see Lennon arrive. But his words bothered me for hours.

Chapter Twenty

Lennon

"Please, please, please come over," Dylan begged on the other end of the line. "I need your help before this afternoon."

I was so tired all I wanted to do was close my eyes and go back to sleep, but I hadn't spent time with my best friend in weeks, and I didn't want to disappoint her. Deep down, I worried about what would happen when Dean and I told her later.

"Fine," I sighed. "Will there at least be coffee?"

"I can arrange that. Oh! Don't wear pajamas."

"Why? It's Sunday."

"Yeah, I know. Tons of family came in to see Dean's play and some are going to stop by before they head home. You know how conservative my family is."

"How does that have anything to do with me wearing my PJs?"

She scoffed. "Please. They already make snide comments about the way we dress. Dean and Tate are here. If you come over without a bra, they'll be scandalized, and we'll never hear the end of what a bad influence you are."

"Your family loves me."

"They won't when they see you dressed like a charlatan."

"Uh, no. A charlatan," I paused and shook my head. I didn't have it in me to explain what a charlatan actually was, or how I definitely wouldn't be dressed like one. "Fine. I'll get dressed and be over in a few. Can you make me coffee? Please?"

My parents were nowhere to be found when I made my way downstairs a few minutes later. I sent my mom a text to tell her I'd be at Dylan's, fired off a quick message to Dean to tell him I'd be coming over earlier than planned, and headed across the street. It felt weird, taking the first step up onto their stoop, almost like I was doing something wrong. I half-expected my dad to come running after me.

I didn't bother knocking. I'd been walking in without invitation most of my life and didn't think anything of it. As I turned the knob, I closed my eyes and said a little prayer that Dylan had actually started coffee.

"Surprise!"

Someone blew a noisemaker.

It took me longer to understand what was happening than it normally would because not only was I exhausted, I was in the wrong house. Confused, I glanced behind me, certain I'd see someone else there.

"Happy birthday, lil' miss."

I'd recognize that voice anywhere, even without the nickname attached. I forced myself to take a deep breath and relax, knowing that if Shaun was there, so were the other two that made up their own merry band of musketeers. Before I could lay eyes on them, Dylan pushed her way through the small crowd of our friends and family and grabbed my hand. "Were you surprised?"

"That's not even the word I'd use," I assured her, forcing a smile.

Her face lit in pride. "Come on. You need to see out back."

I barely had a chance to wave in Dean's direction as his sister hauled me through the house behind her.

. . .

I t felt like hours later when he stepped up beside me at the snack table. I was pretending to weigh my options when, in reality, I was simply agitated by the lack of coffee and attempting to get a moment to myself. He stepped so close there was only a hair's width between us, and after a quick glance to make sure we were alone, the back of his hand caressed mine.

"Having fun?"

"So much," I nodded, eyes wide. "I mean, it's not quite as fun as having to pee while you're stuck in the middle lane of the highway during a traffic jam on your way to present a group project when half the members didn't contribute, but it is better than folding a fitted sheet or sweating, so there's that."

Dean raised a single brow. "That's oddly specific."

"Eh," I shrugged. "I'm a girl who knows how to have a good time."

"Doesn't sound like it. Thankfully, you have me now. And I know how to have a very, very good time." He chuckled as a blush creeped its way up my cheeks. "Sorry. I should have warned you."

"Why didn't you?"

"A few months ago, I explained this wasn't a good idea. Especially since you explicitly said you didn't want a party. Dylan told me to back off because I didn't know you as well as she did."

"I'd laugh at that if I weren't so miserable. You still could have told me."

"It was important to my sister, Len. I didn't want to take that away, especially since I've already got you."

Sometimes I hated how logical he was because it was hard for me to be mad at him when he made sense.

"Come on, it's not that bad," he attempted. He looked around the decorated backyard before finally settling his gaze on me again. "At least the music's good."

I pinched my lips together as I nodded. "Thanks." I bumped his shoulder with mine. "It's my playlist."

He snorted. "I know."

"Any chance I can convince you to rescue me?"

He met my stare. "Absolutely. If you really wanna go."

I sighed. "Your parents said they wanted to talk, so we can't."

"Yeah, that's not happening today."

"Because of the party?"

It made sense. Their house was full, with not just my friends, but people we all knew. It would be hours before everyone cleared out, and by that time, we'd all be too tired to deal with it.

"No. I'll fill you in later. Let's go before someone else spots you. Do you need to say goodbye, or can we sneak out?"

"Is that a trick question?" I snorted. "I've got to thank Dylan, then find my mom. I'll meet you out front in five?"

He nodded as he walked away.

I couldn't find Dylan anywhere. No one I asked had seen her, which was extremely weird and unlike her. I'd expected to find her enjoying being the center of attention, letting us gush over all her hard work.

Mom, on the other hand, was easy. She and Aunt Tasha were with the other adults, lounging on a chaise around a makeshift horseshoe pit, drinks in hand, as they cheered on my dad and Uncle Chad. I stood, watching for a moment as they laughed and gossiped. At least someone was enjoying the night.

Mom spotted me first. "There's the birthday girl," she smiled and reached out a hand. "Having fun?"

Before I could answer, Uncle Chad joined us. "She doesn't look like it."

Dad crossed his arms over his chest. "What's wrong, Lenny?"

I rubbed my hands on my thighs. "I'm just tired." I lifted a thumb toward the road. "So, I'm gonna go."

The four exchanged glances. Some filled with worry, others conspiratorial. Awkward silence didn't begin to describe the quiet that settled around us.

"Okay." My dad threw an arm around my shoulders and tucked me into his side. "Sixteen, huh? When did that happen?"

"When we weren't looking. Yesterday we had three kids in diapers, running around the back yard naked. The day before that we were in college."

"Just be thankful their running around naked days are behind them," Mrs. Eastman said with a laugh. "I can't say that for Shaun."

I'd been wrong before. A heavier, truly uncomfortable, and incredibly awkward silence hit as Aunt Tash gave my mother a horrified look, and Uncle Chad bit his lip and stared at the ground. The only one who didn't react was my dad.

"I'm going to walk Lenny out." He pointed at his friends. "No cheating."

Before anyone could comment, he turned us toward the back of the house. "I need to say goodbye to Dylan."

His head swiveled as he looked for her. "Do you know where she is?"

"No, actually. I thought I'd look inside."

He stopped at the deck steps. "Are you and Dean going out or home?"

I didn't ask how he knew. "I'm not sure."

"Phone on. Door open, if you're home. It's a school night, so be back early." He pushed a kiss to my temple. "Have fun." He started to move away when he stopped suddenly. "Oh, this is yours."

I took the envelope he offered almost cautiously. "What is it?"

"A present. People exchange them on holidays, anniversaries, and birthdays."

My parents had already given me a gift, but I didn't argue. Instead, I ripped open the flap and pulled a small piece of cardstock from inside.

"It's a gift certificate to a clean and reputable body piercer. Their reviews are impeccable. Make the appointment for this summer, and I'll take you to have your nose done."

My mouth fell open as I stared at the gift in my hands. "Are you serious?"

"It's just a small hole, right? If you don't like it, you can take it out, and it'll heal."

I turned, eyeing him cautiously. "Who are you, and what did you do with my dad?"

Thankfully, he smiled. "I'm just a dad, standing in front of his daughter, asking her to stop growing up so damn fast."

My lips twitched. "*Notting Hill*, really?"

"Your mother made me watch it twice the other night after you went to bed."

I groaned in sympathy for him. "Ugh. Not again."

"Yeah. I almost said 'whoopsie daisies,' when I missed a shot earlier."

I snorted at the thought of my rough, rugged dad repeating words he'd heard from my mom's favorite British romcom. "I need to tell Dean that one. He'll die."

"No need," Dad smiled. "Something tells me he heard the whole conversation."

I glanced over my shoulder to find the most handsome boy in the world leaning against his house, fingertips tucked into the pockets of his jeans, watching me with hooded eyes. I was caught in the moment, staring at him when Dad cleared his throat.

I spun back around and launched myself at him, "Thank you!" I didn't know what else to say, but I hoped he understood how much gratitude and emotion was in those two words.

"Night, you two." Dad ruffled my hair as he backed away.

"I feel like I'm in an alternate reality right now."

"We totally are. It's the only explanation. Either that, or the parentals are high." Dean's hand found the small of my back as soon as I stepped onto the porch. "Ready?"

"I need to go inside to find Dylan."

He jerked to an abrupt stop, his eyes narrowed on the back yard. "She's not out here?"

I followed his gaze, searching. "Not unless I missed her."

His frown deepened. "She's not inside, either."

"You sure?"

"Yeah. I was just in there, getting stuff for tonight."

I tugged my phone from my back pocket and typed a quick message. Where r u?

When she didn't read it right away, I fired off another. I'm going home. Thank you for the party! Love u!

I stalled as we made our way out front, hoping she'd see the messages and respond so I could hug her. After five minutes, I gave up.

"Where we going?"

"It's a surprise."

"Okay. I'm lost. Where are we?"

"You don't need to know where we are. All that matters is that I do."

Dean hadn't given away one single clue in the half hour we'd been in the car. When we'd gotten to the almost non-existent dirt road, I'd started to ask questions. After he'd parked in a rag-tag lot and grabbed a backpack from the trunk, I'd demanded answers. He'd only clutched my hand and started up a trail, a quick wink in my direction. Until now, he'd remained mum.

"Do you?" I panted, completely out of breath from the steep climb on the twisty path. "Or are we lost and you're trying to cover?"

He held a finger to his lips. "What do you hear?"

I paused, straining to hear anything other than crickets. Or maybe it was... "Tree frogs?"

He snorted. "Are you asking or telling?"

"I actually have no idea how to tell them apart."

"There's something you don't know? Stop the presses."

"Shut up." I smacked him playfully. "It's not something you learn in a book."

"Sure." He nodded in disbelief. "Try to drown 'em out. Hear what's under their song."

I closed my eyes, listening again. Disappointed, I opened them again a few minutes later. "I can't hear anything else other than a few birds."

"Exactly."

His eyes twinkled in the late afternoon sun. He took my hand, and we started walking again. "This is my favorite place."

"I would have assumed the stage was."

"I think everyone would guess that."

"Not the treehouse?"

"The treehouse is my happy place. The one that seems to be included in too many great childhood memories to count. It's too loud now. And I don't fit as well as I once did." I couldn't see his face, but I could hear the smile. "I come here when I need to run lines, to think, or to get away. This is my spot."

Just as he said the words, we stepped into a large clearing. He moved to the center of the field, pulled a blanket from the bag, and within moments had it laid out, a small pillow and a large thermos sitting on top. He dropped down and beckoned to me like it was second nature.

"Done that a few times, huh?" I teased.

"More than a few. I come here," he trailed off, "a lot. No one knows about it."

"No one?" I asked curiously, as I crawled into the middle with him.

"Nope. You're the first." He gripped my chin, but he didn't move in. "I can see those wheels turning, Len. Go ahead, ask me why."

I thought about not playing along, but I wanted to know, damn it. "Why?"

"Because you bring the quiet. You don't steal it."

I searched his face for signs of insincerity. There weren't any. "I don't know what that means."

"When I'm with you, the stress melts away. I don't worry about anything because it feels like everything will work out. I don't have to focus on tomorrow or wonder what's coming because I'm happy right here. When you're gone, the chaos and turmoil from everyone else invades my head, and sometimes it's just too much. When you're near me, I'm happy."

I understood because I felt it, too. On a much smaller scale, but Dean had always been intense.

I didn't wait for him to kiss me. I leaned forward and pushed my lips against his.

When we came up for air a few minutes later, I had to ask. "What about when I kiss you? Is it still quiet then?"

He laughed, a forced and uncomfortable sound. "No." His eyes never left my lips. "When you kiss me, every single inch of me catches on fire. Sometimes I worry that if I can't stop it, it'll consume you too. Then I realized, I think you're the only one who can put it out."

"You are such a drama king."

"Yeah? Well, you're a know-it-all. Shut up and kiss me." His fist closed around my shirt, and he pulled me down on top of him as he fell backward.

When the sun started to sink low in the sky, and a breeze made me shiver, Dean broke away and pressed a kiss to my forehead. "We should go."

"Mmm. I could stay here forever, lost in this moment with you."

He grinned against my temple. "I'd love that."

Needing to stretch the time with him, I laid my head on his chest and smiled when his arms automatically adjusted around me as if they belonged there. Fingers twirled in my hair, relaxing me almost instantly as I listened to his heart beat a steady rhythm. The birds sang, the tree-tops danced in a breeze, and the crickets chirped. If there were a heaven, I hoped it was just like this.

"Have you seen any reviews of the play?"

For someone who said he liked the quiet, he was awfully chatty when I was around. I nodded. "I've devoured every single one I could find. You?"

"Some of the early ones. I stopped paying attention after that. They were decent, I just didn't have the time to read them. It seems everyone agrees that Nilo earned every penny and then some."

"Nilo may have given you direction, helped, but the actors made that play the success it was. I don't know how you do it."

His fingertips traced patterns on my skin as he caressed my arm slowly. "We all worked our asses off for sure."

"So, what's next? Catch up on schoolwork and get ready for the summer program? Spend every spare second you can with me?" The last part was me teasing, but he didn't play along.

"About the workshop," he cleared his throat. "I'm not sure I'm going to go. It's gonna be rough. I have to surrender my phone when I get there. I get one call a week to my family. We work all seven days, whether it's rehearsing, learning the choreography, or building the set. It's like military school for drama geeks."

"Sounds miserable."

"Yeah. They're tough. They need to squeeze months of prep work into a few weeks. But Nilo says it's the best education I'll ever get. A connection builder. If I don't go, I may never get the chance again."

"I agree with him. You have to go. It's an amazing opportunity."

"I know."

"Then why are you so upset about it?"

"Because I don't want to leave you. I'm terrified you won't be here when I get back."

I lifted my head and glared down at him. "Don't be stupid. I live next door. Our parents are best friends. Our lives are completely intertwined. It's not like I'm going anywhere."

He turned his head slightly, eyes on the clouds, avoiding me. "Have you talked to McKinney lately?"

It was the last thing I expected him to say. "At the party."

"That's not what I mean, and you know it."

I did. "If you've got something on your mind, say it. I'm not a mind reader." I teased, using his words.

He swallowed. "The longest we've ever been apart is that summer I went to my grandparents'. You were just my little Len then, not my girlfriend, and it killed me, being away from you."

"You hated being away from Shaun and Tate. I was an afterthought, if that."

"No." His eyes slid to mine. "Do you remember the weekend I came home?"

I pursed my lips while I tried to recall the details. "There was a huge party at Chelsea's to welcome you back, but your parents made you stay with us instead." I smiled as the scene danced across my mind. "Dylan was pissed because they'd let us stay alone all summer, but the minute you came home, they acted like we needed a babysitter. She wouldn't leave her room or talk to you all night, and I felt bad, so I stayed up and watched movies with you."

"It was a great night," he nodded. "My parents didn't tell me I had to stay. I wanted to. I missed you."

My gaze narrowed, a vague memory drifting forward. "Your dad told us that. We thought he was teasing. Dylan claimed the only thing you missed was bossing us around."

"She would say that." His smile was slow and hot as hell as he reached up and twirled a piece of my hair. "Shaun and I were at the lake when he told me he'd spent the entire time following you around, 'cause you had a boyfriend he didn't trust. He wanted to know what we should do about it. I was so angry I went straight home. I didn't let you out of my sight until school started. I'd only been gone a month and so much happened here, I felt helpless." He sighed. "There's more at stake now."

I wanted to laugh at his ridiculousness. It'd been years ago. Things were different now. We were different.

Yet only one thought dominated my mind. "You're really worried about this."

"Yeah, crazy. I am." He chuckled, but there was no humor in it. "I see the way he watches you. McKinney's gonna move in before I've even reached Emerson. I can't handle the idea of Shaun telling me you're taken, again."

I rolled my lips. "Way to give a girl some credit."

"Out of sight, out of mind, right? This thing between us is so new, how are we going to hold it together if we have to go two months without talking?"

"I dream about you. Every night, you haunt my sleep. Sometimes even when you're in the bed beside me. You'll never be off my mind. So, we don't get to talk. Plenty of couples go through worse."

He made a face, ready to argue. I kept talking.

"Basic training is ten weeks. Hiking the Appalachian takes six months. Then there's jail, and depending on what crime you committed, we could be forced apart for years. Fifty-six days is really a walk in the park if you think about it. It'll be over before we know it. I'll be right here waiting. With my dreams of you to keep me company."

I sounded like a psychotic stalker. He should have pulled away. Or looked at me like I was insane.

Instead, his lips pulled back in a slow and easy smile. "Promise?"

"Cross my heart."

"Just one question," he tugged on the hair in his fingertips. "Why am I the one who commits a crime? You're the one with the unstable temper."

I shook my head. "Shut up and kiss me, you ass."

With a swift tug, he pulled me down onto him and rolled us, until we were side by side. One hand cupped my jaw as he kissed the side of my mouth. My fingernails scratched his scalp as he started to explore. He nipped a path down my neck until he found the spot between my shoulder and neck that drove me absolutely wild.

I gasped and shifted, unable to keep quiet as his tongue drew shapes over my collarbone. When he lifted his head just enough to blow a cool breath over it, goosebumps covered my skin. His empty hand slid under my shirt, and his fingernails mimicked mine, digging lightly into my skin. It was too much; I was feeling too much. I needed his lips on mine or I was going to lose my mind.

"Kiss me," I managed to squeak out, making it sound more like a plea than a command.

His lips curled against my neck. "I thought I was." His chuckle against my overheated flesh made me shiver in anticipation.

Dean broke the kiss with a tortured groan. Bracing his forehead against mine, he circled the tip of my nose with his. "It's getting late. We should go."

I combed my fingers through his hair, holding him close, not ready for him to pull away. "I don't want to."

I was lost in his eyes, too busy staring at him to see anything else, but I heard his smile. It did nothing to help me calm down.

"I know you don't," his voice was rough. "I don't want to either. But we have to."

"Why?" I whined, hating how I sounded.

"Greedy little thing," he muttered with a laugh and kissed me again. "I've created a monster."

With one more press of his lips to mine, he broke my hold on him and sat up, slightly out of breath. I let him pull me up, even though there was nothing I wanted more than to be on the blanket, lost in him.

"It's getting dark," he smirked at my pout as he pushed a lock of hair behind my ear and leaned in close. "I love you, Lennon James. One day, it'll just be you and me, lost in our own little world. One day I'll give you everything you want. I'll do anything for you. Right now, though, I need to get you home."

I love you, Lennon James.

The words were no more than a whisper, but he might as well have screamed them for the universe to hear. They had the same effect. My body shook as he grabbed the back of my head and pressed a kiss to my temple.

"One day. Soon."

Soon.

One word held so many different meanings.

Chapter Twenty-One

Dean

"Where have you been?"

The words, sharp and full of accusation, startled me. I chuckled to myself, thinking of how damn jumpy Len was. Apparently, some of her awkwardness had started to rub off on me.

The thought turned my laugh into a snort as ideas of all the other things I'd like to rub drifted through my mind. Preferably with Lennon in the room. Her hands on me.

"Dean Fitzgerald Cullen!" My mother's angry snarl brought me back to the moment, and my face heated, slightly ashamed. "Answer me."

"Out," my tone had an unintentional bite as I started toward the kitchen. I'd meant to take Len to dinner, but time had just slipped away.

"Out where?" she demanded as she followed, hot on my heels.

"With Lennon," I explained, pulling open the refrigerator door.

"With Lennon where?" She insisted.

"Around." I glanced at her. She was being weirder than normal, and it made a shiver of unease race up my spine. She could demand answers all night, but I wasn't about to spill my secrets.

Mom reached around me and slammed the door shut, moving in front of me to block it, hands on her hips. I took a cautionary step back. Her eyes were wild, face tight, and fury radiated off her in waves I would have sworn were visible. My mom never got mad. Irritated sometimes, yeah, but never crazy infuriated.

"I've been calling you."

I tapped my pockets, not feeling a phone. "Shit, Ma. I must have left my cell upstairs." I hadn't needed it. I'd been with the only person I'd wanted to talk to.

"Of course you did," she scoffed bitterly and rolled her eyes. "I thought you were going to talk to him." The question was directed at someone behind me, but I didn't have to turn to know it was my dad.

"Tash," he started slowly, but she stopped him with an angry slash of her finger through the air.

She pointed at him. "Don't you 'Tash' me." Her eyes slid back to me. "Break up with her. The two of you are done."

For a long moment all I could do was stare. I'd never considered myself to be stupid, yet I didn't understand what in the hell was happening. I simply wasn't following. "Are you drunk?"

I regretted the words as soon as I said them. Not for asking the one question burning through my mind, but how accusatory they sounded. From the way Mom's eyes narrowed into slits so thin I doubted she could see, I knew she'd taken offense.

"Dean," my dad's voice was softer than I'd heard in a long time. "Why don't you head to bed? We'll talk in the morning."

"No," Mom slammed a hand down on the counter. "We're going to do this right now. Break up with Lennon. Tonight."

"What? No," I shook my head as my own rage started to boil. "This is my life."

"You could have any girl in town. Oh, don't act like you don't know," she snapped when I opened my mouth to argue. "You've never been one for false modesty, so let's not start now. You could date anyone. Girls follow you around like strays begging for scraps. You don't need to boost your ego by going after the one girl you thought you couldn't have."

"You think that's..." I shook my head, not bothering to finish. I knew my dad didn't have a high opinion of me, he never had. I'd expected this shit from him. Never from my mom. "I'm in love with her."

Mom didn't even blink at my announcement before she laughed bitterly. "No, you aren't."

I watched her, horrified. I didn't know what to say. She'd always been the one who encouraged me to trust my gut, to make decisions based on not just my head, but my heart too. She'd been drinking pretty heavily with Aunt Gayle when we'd left. Clearly, she'd had entirely too much.

I glanced at my dad for help, but he was staring at her with the same horrified expression I was sure I wore. I turned back to Mom. "I am. I love everything about her. I want forever with her."

Mom shook her head and rolled her eyes again. "You're seventeen. Five minutes from now, you'll want a different forever, have a different plan. One that doesn't involve Len."

"That's what you said about acting. Ten years later, it's still what I want. I know the difference between a phase and forever. Len's not a phase for me. If it's up to me, I'm going to marry her one day."

"We wanted you to have a fallback, in case acting didn't work. There's never been any doubt you'd follow your dreams, but it's our job, as your parents, to make sure you go out into the world armed with realistic expectations. You never think before you leap. You don't worry about consequences. This is no different. What will happen to the rest of us when you break Len's heart into a million pieces?"

"That's never going to happen."

"It is. When it does, you're going to decimate her. And destroy the rest of us in the process."

"You don't know that."

"You forget I didn't raise just you and your sister. I helped raise her too. I know that girl as well as I know you two. One of the hardest parts about being a parent is not simply realizing your child has faults but acknowledging them. I look at you and I see a million amazing things. But I also see the negatives. Acting will always be your first love. She will never compete. Loving you will destroy her."

My hands started to shake, unbridled anger oozing through me. "I would never let that happen."

"Not at first. You'll be happy, and everything will feel like it's meant to be. What about when you start getting roles and have to fly all over the world or relocate to the West Coast? Are you going to leave her all alone, or do you expect her to give up her dreams to follow you while you chase yours? When things start to fall apart, Len won't feel like she can go to your sister or come home because she'll want to protect you and won't want anyone to know you're not perfect. She'll hold it in, wait for you to talk it through because that's what she does. You'll know she's unhappy, but work will need you, so you'll start to stay away longer and longer until you don't go home anymore, leaving her on her own. She'll hold on as long as she can. Once she reaches her breaking point, there's no coming back."

My heart cracked a little. Her words painted a picture I didn't want to see, one that echoed my greatest fears.

Fuck that noise.

"Must be nice to have a crystal ball, Mom. You can stand there and make insane accusations, have crazy theories, but that's all they are. You don't know Lennon or me as well as you seem to think. You have no idea what will happen."

"It's called life experience, Dean. It's what happens when you grow up. I was—"

"Natasha," my dad's voice held a note of warning I didn't understand.

She ignored him, voice full of emotion. "I *was* Lennon. The girl who loved a boy more than she loved herself. I know a little something about giving up a piece of yourself, only to have your heart broken, again and again."

I glanced at my dad. He gripped the counter, shoulders tense, as he watched her with a sadness on his face I'd rarely seen before. Maybe her words were as surprising to him as they were to me. I'd always thought my parents were blissfully happy and utterly in love, but maybe I'd misread that entirely.

"It's not even close to the same thing," I argued. "Len and I share a history. We have a bond that's been there our entire lives. You raised me to love her. That won't ever go away. It's a part of who I am. It's not anything like you and dad. It's not something you could understand."

"Wrong again. I was the girl next door, the lucky one who swore she'd met the love of her life when she was six, the one who bought into the happily-ever-after theory of first loves. I had this same argument with my mom when she tried to warn me against it."

"You met Dad in college," I muttered, not following.

"I did. He saved me. Not just from the pit I was in but from myself." Her eyes softened as looked in his direction. "Clearly, he's not a magician, the scars are still there, the hurt just below the surface. I don't want that for you. Or for Lennon."

Dad no longer looked surprised, so none of this was news to him, but I didn't understand. She'd always told us how great their love was.

"Hey," Dylan interrupted from the hall, her confusion and worry clear. "I heard yelling. What's going on?"

I wanted to rush to her, usher her back to her room, assure her it was a misunderstanding, that she didn't need to worry, the way I had a hundred times before. This was nothing like those other fights. Dad raged at me sometimes, yeah, but never Mom. This was new for all of us. If the roles had been reversed, I'd be just as worried and bewildered as Dylan seemed.

Mom didn't even glance her way, too angry with me, too lost in our argument. I ignored my sister too as my mind whirled. I'd apologize later, make it up to her.

We'd all heard Mom's girl-next-door stories and knew how close she'd been with her neighbor. They'd just been best friends, nothing more. Hell, they were still best friends.

An uneasy feeling nudged me. Somehow, I knew it had all been a lie before I asked the question, dreading the answer.

"Uncle Trev?" The words barely made it out. "You're talking about Uncle Trev, aren't you?"

"Yes."

It was so quiet in the room that Dylan's sharp inhale of surprise practically echoed off the walls. I didn't know how much of our fight she'd heard, but I knew she understood just enough to realize what my mother's answer meant.

"You need to think about the bigger picture, Dean. When it all went sideways, none of us were okay. Hearts broke. Friendships were destroyed. Never in my wildest dreams did I think my son would be in the same position I was twenty-five years ago."

"It's not the same," Dylan's voice held a firmness I wasn't used to hearing from her. "Uncle Trevor asked you to marry him. You said yes. That means you were engaged when you went to Ireland to work that dig site. The one where you met Dad." She eyed our father sadly. "That's how Trev met Aunt Gayle. Her boyfriend slept with his fiancée. Not just once or twice, but they cheated for a really long time."

My first reaction was to defend my parents, to tell my sister she had bad intel. I'd never heard any hint of anything like that. I glanced at my dad. The look of shame on his face was enough to keep me quiet. Disgust filled my stomach.

"That's not true. Tell her that's not true."

Neither parent denied Dylan's accusation.

After a few heartbeats, Dad's eyes moved over each of us slowly before settling on my mom. "Trevor and Gayle are our best friends. We decided a long time ago to let the past stay in the past. We've all moved on, forgiven mistakes, made amends. Because a life with each other in it, is better than one without."

I didn't know what to say. I couldn't wrap my head around any of it.

"So, you not only dated Uncle Trevor, but you were supposed to marry him?" I turned to my dad. "And you dated Aunt Gayle but cheated on her with Mom?"

"It's much more complicated than that, son. You should know nothing involving the heart is simple. But yes. That's the CliffsNotes version."

I was stuck in an alternate universe.

If what they were saying was true, I didn't know how the man I'd always called Uncle Trev could look at my mom with anything but

hatred, let alone be one of her dearest friends. I really couldn't understand why he'd support me dating his daughter. He'd been the one hurt
all those years ago, yet he was still willing to trust me with Lennon's
heart.

"As horrifying as all of this is, it doesn't change anything for me and
Len."

"It changes everything," Mom's screech pierced the air and made
me wince.

A different fear hit me like a bucket of cold water. Acid roiled in my
gut. "Are you trying to tell me that Lennon is my sister?"

"Jesus, Dean." My dad's face pinched in disgust. "Really?"

"It's a valid fucking question," I seethed back.

"Not by blood. But she's family just the same." Mom growled. "History has a way of repeating itself unless someone is willing to make
hard choices and force change. I won't stand here and let you relive my
mistakes."

"I'm not you." I let my voice rise again. "I won't make the decisions
you did. I will never hurt the person I love."

"We always hurt the people we love. Sometimes, there's no coming
back from it. When you hurt her—not if, Dean, when—you'll be
breaking more hearts than hers. And I won't be able to forgive you for
that."

The words stung like a physical blow. I took a deep breath, refusing
to respond in anger. "That's on you, then. Not me. I have no power over
whom you forgive and who you don't. Just like you can't choose who I
love."

I started to turn, hunger forgotten, ready to get away from her, when
Mom spoke again. "Maybe I can't make you break up with her. But I can
make it impossible for you to see her. You're grounded."

I spun to face her. "For what? I haven't done anything wrong."

She gave my dad a pointed look. "You haven't? We have months of
security footage that says otherwise." She held out a hand. "Car keys.
Phone. From this moment forward, you're on lockdown. No driving. No
cell."

"You're fucking kidding me."

Her head tilted slightly, and she motioned me with her empty hand. "Now."

I yanked my keys from my pocket and slammed them on the counter. "For how long?"

"Until you get back in August."

"You're serious?"

"Be grateful we didn't take away the camp."

Without another word, I turned and strode from the kitchen, my anger barely in check.

"That's harsh, even for you. And totally unfair." I heard Dylan argue as I reached the hall. "You, of all people, should know we don't get to pick who we love. Way to be the adult in this situation."

Moments later, just as I was about to open my bedroom door, my little sister tackled me from behind. Her arms closed around me and squeezed tight. "I'm sorry our parents are assholes."

I turned as much as I could and hugged her back. "I'm sorry I didn't tell you about me and Len. And that you had to find out that way."

"Is it true?"

"Which part?" I asked with a chuckle I didn't feel as I led her into my room.

"Are you really in love with her?"

I nodded as I dropped into my chair. "I am."

"Wow." She sat on the bed and pulled her knees up to her chest. "How long? I mean, how long have you been together?"

"We had a thing during spring break, while you were gone. I don't even know what to call it. Then Len got grounded. We went on our first real date last night."

She frowned. "Why didn't you just tell me?"

"Because apparently secrets and lies and hidden relationships are in our DNA."

Her laugh surprised me. "Smartass." She smacked me with a pillow. "I'm serious."

"So am I. Did you hear her down there? Jesus." I shook my head. "If you listen to our mom, I'm a piece of shit destined to destroy Lennon. Worse than that, you and I are doomed to become cheaters."

"She doesn't really mean any of that, and you know it. She's clearly had too much to drink and the idea of you and Len together threw her. She's probably just working through her own shit. I mean, seriously. She's been living next to two people who were hurt immensely by her actions. Oh em gee. Can you imagine? Not only having to face your indiscretions daily, but have them be a huge part of your life, and then find out your son is dating their only daughter? You know how Mom is, with her 'everything happens for a reason,' 'the universe provides' bullshit. She's probably freaking out because she thinks it's some sort of cosmic payback. Sins of the father visited upon the child. In this case, mother." She twisted her lips. "Well, maybe mother and father?"

"How did you know? About what they did?"

"I didn't, not really." She chewed on her lip. "Do you remember a couple summers ago when Len's Aunt Heather came to stay, and she took us to the beach every day?"

I did. Len's Aunt Heather was another relative in name only. As Aunt Gayle's oldest friend, she was Lennon's Godmother and came to visit every few years. I didn't know her that well because she didn't like my mom. Shocker, really. We never spent much time with her.

"She kind of told us. She never said it was Mom and Dad who were the cheaters, but she did say that Trevor had been engaged and was so head over heels that he couldn't see his fiancée was cheating. Meanwhile, Gayle's boyfriend hooked up with another student when he was studying overseas. When they came home the next semester, they kept sneaking around and seeing each other.

"Months later, Gayle's boyfriend felt bad and came clean, admitting that the other woman was engaged. Broken hearted, Gayle took matters into her own hands. She found out who mom was, then tracked down Trevor and told him. He didn't believe her at first.

"Later, he confronted his fiancé. When he found out that it was true, he went to Gayle and asked her out for coffee to apologize. They became friends and eventually fell in love." She shrugged. "Tonight, when I heard Mom, I put two and two together. I hoped they'd deny it."

"Fuck. How are they all still friends?"

Dylan shrugged. "Heather said that both Aunt Gayle and Uncle Trev were so happy with each other they believed it was for the best. They're the forgive and forget kind of people and don't hold a grudge. Which is why Heather holds one for them."

"Touché." I ran my hand through my hair. "What am I going to tell Len?"

"Do you have to tell her anything?"

It was a damn good question.

"Never mind. I take it back. You don't *have* to tell her anything, but we *should*. We stumbled into this den of secrets our families are keeping, but that doesn't mean we have to be part of it. I don't want to keep anything from her. Do you?"

"Hell, no."

"Then let's not. Len needs to know what we know." She sighed as she flopped back onto my mattress. "Speaking of, when did you and I stop telling each other everything? We used to share it all."

"When we reached puberty and you started crushing on my friends."

"Valid point. Can we promise that from this point forward, we'll be brutally honest about the things that matter?"

I was tempted to ask what classified as something that mattered, but it was just nitpicking, and I didn't need to clarify. I'd play it safe. If it were something that she should know, something that made me feel like I was keeping a secret from her, she'd be the first one I told.

"For real, why didn't you guys tell me about you two?"

"I didn't know how. We didn't want to hurt you. Len was convinced she was a spring break fling. You've been pretty adamant that your friends are off limits. More than that, I didn't want you to hate her."

"I'd never hate Lennon. You, maybe, but never Len. It's actually pretty cool, my brother dating my best friend. Like, you'll never exclude us from parties again. And wherever you are, Tate is sure to follow, and I can think of worse people to be around. Plus, if my friend isn't off limits anymore, neither are yours."

"Dylan," I sighed, the dread heavy on my shoulders. I'd just promised to be honest. "Tate won't ever—"

"I know," she interrupted. "Just let me have my fantasy, okay?" When I didn't argue, she continued her earlier thought. "You'll have to stop with that stupid nickname now."

A real smile bent the corners of my mouth. "Hate to break it to you, kid, but you'll always be the little sister."

She groaned. "Of course, I will." She sat up suddenly, eyes wide. "Oh my God. How cool would it be if you got married and had kids? I know, I know," she rolled her eyes, "I'm getting ahead of myself. How cute would they be though?"

"Pretty fucking adorable," I agreed.

"Holy shit." Her mouth dropped open. "You really are serious about her, aren't you?"

I didn't answer.

"Does she know?"

"I don't know. The world seems against us right now." I'd been worried about leaving Len for the summer when we had another few weeks together. Now that we were being robbed of that, my fears were in overdrive.

The knock on my door stopped my spiraling thoughts. I didn't want to go another round with Mommy Dearest.

"Dean? Can I come in?"

Dad's voice made me relax a notch.

"I was just leaving." Dylan popped off my bed like the little bundle of energy she was, gave me a half hug, and squeezed by our dad without a word. "Night, Dean."

Dad gave me a small smile once we were alone. "I'm a little envious that you're leaving for the summer. I have a feeling your sister is going to hold a grudge on your behalf. Should be fun around here."

I couldn't find it in me to feel sorry for him. "What did you need?"

"Your phone."

I glanced at the nightstand where I'd left it charging earlier. "Can I give it to you tomorrow? I'm supposed to call Len in a bit."

He shook his head. "Your mom wants to put it away before she turns in for the night. She's pretty upset."

"Yeah." I didn't have the energy to argue. Instead, I leaned over my bed and grabbed the phone before tossing it in his direction. "When do I get it back?"

"Not before you leave."

Fantastic.

"Trevor and I were talking about the security cameras earlier. It seems that he had to turn his off because the software was glitching." He watched, waiting, but I didn't give two shits about the damn cameras. When I just stared back, he continued. "I'm going to be up for a while working on a project and told Mom I'd check on you and your sister before I go to bed, so she didn't have to."

I frowned at his totally random statements. I hadn't known they still checked on Dylan and me.

"I noticed that most of the lights in the James' house are out."

I crossed my arms. Now he was just being weird. "Are you creeping on the neighbors, Dad?"

His look turned pointed, and he sighed. "If someone wanted to, I don't know, say sneak out, this would be a great chance."

"Really?" My tone was flat, not believing him.

"Yeah."

"You're not joking?"

"Son, I can promise you, there are three things I will never joke about with you. Death, taxes, and Lennon James. Everything else is fair game and open to creative interpretation."

"You're not going to narc if I leave?"

"Dads don't 'narc.'" He lifted a single brow. "Put that in the category of shit people should never say about dads, right up there with a 'father babysitting his kids.' *Pshh.*"

"Fine. You're not going to tell your wife I left? Or is this just one more secret to keep?"

"I'm the lucky bastard who got to fall in love twice in my life. Once with a brilliant beauty who has a heart of gold and a rare laugh that still makes me smile and continues to be my friend twenty-five years after I broke her heart. The second with a dash of chaos who keeps me on my toes and makes my heart beat a little faster every day. Dylan's right. You can't pick who you love. And no one else gets to pick for you either. Spend every second you can with the ones you love because no one knows what the future holds." He turned for the door. "Night."

I counted to a hundred and crept to my door, pushing an ear against it. When I didn't hear anything, I leaned into the hall and checked both ways. Leaving my room, I spy-walked all the way down the stairs and out onto the stoop, feeling like an idiot the entire way.

I closed the front door quietly behind me and ran for the road. Once I was on Len's side of the street, I let out the breath I'd been holding.

I was almost to the tree that would take me to Lennon's window when I hesitated. I didn't know everything about their history, but it seemed like my parents royally screwed over Lennon's. Maybe my parents could justify it by saying it all worked out because my aunt and uncle were so happy, but I didn't know if Trevor and Gayle felt the same.

Yet, they hadn't been the ones freaked out about Len and me. I stared up at their house, feet frozen to the ground. I couldn't do it.

I wanted to spend the night with Lennon, to have that extra time with her, but it wasn't worth the cost we'd have to pay if we betrayed her parent's trust. I wanted to do things the right way. With a sad sigh, I turned around.

"Just a sec."

Len answered my knock and did a double take. Her gaze darted from my face to the hall behind me, as if she was searching for something.

"Your dad let me in."

"That's random." She ran her fingers through her strands and pushed the hair back. "Everything okay?"

"We need to talk. Can I come in?"

Again, her gaze went to the hall, as if she expected to see one of her parents lurking.

"They know I'm here."

"It's really late." She stepped back, giving me room to enter. "What's wrong?"

I snagged her hand as I walked in, the door open behind me, and lead her to the bed. "Maybe you should sit down."

Chapter Twenty-Two

Lennon

Three Months Later

A horn blew twice, letting me know that he'd gotten to the street and that it was almost time to go. I grabbed my towel and bag and hurried down the stairs. My parents were in the kitchen, having a quiet conversation as Mom drank her coffee and Dad scanned the paper.

"Morning."

"Good morning, sweetie." Mom's eyebrows rose when she glanced my way. "Still not sleeping?"

I shook my head.

The dreams had gotten bad again. Nightmares that didn't make sense. A kaleidoscope of flashing lights coupled with the echo of screeching horns. Warning bells, telling me something was wrong, that left me feeling disoriented and nauseous.

Every day I waited to hear from Dean so my worried psyche could rest. And every night I went to bed wondering if I'd imagined the way he'd looked at me, questioning if the words he'd whispered had truly been spoken, and second guessing my sanity.

"It's getting worse."

"I'll call the doctor first thing Monday and see if they can see us. Maybe there's a new medicine we can try to help your anxiety." She gave me a small, worried smile. "New suit?"

I let her change the subject as I reached for an apple. "You like it?"

"I do." She held her large mug with both hands as she watched me. "I just wish there was more of it." *Me too, Mom. Me too.* She turned to my dad. "What do you think, Trev?"

Dad and I had made leaps and bounds over the summer, trying to find some middle ground and get along again. We weren't where we'd once been, but I wasn't a little girl anymore either. He claimed I was in transition, in the middle of my journey to adulthood and that I'd understand when I made it to the other side.

I had to give him credit. He'd started taking a deep breath or "tabling" discussions, when before, he would have yelled or locked himself in his office. I was trying not to be such a brat and hear the words he spoke, instead of just letting them wash over me.

I'd expected a fight from him today. He wanted to be the dad that didn't care what his daughter wore as long as she was comfortable, but sometimes he struggled with my choices. Since I was stressed about my outfit, I assumed he'd tell me I wasn't leaving the house until I changed.

I wouldn't object to that.

He slowly snapped the paper backward and looked at me, his gaze never dipping below my neck. "New nose ring?"

I leaned back against the counter, facing them, and snorted. "No. It's the same starter stud, Daddy." The word slipped out on accident. As I tried to recall the last time I'd used it, I reached up to turn the ball, a trait I'd developed over the last few weeks. Remembering it drove my parents crazy, I forced my hand to fall limp at my side.

"Daddy?" Mom smirked and gave Dad the side-eye, clearly amused. Thankfully, she didn't push.

"It's Dylan's," I explained as I took a giant bite of the Red Delicious. "The bikini, I mean. I lost a bet."

Dad's shock was almost laughable as he dropped the paper and gawked. "Don't take this the wrong way, Lenny, but I find that really hard to believe."

"Unless it was something physical," Mom countered, her worry palpable. "But even then..."

I waved a hand. "It wasn't anything dangerous." I assured her before shifting my jaw as I looked at my dad. "It wasn't anything academic either." I rolled my eyes. "It was stupid."

"How stupid? Like 'wasting money on track ponies' dumb or 'trying to light your flatulence on fire' idiotic?"

Mom and I both gaped at him like he was the strangest man on the planet. "Is that even a real thing?"

He nodded. "It is."

"Eww." I couldn't hide my disgust. "Do I look like someone who would try to light a fart on fire?"

He shrugged. "You never know. Smart people do idiotic things when there's a wager on the line."

"I have no words. I'm not even going to ask how you know that." Mom shook her head as she put her cup down. "I was thinking more along the line of smoking smarties or walking over the arch of the old stone bridge."

"Nothing like that, I swear." People had died doing both. I tore off the last bit of apple with my teeth and tossed the core. "Dylan bet I couldn't eat an entire meal by myself."

"Please don't take this the wrong way, I can't believe you lost."

No offense was taken. I could eat. Dean once laughingly predicted I'd grow up to be a competitive eater. The random thought made me miss him.

It seemed like every time I started to feel settled, or I started to ignore the Dean-shaped hole in my heart, a memory came along and knocked everything sideways.

"How'd you lose?"

"Because they're dirty cheats."

The small roadside diner was packed full, which wasn't unexpected on a Friday night. Oceanside villages were the number one tourist destination every summer in Maine. Toward the end of August, locals came out in full force, desperate to squeeze in a few more adventures with their families. I'd expected a long wait when Shaun pulled in, but a waitress with a tired smile ushered us to an empty table almost immediately, handing us menus and promising our server would be with us soon.

"Is that Preo?" Tate asked as he slid into the booth next to me, his attention on someone across the room.

Shaun narrowed his eyes in the direction Tate pointed. "No shit. It is." He turned back to us. "We'll only be a minute, okay?"

After they left, I scanned the menu, past the seafood, over pasta and salads, right to the holy grail of burgers and fries. We'd been at the beach all day, playing in the water and chasing the frisbee and football over hot sand. Famished didn't begin to explain how hungry I was.

"Whatcha getting?"

"The southwest barbeque bacon burger with homemade onion rings. You?"

"That sounds good. Wanna share?"

"Not even a little bit. I could eat everything on the menu, all at once." I snorted as I looked around, making sure no one heard us as I dropped my voice. "If you didn't bring money, I can spot you."

"Seriously? Of course, I have money," she rolled her eyes dismissively. "I'm just not that hungry."

I narrowed my eyes. "You barely ate lunch. I don't know what you had for breakfast, but there's no way you're not starving right now."

"I'll eat later when I get home."

I grabbed her wrist. "What's going on?"

"I'm not going to binge in front of Tate. All I need is for him to imagine Miss Piggy when he thinks of me. That's real sexy."

"You're insane. All you've done this summer is lose weight. It's Tate. He's seen you eat your entire life."

"Whatever. Some of us are single and don't want to be. If we're not careful, we'll end up fat and alone." She lifted a shoulder.

I shook my head, utterly flabbergasted. "Okay, one, fat and alone seems like a happier way to live than not being able to eat when you're hungry. Two, you're not even close to being overweight, and even if you were, your size doesn't define you. A size is just a number on a tag, not a reflection of who you are. Three, you've been half-naked all summer, throwing yourself at him. If it hasn't worked yet, he's not going to care what you're eating. Give the guy a break."

She huffed, angry at my harsh words. "It's not like you're going to eat it all."

"Yeah, I am. Every last bite."

"I bet you can't. There's not enough room in your tiny stomach to fit it all."

"And you'd be wrong."

"Then let's make a little challenge, shall we? If I win, you stop hiding that banging body of yours—"

"I don't hide my body," I interrupted, looking down at my tight white tank and small jean shorts that left very little to the imagination.

"You stop hiding all that fantasticness," she repeated, talking over me, "and let me pick your outfit for the beach tomorrow."

"Fine. If I win, I get to pick what you wear. Then maybe you'll realize you'll turn just as many heads in a regular suit."

"Deal."

"Deal."

We shook hands.

The boys came back to our table a few minutes later, laughing and talking about football. Usually, I'd try to drown them out, but I didn't want to talk to Dylan and one word piqued my interest. "Scouts are really coming to see you this season?"

Tate beamed, unable to hide his excitement. "That's what Coach says. Not huge schools, but all the state universities and a couple of other New England colleges. The same ones that came last season."

"That's amazing."

"Well, they still need to show. And we still need to kick ass. Everyone is convinced it's just a formality, that I'll be getting offers soon, but I need to bring my A-game. I can't screw anything up."

I was excited for him. As much as I dreaded the idea of him not being *right across the street anymore, I knew that football was his only chance to get out. He needed a scholarship.*

The waitress still hadn't come by the time I'd finished my water, and I couldn't wait anymore. "I have to pee. If she comes, will you order for me?"

Tate and Dylan both nodded.

The line seemed to stretch on forever. We may have gotten there in time to get a table, but it seemed like we'd hit the tail end of the dinner rush. Every single woman in the restaurant had chosen that moment to powder her nose or use the bathroom.

Almost twenty minutes later, I made my way back to a now much less crowded dining area. Our food arrived not long after. I stared at the mounded plate in front of me for only a second before I confronted my best friend.

"Is there a reason I have so much food?"

Dylan's eyes widened in faux innocence, and she lifted a single shoulder in a sassy shrug before she dug into her small garden salad with no dressing.

Shaun, blissfully unaware of our bet, took a sip of his soda and answered. "Lil' sis said you couldn't decide between onion rings and fries so she asked the waitress if you could upsize and get an order of both."

Tate, always the perceptive one, glanced at my plate. "Is something wrong?"

"We made a bet that I couldn't eat my entire meal. And you," I pointed at Dylan with a fry, "cheated."

"That's an easy fix," Shaun explained as he reached for my plate. "I'll take your half your fries and rings. That way, it'll be the size you ordered."

The waitress appeared, a tray of drinks in her hand. She plucked one off and set it on the table in front of me. "Here's your shake, sweetie."

All I could do was glower at Dylan.

She shrugged playfully. "You didn't specify what you wanted to drink."

I was going to kill her.

As if sensing her imminent demise, Tate reached for the glass. "Not part of the bet. You said, eat the meal. Drink doesn't count. I'll take that."

Dylan glared at Tate. "You two can't pick sides; you're supposed to be neutral."

"I'm keeping things fair, lil' sis. That is neutral."

We quieted as the food distracted us. Every bite I took was pure delicious-

ness in my mouth. I closed my eyes, enjoying the savory taste and peaceful quiet of the restaurant.

"What'd you guys bet on?" Shaun asked a few minutes later.

Dylan smirked. "If I win, she has to wear a bikini tomorrow. If I lose, we're both stuck in granny suits."

"It's not a granny suit. It's one piece, but believe me, there is nothing granny about it."

They ignored me. "If she loses, she's wearing a bikini? All day?"

Dylan and I both nodded.

"What were the rules?"

Dylan's eyes met mine. We hadn't made specific rules. "Just that she had to eat her entire meal."

Shaun popped a few more fries in his mouth, then grabbed his burger with one hand while lifting his plate with the other. Once it was positioned over mine, he upended it, filling mine with fries and rings once again.

I gaped at him. "What the hell?"

"Sorry, lil' miss. I'm not missing the chance to see you in a bikini." He grinned at Dylan. "Please make sure it's itsy, bitsy, and covered in yellow polka dots."

"I hate you both."

"You can hate her all you want," Shaun assured me. "But you love the fuck outta me."

My parents watched me with a mixture of humor and horror on their faces as I told a condensed summary of the story.

"Well, that explains that." Mom stood and carried her mug to the coffee pot, refilling it with a laugh. "You've been spending a lot of time with Shaun this summer."

I had. We'd been practically inseparable. Even on days Tate and Dylan were busy, Shaun and I had found something to do. Some days we'd lounge by his pool, him drawing while I jotted story ideas down in my notebook or read. Others, we went on adventures. He joined me at the Padilla's when I babysat, and I tagged along with his family when-ever his parents were in town and insisted on his presence. When I was really bored, I'd even let him haul me on his grueling workouts. I'd grown so attached to him I didn't know how I'd take it if Dean came home and wanted his best friend back.

I couldn't tell my parents any of that. I knew how it must look. Two teens always together, laughing until we cried. Our teasing and constant banter could be easily mistaken for flirting.

It wasn't. We were just friends. Best friends who'd bonded over how much we both missed Dean.

I loved Shaun the way I imagined I'd love a brother. The way I loved Tate. They weren't blood, but they were my family.

"Not just Shaun. Tate and Dylan, too. I feel bad for the boys. I think they felt like they had to entertain and watch over us after Dean left. I'm not going to complain, 'cause they're so fun to be around. Dylan and I are definitely cramping their style though. They've been stuck with us tagging along and haven't been to one party all summer."

"That's impressive. I'm proud of them. Are you babysitting tonight?"

I shook my head. "Nope. The Padilla's gave me the night off. They're going to play mini-golf as a family."

"Oh, that sounds fun. We should do that before school starts. You could bring Shaun."

Dad nodded his agreement.

"Maybe," I muttered, no intention of asking Shaun to join us on a family date.

"Since you're not working, you and Dylan should have a girls' night. Tell the guys to go do their own thing for a change."

"Your mother's right. We're not going to be home. Why don't you see if any of your other friends want to come over? I'll leave money for pizzas and the card is already programmed into Amazon for you to rent a movie or two."

They'd never asked why Dylan and I had suddenly chosen our house to be our base or said anything about my constant presence at home. I was sure they'd guessed by my lack of time across the street that I didn't want to be there anymore, but they'd never mentioned it. They'd been encouraging Dylan to stay with us as much as possible, which I appreciated.

"Yeah, maybe. Thanks. You guys going out with Tasha and Chad?"

My mom shook her head, ignoring the lack of titles I'd always bestowed on their best friends. "Dad has that company brunch tomorrow, remember? We agreed to meet some of his work friends tonight for drinks and a late dinner. Aunt Heather is going to try to join us." She smiled at the mention of her dearest and oldest friend. "We'll probably head out around four or so. You're okay here?"

I nodded. "Yeah. Dylan's staying and I'll ask some of the other girls if they want to join us."

A horn blew three times in quick succession, letting me know my friends were ready for me. "Gotta go." I pulled a sheer kimono off the chair and slid it on, trying to cover as much of me as possible.

"Have fun. We'll see you tomorrow afternoon, early."

"Love you." I gave each a quick peck on the cheek and waved goodbye over my head as I ran out the door.

Tate and Dylan were already in the back seat of Shaun's topless Wrangler, talking softly, debating something by the looks of it, as they waited for me. Shaun, on the other hand, leaned against the back fender, one flip-flopped foot propped over the other, giant muscled arms crossed over his broad chest. In his tank top and board shorts, shoulder-length hair hanging loose, he looked like he belonged on the opposite coast, a surfboard tucked under his arm.

If I was half the artist Shaun was, I'd paint him in that moment, carefree and happy. Galleries would fight over who would show it and it would sell for millions, making me a household name. He was just that beautiful.

I couldn't draw if my life depended on it. Reaching in my bag, I grabbed my phone, aimed it in his direction, and captured the moment before he could move. He frowned slightly and then shook his head with a laugh.

"You trying to gauge my reaction? Stop stalling. Let's see it."

With an eye roll and a smirk, I pulled open the sides of my cover-up and flashed him the teeny, tiny black string bikini with absurdly large yellow polka dots.

"Holy fuck," He dragged out the words as he pushed off the Jeep and walked toward me. "You really did it."

"A bet's a bet."

His eyes roamed over me quickly, not lingering too long. "You look good."

"You don't look so bad yourself." As I said the words, movement at the house across the street caught my eye. Without thinking, I looked.

It wasn't Dean. Deep down, I'd known it wasn't going to be him. But that didn't mean I'd stopped hoping.

It'd been over a month since I'd gotten one of the weekly letters he'd promised to write. Three weeks since he'd called home to talk to his family. Dylan was just as concerned as I was, although she tried to brush it off and act like everything was normal.

We'd never gotten tickets for the family and friends dress rehearsal. His parents I could understand, but he'd left the rest of us out, too. None of us understood why.

As much as I tried to ignore it, it felt like we were his past, that Dean had outgrown us. Maybe he had. Maybe this was just a taste of what our future would be.

I kept hoping that no news was good news. I'd convinced myself that we didn't get tickets because he'd dropped out and decided to come home early. Anything to keep my mind from fixating on other possible reasons like the idea he might not want me anymore, that it had all been a fluke.

It wasn't all about me. I needed to remember that.

"Hey," Shaun's voice was soft as if he understood where my mind had gone. "You know what you need? Sun, waves, and the peace that only the ocean can provide."

I took the hand he offered and let him haul me to his ride. Peace sounded wonderful. If only I could find some.

"What're we searching the skies for today, lil' miss?" Shaun asked as he dropped down onto the blanket next to me.

We had the perfect spot in the corner of the beach. Shaded by the trees growing on the rocks high above us as well as close to the water where Tate and Dylan splashed each other mercilessly. The truth was, I'd picked it every time we came because for a few minutes I could pretend I was on top of Dean's hill, in his favorite place, staring at the sky with him.

I sighed and watched another cotton-ball cloud shift and morph from a perfect heart into a dozen birds streaking across the sky. Fitting, really. Since my heart was in smithereens and half of it had flown the coop. "Answers."

"Before you can find answers, you need to ask the right questions." He lifted an arm and pointed. "Look, a bunny."

I followed his aim to where the most adorable rabbit sat easily identifiable amongst a rocky sea of cumulus. "You know what question keeps running through my mind, over and over?"

"Whether clouds ever look down on people and think, 'hey, that one looks like an idiot?'"

I snorted. He'd deadpanned so perfectly if I hadn't known him as well as I did, I would've assumed he was serious. Totally thrown off-topic, away from my forlorn state of mind, I laughed at his absurdity until tears burned my eyes and I couldn't breathe.

"I love you," I finally wheezed out.

"As I love you." He nudged my arm with his and then lifted my camera above our faces, "smile." I didn't have a moment to think before I flashed a quick grin. He dropped the camera as quickly as he'd picked it up, before pointing toward the sky once more. "Kitty cat."

For a few minutes, we laid in silence, watching clouds move across the sky. He'd been right, damn it. Being there, with him, doing nothing more than soaking up the warmth and quiet, calmed my mind.

"Butterfly." I pointed toward the right.

"Baby chicken." He moved his fingers through the air, outlining the shape for me to see. "Why do we see shapes in the clouds? Is it like dreams where our subconscious is trying to tell us something by allowing us to see certain images?"

"Are you asking if there's some underlining reason to explain why you keep finding cute and cuddly farm animals?"

He chuckled. "Sure, we'll go with that."

"The human brain is so complex that it seeks out patterns in all things to help us function. Half the time, we don't even realize it. It's why we're able to anticipate certain behaviors or accept random things that shouldn't make any sense. If the eyes see something that has no familiar pattern, the brain invents one. Hence, the reason we see shapes in things like clouds and stars."

He was quiet for a moment. "Is there anything you don't know?"

My mind filtered through all the questions that had been plaguing it lately. He was talking about the random, useless facts I could spout at a moment's notice, not my inability to understand basic human nature, but my thoughts still went directly to Dean. "So, so many things. The rest came from PBS."

"Liar." He snorted. "You're my favorite person in the entire world, Lennon James. Don't ever forget that."

"Yeah?" I adjusted my arm under my head as I turned onto my side. "I bet you say that to all the girls."

"I do." Shaun tipped his face toward me, a semi smirk tugging at his lips. "But I actually mean it when I say it to you. If I could spend the rest of my life here on this beach, staring at clouds with you, I'd die knowing I'd spent every second well." He winked. "Seriously, this has been the best summer I've ever had."

"That's only because you can actually remember it."

"Ha, ha." He shook his head in mock disappointment before he wrinkled his nose. "You have a good point. I've been painfully sober all summer."

"And yet, best summer of your life. Coincidence? I think not," I teased.

"I've been meaning to talk to you," he pushed himself up on an elbow and looked down at me. "There's a party tonight and I want you to come with…"

I shook my head before the word party had finished passing his lips. "Nope. I'm good."

"You didn't let me finish."

"I'm not going to another party. Maybe not ever."

"Len." He said my name like he was trying to reason with an unreasonable child. "I'll be with you the whole time. Never let you out of my sight. Be stuck to you like glue."

"Do you know what a group of people is called?" I asked, flopping back onto my back again as I raised my eyes to the sky.

"Uh, a crowd?"

"Good point." I nodded, chuckling. "To me, a group of people is called a 'no thanks.'"

He laughed again, lowering himself down next to me. "Okay. We'll do something else."

"You don't have to babysit me. You and Tate should do your thing. Go to the party. Take that girl you've been talking to on a real date instead of sneaking around."

His only answer was an eyeroll. I grinned. I'd get the truth out of him, one way or another. He couldn't hide her from me forever, even though he'd done a great job over the last few weeks. I didn't even have a solid lead.

"Seriously. It'll give Dylan and me a chance to have a girls' night."

"Do you ever feel like you're running out of time?" His voice was so sincere it shocked me.

It was my turn to sit up and look down at him, concerned. "What do you mean? 'Cause you're going to be a senior? Like this is your last hoorah?"

He released a long breath and sat, stretching his muscular legs out in front of us. "I don't know. Maybe? It's just a nagging feeling in the back of my mind I can't explain. Something telling me I need to spend time with you now or I won't get a chance later. It's not just you. It's all of you. Cullen, Tate, lil' sis. I don't know what it is."

"It's normal to want to hold on. Change is hard. With Dean gone, the reality of life after high school feels that much closer. On one hand, we're ready to grow up. On the other, we don't want to face what that means."

He pulled his sunglasses from his eyes and watched me as I talked, nodding in agreement. "I knew you'd get it."

I tipped my head and reached out to hold his hand. "We'll always be family. You know that, right? I'll have your back until the end of time."

"There was never a doubt in my mind. Because I'll always be right here, whenever you need me. You and me? We're soulmates and shit. You're imprinted on my heart." He looked out, watching our friends in the water. "You're sad today." He paused. "You're not starting to resent him, are you?"

"For taking a chance and doing what he loves? Never."

"No." His voice was so soft I had to strain to hear him. "For leaving you behind."

"Dean didn't leave me behind, Shaun. He's gone on an adventure to chase his dreams. Unfortunately, that journey is one we all have to take alone. You'll do it next year, me the year after. The important thing to remember is that even when you feel like no one is around, we're right behind you, cheering. Because even though you're a few steps ahead, the people who love you are pushing you on."

"Wise beyond her years."

I snorted. "The power of reading books. And only in some areas." I sighed. "I'm clueless in others."

I didn't have to spell it out for him to know that I was utterly lost when it came to love.

"Hey, I've got something for you."

"Oh, yeah?" I chuckled nervously. I never knew what to expect from him. He was probably about to throw a hermit crab into my lap.

He nodded, almost sheepishly as he dragged his messenger bag close. Seconds later he'd pulled out his sketchbook. Turning slightly so I couldn't see more than a glimpse of the pages, he opened it and then held a small piece of paper in my direction.

I lifted it from his fingers gingerly, treating it like the priceless work of art it was. I felt extremely special. I loved everything Shaun created, but he rarely showed his pieces to anyone.

The charcoal drawing was beautiful. A giant moon lit up the midnight sky around it. A young couple took center stage, holding each other while they gave off into the wild unknown.

"It's breathtaking." Worried it'd get ruined by the sand or a stray spray of ocean water, I tried to hand it back.

Shaun shook his head, his hand stopping mine. "It's for you."

"Me?" I was honored.

"Whenever you start to forget, look at this and remember. It doesn't matter where you are, you and Dean are under the same moon, loving each other, dreaming of the day you'll be together again."

Tears burned my eyes. "Shaun, I..." I didn't know what to say.

He shot me a wicked grin over his shoulder as he tucked his precious possession beck into his bag. "Lennon James speechless? No fun fact about art? Not going to talk nerdy to me? What is happening right now?"

I laughed, wiping my eyes quickly. "Shut up. I love it."

I reached for my own bag and lifted out my favorite notebook. Using extra stickers I'd tucked into the pocket, I secured his gift to the front cover, next to my favorite picture of Dean and me from when we were kids.

For a moment, I stared at the third picture. Dylan had snapped the perfect shot of her brother kissing my forehead on the last day of school. My fingers traced the teens absentmindedly. Dean had been so worried about leaving me...

I sighed. I missed him so damn much.

"Have you called him?"

I shook my head. "He doesn't have his phone, remember? He got grounded because he wouldn't dump me."

I was still unbelievably bitter about that, even all these months later. It wasn't just that his mother had said and done all the things she had, because that was bad enough. It was because I'd always thought she genuinely liked me.

"I meant at the school. He wasn't allowed calls before the play, but that was last week."

"The Friends and Family performance was last week. Tonight's the big show. Dylan said it's some black-tie event with famous actors and agents in the audience."

"Oooh. Fancy." He twisted his lips. "I still think someone should try to call just to make sure he's okay." He popped an eyebrow. "Unless you want to drive down there and crash the show tonight. I look utterly fuckable in a tux. I can only imagine how banging you'd look in a little black dress and sky-high heels."

"Not a chance," I chortled at the idea. "But thank you for suggesting it. And offering. It means a lot. Besides, you have that party."

"You really don't mind if I go?"

I quirked a brow. "Why would I care? Unless of course, you secretly want to see a chick flick with Dylan and me."

"Fuck no. I'm good." He snorted. "What are we doing tomorrow? Shopping for school or a lazy day by the pool?"

"Can we hit the mall?"

"Holy shit. Has hell finally frozen? Lennon James is *asking* me to take her to the mall?"

"Shut up." I smacked his arm. "I ordered something that I couldn't get anywhere else. It's ready to be picked up. Unfortunately, that means a trip to the torture chamber."

"Then, absolutely." He fell back onto the blanket. After a minute, he pointed at the sky again. "That's not a soft and cuddly animal. Look at that wolf baring his fangs. It's badass."

I tried to see what he did, but all I could see was a giant, jagged, broken heart. Yet, for the first time all day, I didn't feel dread. I wasn't worried. Shaun's presence always brought me calm.

Chapter Twenty-Three

Dean

"James?" Someone called loudly from the hall, making me cringe. Every student in this program knew better than to talk backstage while there was a performance happening mere feet from us. "Someone tell me where in the hell Cullen James is."

It took me a few heartbeats to realize the voice was calling for me.

As soon as we'd arrived at camp we'd been thrown directly into classes. The first covered stage names. There were many arguments to be made for younger actors to use a moniker for professional purposes, including protecting their future selves as well as their loved ones.

I didn't care about adult-Dean or my parents. It took me less than five minutes to decide I wanted anonymity for Dylan. Even less to decide what my professional name would be going forward.

Cullen James. It had curb appeal. It was unique. It rolled off the tongue. People would remember it. More than that, it allowed me to carry Lennon with me wherever I went.

I couldn't wait to tell her.

I'd written her a letter every single night I'd been at the workshop.

They were sealed in envelopes, hidden in my suitcase. I hadn't had a chance to mail them.

At first, guilt had plagued me. Then I realized I wanted to tell her in person anyway.

When I didn't respond right away, Bell shot me an agitated look. Since she was closest to the door, she reached for the knob, her face scrunched in confusion. Every crew member should know where each actor was waiting, that way they could give us our cue.

"In here." Her voice, in contrast to the other, barely rose above a whisper.

Julian, the Assistant Stage Manager, pushed open the door, searching the room until his eyes stopped on me. He ran a hand through his disheveled hair, appearing more frantic than usual. Considering we were in the midst of the show—the most important performance of our careers thus far—and he had more responsibilities than most, I understood his stress.

A nagging thought in the back of my mind told me his behavior had nothing to do with the production.

"I'm not on yet," I muttered, just in case I was misreading him.

"I know." He held out a phone I didn't recognize. "You have a call."

I hesitated a moment, eyeing the cell in his hand, feeling like I was facing a trap. We were allowed weekly check-ins to let our parents know we were still alive and hadn't run off to join a cult, but I was one of the few who had decided to cease all outside contact and immerse myself fully in the program. Any phone use other than that one call was forbidden.

When I didn't take it, he shoved it into my hands. "I don't have time for this. Professor told me to get it to you. You need to take it and then go see him right away."

He spun and raced back into the hall before I'd even processed what was going on. I looked at my new friends, but they were just as baffled as I was.

Whoever it was better have a valid reason for calling. The audience was filled with the people who would help make my dreams come true and I needed a flawless performance.

"Hello?"

Chapter Twenty-Four

Lennon

"Why can't every boy we know be that perfect?" Dylan asked with a sigh as we left the movie theater and strolled slowly through the lobby.

"Because those are grown men with muscles for days and we spend all our time with teenagers," I answered with a chuckle as I looped my arm through hers. "Plus, it's a movie." Together we pushed open the front doors of the cinema and walked into the parking lot. "Dean said most agents create an image for their clients, something that they can sell, and then shop for roles that help boost that image. The comedy relief may be the biggest douche in real life, but we'd never know because of what we see in the tabloids and on the screen. Same goes for the villains we love to hate. Most are genuinely the kindest people but are typecast because of their looks. Then their agents create that persona to keep their client working."

"Of course, Dean would say that. He takes the fun out of everything," she sighed. "Think the guys will be mad when they hear we went to see an action movie without them?"

"Maybe." I chuckled. "Guess they should've come to see our movie with us."

We hadn't planned to spend all evening at the movies. In fact, we'd chosen the early showing of the latest romantic drama, so we could grab dinner afterward, and then go back to my house to have a stereo-typical girls' night; facials, foot scrubs, maybe even our do nails. A few friends said they'd call us later.

That's what we'd told the guys when they'd dropped us off almost five hours before.

We also hadn't expected to be completely and utterly devastated by the first movie. I'd started to cry ten minutes in, when a car accident killed a major character. The tears hadn't stopped until the end credits rolled. My heart still hurt.

We'd needed something to take away the pain. Distract us for a little while. On our way out, we saw a group of girls a few years younger than us coming out of another theater, giggling. We assumed it was a comedy and were shocked when we realized it was a rated-R action about a bank robber.

Thankfully, Dylan flirted with the freshman working at the box office, and he snuck us tickets without our parents being there to buy them. We'd loaded up on snacks from the concession stand and gone in blind. The blood, gore, and hot actors had definitely gotten our minds off the first movie.

"I don't remember the last time we saw two movies back-to-back. Do you?"

"No. But I'm so sore I don't think I ever want to again." I lifted my arms and arched my back, stretching.

"I swear you're sixteen going on sixty." We both chuckled. "What do you think the guys are doing?"

"They're at Chelsea's party. Drinking and doing things I don't want to think about."

"True story." She sucked on her front teeth as we hit the sidewalk. It had gotten dark while we were inside, but thankfully, the walk home wasn't that long, and we had each other. "It feels like we've been double dating all summer. It's weird to be without them."

Oddly, it had. Well, if normal double dates didn't include anything romantic and zero kissing. Something definitely felt like it was missing tonight. Like a part of me was gone. I'd thought it had been because of the sad movie, but the ache lingered.

Apparently, I couldn't get away from missing Dean no matter where I went.

When I didn't say anything, Dylan kept talking. "It's going to be so weird when Dean comes back. He'll be like a fifth wheel now."

"Maybe."

I didn't want to think about how different things would be when he finally came home. Not only with him but with all of us. I missed him, yet there was no way to know if he'd be the same boy who'd left. Chances were, we'd get a new and not necessarily improved version.

"Ugh," she groaned as I was lost in thought. "I don't want to walk all the way home this late. Think they'll come get us if I ask nicely?"

"Not if they've been drinking. But it's still early, right? Maybe they haven't started yet." There was no doubt in my mind that she'd find any reason she could to call Tate, so we might as well get it over with.

"What time is it?" She stopped walking and pulled open her bag. "I never turned my ringer back on after the movie."

I tugged my cell from the back pocket of my jeans. "I didn't either."

"That's weird." She lifted her eyes toward mine, the blue light from her screen illuminating her face. "My parents have been blowing up my phone."

"Want to know something even weirder? They've been blowing up mine too." I held my missed call list up for her to see her. Both her mom and dad had been calling me for hours. "Shaun called, too."

Her expression morphed into worried panic as she hit a contact button and held the phone to her ear. She shook her head after a minute. "Voicemail." She tried again just as I was about to ask her if she wanted me to call my parents. I heard her father answer on the first ring.

"Jesus, Dylan. Please tell me that's you."

"Daddy? What's going on?"

Not wanting to eavesdrop on their conversation, I typed a quick message to Shaun to tell him we were out of the movies. I didn't know why he'd wanted to know, but when he'd dropped us off, he'd made me promise to text him. As a quick warning, I also let him know that Dylan was about to start calling Tate.

I sent it just before I heard Dylan gasp. I looked up.

I could normally read Dylan like a book. When her face drained of all color and she went so completely still not even her gaze moved from the sidewalk, even a blind man would have known something horrible had happened. I wished I could hear what he was saying. I really hoped she hadn't gotten in trouble for going to the movies with me.

"No, we're fine." She shook her head. "I'm so sorry. We're okay." She glanced behind us, back toward the town we'd just walked away from. "No, we're not far. We'll be there in maybe fifteen minutes. I love you, too."

Before I could ask what was wrong, she fell into my arms and started to shake. "There was an accident, and when they couldn't find us, they'd worried."

"Accident?" I demanded. "Who was in an accident?"

I didn't understand why they'd be worried about us. Neither of us drove. Unless... my heart practically stopped.

She stepped back, still pale, eyes now wide, almost as if she could read my thoughts but didn't want to acknowledge them. "He didn't say. Oh my God. Maybe it was them? He said that they were at the hospital and needed us to come right down. But he also said that he'd go find my mom and tell her. Do you think she's hurt?"

I locked her fingers between mine. "We don't know what's going on, so let's not get ahead of ourselves. Come on, we can be there in ten minutes, if we cut through the back lot of the grocery store."

She swatted a tear away and nodded. "You're right. It's all going to be okay."

I didn't repeat the phrase because, at that moment, it didn't feel like anything was going to be okay again. Memories from a dream I'd had a few weeks before started to poke my subconscious like a magnet was pulling them from their hiding spot against their will.

I'd woken in a sweat-soaked bed, screaming so loudly my parents had invaded my room, panicked. I couldn't tell them what had happened because for the first time, the details were painfully blank. It was something dark that stood just out of reach. I'd been left with nothing but a feeling of doom that I'd quickly forced away.

At the time, I'd associated it with Dean's absence. It scared me. Not wanting to face truths I wasn't ready for, I'd closed it off.

As Dylan and I walked, clutching each other tightly, I had to wonder if it hadn't been anxiety over Dean at all.

A middle-aged woman with a kind smile and an RN label on her nametag was waiting for us at the information desk right inside the main entrance. Dylan seemed relieved, but I knew that nurses were short-staffed. There'd been a fascinating expose in the paper outlining the problems hospital personnel faced over the summer. They barely had enough manpower to cover shifts. If they'd spared a nurse to come greet two random teenagers, we weren't so random after all.

The RN led us down a maze of halls but was unable to tell us where we were going or answer any questions. My mind swam with possibilities, none of them good. I needed to call my parents soon. I didn't want to interrupt their dinner, but this entire experience was something they needed to hear from me.

Plus, I was so shaken, I needed to hear their voices.

Shaun's parents were the first people I saw. Huddled together in a corner, gripping each other's hands like it was the only way to keep the other there. Mrs. Eastman sobbed uncontrollably while tears formed rivers and flowed down Mr. Eastman's cheeks.

I frowned, confused.

When they saw me, Mrs. Eastman stood abruptly, her mouth forming words I couldn't hear over the thundering pulse in my ears. I glanced away, surprised to see both Chad and Tasha standing in the middle of the room, talking to a man in scrubs. As soon as they saw us, they lunged.

It felt like my mind had been filled with sludge, each thought coming slower than the one before, eerily similar to, and just as exhausting as walking through mud. I wondered if I'd been drugged because everyone was moving in slow motion.

Chad got to me first. His lips moved, saying my name, yet no sound reached me. His hands closed around my shoulders, shaking me slightly.

I turned, trying to find my best friend, wondering if she felt the same way I did. She was right there, next to me, her mom leaning over, cupping her face as she spoke words I couldn't make out despite their closeness. Dylan shook her head over and over, tears running freely as her eyeliner and mascara stained her skin.

"Lennon."

The voice I knew better than my own, the one I'd missed with every part of my heart and soul, pierced the white noise. I spun, pulling away from Chad as relief poured through me. Dean ran down the corridor, his clothes not from this century, his face a mask of cool, calm terror. I'd known something was wrong before we'd walked into the hospital, but in that moment, I knew it was something horrible.

I stepped back when the last part penetrated my mind, only to find a solid wall blocking me.

I didn't want to know whatever Dean was going to tell me. He wasn't supposed to be there. He was supposed to be hours away at his play.

If he was there with us, so close I could almost touch, and he was upset, whatever he was going to say wasn't something I wanted to hear.

Movement behind him distracted me, pulling my attention away from the boy I loved. "Tate?" My eyes landed on Dean once again, hoping he could make sense of the chaos. "Why is Tate here? Is he hurt?"

I didn't need anyone to answer me. Not really. The proof was sitting in the wheelchair behind Dean.

Half Tate's handsome face was beat to hell. One cheek was scraped raw, lips cracked, fat, and bloody, and even though someone had attempted to clean him up, his eye was swollen and would be jet black come morning. It was a wonder he could see.

The worst part wasn't his awful appearance, or the fact that someone had removed his clothes and put him in a hospital gown, or even the horrifying realization that one of his ankles was propped high, the swelling too obvious to miss. No, the worst part was the sling that cradled his right arm and the tip of the cast I could see poking out.

If he'd broken his arm, he couldn't play ball. If he didn't play football this season, scouts would never see him. *If I get hurt, or I fuck one thing up, my career will end in high school.* His words from months before came back to me and I wanted to cry, devastated for my friend.

I realized the awful truth in that moment.

There had been an accident, but it hadn't been Dylan's parents.

The boys. My boys.

I forced the thoughts away, refusing to acknowledge them.

The Cullens had probably been worried when they couldn't find us because they'd watched us drive off with Shaun and Tate only hours before. Dylan and I were fine though. We didn't have a scratch.

Tate's bones would heal. He would play ball again, chase his dreams. We were alive.

Dean reached me, and whoever had been holding me released me almost immediately. His red-rimmed and puffy eyes and smeared stage paint told me he'd been crying too. I wanted to comfort him, to hold him and make the hurt go away, but I still didn't understand why everyone was crying.

We were alive.

"You're here." My boyfriend cupped one cheek while his other hand clutched my shoulder, the back of my head, my hand. It felt like he was inspecting me, making sure I was in one piece. "Thank God." The relief in his voice was clear.

He pressed a kiss to the middle of my forehead before he wrapped his arms around me so tight I struggled to breath. As soon as Dean stepped back, I looked around, searching for the one missing piece. I didn't want to ask, some deep part of me begged me not to, but I had to know.

"Where's Shaun? Was he driving? How bad is it?"

Dean shook his head as if he didn't want to answer me. I pushed him further away. I loved him more than I loved words, but Shaun needed me. I'd promised him I'd have his back.

"Lennon," Tate spoke, voice so full of sadness I was afraid he'd break. The pure misery and loss etched on his face told me everything I needed to know.

No. I stepped backward, shaking my head. *No.* Shaun was in another room, down the hall. Tears burned my eyes, and blood began to ooze from the lip I'd bitten too hard, trying to stop its tremble. The familiar metallic taste bitter on my tongue. *No.*

"Where is Shaun?" The words came out too loud, a scream I hadn't intended.

In some distant corner, Mrs. Eastman began to wail. I wanted to join her. But I couldn't. Because any minute her son was going to come strolling down the hall, a stupid joke ready, and ask me questions about his stitches or how long it would take before he could have sex again.

Dean shook his head, his expression filled with so much pain I could almost feel his heart breaking. "Len." His gaze left mine, moving over my shoulder, as tears filled his eyes. His head moved in a quick, sharp shake. "I can't—"

"Len, honey." A soft feminine voice I recognized as Mrs. Eastman's spoke from behind me, thick with emotion. "Shaun is gone, honey. They did everything they could." A hand rubbed my back.

I started to shake again, my entire body quaking. I was suddenly so cold I didn't know if I'd ever get warm again, but unfathomable anger was all I felt. Every single person in this room was brutally cruel to attempt such a prank. It wasn't funny.

I would know if Shaun was gone. He was my person. He held a piece of my heart no one else had touched. Shaun had been my saving grace. My everything while Dean was away.

I would know if he were gone. I would feel him missing. A hole that could never be filled.

I blinked and looked around the room. Familiar faces watched me with fear-filled eyes, waiting for me to break. Their little Lennon. I could see it, the concern mixed with the worry.

It was fine. We'd laugh about this later. That insane moment when I'd feared the worst, when, in fact, Shaun was just getting a bone set or a gash sewn. Shaun and I would find it hilarious, even if no one else would.

A giggle escaped, small at first, but the laughter grew uncontrollable as I envisioned my friend howling at how sad everyone was in that moment. I could practically see him strolling into the waiting room, clothes torn, a few bumps and bruises, but no worse for wear. He'd plop down onto the chair and say something stupid, because that's just what he did.

"They're crying for me, lil' miss. Buncha pussies. Don't they know there's no crying in baseball?"

I grinned at the set of empty seats, the laughter dying on my lips as my imaginary Shaun vanished, leaving only heartbreak and devastation in his wake. My eyes danced around the room finding nothing but tears and alarm.

No one said a word.

Finally, Dean held out a hand. Not to offer me comfort, but to plead. "Lenny, you're scaring me. Scaring us."

He never called me Lenny. That wasn't his name to use. I shrank away, curling into myself.

I wanted my mom and dad. They'd know what to do. They'd help me clear up this horrible mistake.

The sudden realization that the people who surrounded me, those I'd known my entire life, would never joke about something as devastating as losing one of our own, stabbed me like a knife. I was going to throw up. The tears I'd been trying to keep at bay broke, scorching my skin as they flowed. I could barely see as everything blurred.

"Dylan?" I reached blindly for her. "Can you call my parents? I really need them to come home. I need my mom and dad."

Strong arms wrapped around me and pulled me hard, holding me tight against a solid chest. Dean's familiar scent enveloped me as his wide hand braced the back of my head. For a few heartbeats, I felt safe, like everything might be okay.

But it wasn't. Nothing was going to be okay ever again. The knowledge brought another wave of heartbreak.

Dean leaned down and whispered words of comfort as I cried. He never let go, no matter how hard I hit, or how much I shook. Finally, when I knew for sure he wasn't going anywhere, when I knew he wouldn't make me face this nightmare alone, I fisted my hands in his shirt and held tight. "Don't leave me."

"Never. I will never leave you, Len."

My words, his promise, were far too close to the one I'd given Shaun. *"Do you ever feel like you're running out of time?"* Had he known? Had he felt his time was almost over? I sobbed harder.

There was so much I hadn't said to him. If I had known, I would have held on just a little tighter, a little longer. Had Shaun known how much we loved him? How much he mattered to us? Had he ever realized how much he truly mattered to me?

"Lennon James?"

It took a few moments for the voice to cut through the fog in my brain. I couldn't see who had spoken my name, but the way he'd done it with a formality I'd rarely heard, made me go still in Dean's arms.

"Do you have to do this right now?" Someone asked in a hushed whisper. "She just found out her friend..."

A throat cleared. "She just found out her friend didn't survive."

The words were so final. So much worse than him just being gone. Gone could mean he'd finally run away and was painting one of his masterpieces on the sidewalks of Paris. Or surfing the Banzai Pipeline in Hawaii. Gone meant I'd see him again.

Didn't survive meant he was never coming back.

"We're all mourning right now," a deep voice snarled. "Can't you just give her a little more time?"

"Give her time, please. She's only sixteen. Let her have a minute to digest one tragedy before you add more."

I didn't know who was talking or why, but I needed to go home, crawl into bed, and wait for my parents. They'd know what to do. They'd help me through.

"I'm afraid we can't do that," another voice, much more severe than the first, answered. "Ms. James, we need to speak with you."

I wanted to lie down, go to sleep, and pretend everything was okay for a few hours. Guilt hit when I realized that Dean, Dylan, and Tate were going through the same thing I was, feeling the same way.

We'd all lost our friend tonight.

Knowing I needed to check on them, that they needed me to get my shit together and be strong for them, was the only thing that made me sniff back the rest of my tears, wipe the streaks off my face, and turn to see who wanted to talk to me so damn badly.

I did a double take and recoiled slightly when I found two uniformed police officers. Both watched me, one with sadness, the other with pity. I swallowed and shook my head as Dean's hand found mine and gave a squeeze of support.

"I'm sorry I can't help you. I was at the movies with Dylan." I closed my eyes, realizing my mistake. They didn't know who in the hell Dylan was. "I mean, with one of my best friends." I pointed in her direction, but the words hit me hard.

I was at the movies with one best friend while the other died. Had he gone quick? Had he been in pain? Would he still be with us if I'd begged him to come to the movies?

The thoughts hit me like punches to the gut. I grabbed my stomach, almost doubling over. *Please God*, I prayed like it would actually matter, *please have made it painless.*

The older officer's face fell, but it was the younger one who looked taken aback. They exchanged a quick glance, and the older one cleared his throat as he dipped his head to meet my eyes.

"Ms. James, I'm Officer Brooks. This is Officer Sanchez. Let's have a seat."

I glanced at Dean over my shoulder, confused. At his nod, Officer Sanchez led me to a row of chairs against the wall. He sat across from me while Officer Brooks sat on my right, Dean on my left.

I scanned the room, wondering why everyone didn't have to sit down. Dylan was crying on her mother's shoulder, while Chad was crouched next to Tate's wheelchair, talking quietly just like he would if he was giving him advice on the football field. Shaun's parents had disappeared. Probably because of my outburst, which made me feel even worse.

I'd lost a friend. They'd lost a child. *"It's against the natural order of things for a parent to bury their baby,"* My grandmother told me once. *"If you were there when they were born, you shouldn't be there when they die."*

Gram was a tough old broad. She'd only been a teen when her parents had passed, but she'd insisted it hadn't changed her. *"Doesn't matter how old you are when your parents die because that's what was supposed to happen. They're supposed to go first."*

I frowned at the random memory.

Officer Brooks took my hand, which surprised me. I'd always assumed the police didn't like to touch or be touched. His hand was warm and oddly comforting.

"Lennon, we're here to deliver bad news."

I shook my head. I didn't understand. My lips were so dry they felt like they might crack and bleed more. My throat burned, but I forced out the words anyway. "I already know. Someone told me he di..." my voice broke, and another round of tears made their way down my cheeks. "He died." The word was a sob.

For a moment, I thought Officer Brooks might cry too. I glanced at Sanchez to find that he'd also teared up. It couldn't be easy, giving a death notification for a teenage boy. I couldn't imagine how hard it must have been to tell his parents.

"No, Lennon."

I hated the way he kept using my name, as if afraid he had the wrong person. I was confused about why he wanted to talk to me specifically; we were all here for the same reason.

"Your parents, Trevor and Gayle James, were killed in a car crash earlier today."

Chapter Twenty-Five

Cullen

Present Day

I stared out the window as memories of moments we'd shared assaulted me. The crushing weight on my chest was familiar. It came every time I thought about that summer. It was the look on Lennon's face, one I could still see vividly whenever I let myself remember, in that moment all those years ago—one of utter heartache and hopelessness—that always shredded my heart the most.

She'd been through more than most would ever realize. And she'd come out the other side better. So much stronger than anyone could have ever imagined. Even her.

Joan cleared her throat, bringing my attention back to my manager, as she listened to whatever my wife was saying on the other end of the line.

"Stop being so cruel. Take the damn phone and put her out of her misery."

Briar's voice had been too loud, the car almost silent. I had no idea how much Len had heard, but from the look on Joan's face, it hadn't been good.

It didn't matter what Briar thought. I couldn't simply pick up the phone and talk to Lennon. This was not a conversation I was going to have without flying home and facing my demons. There was too much history between us. I owed Len that much. More, actually. So much more than I could ever repay. I'd give her the world if I could.

There wasn't anything I wouldn't do for her.

I'd happily sold myself to the devil. I'd do it all over again. There wasn't a single thing I wouldn't do to protect Lennon James Cullen, even if it meant breaking her heart.

Joan's piercing gaze met mine as she nodded absentmindedly, as if Lennon was in the car and could see her. Then she looked away. "Take care of yourself, Lenny."

The words threw me. Not only because they'd been spoken softly, an almost maternal sound I'd never heard Joan use before, but also because of the finality to them. I knew that if my manager said something in that tone, it was sincere, and she meant every word. Yet, it sounded suspiciously like a real goodbye.

She dropped the phone to her lap, stabbing the end button with an angry finger. I watched, waiting.

"Lennon would like me to extend her congratulations on your engagement. She has no doubt you'll be very happy together and hopes you have a long marriage blessed with excitement, adventure, and a house full of children."

The words, chosen no doubt to twist the knife I could physically feel in my heart, hit their mark. *All things I had promised to give her.* I clenched my fists.

"She apologized that it would be late but said you could expect your engagement present to arrive next week."

I saw Briar glance at me out of my peripheral, her trepidation obvious. "Cullen?"

I couldn't take my eyes off Joan, waiting for the other shoe to drop.

Joan cleared her throat uncomfortably. "She'll be filing for divorce first thing Monday to save you the trouble."

The fuck she was

Sadness crept into Joan's voice. "She'll have your sister fly out the necessary paperwork in order to expedite the process and keep prying eyes away. Her only request is that you sign them immediately and send them back with Dylan."

She wasn't getting out of it that easily. Lennon James had never backed away from a confrontation in her life and she sure as hell didn't get to start now.

"Take me to the airport." I snarled loud enough for the driver to hear.

"Um, no." Briar's voice was filled with worry. "We just announced the engagement. You can't fly across the country tonight."

Briar was one of the most important people in my life. I didn't know where I'd be without her and there wasn't much I wouldn't do for her. However, this was where I drew the line.

Lennon James was a part of me, just like I was a part of her. A piece of paper hadn't been the tie that bound us together. One sure as hell would never be able to tear us apart.

She may be ready to give up, but I wasn't done. The curtain may have fallen on this act, but there were plenty more to go. Our story was far from over.

Chapter Twenty-Six

Tate Griffin

The Past

"Someone really wants your attention. Hot date?" I mused with a chuckle, glancing at Shaun.

His phone had been blowing up for the last five minutes. We'd dropped the girls off at the movies twenty minutes before, so I knew it wasn't them.

Yet.

Give it a couple hours and Dylan would be texting me nonstop. That was if she even made it through the movie without checking on us, the nosey little brat.

"Yeah, I do. He's sitting right beside me." Shaun slowed to a stop at a red light and snagged his cell. "Fuck. My parents are back early," he dropped it into the cup holder between us and turned his focus back to the road.

"They want you to come home tonight?" The Eastman's traveled most of the time, but when they were home, they tended to demand an audience with their only child, regardless of his plans. "We can bail on the party."

"Nah. They requested Len's presence for brunch at the club in the morning. They want to introduce her to some of their friends."

"Brunch at the club? But of course, why wouldn't they?" I asked in my snottiest voice before I laughed. "They know you and Lenny aren't a couple, right?"

He snorted. "Yeah, asshole. They know. Even if she was single, lil' miss isn't exactly my type. I don't go for the innocent virgins, remember?"

I knew that. Everyone did. Just like everyone knew Eastman didn't do relationships. At least, that's what I would have said last spring.

There'd been too many times over the summer I'd almost called bullshit.

Watching them together, listening to them laugh and bicker... sometimes it was easy to forget they weren't dating. If Lenny had been some random single chick hanging with us, I would have sworn my best friend had finally met his match. Hell, if she'd belonged to anyone else, I would have assumed Eastman was buying time until he made his move and stole her away.

Every time I'd start to get a little suspicious, I'd remember two very important facts. One, Lennon was Cullen's girl. She was unapologetically head over heels for the boy next door. And two, Shaun was loyal to a fault. He'd cut off his left nut before he betrayed either Dean or me.

If you'd ever had the privilege to be in the locker room after a win, you'd know how big of a statement that was; the man loved his balls, and he was partial to the left.

"Then why do they want to introduce her to people?"

"They really like her," he shrugged. "They think she's articulate and brilliant beyond her years."

All things I agreed with.

The light turned green, and he pulled into the intersection, waiting for the line of traffic to clear so he could turn left. We were headed a few towns over to meet his cousins before the party.

"They want to help her make connections that will help her later." He sighed. "I don't know. Maybe it is wishful thinking on their part and they're hoping one day I'll settle down with someone like her. Or maybe they know her parents are gone for the weekend and don't want her to be alone. They're still pissed at Chad and Tash."

"Mom, too." I shook my head. "She's barely said two words to Tasha all summer, yet she and Gayle have been inseparable when she's home. They're going shopping next weekend."

"Fuck. That's cold, bro."

It was. Mom had been close friends with both sets of our neighbors for as long as I could remember. Dean, Dylan, Len and I had been raised together. We'd always joked that if you lived in our cul-de-sac, you didn't have just one mom, you had three.

I thought they'd always be tight. Then Tasha pulled her over-the-top psycho-mom crap and every adult we knew disagreed with how she handled it. Shit on our street got tense.

I'd been overprotective of Lennon from the moment I'd met her. She wasn't just the youngest. She was the sweet kid with an easy smile who saw the best in every situation. She'd been my shadow for years, never afraid to try anything, no matter how dangerous. Protecting her wasn't a choice. It was pure instinct.

I didn't have a little sister. The universe had given me Lennon James instead. I couldn't have loved her more if she was blood.

What I hadn't realized was that my mom felt the same. When she heard what happened with Tasha and Dean, she'd gotten angrier than I'd seen her in years. She raved and ranted for days. It was funny as hell at first.

I didn't see the humor in it anymore. It had been weeks and mom was still angry. Part of me worried that she might not get over it, and we'd never get back to normal.

Not that anything was going to be the same again anyway.

I sighed and forced the thoughts away. *One more year.* With the help of a standout season, by next fall, I'd be in college as far away as I could get. It was a bittersweet idea.

"You going to ask Len if she wants to go?"

"I dunno. I like it when she's there because they lay off for five fucking minutes. If they start talking about anything heavy, she butts in and changes the subject. They let her. Plus, she makes me laugh."

"You should take her. It's the perfect distraction. Just have her back before the big surprise."

He smiled, all seriousness fading. "Our boy is finally coming home."

It had been a long summer without Dean. Fun. Crazy. One I'd never forget. But I was ready for senior shenanigans, as Len called them. One last hurrah with my favorite people. I was ready for Cullen to be home.

"I can't believe we pulled it off and Lenny has no idea he's coming home tomorrow."

"Dude, she's going to lose her mind." His smile vanished, replaced by a frown.

It was so rare that it immediately made me uneasy.

"What's wrong?"

"It's our last night with the girls. Tomorrow, everything goes back to the way it was before."

He didn't have to spell it out for me. I felt the same way. "It's gonna be a gorgeous night. Perfect for a bonfire on the beach."

"Stargazing and S'mores with lil' miss," he added, nodding.

"Starlight swimming with the lil' sis."

"So you can torment her about all the creatures she can't see in the water?"

"Hell, yeah." I laughed.

It was funny because it was true. The girl was afraid of everything. Seeing Dylan scared but knowing she wasn't in any real danger gave me a twisted sense of joy.

Can't wait to explain that fucked up tidbit to her brother.

Shaun nodded. "What about Chelsea's party?"

"There's always going to be another party."

"You sure?"

I nodded.

"Fuck it. Let's go back and get them."

The backroad we were on was heavily traveled because it was the shortest route to the city and the freeway. Houses, however, were few and far between. Probably because no one wanted to live where everyone else drove like they were on the Autobahn.

He handed me his cell. "Call Lennon, will you? Let her know we're coming back."

I got voicemail. "Hey, Lenny Lou." I snorted, knowing she'd hate the nickname I'd made up on the fly. "Change of plans, kid. We decided that you two don't need a night off after all. We're coming to get you."

"Lenny Lou!" Shaun hollered with a hoot. "We love you!"

Chuckling, I shook my head. "We're not going to the party. Just in case you're thinking of dodging us, we're thinking beach, bonfire, best night ever. Call me if you get this before we get there. See ya soon."

Shaun slammed on the brakes before I could hit the end button. My body flew forward before my seat belt painfully jerked me to a stop. That was going to leave a mark. "The fuck?"

I snapped my head up, too shocked for words.

Before I could process the scene in front of us, Shaun had jerked the Jeep to the side of the road, thrown open his door, and leapt from the truck. "Call 911!" He screamed before he ran toward the accident in front of us.

I dropped his phone, my brain struggling to process what I was seeing.

What had once been a white SUV was half buried in the woods that lined the road. Its hood had crinkled like paper, the rest of the front end split down either side of an ancient tree. It looked like a monster the size of Godzilla had picked it up, twisted the frame so the back end was now on an angle, then stomped on it.

I didn't think I'd ever seen anything so destroyed. Until I looked at the other car.

Upside down, lying across both lanes right before the road veered left in one of its many sharp turns, it resembled an aluminum can that had been squished. All the windows had been shattered. Every tire was flat. I couldn't see the driver's side, but the passenger's side had been T-boned.

I didn't know what had happened to cause a wreck that extensive, but it must have been something horrible. I wasn't a medical professional, but I knew instantly there was no way anyone could have survived this crash. Not without divine intervention.

The thought made me sick to my stomach.

Shaun didn't seem to realize it was a lost cause. He was yelling, tugging on what was once the passenger door of the car. He had to know that even if he could get anyone out, they'd never make it. We should sit tight and wait for the emergency crews to arrive.

Panicked, I popped open my seatbelt and rushed out of the jeep toward him. It only took me two steps to realize why he was so frantic.

My blood went cold.

I knew that car.

I saw it every day. I waved automatically when it passed me on my morning run. I checked to see if it was parked in the garage each night before I went to bed.

I broke into a run, desperate to get to them, to get Lennon's parents out.

I fell to my knees next to Shaun, ignoring the bite of debris and glass that tore my skin.

"I can't get the door open," my friend screamed in pure agony. "She's crushed. I can't get her out through the window."

At his words, I leaned closer to the ground and reached for anything I could get my hands on. Maybe together we could wrench the door free.

For the first time in my life, real terror consumed me. Gayle James, covered in blood, was trapped upside down, her body twisted in unnatural ways as it almost folded over on itself. Fear filled eyes met mine.

She was alive. Next to her, the seat was empty.

"Boys," her voice was weak, hoarse, barely a whisper. But there was light and recognition in her eyes. She knew who we were. "Go."

"No," Shaun insisted, dropping to his stomach and sliding as close to the car as he could get. "We're going to get you out."

I watched in horror as he reached inside the empty space where a window had once been, impervious to the jagged metal that tore at his flesh.

"Gas." The rattle gasp was like nothing I'd ever heard. It had to hurt her to speak. Blood dribbled out the corner of her mouth and covered her teeth. "Go."

"I can get you out!" Shaun yelled. "Let me get you."

He'd no more than said the words when the fire started. It wasn't like the movies. There was no explosion. The entire car didn't engulf at once.

Instead, a small spark sprung from the engine area, a bright light from where we laid in the shadow of the devastation. Almost instantly, flame spread over the hood. Shaun swore.

He stood up, frantically spinning. "I need a... a... a crowbar. Something to pry open the door." He rushed away.

Helpless, I reached for the pale, white hand that lay limp on the pavement. I didn't know how much time she had, but I needed her to know she wasn't alone. I prayed for a miracle. For the fire department to arrive. For anything.

The hand in mine moved, squeezing slightly. "Lennon." A single tear dripped from her eye down her forehead.

"Hold on. Shaun's coming. We're getting you out."

"Go."

Her hand went slack. I clung to hers harder, desperate to give her comfort. Gayle's eyes drifted closed, slowly, yet it wasn't until the rasping stopped that I realized what was happening.

We were losing her.

The silence was deafening. I hadn't noticed how quiet it was before that moment. Even the birds refused to sing. A peace I didn't welcome settled over us.

"No. No, no, no." I shook her hand, hoping she'd open her eyes. "Shaun!" I screamed as sheer panic consumed me. Refusing to let go of her hand, I grabbed the door with my other and yanked with every ounce of determination and energy I had.

It didn't budge.

I heard a motor, a car somewhere off in the distance, speeding up instead of slowing down. Maybe it was the ambulance. Maybe there was still time.

I needed to get her out. We could save her.

"Tate!" I heard Shaun's feet pounding the pavement behind me. He must have found something we could use.

"Hurry. She's dying!" I cried over my shoulder, my heart breaking.

His hands were empty.

"Move!"

It all happened so fast. Two hands grabbed me. I was in the air, flying backward. Bright lights blinded me. Brakes screeched. Another sound, like nothing I'd ever heard, echoed all around me.

Suddenly I was on the football field, in the middle of a game. I could hear the crowd cheering. The smells of sweat and grass mixed with steamed hotdogs.

Something was wrong. It wasn't a normal game. I was getting my ass handed to me.

I took a tackle, landing in a heap, head hitting the ground so hard it bounced. Sharp knives dug into my skin. Other players fell on me, crushing my arm and leg. Excruciating pain vibrated over my entire body.

Sadness filled me. Overwhelming devastation. Loss. So much loss.

Then, there was nothing but blissful black.

Note For The Reader:

Cliffhanger's suck. They're awful. I once swore I'd never write one.

Yet here we are.

I'm a wordy girl. If this is the first book of mine you've read, I can't just tell a story; I need you to feel it. Lennon and Cullen's story, unfortunately, is not a cut and dried tale that can be experienced fully in a short hundred thousand words. There are just too many layers.

Usually, I can tell you the exact moment a character walked into my life. Nate Kelly, for instance, strode across stage in the middle of a Jarrod Niemann concert and refused to leave. I literally bumped into an old friend one morning and Declan Callaghan's book was born. The Bastards came to life while I had lunch with my husband and his best friend.

I can't recall when or where I met them, but I can tell you that Lennon, Cullen, and company came into my life and refused to leave. Over the years (yes, years) I've seen glimpses of them as they teased me.

These five crazy kiddos have been a constant in my life, popping up when I least expected it. I'd get clips of their lives during a random song, walking on an island, or looking at the clouds. When I saw a tabloid headline about an actor and my heart started to ache because I felt what Len would have if she'd seen Dean on the cover, I knew it was time to focus on them.

At one point I didn't think I'd ever be able to write the enormity that is their story. It was too much. Too much history, too much pain, too much loss and self-sacrifice. I was going through too much with my own son to focus on anything else.

To top that off, this story isn't what sells. There's no market for teenagers who aren't overly naughty and fall in love as if it was the most natural thing in the world. There really isn't a market to watch those teens grow into married adults who are either in denial or hate each other—I'm not sure which—either. That worried my team. If I was going to try to salvage my career and break back in, I should write something that was hot. Something that would sell.

My friend Stephie encouraged me every step of the way. She reminded me again and again that I loved these characters as if they were real and I needed to write this story for them and for me, not anything else. So, I did. I love them so damn much that I want to talk about them all the time.

Early on, Shaun claimed his spot as my favorite character. Maybe all-time favorite. I could see him with his own book, covered in tattoos, long hair in a man bun, giant arms crossed over his chest as he smirked sardonically at the woman he'd love eventually. I had big plans for Eastman.

One day I was in the shower, working out the plot, and I saw his future. This ending. It physically hurt me. I shook my head in denial and actually spoke the word no. It wasn't happening. I knew what happened to Len's parents. It had always been there, but the details were a little murky.

Yet suddenly it was clear. I saw their accident, felt the fear and adrenaline. I cried real tears as if I'd just lost my own dear friend. I didn't want to write that version because I wasn't going to accept it.

As the months went by, I fought against my characters. That wasn't how this book would end. I wasn't going to write it that way.

I put it off as long as I could, determined to find another way. When

I couldn't wait any longer, I sobbed the entire time I wrote the chapter, because in those moments, I was Lennon.

I lost my dad at seventeen. My best friend at nineteen. My husband's best friend at twenty-five. I felt what she did.

Some losses you never recover from.

If you're reading this before the next two books are released, I hope you'll stick around for them. I was adamant that Dreams wouldn't be released until Echoes was finished because I didn't want you to wait long or wonder if I'd ever finish. Let's be real. Sometimes I promise books and then characters don't talk. Sometimes, my words get stolen before I publish them, and I throw a tantrum and cancel the book (hey, I'm human).

If you loved this book, I promise you, you'll love the next two just as much. Click here to pre-order Glimmers of Me.

Thank you for coming on this journey with me! It's my hope that you will fall in love with Len and Cullen as they fall for each other. Their love, while not over the top or dramatic, warms my cold black heart and makes me believe that everything happens for a reason.

I love to hear from my readers. Please get in touch.

carinaadamswrites@gmail.com

Or find me on Facebook: Carina Adams

Acknowledgments

Melissa Lambert Derda: Without you, this book would not exist. I never would have published it. I would have walked away, letting the insanity of the book world beat me. If there is ever a day when you need a reminder, call me. I'll spend hours explaining what a blessing you are. There is the family you're born into. Then there's the family you choose. Thank you for being my chosen family.

The Hubs: There were days you wondered if I'd written anything at all and others when you begged me to go to bed. I promised a quick, easy, short and lighthearted story that wouldn't impact us in the least but gave you Lennon and Cullen instead. Thank you for loving me enough to share me with fictional people, helping me chase my dreams wherever they go, and holding my hand through this crazy ride we call parenting. I love you more with each passing year, if that is even possible.

Boys: They say if you do what you love you never work a day in your life. Lies. Vicious lies. You will work every single minute of every day. And if you're not working, you're thinking about work. It's worth every second. I hope you find the perfect balance because I don't want you to miss a thing.

Mi Madre: You might not understand my need to write and create, but you spent the last few years encouraging me to not give up on my dreams. Artists are called moody for a reason, that's especially true for authors who aren't writing. I'm sorry.

Scuttlebutt: Sleepovers with you now are just as fun as they were when we were little. I was falling asleep when I told you about this idea, but a few days later you told me you'd spent hours trying to find the book on Amazon and my heart was happy. You are the best sister in the world.

Trouble: There are Ride or Die friends. Those aren't our kind of people. Nah. We're hardcore. We're Ride *Until* We Die friends. Rebels *with* a cause. Stephie Walls, you're the Thelma to my Louise—only on Harley's and with a better ending. Thank you for being my unbiological big sister and the world's best aunt. You are simply a blessing.

Grey Ditto: I love our friendship. I don't know what I'd do without you. Not only are you a constant support for the writer in me, you have the best book recommendations, and our texts let me know I'm not alone in this crazy world. I hope that I'm half the friend to you that you are to me.

Jeannine Colette: Thank you for answering a million questions about news channels and jobs. You always have my back in the book world. That's only one of the reasons I call you my friend and love you to pieces.

Heather South: Your gifts of coffee, messages of encouragement, and overall friendship is more than I can ever repay. Thank you for being my BBFF.

Margaret Hassebrock: Your friendship and support means the world to me. You keep me writing just by being you. I hate that you live in Scotland and I live in Maine. They should be next to each other so I can see you all the time. I love you, my friend! I can't wait to hug you again.

Marcie Shumway: I call you my Book Bestie because you are. Maybe it's because we're almost neighbors. Maybe it's because you just get me. Or maybe it's because you're simply amazing. Whatever the reason, I'm so grateful you're in my corner.

Design Team at BAd Designs: This is my favorite cover yet! You took Lennon James and created her notebook to perfection. This cover screams Len, Dean, and the gang. Thank you!

The Adams Family Group: I love our little group. I miss you so much when I'm away in the writing cave. Don't ever underestimate how much your messages mean. Thank you for putting up with my insanity!

Readers and bloggers: Without you, I'd be nothing. Thank you for helping me follow my dream. Please consider taking a moment to leave a review, even if it's only a few words. They matter so much for Indies like me.

About the Author

Carina Adams, an Amazon and international best selling author, is an avid reader who loves the epic and unconventional, has an unhealthy obsession with Stanley Tucci, loves the sound of Johnny Cash, is the crazy friend your mom warned you about, has a heart and soul as black as the coffee she drinks, believes you'll see her compete on Survivor one day, and hopes to go through the stones and find Jamie Fraser.

Carina has been writing and creating characters for as long as she can remember, allowing her to fall in love with the next man of her dreams with every new story. None of which are anything like boring Prince Charming.

Carina lives in a tiny Maine town with her biker-turned-businessman husband who keeps her on her toes and their two heathens who made her realize that wicked chicks lay deviled eggs.

Printed in Great Britain
by Amazon